PIONEER SUMMER

PIONEER SUMMER

A NOVEL

ELENA MALISOVA
& KATERYNA SYLVANOVA

TRANSLATED FROM THE RUSSIAN BY
ANNE O. FISHER

THE OVERLOOK PRESS, NEW YORK

Originally published in Russian in 2021 by Popcorn Books as *Leto v Pionerskom Galstyke*.

This English-language edition first published in hardcover in 2025 by
The Overlook Press, an imprint of ABRAMS

Abrams books are available at special discounts when purchased in quantity
for premiums and promotions as well as fundraising or educational use.
Special editions can also be created to specification. For details,
contact specialsales@abramsbooks.com or the address above.

Copyright © 2021 Elena Malisova and Kateryna Sylvanova
English translation © 2025 Anne O. Fisher
Jacket © 2025 Abrams

The authors are represented by Meow Literary Agency.

All rights reserved. No part of this publication may be reproduced or transmitted in any form or by any means, electronic or mechanical, including photocopy, recording, or any information storage and retrieval system now known or to be invented, without permission in writing from the publisher, except by a reviewer who wishes to quote brief passages in connection with a review written for inclusion in a magazine, newspaper, or broadcast.

This book is a work of fiction. Names, characters, places, and incidents are products
of the authors' imagination or are used fictitiously. Any resemblance to actual events
or locales or persons, living or dead, is entirely coincidental.

Library of Congress Control Number: TK

Printed and bound in the United States

1 3 5 7 9 10 8 6 4 2

ISBN: 978-1-4197-7310-5
eISBN: 979-8-88707-253-1

ABRAMS The Art of Books
195 Broadway, New York, NY 10007
abramsbooks.com

CHAPTER ONE

COMING BACK TO CAMP BARN SWALLOW

Yes, there was a shovel in his trunk. Why shouldn't there be? After all, it was a perfectly natural place for someone who grew up in the USSR to keep one. What if it was winter out? Deep snow? But even in September, there could still be lots of reasons: he could get stuck in the mud, or in a pothole. Would they get worked up about the rubber boots, too? What about the windshield washer fluid?

As he met the traffic cops' questioning gazes, Yura couldn't tell whether they were pulling his leg or not. Come on, they were local guys—how did they not get the need for a shovel?

After listening to his explanation, the Ukrainian traffic cops nodded in unison, but they didn't let him go. They could tell from his German driver's license that he was a foreigner, so the conversation took a predictable turn. There was a sign right there showing the speed limit, right? Right, agreed Yura. And the speed limit shown on the sign was exceeded, right? Right, agreed Yura. So the infraction of the law was self-evident, right? Right, agreed Yura. But Yura didn't want any, ahem, extra hassle because of it, right? Right, agreed Yura again. And therefore . . . ?

This is what finally made Yura mad. How could he have avoided an infraction, with the sign at the very bottom of a steep downhill and covered by a big feathery poplar branch?

"You should be cutting down that branch, not putting radar traps at the bottom of the hill," Yura said. "Because if the speed limit's lower there, it must be for a reason. It must be a dangerous stretch of road!"

The traffic cops, evidently indifferent to matters of traffic safety, were less than enthusiastic about his observation. Cutting down tree branches wasn't their job, and telling them what to do wasn't his.

The taller cop turned Yura's driver's license over in his hands a few times. "Okay. Looks like it'll be an infraction, then," he sighed. "Of course, you could also just pay the fine now . . . unless you want the extra hassle?"

Inside Yura, a battle was raging between a principled European stance—he'd lived half his life in Germany, after all—and common sense. Insist on justice, demanding they cut down the branch and drop the charge against him? Or hand over the "fine"—a bribe—and save time? The battle was brief. Common sense prevailed. Yura did not, in fact, want the extra hassle.

"How much?"

The men exchanged a crafty look: "Five hundred hryvnias!" Half a month's salary in Ukraine. They obviously took him for a fool.

Yura started digging out his wallet. Seeing this, the stalwart traffic cops softened. All smiles now, they inquired as to where he was headed, eagerly offering to show him the way so "Herr Foreigner" wouldn't accidentally get lost out here in the back end of beyond.

"How do I get to the village of Horetivka? The village is on the map, but the road isn't. I remember it, but I can't find it."

"Horetivka?" the tall one asked. "That hasn't been a village for a long time. It's a fancy cottage community now."

"Okay, so it's not a village, but there's still a way to get there, right?"

"You can get there all right, but you probably can't get in. It's a gated community with a guardhouse. They don't let in just anybody."

Yura gave it some thought. Before the conversation with the traffic cops, he'd had a clear plan for finding the special spot that was the goal of his trip: get to Horetivka and walk through the fields of the former collective farm down to the river. But now, if he couldn't get into the village . . . maybe he should give it a chance anyway? He could make a deal with one of the guards? Yura shook his head. No, he'd lose too much time if it didn't work out. His only remaining option was to get there through the camp. "Okay. Then how do I get to Camp Barn Swallow?"

"To what?"

"The Zina Portnova Barn Swallow Pioneer Camp. It was around here somewhere back in Soviet times."

The shorter cop brightened.

"Oh, yeah, that camp. Yeah, it was here . . ."

The taller one eyed Yura: "But what do you want to go there for?"

"I was born in the USSR, you know. I went to that camp. I spent my childhood there. Das Heimweh, Nostalgie . . ." He caught himself. "Homesickness, nostalgia!"

"Ah, right, we get it." The cops exchanged a look. "Where's your map?"

Yura handed it over and watched attentively as one of the men traced a finger across it.

"You need to go along R-295 until the sign for the village Richne. About twenty meters after that, there'll be a turn off to the right. Take that and follow it to the end."

"Thank you."

Yura got his map back, got a "Have a good one" in exchange for his cash, and set out.

"I knew it! I knew I'd get stopped at least once!" he groused, stepping on the gas.

He recognized absolutely nothing in the area and had to depend completely on the map to know where he was. Twenty years ago this area along the road had been lined with dense, dark undergrowth interspersed with sunflower fields, but now the town was creeping this way, step by long, slow step. The woods were being cut down, the fields were being leveled, and several plots of land had been fenced off. In the loud construction sites behind the fences he glimpsed cranes, tractors, and backhoes. The horizon, which Yura remembered being clear and incredibly distant, now seemed dismal and cramped, and the entire landscape stretching along it bristled with upscale summer homes—dachas—and gated communities everywhere he looked.

After the sign for the village of Richne he turned, just like they'd said. The paved road ended as abruptly as though it'd broken off. The car jolted. The shovel in the trunk clanked loudly, like it was alive and reminding him of its presence.

He had absolutely no recollection of how to get to the camp. The last time Yura had seen Camp Barn Swallow was twenty years ago, and even then he'd never driven there himself; he'd always been bused in. It had been so much fun that first summer, riding in a column of identical, iconic Likinsky

Bus Plant buses, white with their red stripe and decked out with flags and traditional signs indicating there were children on board. It had been especially fun riding in the very first bus, right behind the official traffic police car, where he could see everything spread out before him, both road and sky . . . and listening to the blaring siren, and singing children's songs with everyone . . . but then there were later years, looking out the window, bored, because he'd outgrown the silly songs . . . Yura remembered his last camp session, when he just listened instead of singing: "We ride along with flags and songs, we sing and clap and stamp! This is how our fearless troop goes to Pioneer camp . . ."

Now, twenty years later, all he heard was the jangling of the shovel bouncing around in the trunk. He cursed through gritted teeth at the ruts and potholes. Praying he wouldn't get stuck somewhere, he peered up, not at blue sky but at gray storm clouds: "Just don't drench me, now!"

His plan of action had been thoroughly weighed and considered. He'd left during the day, figuring he'd make it to the village while it was still light but would then wait until late at night to get into the camp itself and from there to his special spot. He'd thought everything through: it was September, so the last camp session of the season would be over and there wouldn't be any kids there, and there would probably be just one watchman, whom Yura could easily sneak past—the woods at night were pitch black. And even if he did get caught, he'd think of something. The watchman, who'd be an old man, might initially be scared of this random guy sneaking around in the bushes with a shovel over his shoulder, but he'd come around eventually, see that Yura was a normal guy, not some alcoholic or bum. Of course they'd come to an agreement.

The Pioneers . . . the Vladimir Lenin All-Union Pioneer Organization . . . red neckerchiefs, calisthenics, assemblies, swimming, campfires . . . how long ago that had all been. Everything must be completely different now: it was Ukraine now, not the USSR . . . a different country, different anthems, different slogans and songs . . . The kids wouldn't have the neckerchiefs and pins anymore, but kids are kids and camp is camp. And soon, very soon, Yura would be back there, and he would remember the most important time, the most important person, of his whole life. Maybe Yura would even find out what happened to him. Which meant that maybe Yura would even see him again, that person who had been his one true friend.

But when he pulled up to the familiar sign, it was hanging by a thread and so faded he could barely make out the letters. Yura saw what he'd dreaded most: there was almost nothing left of the chain-link fence that used to run the entire perimeter of the camp. Only the metal fence posts were still there. The handsome double-door gate was broken. One red and yellow door was somehow still hanging on its rusted, mangled hinges, but the other door was flat on the ground and had been that way, judging by the weeds surrounding it, for quite a few years. The guardhouse was now dilapidated; the original painted patterns of blue and green had come off long ago, the wooden walls had rotted in the rain, and the roof had fallen in.

Yura heaved a heavy sigh. So the devastation had reached all the way out here, too. Deep in his subconscious he'd suspected it, given what happened in Ukraine after the collapse of the Soviet Union; he lived in Germany, after all, not under a rock. He knew that factories had been shut down left and right. And, like all the Pioneer camps, this one had been affiliated with one of those same factories, the one where his mom had been an engineer. But Yura hadn't wanted to think about the same sad fate befalling Camp Barn Swallow: it was the brightest spot of his whole childhood, a searing solar flare of memory. This was where he'd left more than half of himself behind . . . but now Yura could feel that memory fading, as though it were the paint on the guardhouse, damp flakes of it sloughing off into the tall weeds.

The inspiration he'd felt during the drive drained away, leaving him sad and wistful, his mood matching the dreary weather and the fine drizzle misting down from the sky.

When he got back to his car, Yura changed into his boots, got the shovel from the trunk, and swung it onto his shoulder. He stepped over the rusty metal panels that had once been a gate and entered the camp: the Pioneer Hero Zina Portnova Barn Swallow Pioneer Camp.

His forward steps took him backward in time, moving in reverse to his half-forgotten past, to those happy days when he'd been in love. The big square concrete pavers were cracked and dark under his feet, while the trees, disturbed by rain, were rustling all around him, but dappled sunlight glimmered in his mind's eye, flickering faster and faster down the old camp's main avenue, pulling him into the last summer of his childhood.

He stopped at the intersection where the path to the mess hall went off to the left, the trail he remembered leading to the unfinished barracks—had they ever been finished?—went off to the right, and the once-broad Avenue of Pioneer Heroes led straight ahead to the main square in the center of camp. Most of the pavers were broken and huddled in random piles, but there was a tiny spot by the flower bed at the intersection that had remained intact.

"This is where it was! Yes, it was right here!" Yura smiled, remembering how late one night, when the whole camp was asleep, he'd sneaked out here with some chalk and drawn the most beautiful letter in the world: V.

Then the following morning, as they were going to breakfast, all the kids had tried to guess the shape drawn around the letter V.

Rylkin from Troop Two, the second-oldest troop at camp, had been sure he'd figured it out: "It's an apple, guys!"

"But what type of apple starts with V?" asked his troopmate Vasya Petlitsyn.

It hadn't occurred to a single one of them that the shape traced around the letter V wasn't supposed to be an apple but a heart. The shape had gone wonky because, while Yurka was drawing it, he'd suddenly heard those cherished footsteps through the rest of the general nocturnal rustling, and he'd been so overcome with shyness that his hand started trembling. So that's what he'd ended up with: an apple.

Yura nudged a broken hunk of paver with the toe of his boot and looked around. Time had spared neither avenue nor flower bed. Scattered over the ground were twisted, rusting lengths of metal—the remnants of the frame around the gate—as well as rotten boards and slivers of wood and broken bricks! He picked up the pointiest piece and crouched down. In one sure movement he drew a big, beautiful V with decorative flourishes. Then he enclosed it in a heart, one that was crooked and lopsided, again, but still *his*. Yurka's. The cynical, grown-up Yura suppressed his skepticism and mentally nodded to his younger self: that which should be preserved in this place was now restored.

His memories drew him farther along the Avenue of Pioneer Heroes. In the distance he saw the three broad steps leading up to the camp's main square. Along the way, moss-covered pedestals and statues stuck up randomly out of the undergrowth, just like headstones. It sure felt like he was wandering through a cemetery—an old, abandoned one. Once there had been seven statues of Pioneer Heroes here, glaring fiercely westward, and once Yura, like thousands of other Pioneers, had known not only their names but their accomplishments. He'd also done his best to be like those seven heroic children and follow their example. There was Lyonya Golikov, a sixteen-year-old Soviet Russian who had joined the partisans—the bands of organized, armed resistance fighters hiding in the countryside—and killed something like eighty German soldiers before they got him; there was Marat Kazey, a Soviet Belorussian spy and scout who, at fourteen years old, blew himself up with a hand grenade rather than be captured by the Germans; there was Soviet Ukrainian Valya Kotik, the youngest person to be made a Hero of the Soviet Union (albeit posthumously, like all the other Pioneer Heroes), who died just after his fourteenth birthday fighting the Germans in Volhynia in northwestern Ukraine; there was Tolya Shumov, a Soviet Russian who was seventeen when he fought alongside the partisans until he was captured, tortured, and killed; but the most heroic of them all was Zinaida Portnova from Leningrad, who was a member of a partisan band called the Young Avengers. At the age of seventeen, Portnova had spied, distributed leaflets, sabotaged factories, and poisoned a whole enemy garrison. The Germans eventually captured and interrogated her, but she got hold of her interrogator's pistol and shot her way out, only to be recaptured, tortured, and executed . . . But now, some twenty-odd years later, Yura found himself grasping for all of these details. He had forgotten everything he'd once known so well.

Yura walked farther along the crumbling avenue. The only traces of the clean, smooth path that used to be here were the gray remnants of asphalt among the thick weeds. Yura kept going, strolling past the crumbling pedestals and gazing with pity at the plaster arms, legs, and heads sticking up out of the undergrowth. As his gaze lingered on some dingy, lifeless torsos with metal armatures poking out of them, he caught sight of their worn plaques. There they were: Marat Kazey, Valya Kotik, Tolya Shumov . . .

But there, right by the steps at the end of the avenue, the honor board had remained intact. Back then the honor board had been in a rectangular glassed-in frame, but the only glass left now was a few sharp shards poking out of the corners. Still, thanks to the frame's shallow overhang, a few of the captions on the honor board were still fairly legible, and there were even three black-and-white photographs left.

"Session Three, August 1992: Achievements and Distinctions," Yura read at the very top of the board. So that was the very last session. Had the camp really gone on for just six more years after the last time he'd attended?

As he walked up the three steps leading to the main square, Yura's heart almost burst in a surge of sad longing. The awful thing wasn't the old being replaced by the new; it was the old being forgotten and abandoned. But this was much worse, because the one who'd forgotten and abandoned everything had been him, even though he'd earnestly sworn back then to remember the child heroes, and his fellow Pioneers, and especially V. So why hadn't he looked for this damned place before now? Why hadn't he come back until now? To hell with Lenin's maxims, the red banners, the oaths he'd been forced to take—to hell with all that! How had he allowed himself to break his word to V., his one true friend?

Yura tripped over a faded, broken-off section of a wooden sign reading OUR FUTURE IS BRIGHT AND SPLEND—. "It's not all that bright, and it's certainly not splendid," he grumbled, stepping up the last step.

The main square, the most important place in the whole camp, was just as decrepit as everything else. It was littered with trash and fallen leaves. Clumps of weeds pushed through holes in the asphalt, seeking the wan sun. Smack in the middle, surrounded by broken concrete and rock, lay a beheaded statue: the monument to Zina Portnova, Pioneer Hero of the Soviet Union, after whom the camp had been named. Yura recognized Zina and swore through gritted teeth. Even though the girl was just plaster, he still felt sorry for her. She'd accomplished genuine feats, after all, so what did people have to go and do that for? He wanted to try and stand her back up, but couldn't, due to the rusty metal struts sticking out where her legs had been broken off at the shins. Instead, he leaned the statue's torso against its pedestal, set the head next to it, and turned around to consider the one thing on the whole square that had remained intact: the bare flagpole, stretching proudly to the sky, same as it had twenty years ago.

Yura had first gone to Barn Swallow Pioneer Camp when he was eleven. He'd been so delighted by the camp that his parents started signing him up every year. Yura had adored the place when he was little, but every year, when he came back for another camp session, he got less joy from it. Nothing changed here. From year to year it was the exact same well-worn paths, the exact same troop leaders with the exact same tasks, the exact same Pioneers following the exact same daily schedule. The same old stuff. The clubs: model airplanes, sewing, art, sports, and computer science. The river where the water never went below twenty-two degrees Celsius. The camp cook, Svetlana Viktorovna, and her Friday lunch of buckwheat soup. Even the smash hits on the dance floor were repeats, the same songs year in and year out. And his last camp session had also begun same as usual: with an assembly.

The children began gathering into their assigned troop locations on the main square. Dust motes danced in sunlight and there was exaltation in the air. The Pioneers stood in their places, happy from new meetings with old friends. The troop leaders issued orders to their charges and surveyed the square sternly, just the barest hint of glee in their eyes. The camp director was swaggering and preening: that spring they'd managed to remodel four whole cabins and had even almost finished building a big new barracks. And only Yurka was the odd one out, again; the only one who didn't feel like joining in the fun and games; the only one who was sick to death of camp by now. It was all almost offensive to him, somehow. And there wasn't anything to take his mind off it.

No, wait—there was something, after all. A new troop leader was standing over to the right of the flagpole, in the middle of Troop Five. He wore navy blue shorts, a white shirt, a red neckerchief, a red flight cap, and glasses. A college student, maybe even a first-year; certainly the youngest and tensest of all the troop leaders. The breeze smoothed the unruly locks escaping from his scarlet cap; freshly scratched mosquito bites glowed red on his pale legs; his focused gaze moved along the backs of children's heads as he counted them off, his lips moving reflexively: "... eleven ... twelve ... thir ... thirteen." He must've been the one named Volodya, Yurka reasoned; he had heard something to that effect back by the bus.

The bugle sounded, hands flew up in the Pioneer salute, and the camp administration took the stage. The air reverberated with words of welcome and shook with the same thunderous, passionate speeches about Pioneers, patriotism, and Communist ideals that had been repeated a thousand times. Yurka knew them so well he could've recited them verbatim. He tried to keep himself from scowling, but couldn't. He didn't believe the educational specialist's smile, or her burning eyes, or her fiery speeches. Yurka could tell there wasn't anything real in them, or even in Olga Leonidovna herself; otherwise why repeat the same thing over and over? Sincerity would have been able to find new words. It felt like everyone in the whole country was living by inertia, reciting slogans and swearing oaths out of old habit without really feeling it. That's certainly what Olga Leonidovna was doing; officially, her job at the camp was to ensure that camp was educational, so that all campers learned how to be good Soviet citizens, but he knew she just liked ruining people's fun. All this passion felt like it was just for show. He felt like he, Yurka, was real, but everyone else was a robot. Especially that Volodya.

Because come on, could somebody like that, somebody who looked like a film still, really be a living, breathing person? So perfectly perfect, such a model member of the Komsomol—the Young Communist League ... like he had been cultivated in a greenhouse under a bell jar! He could have stepped out of a Communist Party poster: tall, trim, self-possessed, dimples in his cheeks, skin glowing in the sun ... "The only little hitch here's the hair color," Yurka scoffed spitefully. "He's not blond." Even so, his hair was perfect, not a strand out of place. The same couldn't be said for tousle-headed Yurka. "There's a robot for you," Yura rationalized, abashedly smoothing down his own mop of hair. "Normal people's hair gets messed up in the wind, but get a load of this guy: his hair just gets better."

Yurka was so lost in thought, so dissolved in his contemplation of Volodya, that he almost missed the most important part of the morning: the flag-raising ceremony. Good thing the girl next to him nudged him. He, too, looked at the flag and sang the Pioneer anthem, as required, with its evocation of blazing campfires, midnight blue skies, and workers' children marching and singing happily. Except that after the last words—"always be prepared!"—he fixed his eyes on Volodya again and stood still as a post. Eventually, Troop Five started falling out. The leader of Troop Five was poking at the bridge of his nose as they did, attempting to push up his glasses, as he counted to himself: "Twelve . . . oh! Thirteen . . ." Then he followed the children away.

Yura shook his head morosely, surveying the square again. Time spares nothing and no one; even this square, full of deep meaning for him as the place where he'd first seen his V, was getting overgrown with trees. Give it ten more years and it'd be impossible to push through the bushy, bright-leafed maple branches, and the Pioneers' plaster body parts peeking out of the underbrush would scare random explorers half to death. Or worse: the new development would reach all the way out here, and his beloved camp would be bulldozed and replaced by an elite cottage community.

Yura wandered over to the western corner of the square, to the path along which the junior troop leaders led their charges back to the junior cabins after assembly. The path went on down to the river, but he stood where he was and looked around for the trail hidden in the grass. Relying more on his memory than on what his eyes told him, he spied the fork he was looking for: to the left he could make out the outlines of the athletic fields and courts, while to the right, a little farther off, he could see the remains of the junior cabins. But Yura turned back to the square and walked across it in the other direction, toward the outdoor stage and the movie theater. He strolled slowly, looking up at the tall trees, feeling like he was in some kind of weird dream. He was pretty sure he recognized this area: the power shed was over there on that little rise, and if he kept going, he'd wind up at the storage shed. As he recalled those old scenes in his mind, he experienced that poignant ache again, warm and familiar despite the bitter strangeness of what this place had become.

He quickly made it to the outdoor stage, the place where his story—their story—had begun.

The dance floor and stage, partially covered by a band shell, was enclosed by a low railing that was now falling apart. The area had once been decorated by red flags and colorful posters reading GLORY TO THE COMMUNIST PARTY OF THE SOVIET UNION and WE ARE YOUNG LENINISTS that had already been old back when Yura was a camper. A long, dirty-orange banner with poetry on it lay ripped and faded on the ground. Yura looked down at the torn rag underfoot and read the part he could see: PIONEER, REMEMBER TO TREAT YOUR SCARF WELL . . . He turned away. A copy of the day's schedule had traditionally hung to the right of the stage. Now its single remaining line informed him that at four thirty it was time to do civic duty work.

To the left, at the very edge of the dance floor, Yurka's old observation point, a magnificent triple-trunked apple tree, still stood. At one time it had been adorned by heavy, plump fruit and strings of lights, but now it was desiccated, bent, and cracked. No one could've climbed it now, it'd break. Although Yurka had already fallen out of it, twenty years ago, when his troop leader assigned him to hang strings of multicolored lights on it.

That had been his first task, assigned right at the beginning of the session. Yurka never even knew what hit him.

After the opening assembly he got moved into his cabin; then—in body, but not in spirit—he attended the troop council, where delegates from each troop met to plan the upcoming camp session. After lunch he made a beeline for the athletic fields to meet the new kids and find the people he knew from past camp sessions. The loudspeakers blared out a welcome to all the new arrivals, informing them that meteorologists did not foresee any heavy precipitation over the next week and exhorting them to have an active and beneficial stay and to bask in the sun. Yurka immediately recognized the sonorous voice of Mitka, a good singer and guitarist who'd been the announcer last year, too.

He caught sight of some familiar faces scattered among the new campers. Polina, Ulyana, and Ksyusha were chattering by the tennis court. Yurka had already seen them at the assembly. He'd been in the same troop as them for five years in a row. For some reason Yurka and the girls had disliked each other from the get-go. He remembered them as snot-nosed ten-year-olds;

now they had grown up and blossomed into actual young women. Even so, Yurka still couldn't bring himself to feel friendly toward them, stubbornly continuing his animosity toward the trio of gabby gossips.

Vanka and Mikha, also Yurka's longtime troopmates, waved at him in unison. Yurka nodded in response but didn't go over to them. They'd start pestering him with questions about how his year had gone, and Yurka had no interest in answering, "Not that great, as usual," then having to explain why. He'd known the pair of them since he was little, too, just like the trio of girls. But these two were the only ones he talked to, when he talked to anyone at all. Vanka and Mikha were nerds, meek and pimply, but funny. They weren't exactly girl magnets, but they did respect Yurka. He bought their respect with the cigarettes he shared sometimes during quiet hour when they sneaked out and hid behind the camp fence.

Masha Sidorova was also standing nearby, looking baffled as she searched the crowd. Yura had known her for four years now. She had it in for Polina, Ulyana, and Ksyusha, and she was condescending, and she always talked down to Yurka. But last summer she'd gotten along really well with Anyuta.

And Anyuta was awesome. Yurka really liked her. He was friends with her and had even asked her to dance—twice. And the best part was that she had! Both times! Yura liked her pealing cascades of laughter. And also Anyuta was one of the only ones who hadn't turned away from him last year, after—

Yurka clamped down on that thought. He had no desire to recall what had happened then and how he'd had to apologize afterward. He surveyed the athletic fields again, hoping Anyuta was here somewhere, but she was nowhere to be found. He hadn't seen her at assembly, either. And judging from the way Masha was looking around, baffled, as she searched for her friend, it seemed unlikely that Anyuta was here.

Yurka asked Masha about Anya, who snapped: "Looks like she's not coming." So he shoved his hands in his pockets, scowled, and wandered up the path, thinking about Anyuta. Why hadn't she come? It was too bad they'd become friends only as their camp session was ending. Then they'd parted ways, and that was it. That year, Anyuta had been his only happy memory from Camp Barn Swallow. She'd said she really wanted to come to camp again but wasn't sure she'd be able to. Something about her father having some kind of problem with the Party, or maybe his job . . .

Yurka wandered over to the power shed. He kicked the lower branches of a thick cluster of lilacs growing there. He was annoyed at it. He didn't like the smell; it was cloying and clung to the nose. But, for lack of anything better to do, he stopped to look for flowers with five petals. Once his mother had told him that if you find one, you should make a wish and eat it, and then your wish will come true. As if he had anything to wish for, though. A year or so ago, he'd had both dreams and plans . . . but now . . .

"Konev!" The stern voice of Irina, Yurka's troop leader, rang out behind him. Yurka gritted his teeth and glanced over his shoulder. A pair of bright green eyes drilled suspiciously into him. "What are you doing walking around here by yourself?"

Irina had been his troop leader for three years now. The short brunette, tough but fair, was one of the few people at Camp Barn Swallow who Yurka got along with.

Yurka ducked his head. "Aw, MarIvanna . . . ," he began pleadingly, without turning around.

"What did you say?"

His little joke of calling her Marya Ivanovna, the archetypal stern schoolteacher name, had backfired. With a small crack Yurka broke off the lilac branch that had the biggest, most luxurious bunch of flowers. He turned around and held it out to the troop leader with a flourish: "I'm enjoying the flowers. Here, Ira Petrovna, this is for you!"

"Konev!" Ira turned red and was obviously taken aback, but made her voice even stricter. "You are disturbing the public order! Good thing I'm the one who saw you over here. What if it'd been one of the senior staff?!"

Yurka knew his troop leader wouldn't tell on him to anyone. First of all, because she felt sorry for him, for some reason, and so she was indulgent even in her strictness, and second of all because the troop leaders themselves could get reprimanded when their charges got out of line, so they tried to resolve things without getting the administration involved.

Ira sighed and put her hands on her hips.

"Well then, as long as you're over here goofing off, I have an important public duty for you. Go find Alyosha Matveyev, in Troop Three, the redhead with freckles. Take him and go get two ladders from the facilities manager and bring them to the outdoor stage. Once you're there, I'll give you some strings of lights to hang for tonight's dance. Got it?"

Yurka was more than a little disappointed: he'd been planning on going to the river, but now he had to try not to fall off a ladder instead. But he nodded. Grudgingly. Still, Irina narrowed her eyes at him: "Are you sure you've got it?"

"Yes, Marya Iva—dang it! Yes, ma'am, Ira Petrovna, ma'am!" Yurka drew himself up and clicked the heels of his nonexistent boots together. He was the only one who addressed her formally, using her patronymic as well as her first name, utterly clueless that doing this really hurt her feelings.

"Konev, you're on thin ice here! I was already tired of your little jokes last session!"

"I'm sorry, Ira Petrovna. Understood, Ira Petrovna. Consider it done, Ira Petrovna!"

"Go on, you troublemaker. Hop to it!"

Alyosha Matveyev turned out to be not only redheaded and freckled but jug-eared to boot. He wasn't a first-time camper, either, and babbled endlessly about past camp sessions. He bounced chaotically from one topic to the next, tossing out names, occasionally asking, "Do you know so-and-so? What about so-and-so, remember him?" And Alyosha's red curls and ears weren't the only things that stuck out: his teeth did, too, especially when he smiled, which was all the time. Alyosha, funny and sunny, literally radiated energy and a thirst for life. And he was devastatingly industrious— "devastatingly" because five minutes of his help was worse than an hour of anyone else's hindrance. As a result, Yurka quickly came to learn why everyone at camp thought long and hard before giving him even the smallest assignment.

Hanging the strings of lights wasn't hard. It only took them an hour to wrap several of the surrounding trees in lights and stretch the best strings of lights above the stage. The only thing left was to put up some lights on the apple tree. Yurka appraised the tree with a professional eye and got on the ladder. He wanted to make his beloved apple tree not only the prettiest tree there but also the most accessible one, so that when he was climbing it later he wouldn't get tangled in the lights. Holding one of the bulbs in one hand, he firmly grasped a tree branch with the other. Then he stepped off the ladder up onto a limb so he could set the string of lights as high as possible.

There was a dry crack. Alyosha shouted, and then something scratched Yurka's cheek hard and the world went blurry for a couple of seconds, and then pain shot through his back and backside. Everything briefly went black.

"Oh my goodness! Konev! Yurka! Yur, are you hurt? Are you alive?" Ira was bent over him, both hands over her mouth.

"I'm alive . . . ," he croaked, sitting up and holding his back. "I landed hard . . . It hurts . . ."

"What hurts? Where does it hurt?! Your arm? Your leg? What?! There?!"

"Ahhh, I broke it!"

"What did you break?! Yura, what's broken?!"

"I broke the string of lights, that's what . . ."

"Who cares about that?! The main thing is—"

Yurka got to his feet. All twenty-odd people who'd been decorating the main square for the celebration had surrounded the victim and were gazing at him expectantly. Rubbing his scraped, bruised palm, Yurka grinned, trying to hide the pain behind a smile. He was deeply afraid of losing his reputation as a brave, unflappable guy. The last thing he needed to do now was complain about his boo-boo and look like a crybaby. It'd be fine if it were just his hand and his back that hurt, but his damn tailbone was aching, too. No way he could admit that, though, since everyone would just make fun of him: Konev busted his butt!

"What's that you said? 'Who cares about that'?" interjected Olga Leonidovna, the educational specialist. She was tough as nails and had been out to get Yurka for two years now. "What's that supposed to mean, Irina?! That string of lights is camp property! Who's going to pay for it? Me? Or maybe you? Or *you*, Konev?!"

"What am I supposed to do if your ladders are rickety?"

"Oh, so the ladders are rickety! Is that it?! Or is it your own fault, you good-for-nothing! Just look at yourself!" She jabbed her finger sternly in Yurka's chest. "A Pioneer's neckerchief is one of his most valued possessions, but yours is dirty and torn, and the knot is crooked! You should be ashamed, walking around camp looking like that . . . attending *assembly* like that!"

Yurka hastily plucked up one of the ends of his swatch of red fabric and examined it. It *was* dirty, actually. But how'd that happen? Was it from falling out of the apple tree? He defended himself: "It was straight when I was at assembly! It got crooked because I fell!"

"Because you're a parasite and a vandal!" Olga Leonidovna's spit was flying. Yurka was flabbergasted. Unable to think of anything to say in reply, he stood listening mutely as she belittled him. "You outgrew the Pioneers two years ago! But here you are, a great big sixteen-year-old lug, and you're not even *thinking* about joining the Komsomol! Or is it that they won't take you? Is that it, Konev? You haven't earned it? You don't do any public service work, your grades are abysmal—of course they won't take you! The Komsomol doesn't take hooligans!"

Yurka would've been gleeful—at last, he'd gotten the senior specialist to show her true colors, and in front of everyone!—but that last bit made him too mad.

"I'm not a hooligan! It's your fault that everything in this camp of yours is all flimsy, all creaky, but you—you—"

He was about to let loose and tell her exactly what he thought of her. Yurka leaped to his feet, took a lungful of air, got ready to yell, and—abruptly choked it all back when somebody poked him right in his aching spine, hard. It was Ira. She widened her eyes at him and hissed: "Quiet!"

"What did you stop for, Yura?" the educational specialist said, narrowing her eyes. "Keep going. We're all listening to you very attentively. And after this, I'll call your parents, and I'll write you up a character reference that'll keep you from ever seeing the Komsomol, much less the Party!"

The very skinny, very tall Olga Leonidovna towered over him, furrowing her eyebrows and emitting sparks of fury from her eyes. She was showing zero signs of subsiding. "You're going to end up sweeping floors your whole life! You should be ashamed of yourself for disgracing your name!"

Yura flushed; it wasn't his fault he had the same last name as the great general Ivan Konev.

"But, Olga Leonidovna . . . you told us yourself never to shout at a child . . . ," Ira ventured reproachfully.

There had already been a large group around them from Yurka's fall, but more people gathered when they heard the shouting. The educational specialist was chewing out not only Yurka but a troop leader, too, in front of all of them.

"It's the only thing he understands!" the tall woman countered, then continued her accusations: "Earlier today you went on a rampage in the mess hall, and now you're breaking our lights!"

"That was an accident! I didn't mean to!"

Yurka truly hadn't meant to cause a fuss, and certainly not in the mess hall. But while he was clearing his plate at lunch, he'd accidentally smashed half the camp's dishes. He'd dropped his plate on a wobbly stack of other people's dirty dishes, and it slid off and crashed into other dishes, which then also slid and crashed into more dishes, and finally everything spilled to the floor and smashed to pieces, making a huge racket. Of course, everyone noticed. Half the camp had come running at the noise. But he just stood there, open-mouthed and red-faced. Yura never wanted any attention, to the point that back home he even went to the store in the next village over, not the closest one, just to avoid seeing people he knew. And now this: he'd fallen out of a tree and was getting a tongue-lashing over some lights while everybody watched.

"Olga Leonidovna, please go easy on him," Ira intervened again. "Yura's a good kid. He's grown up since last year, he's gotten better, right, Yur? It wasn't his fault,: the ladder was rickety. He should go to the first aid station—"

"Irina! Now, that's too much! You should be ashamed of yourself, lying right to my face—and me a thirty-year member of the Communist Party!"

"No—I didn't—"

"I saw Konev step off that ladder onto the tree limb with my own two eyes. I'm officially issuing you a severe reprimand, Irina! That'll teach you to cover for sabotage!"

"What are you talking about, Olga Leonidovna?! What sabotage?"

"One reprimand's not enough? You want a matched set on your record?!"

"No. Of course not. It's just that Yura—he's still a child, after all, and he has a lot of energy. He needs to direct that energy into the proper channel..."

"Some child! He's almost two meters tall!"

She was exaggerating his height, of course. One meter seventy-five centimeters, they'd announced at his last checkup, and not a centimeter more.

Yurka hoped to god he'd eventually hit two meters. Although there was no god in the USSR.

"He's a creative boy, he needs a club that's a little more active." Ira Petrovna wouldn't let it go. "We have an athletics group, right, Yura? Or else we have a drama club that just started, and Volodya does need more boys. Please, Olga Leonidovna, give him a chance! I'll take full responsibility."

"You'll take full responsibility?" the educational specialist said, showing her teeth in a sneer.

Yurka was sure this was the end, but all of a sudden Olga Leonidovna scoffed.

"Fine. I'm holding you personally responsible. And no more warnings." She glanced at Yurka. "Konev, if a single thing goes wrong, you'll both answer for it. That's right, you heard me: Irina will be punished for your mistakes. Maybe that'll keep you in line." Then she barked, "Volodya!"

Volodya had been hauling the music equipment out of the movie theater to set it up for the dance. When he heard his name, he stopped, blanching and blinking nervously. But then his darting glance shifted to Yurka, and in a flash Volodya changed completely: the color came back to his face, he squared his shoulders, and he marched boldly over to the instructor.

"Yes, Olga Leonidovna?"

"You're getting a new actor. And to make sure he doesn't sit around twiddling his thumbs when you need help with your drama club, we're going to broaden the scope of Konev's responsibilities. I want daily reports on his progress."

"Yes, Olga Leonidovna. Konev . . . it's Yura, right? Rehearsal's in the movie theater right after snack. Don't be tardy, please."

Taaaaardy, Yurka laughed to himself, mocking Volodya's pretentious Moscow accent with its long, drawn-out *a*'s. But Volodya actually had a nice voice. It was a little deeper than the standard baritone, silky and pleasant, yet not at all singsongy or trained.

Up close, the troop leader didn't look scared anymore. Quite the opposite. As Volodya walked up to Yurka and looked closely at him, Volodya seemed a completely different person, calmly taking hold of his glasses by both arms and resettling them on the bridge of his nose, then lifting his chin and looking down at Yurka a trifle superciliously. Yurka—who came up to Volodya's nose, as it happened—leaned back on his heels and confirmed, "Understood. I'll be on time."

Volodya nodded and looked away, his gaze landing on some kids poking around the speaker cables. He ran over to them, sternly shouting: "Hey, what are you doing? Those cables are for the light and sound equipment!"

Yurka turned away. The dance floor was humming like a disturbed beehive. The Pioneers were getting back to business, each with a different task: hanging things, fixing things, painting, washing, sweeping . . . and behind Yurka, in the band shell, he heard the creak of stretching cord. The kids were getting ready to hang up the big cloth banner that was spread out flat on the stage. San Sanych, the facilities manager, thundered, "Pull!" The cord twanged taut and the broad, bright red length of cloth with snow-white letters snapped into the air right over Yurka's head.

Yurka scoffed, picked at the considerably frayed edge of his own Pioneer neckerchief, and chanted the ubiquitous Pioneer poem scornfully: "Pioneer, remember to treat your scarf well, and honor the story of duty it tells . . ."

CHAPTER TWO

A STRAIGHT-UP CLOWN SHOW

The intermittent sprinkles of rain had turned into a steady shower, and the wind had picked up, blowing the choking smell of burnt diesel over from the construction site. The odor felt so out of place here that he had to get away from it, so Yura hurried over to the movie theater. He wouldn't have been able to stay away from it anyway, even if he hadn't been caught in the noxious wind and cold rain, since the theater was the place that brimmed most with memories of that summer.

The tall wooden building stood just next door to the outdoor stage. It was surprisingly well-preserved, except for the gaping black holes and protruding shards of glass where the large windows had been.

The steps leading up to the entrance creaked exactly as they had two decades ago, the evening they'd first met. Deep down, Yura was even glad to hear the creaking: How often do you get the chance to hear the pure, undistorted sounds of your childhood? If only he could hear the piano, too, Tchaikovsky's deep, tender "Lullaby," the leitmotif of that summer. This building was forever associated with music for Yura.

The outside of the movie theater was well-preserved; the inside, not so much. Thick, moth-eaten curtains fluttered at the windows. The door, insulated with felt padding, had at some point been broken down, and through the empty doorframe a strip of daylight pierced the large dim room. The light spread across the backs of the green seats that still stood in even rows. It fell on the bare wall, throwing the texture of the peeling paint into relief. It illuminated the dirty parquet floor. Yura's gaze slipped along the band of light and landed on some parquet tiles that had been pulled out of the floor. Some of the light-brown wooden rectangles lay in jumbled piles, but others were placed next to each other, for all the world like broken-off piano keys. Like the keys of the piano that had been here, inside this very theater.

The stage. A birch sapling had forced its way up through the foundation over on the left, exactly where Volodya had been sitting on that fateful evening. It had broken through the rotten parquet floor and was reaching for the light, stretching toward the hole in the ceiling through which pale rays slanted into the large, dark room. The young tree's unusually lush foliage only emphasized the surrounding emptiness, the absence of the piano that had once stood there.

Yura picked his way along the piano-key parquet tiles toward the birch. The moment he touched its slightly dusty leaves, he knew he didn't want to leave. Not for anything. He wanted to stay here until it got dark, and look at the birch, and wait until the heavy curtain parted and the actors came out onto the stage. He leaned his shovel against the wall and sat in one of the decrepit seats. It creaked. Yura smiled, remembering the way the floor had squealed piteously underfoot during their first rehearsal, when Yurka had hesitated behind the felt-padded door that now lay flat on the porch. He'd been furious at Ira Petrovna then—so furious!

"No way, Ira! Aw, come on, Petrovna! What do I need your dumb theater for?!" Yurka had just gotten back from visiting the nurse and was in the worst mood ever. No surprise, given how many people had seen him not only get chewed out but made to look like a total idiot, too. That Olga Leonidovna could just go to hell and take her moralizing with her! All day Yurka was outraged and insulted and tried to think of a way to get out of attending rehearsal. But he couldn't. So he had to clamp down on his cantankerousness, knowing that if he didn't go to the theater that evening, he'd be betraying Ira Petrovna, who had put her head on the line for him.

But he was still furious—even planning on slamming the door, to show everyone what he thought about this amateur hour nonsense. When he opened it, though, just as that top step had emitted its tiny creak—just as he was poised and ready for action—he froze in the doorway.

Volodya was the only one in the whole theater. He was sitting way over to the left, reading something in a notebook and munching on a pear. A radio next to him was trying to play Pachelbel's Canon, constantly hissing and sputtering from interference. The static kept drowning out the sound of the piano, and Volodya finally laid his notebook on his lap and, without taking his eyes off it, reached over and fiddled with the radio antenna.

Yurka was transfixed. This Volodya was artless, even touching. Hunched over in concentration, without a trace of bravado, the troop leader was sitting on the edge of the stage, swinging one foot back and forth. He bit into the pear with a crunch, chewed thoughtfully, then choked and coughed, giving his head a shake; evidently he'd read something he didn't like. His glasses slid down to the tip of his nose.

No wonder they slide down, on a nose as straight as that, Yura thought. He would've stood there longer, watching and admiring Volodya, wishing he had one like that, too—not a nose, obviously. A pear. Because Yurka really, really liked pears. But without meaning to, he cleared his throat. Volodya looked up, put down the notebook, and reflexively moved his pointer finger to his face, but then caught himself and, with a somewhat condescending expression, instead lightly took hold of the arms of his glasses with both hands and repositioned them.

"Hi. Back from snack already?"

Yura nodded. "Where are they handing out pears? There aren't any in the mess hall."

"Someone gave it to me."

"Who?" asked Yura automatically. Maybe it was someone he knew, and then he could get one, too, or trade for it.

"Masha Sidorova. She's our pianist, she'll be here soon. Want to share?" Volodya proffered the unbitten side of the pear, but Yurka shook his head. "No? Have it your way."

Yurka climbed up onto the stage and crossed his arms matter-of-factly. "So. What am I going to be doing here?" he inquired.

"Cutting to the chase, eh? Good attitude. I like it. And it's a good question . . . What *are* you going to be doing here?" Volodya rose to his feet and gazed thoughtfully at the clean white ceiling. "I'm looking at the script and thinking what part to give you."

"Maybe a tree? Or a wolf? Every kid's show has either a wolf or a tree."

"A tree?" Volodya scoffed. "We'll have a hiding place in a log, but that's a prop, not a part."

"Well, just—think about it. If there's one thing I know how to do, it's play a log really well, like a professional. Want to see?"

Without waiting for a reply, Yurka lay flat on the floor and stretched his arms along his sides.

"What do you think?" he asked, sitting up and looking up at Volodya.

"Not funny," Volodya shot back bluntly. "Let me fill you in on something. This isn't a light-hearted comedy, it's a drama. A tragedy, even. The camp has a big anniversary this year: thirty years since the day it was founded. Olga Leonidovna was talking about it at assembly."

"Yeah, I know she was," Yurka said.

"All right, then. You already know, of course, that this camp was named after Zina Portnova, Pioneer Hero of the Soviet Union and one of the bravest Young Avengers. But the fact that the first big event held here was a show about Portnova's life—that's probably news to you. Well, that show is what we're performing for Camp Barn Swallow Day. So no logs for you this time, Yura."

Volodya spoke animatedly, with the air of someone intent on doing something special and meaningful.

"Bleah!" Yurka grimaced. "Boring."

Volodya frowned at first, but then took a good, long look at Yurka and finally replied: "I think not. Boring is just what it won't be—not for you, anyway. Since there's no role for you, you'll help me with the actors. Why not? The only other grown-up here, apart from me, is—"

Yurka rolled his eyes and scoffed in exasperation. "Yeah, some grown-up!" he broke in. "How old are you, even? Seventeen, if that! You're in your first year of college; you're just a year older than me."

Volodya cleared his throat and repositioned his glasses, then said quietly: "I'm basically nineteen. Almost. My birthday's in November." Then he collected himself and added sternly: "And if I were you, Konev, I wouldn't forget myself when I was talking with a troop leader!"

He looked more disappointed than formidable, and Yurka found himself embarrassed. Volodya really was a troop leader, after all, just like Ira Petrovna. Chastened, Yurka admitted, "Okay, I overdid it . . . But who else in drama club is a grown-up, apart from you?"

"Masha," replied Volodya. Yurka felt that Volodya had been more offended than he let on, but Volodya continued as though nothing had happened. "She's from Troop One, same as you. The rest are all little boys. With girls, see, you don't have to take care of them—they're obedient by nature—but boys . . . boys are completely wild. With boys, it's not just watching them like a hawk, you also need authority."

"Pfft . . . let Masha babysit them, then. What am I, their mommy?"

"That's what I'm saying, is that Masha can't. These boys don't need just anybody, they need somebody with authority. I don't have the time to—"

"And what makes you think I'll do it?"

Volodya sighed heavily. "You'll do it because you don't have a choice."

"Oh, really?"

"Yes, really. If I were in your shoes, I'd be working on my self-discipline, or else . . ."

"Or else what?"

"Or else you'll get yourself kicked out of camp if you cause trouble again!" Volodya raised his voice, a note of anger sounding in it. "I'm serious. Do you have any idea how much trouble Irina got in today because of those lights? Oh, and on that note, Olga Leonidovna asked me to remind you that that was your final warning."

Yurka had nothing to say in reply. He jumped to his feet and started walking in little circles. Then he stopped, lost in thought. Was camp boring? Yeah, of course. But did he want to leave? Not really, no. To tell the truth, Yurka couldn't figure out what he wanted, but to be kicked out in disgrace . . . Well, he didn't care that much, even if it was in disgrace, but what about Ira Petrovna? What if she got a reprimand in her personal file and a terrible character reference? What a great guy he was: not only had he hidden behind his troop leader's skirts, he'd also let her down. No, this was definitely not what he'd had in mind.

"So you vouched for me and now you're blackmailing me?" he huffed, though it wasn't clear who he was angry at, Ira and Volodya or himself.

"Nobody's blackmailing you, much less trying to get you kicked out. Just be on your best behavior, do what your troop leaders say, and be helpful."

"Do what they say?" spat Yurka.

He'd been backed into a corner. It felt like everyone had banded together against him and now they were looking for an opportunity to rub it in, finding ways to harass him, suffocate him . . . He'd just arrived and they were already attacking him, accusing him, yelling at him, lecturing him. It wasn't fair!

It was like Yura turned into a wild beast, with no awareness of what he was saying. He needed to unleash his suppressed rage, to smash and crush everything in his path.

"But who are you, anyway, that I should do what you say? Ha! I'll show you! You want a performance? Fine! I'll give you a performance—one you won't forget!"

"Aaaaand here come the threats," chuckled Volodya, as though Yurka's tirade hadn't moved him in the slightest. "Go ahead, give your performance. You'll get kicked out, and that'll be the last we hear of you. Just know who'll get the blame for it. You. Not me. Like you don't already know the way you stick in the administration's craw."

"But I didn't do anything bad!" Yurka shot back. Then he sighed, dejected. "It just . . . it all just happened, the plates, and the lights . . . I didn't mean to! And I didn't mean for Ira to get involved, either . . ."

"It's obvious you didn't mean to," said Volodya, so sincerely that Yurka gaped in astonishment.

"Come again?"

"I believe you," Volodya said. "Other people would, too, if Yura Konev didn't have such a bad reputation. Ever since you almost got thrown out after your fight last year, we've been getting a ton of inspections, one after the other. You give Leonidovna the least opportunity and she'll throw you out. So here's the thing, Yura . . . be a man. Irina vouched for you, and now I'm answering for you, too. Don't let us down."

There was an upright piano on the right side of the stage. In center stage stood a bust of Lenin on a pedestal. Yura was so frustrated he felt like hurling the leader of the proletariat to the floor and shattering the sculpture into a million pieces, but he tried to calm down and steady his breathing. He walked up to the bust, propped his elbows on the pedestal, and rested his forehead on Ilych's cold balding pate. With his forehead still pressed to the statue, he swiveled his head to look sadly at Volodya.

"Since you're being so honest and all, tell me this: Are you not giving me a part so that nobody'll see my ugly mug and I won't embarrass the camp?"

"What kind of nonsense is that? There's no part for you because I haven't thought of one yet. Our boy actors are all little. You'd look like a giant in the land of the Lilliputians out there with them, but there aren't any giants in the script." He smiled. "Look, is there something else you can do? Can you sing? Dance? Play an instrument?"

Yurka glanced at the piano, an Elegy, a typical Soviet upright model. His chest constricted painfully. He scowled and fixed his gaze on the floor.

"I can't do anything and I don't want to do anything," he lied, knowing full well that right now he wasn't lying to Volodya as much as to himself.

"I see. In that case we'll go back to where we started: you'll be my helper, and at the same time you'll work on your own discipline and restore your reputation."

Their conversation ground to a halt. The silence grew. With his left eye Yurka focused on Vladimir Ilych's nose. Then he blew a speck of dust off it. Then Volodya, the other Vladimir in the room—the one who was the leader of Troop Five, not of the world proletariat—buried himself in his notebook again.

Meanwhile, the snack break Yurka had left early was ending and the actors started trickling into the movie theater. The first one to arrive was Masha Sidorova. Smiling at Volodya and ignoring Yurka, her hips swung breezily in her circle skirt as she walked over to the piano and sat down. Yurka looked hard at her: in the intervening year she'd changed completely. She'd gotten taller and thinner. Her hair now hung down to her waist, and she'd learned to flirt, just like a grown woman. Now she was sitting all proud and pretty, her back straight and her legs long and tan.

"Ludwig van Beethoven," she announced quietly. "Piano Sonata No. 14 in C-sharp Minor, Opus 27." She flipped her hair back and touched her fingers to the keys.

Yurka winced. The Moonlight Sonata! Couldn't she have thought of something a little more original? The sonata was already painfully familiar. Everybody and their dog could play it. But Yurka was a tiny bit jealous, despite his grumbling, because it was Volodya, not him, who Masha sought with her timid yet tender gaze, and it was for Volodya, not for him, that she played.

When Masha finished the sonata, she immediately began a new piece, clearly trying to keep Volodya standing right there next to her a little longer, gazing approvingly at her, smiling at her . . . But Mashka's efforts were all for naught, because a swarm of young actors burst into the theater, slamming the door the way good-for-nothing Yurka had wanted to earlier. The group seized both Volodya's attention and Volodya himself: he was trapped inside a circle of yelling children, each of whom simply had to tell the artistic director something of the utmost importance.

Volodya tried to calm their agitation, but a moment later he was the one who was agitated: the trinity had come to the theater! No fathers, sons, or holy ghosts here, of course—although, speaking of things celestial, it did smell to high heaven from their perfume. It was Polina, Ulyana, and Ksyusha. Yurka privately called them the Pukes, after the first letters of their names. These three girls were the living embodiment of the three "See no evil, hear no evil, speak no evil" monkeys but in reverse: "See everything, hear everything, and blab everything." Even now they eagerly surveyed the theater as they fluttered grandly up to the stage. All dressed up, even overdressed, and each with the exact same lipstick and the exact same smell: the Polish perfume Być Może, "Perhaps." Yurka knew the scent well, since half the country used it.

At first he thought Volodya had made up the "I'm the only grown-up in drama club" stuff, but as soon as Yurka looked over at the nervously sweating artistic director, he realized that Volodya himself was surprised at the club's newfound popularity. And Polina was making matters worse, grabbing Volodya's elbow and enthusing: "Volodya, let's put on a modern play! There's this one really interesting play about love, and actually I could even play the role of—"

"Girls! You do know that clubs have already been assigned?!" interrupted Masha, pale with rage. Apparently she'd realized it was the club leader, not the club, that had gotten so popular. "Go away. You're too late."

"N-no, it's okay," Volodya said, disconcerted, his cheeks burning. Small wonder: so many beautiful girls around, and all of them gazing at him . . . Yurka would be disconcerted too! "There were a lot of girls in the Young Avengers, not just Zina Portnova. We'll find parts for you. We need someone to play Fruza Zenkova, for example . . ."

"So that's how it is! You'll find parts for them, but I have to babysit?!" Yurka raged.

His protest went unheeded. The shouting of the older teens joined the chorus of shrieking children. A straight-up clown show ensued.

"So can I be the costumer?" shrilled Ksyusha. "I'll make such pretty dresses!"

"What kind of pretty dresses are there during a war?" asked Yurka indignantly.

"The show's about war?" Ksyusha whined in disappointment. "Awww . . ."

"Ha!" barked Yurka. "Obviously it's about war—it's about Portnova! Hmph . . . signs up to do the show without even knowing what it's about . . . Volodya! Why am I the one who has to babysit?!"

"Vovchik, come on, let's do something modern!" Polina wasn't giving up. "Let's do *Athena and Venture*!"

Yurka snorted. The spectacular, wildly popular Soviet Russian rock opera was a little bit out of their league.

"But who was just saying that doing a show was boring, Pol?! Who was that, hm?!" Masha, disheveled from rage, yanked down the hem of her cotton dress. "And what are you laughing at, Ulya? Like you weren't egging her on!"

"What do you care! Afraid we're going to steal him?" jeered Ulyana.

"Volodya! Volodya! Volodya! Look at me! Is it my turn? Can I say something? Volodya!" The little kids were jumping up and down and grabbing the artistic director's arm.

"We should have the metro in the show! I've been on the Moscow metro. It's so beautiful," bragged Sasha, a chubby boy little from Volodya's troop.

"Now just hold on a minute. One at a time, children . . . ," the troop leader said, trying to calm them, but the room kept escalating.

"I stood on the very edge of the platform and the trains went by all shoom! fshoom! fshoom! Right on the very edge, like this . . . and shoom!" said the pudgy showoff, spinning around to demonstrate speed.

"Sasha, get back from the edge of the stage! You'll fall!"

"Shoom! Fshoom!"

"You miserable frump!"

"Can I say something?"

"That's not fair!"

"I'll do the costumes!"

"Good god, that's enough!" Volodya's roar reverberated through the theater, drowning out the hubbub.

It got quiet. So quiet, Yura could hear the dust motes floating to the floor, and his heart beating (ba-bump), and Masha's furious breathing. Everyone froze . . . except the chubby showoff, who was spinning in circles on the very edge of the stage . . . It was tall, at least a meter off the ground . . .

. . . ba-bump . . . ba-bump . . . ba—

. . . and suddenly the boy's ankle twisted, he awkwardly threw his arms wide, and he fell, slowly and heavily, off the stage. Yurka's heart skipped a beat, Masha squeezed her eyes shut in horror, and Volodya's glasses flashed—

—bump!

"Aaagh! My foot!!"

"Sasha!"

It hurt just to look at the showoff, but it hurt even more to look at Volodya and see how he ran in circles around the injured boy, how his hands shook, how he started cursing himself: "But this is something I could've stopped . . . I could've stopped this . . ." Even though Yurka was mad at Volodya, he still found himself the first one rushing forward to help.

"Let me through! My father's a doctor!" Yurka yelled, quoting a line from a popular foreign film as he elbowed through the crowd of gaping actors that had immediately collected around Sasha and knelt beside the chubby little tyke. In a way, Yurka wasn't kidding: his father had showed him a thousand times how to examine a patient. So now he examined the scraped ankle and skinned knee, then concluded with an air of expertise that the patient needed to be taken to the first aid station, and quickly, adding authoritatively that a stretcher wouldn't be necessary.

Volodya grasped Sasha under the armpits and tried to heave him to his feet, but the victim burst into tears, categorically refusing to stand on his uninjured leg.

"Yur, help me. Get on his left. I can't . . . phew . . . I can't do it myself . . ." panted Volodya. It was bad enough that the squirming, sobbing Sashka weighed as much as Volodya himself, but his panicked flailing was making things worse.

"Mommy! Mooommmyyyy!" Sasha groaned.

"Okay, take his arm: one, two, three, up!" said Yurka brusquely, doggedly acting like nothing hurt and he hadn't gotten all banged up earlier that day falling out of the apple tree. Although even just bending over hurt.

"Masha, you're in charge," said Volodya.

Masha glared triumphantly at her rivals.

"Can I be the costumer?" the pesky Ksyusha butted in.

"All right, fine!" replied Volodya irritably. He took a moment; then, calmer, he instructed: "Read the play out loud until I get back, and—good god, Sasha! I know it hurts, but quit yelling your head off!"

Their journey to the first aid station was long and slow, accompanied the whole way by the victim's wails. But anybody with eyes could tell Sasha was screeching not from pain but from fear, and also to be the center of attention. Yurka was silent, focused on his own tailbone, while Volodya urged Sasha on: "Come on, Sanya, you can do it, hang on, just a little more . . ."

The nurse came out when she heard the wailing and immediately set to fussing and clucking like a mother hen over the pitiful creature. She rudely shoved Yurka aside and shot a stern, even threatening look at the troop leader. Yurka shrugged and didn't bother going into the first aid station. What if Larisa Sergeyevna inquired whether the ointment she gave him earlier had helped? Then Volodya would find out about Yurka's injury. Not a major concern, but still annoying. At any rate, Yurka decided to wait for Volodya, who had followed the nurse and her patient inside. Yurka wanted to find out whether he'd correctly diagnosed the patient as suffering from boneheadedness and a few bruises, not strains and sprains.

A comfy little bench nestled under an overgrown wild rose in full bloom by the porch. Yurka lay down on the bench, gazed up at the sky, and took in a lungful of fresh, flower-scented air, appreciating how stuffy it had been in the movie theater and how good he felt now.

Volodya came out after ten minutes or so. He pushed Yurka's feet away and plopped down on the bench in exhaustion. He heaved a heavy sigh.

"How is the victim? Will he live?" Yurka asked lazily, still luxuriating in the air: it was so good, so pure and cool, you could all but drink it.

"Ah, it's just a scratched knee and a couple of bruises, nothing serious. So what'd he scream bloody murder like that for?"

"What for?" Yurka repeated, raising his head off the bench but holding off from sitting up all the way. "You had auditions today, right? Well, now he stands out from the rest. Clearly he wanted to demonstrate all his many talents at once. You should make a note of it. There's gotta be a way to use a voice like that!"

Volodya smiled. On his tired face, the smile looked so genuine that Yurka was taken aback: Had he really been the cause of it? That felt good; he was glad. But Volodya's smile vanished as quickly as it had appeared.

"I'm so sick of all this!" Volodya said, rubbing his temples.

"What are you sick of? Being in charge?" Yurka stretched, then put his hands behind his head and looked up at the sky. The blue was so bright he had to squint.

"It's only the first day of the session and I'm already sick of it! Running around taking care of the small fry, justifying every little thing I do to the senior staff, and then they chew me out for every little thing anyway. And then they saddled me with this club . . . and now, to top it all off, a kid's been injured . . ."

"So why are you doing it? Didn't you know it'd be hard?"

"I knew it'd be hard; I just didn't know it'd be this hard. When I was at Pioneer camp, it looked easy: just taking care of little kids. Nothing to it! And I thought it'd be useful, too: you get paid for it, and you get to relax out in nature, and it's great for your character reference, which is really handy for the Komsomol or maybe even for the Party, if you're lucky. But the reality of it is completely different." Volodya shifted down the bench toward Yurka and bent closer to him. "They foisted off the youngest troop on me, telling me it's easier to work with the little ones. But it's just the opposite. I count them three times an hour because they keep running off with other troop leaders and they don't do anything I say. What am I supposed to do, scream at them for real?"

"Why not? Even the educational specialist does! Hmph . . . call that 'educating' . . . she can just go and . . ." Yurka pouted.

"She shouldn't have done that, of course," Volodya said. "She taught us not to raise our voice at a child, but that if we do have to bawl someone out, then to focus on the action, not the child. And, most importantly, not to do it in front of other people."

"She said that?" Yurka gave a derisive snort. "No kidding."

"Yes, she did. But that was before we got a surprise inspection yesterday, before you all got here, that uncovered a lot of violations. Now she's stressed. We get inspections every session now. And guess whose fault that is?"

"Oh, come on! Like that's all because of me!" Yurka didn't believe it, but it did ruin his good mood.

"Who had the bright idea of getting into a fistfight at Pioneer camp? You should be grateful the police weren't called in." Volodya's eyes flashed dangerously, but his attempt at teaching Yurka some sense ended when he glanced over at the little green hut of the first aid station. The troop leader suddenly wilted, turning from a model educator into a regular guy. He sighed. Clearly, even just being reminded of the injured Sashka sucked him right back into a whirlpool of misgivings. When Volodya spoke again, his voice was hoarse and lifeless: "I have to take Troop Five to the river tomorrow. Not by myself, of course; Lena, the other troop leader, is coming, and she's more experienced. And the athletic director's coming, too; he'll also help me keep an eye on the kids. And we've already roped off a shallow zone for them. Everything by the book. But I'm still absolutely terrified. And Lena's also terrified. She told me a troop leader she knows was prosecuted last year when one of her girls drowned in the river . . . in the middle of the day, in front of all the troop leaders . . . We didn't make it to the river today. By the time we got everybody out here and got all set up, it was already lunchtime. But tomorrow there's no way out, we have to take them to the beach. If I had my way, we wouldn't even let them get near the water!"

Yurka shifted uncomfortably. Camp Barn Swallow had actually had its share of accidents, too; he'd heard things.

"Well . . . don't let it get you down," he said. Volodya had now become even more dejected, so Yurka decided to cheer him up. "It's just the beginning of the session; there's still a lot of time left. You'll find your rhythm, you'll get used to it. I mean, look at Ira Petrovna—this isn't her first time being a troop leader, so there's got to be something good about all this, right?"

"The only good thing I see so far is the pay and the good character reference, to get into the Party later . . ."

"Why are you so fixated on the Party?!" Yurka burst out. "This is the second time you've brought it up!"

It irritated him when people tried to just live by inertia, going wherever they were led, uninterested in stepping off the beaten path sometimes to do something differently from how they'd been taught.

Volodya just shrugged. "Of course I'm fixated on it! Yura, you know full well that without a Party membership you can't get a good job—I mean a really good job—and that you can't travel anywhere, either. Sure, it's not an ideal political system—in some ways it's outdated, in other ways it's over the top—but it works, after all . . ."

"What do you mean?" Yurka's eyebrow shot up in surprise. He'd never expected to hear something like this from Volodya, a prime example of somebody who, to all appearances, was a zealous follower of that "working" system's orders.

"What I said. Just keep it between us, okay? It's not as bad now as it was back in Stalin's day, but I could still get in deep trouble."

"Of course!" Yura even sat up, then grimaced when his tailbone twinged.

"In this country everybody lives the same way they did fifty years ago: the Pioneers, the Komsomol, the Party . . . I'm sure it's frustrating for any progressive person here. And I'm not blind, either . . . but there's no other way . . ."

"I don't agree!" Yurka actually squared his shoulders as he turned to look Volodya right in the eyes. "There's always a way."

Volodya smiled. The smile was a bit smug and patronizing, but even so, it managed to make Yurka happy again.

"You usually don't agree with anything anyway, Konev. But that's no way to live, either. Of course there's a way. You do what you're supposed to: you join the Komsomol and then the Party, no matter how useless you think it is. But digging your heels in, trying to destroy the indestructible . . . *that's* what's useless."

Yurka, who did tend to argue with everyone and disagree with everything, was suddenly at a loss for words. He had no desire to acknowledge Volodya was right; still, deep down, he abruptly admitted there was a grain of truth to Volodya's words. Especially the part about it being useless for Yurka to resist.

More than that, though, he felt his attitude toward Volodya also change at that same moment. Suddenly the troop leader stopped seeming like a robot and turned into a normal person, one with his own worries and problems, things he didn't always know how to cope with. Yurka liked it that they both had the same thoughts about certain things.

"Want me to help you?" he said, feeling a sudden urge to try and support Volodya.

"Come again?"

"I mean, like, helping with the little guys. So it wouldn't just be this drama club here but your troop, too. Tomorrow, for instance: When you take them to the river, want me to come—" Yurka broke off, surprised at his own fervor. "Well, I just . . . since you're so worried about them . . . ," he added, trailing off awkwardly.

Volodya was also surprised—and delighted: "Really? That would be awesome!" But then he clasped his hands together. "How'd this end up being all about me and my problems, huh? That's no good. Tell me something about you."

Yurka was prevented from talking about himself by a piercing blast from a speaker mounted on a post. It wasn't the trumpets of Jericho, it was the camp bugle calling everyone in for dinner. And the ground shook, but it wasn't the insurmountable walls tumbling down; it was the thundering of Pioneer feet. Troop leaders shouted like generals to their armies: "Pair up! Column formation! Forward march!" The camp burst into lively activity.

As soon as he heard the loudspeaker start crackling, Yurka's conversation partner raced back to the movie theater to collect the rest of the drama club and lead them to the mess hall, while Yurka himself, groaning and sighing, stood up and walked into the first aid station to have Larisa Sergeyevna rub on some more ointment. For better or worse, he was going to have to make an appearance in his swim trunks tomorrow, even though he was embarrassed to show off his bruised backside to everyone.

Yurka knew that Troop One was also going swimming tomorrow, but for some reason, when he was thinking about his backside, he wasn't worried about his own troop but about Troop Five. Or, rather, about the Troop Five leader.

CHAPTER THREE

YURKA MAKES A DEAL

Yurka was especially fond of mornings at Camp Barn Swallow. But only up until the point he had to emerge from under his warm blanket and drag himself outside to the camp washstand. Everything would be just fine . . . The birds would be singing, the trees whispering, and the whole camp would be sleepy and melancholy . . . But then they'd play a recording of the call to reveille over the loudspeaker, and although it was just a bugle, you might think, listening to it, that it was sinners shrieking in hell.

Regardless of the daytime heat, it got very cold at night in the woodsy environs. After warming up during the day, the ground cooled off, and by morning reveille a blanket of mist descended on the camp, along with a damp chill that was especially penetrating in contrast to the warm cabin. Even the kids whose parents had tempered them from birth with cold showers had to gather their courage to wash at the camp washstand, which was nothing more than a roof over a couple of metal troughs with faucets. The water from the washstand faucets came directly out of the ground, like water from a mountain spring, so not only was it not warm, it was so freezing cold it burned and made your teeth ache. But there was one indisputable benefit to washing with it: you definitely weren't sleepy afterward.

Yurka, covered in goose bumps and wishing he could crawl back under his blanket, rubbed his face with his towel, gave an energetic "Brrr," and threw his towel over his shoulder. He didn't realize someone was talking to him until his gaze fell on Ira Petrovna.

"Konev! Are you even listening to me?"

"Ira Petrovna? What is it? Good morning!" Yurka could tell that Ira Petrovna was angry, but he wasn't sure how he could've gotten in trouble already, given that he'd just gotten out of bed.

Irina rolled her eyes and ground through gritted teeth: "I'm asking you for the last time: Why did you tear up the lilacs yesterday? Hm?"

Yurka goggled at her in amazement. "What lilacs?"

"Don't pretend you don't know! The lilacs behind the power shed!"

"I didn't tear anything up, Ira Petrovna!"

"Like hell you didn't! Who did, then?" She looked at him suspiciously.

"I don't kn—"

"You were late to dinner yesterday, and then I saw leaves and petals by the door to the cabin and a bouquet in a jar on Polya's nightstand. And this isn't the first time you've broken off lilac boughs, either! The lilacs are almost done flowering anyway, but now that you've torn them up, they look disgraceful!"

"But why's it automatically me? Polya could've broken off those boughs herself!"

Yurka was horribly hurt: here it all went, again, and for no reason, again. He really and truly hadn't done it, but he was the one being accused. By inertia, apparently. Because the easiest thing, of course, was just to blame him: he was always stirring up trouble anyway, so it must be him this time, too.

Yurka scowled, trying to guess how much trouble he'd get in this time for something he hadn't done.

"Irin, it really wasn't him," came a voice behind him. Yurka turned and saw Volodya. "Yura was in the theater yesterday, and then he was helping me bring a boy to the first aid station. That's why he was late to dinner. So it was someone else who tore up your lilacs."

Ira Petrovna stopped short, gave Yurka a look of amazement, and turned to Volodya. "He was helping you?"

"You heard it at the staff meeting: yesterday there was an accident in my club. Sashka fell off the stage and Yura stepped up to help," Volodya assured her.

If there was one person she had to believe, it was Volodya. Irina was taken aback. Yurka let out a breath and shot Volodya a look of immense gratitude: he'd come not a moment too soon!

"I didn't know that; we didn't talk about it at check-in . . . Never mind, then, Konev," said Ira Petrovna. "If you really were helping, then good work. I'll go ask the girls where they got the lilacs."

"Fine, but couldn't you have gone to them first?" he grumbled resentfully.

She just tousled Yurka's hair as she left, making him huff in annoyance. He was angry enough to snap "What about an apology?" at her back.

She paused for a moment, tossed a "Sorry" over her shoulder, and walked away.

"Thank you," said Yurka, smiling, as he turned to Volodya. "I thought I was really going to get it there."

"No problem. You really *aren't* to blame. It seems Olga Leonidovna's already managed to convince Irina to blame you anytime there's something strange going on. So now she's picking on you."

"But wait—what are you doing over here?"

"I came to tell you we're heading to the river around ten. You volunteered to help yesterday—"

He was interrupted by Ira Petrovna, who'd suddenly reappeared. "Yura, after breakfast, instead of cleanup duty, go get Mitya from Troop Two. You remember him, don't you? Take him and check the mattresses in the junior cabins. The kids were complaining that some of them were damp. Put the unusable ones in storage. I'll get someone to bring new ones to the junior cabins by quiet hour."

Yurka groaned in despair. "Gee, Ira Petrovna, thanks for not hitching me to a plow, at least!"

"Don't clown around with me, or—" She broke off upon catching sight of Ksyusha coming out of the cabin. "Ksyusha, hold on! I have to ask you something about the lilacs..."

"Somebody's sure gonna get raked over the coals now," said Yurka with a smirk.

Volodya sighed. "I'm guessing you're not going to be able to make it to the beach?"

Yurka shrugged. "I'll try to take care of this as fast as I can."

He washed and headed back to his troop cabin to change. He shook hands in greeting with Vanka and Mikha, who were lolling on the bench by the entrance, and gave a short nod to Masha, who was grinning suspiciously. He was on the threshold, about to go into the cabin, when he stopped dead in his tracks. His troop's wall newspaper was posted by the door. Every troop wrote one by hand every week on a large sheet of paper, applauding the good troop members and scolding the bad ones, and posted it publicly on the outside of their troop cabin for all to see. This issue was dedicated to the ceremonial opening of the session and the first day of camp. It was a nice, big, eye-catching wall newspaper, but it made Yurka's mood go sour: he'd been subjected to public censure in the form of a caricature.

Half of the paper was taken up by a cartoon of a great big apple tree. From it, a stick figure version of Yurka was hanging upside-down with a strand of lights wrapped around his ankle, arms and legs flailing. The drawing had actually turned out pretty well, it was funny, but the expression on Yura's face was just too stupid. It wasn't a face so much as an ugly mug, with a wide snout like a pig's and a gaping mouth displaying a missing front tooth. But Yurka had all his teeth! And they were excellent, too! It was offensive. He was grown-up, basically, so stuff like this didn't work on him, but it was still able to hurt his feelings. It already had, so many times . . .

No matter how funny it was, it was still offensive. And since all the troops in camp avidly read each other's wall newspapers, he'd be getting ribbed for his piggy snout all day, all over camp.

Even the delicious tvorog breakfast cake couldn't get rid of the bad taste the wall newspaper left in his mouth. Before he went over to start hauling mattresses, Yurka got the artist's name from his fellow troop members. It was Ksyusha. One of the Pukes. Yurka wasn't going to go get revenge on her or anything—, but he did make note of it.

The Mitka whose voice was broadcast from the radio was the one assigned to help Yurka. Or rather, Yurka was the one doing the helping, because Mitka was sent out on tasks like this all the time, where he was moving, lifting, and carrying things. Mitka not only sang well and had a good speaking voice, he was also big and strong. Yurka, thinking of all the things Mitka was that he wasn't, felt out of sorts all of a sudden.

Sure enough, some of the mattresses were wet. The boys hauled out the six damp ones and dumped them next to the cabin. At first Yurka blamed the kids: they'd gotten scared, they hadn't been able to hold it, they were still just Little Octoberists, these things happened at that age . . . But when it turned out that all the wet mattresses were on beds right next to each other, Yurka walked around with an intent look on his face, then rubbed his chin in contemplation.

"Hey, Mit! Maybe the roof's leaking. I heard there was some rain a few days ago. Maybe something happened to the roof?"

Mitya peered up at the ceiling, examining it closely, but didn't see any stains. "And nobody noticed the water dripping from the ceiling?"

"There was nobody in the cabin then, it was in between sessions . . . Listen, we need to climb up there and take a look."

"You go right ahead. The roof wouldn't hold me, anyway," Mitya said, laughing.

Yurka nimbly ascended to the roof—he didn't even need a ladder—and immediately spotted the issue. Right over the area where the wet beds were, the asphalt roofing material had cracked, so water was evidently getting in through the crack. Yurka crouched down and picked at the tarry surface with his fingernail, talking to himself as he figured it out: "This stuff probably cracked back last winter from the cold, and now, between the pouring rain and the burning heat, it's finally given up the ghost. Need to tell the facilities manager . . ."

"Yuwka! Hi, Yuwka!" he heard suddenly, down beneath him. Yurka was so startled, he jumped out of his skin.

A group of kids in yellow bucket hats was walking past: Troop Five, preceded by both its leaders, was making its way to the river. One of the little boys—Olezhka, who was also in drama club—had stopped, breaking up the column, and was shouting and waving both arms. Olezhka couldn't say his *r*'s right. This flaw in his speech became especially noticeable when he was shouting at the top of his lungs.

"Volodya, look! It's Yuwka up thewe!"

"Hey! You get down off the roof or you'll fall!" Volodya shouted sternly.

"What are you doing up there?" squeaked Sasha, the chubby boy who'd been injured the day before.

"I'm on the lookout for treasure hunters," said Yurka, making it up on the spot. "They come here and poke around. Did you know this area was occupied by the Germans during the war?"

Suddenly he was filled with horror—but it wasn't because he was about to fall. No. Yurka had seen the terrified but furious Ira Petrovna rushing toward him along a dirt path, raising a cloud of dust.

"Come on back to earth, Gagarin," said Volodya. "I mean it. Get down."

"Konev! For goodness' sake—*Konev!*" Ira Petrovna's shriek seemed to carry through the entire camp. "Hurry up and get off that roof! Now!"

"You want me to hurry up? Whatever you say." Yurka stood back up and walked over to the side of the roof, pretending he was about to jump off.

"Oh no, Yurochka, don't! Don't do that! Just go down the same way you went up!" Ira cried. Once she caught sight of Yurka's devious grin, she turned to Volodya and begged, "Volodya, do something!"

Volodya narrowed his eyes, mentally calculating the height of the roof, and then asked, completely calm: "So, are you coming to the river with us?"

The kids bellowed, "Come!" "Yes!" "Yes, he is!" "Come with us, Yuwka!"

"Well, I don't know . . . I still have to move those mattresses . . . Or maybe you'll let me go, Ira Petrovna? Mitka can move them himself . . ." Yurka wobbled precariously on his tiptoes at the very edge of the roof.

In a thin, terrified voice, Ira Petrovna squeaked, "Go wherever you want, Konev! Just climb down from there normally, without jumping!"

Yurka shrugged as if to say, *Why not?* He crouched as though he were about to begin climbing down, but then jumped anyway. Ira Petrovna shrieked. When Konev emerged safe and sound from the bushes by the cabin, she blew out a breath in exasperation.

"We put the pile of wet mattresses over there," Yurka said, smiling. "You don't trust me, Ira Petrovna! You think I'm going to use a self-inflicted injury to get out of work. But you're wrong!"

Ira Petrovna sighed in relief, so shaken that she had to lean against a tree. "Oh, Konev! Get yourself out of my sight!" But she was the one who left.

Twenty pairs of children's shoes were arranged on the yellow sand in two even rows. Nearby, Polina, Ulyana, and Ksyusha were laying out on their towels, bodies arranged in graceful poses to get the most sun. A little farther away, a bored Masha lolled in a bit of shade with a volume of Chekhov. When he looked at Masha, Yurka was reminded of Chekhov's comment about the gun hanging on the wall that eventually will have to be fired. He had no idea why. Nothing about Masha looked threatening—quite the opposite, in fact. She looked very romantic, with her light ruffled dress that fluttered in the breeze, occasionally baring a bit of tawny-gold thigh. "Where does she find the time to sunbathe?" Yurka wondered.

Without coming up with an answer—actually, without even bothering to try—he turned and saw Vanka and Mikha on the other end of the beach. They were also stretched out on towels, so evidently they'd just finished their civic duty work of sweeping all the common areas. But Yurka walked past them. Right now, he wasn't interested in friends or girls. He was interested in Volodya.

Volodya was standing ankle-deep in the water, staring intently at the campers under his care. The river rippled in lazy little wavelets while the sun flashed off the surface and sparkled in the splashes of water sent up by the frolicking children. Troop Five was churning and squealing in the shallow zone, roped off by nets and buoys. It looked like the water was boiling. Zhenya, the handsome physical education instructor, was floating in a boat behind the barrier. Every so often he'd grunt a warning at the daring Olezhka, who kept swimming right up to the buoys. Lena, Troop Five's second leader, was also on the beach, sitting in a chair raised on a platform. She kept an eye on the kids and shouted orders from a megaphone, but she remained perfectly relaxed and calm, unlike Volodya.

"Pcholkin! Quit splashing!" Volodya ordered.

Pcholkin quit, but as soon as the leader looked the other way, he snickered and splashed up gouts of water again.

A few steps and Yurka was next to Volodya, but he didn't even have a chance to open his mouth before Volodya waved him off: "No time. Not now. Sorry." Without turning his head, Volodya's peripheral vision caught another infraction. He shouted, "Pcholkin! One more time and you're out of the water!" right in Yurka's ear.

Yurka blinked helplessly, deafened. Just to be on the safe side, he went back to the beach. He couldn't bring himself to distract Volodya—at least, not until Pcholkin had been ejected from the water back onto dry land. The leader was pale with worry and getting more nervous every minute. Yurka would only have gotten in the way.

Vanka saw his friend and waved at him to come join them. Yurka willingly joined him on his towel. As Yurka listened to his friends with half his now-deaf ear, he kept getting distracted—by Volodya, or the Pukes, or Masha. The last of these was actually only pretending to read; what she was really doing was glaring sternly at the flirtatious girls and then gazing fondly at Volodya, waiting to see whether the businesslike leader would look her way. He didn't. He was watching the splashing kids intently without taking his eyes off them; it even seemed like he was trying to blink as little as possible.

"You up for a game of twenty-one, Yurets?" Mikha pulled a deck of cards out of his pocket.

"Deal," said Yurka absentmindedly. He took off his sandals and sat cross-legged on the sand. "What are we betting? Flicks?" The traditional finger flicks to the loser's forehead were no joke. Unfortunately so, because with Yurka paying attention to anything and everything but the game, he kept losing. Badly. His forehead was burning from all the flicks by the time Mikha suggested a new game.

"Should we play durak next? And for the loser . . . takeoff-and-landing, maybe?" suggested Mikha, eyes narrowed craftily. This punishment was an especially painful one: a slap to the front and then the back of the head. Vanka rubbed his hands together. Yurka nodded.

Yurka was finally able to get into the game while playing durak; no surprise, given what was at stake. But he had rotten luck. He only got two trumps, and they were both low: a two and a six.

Mikha was the first to get rid of all his cards; he eyeballed his companions, flexing his hands in anticipation and smiling an evil little smile. Yurka could tell what he was thinking just looking at him: *I'm gonna give you such a takeoff-and-landing, you'll black out.*

Yurka played his last trump and cringed inwardly: he only had one card left, a ten of spades. He was screwed. Vanka bobbed up and down with glee and flung down the queen of trumps, shouting victoriously, "Wham! Take that!" Yurka scoffed in disgust. He'd been destroyed. He sighed and turned to Mikha.

Whack! Mikha smacked him hard in the forehead with the palm of his hand: takeoff. Yurka's head flew back from the force of it. Then, before he could come to his senses: Thwack! Mikha belted him on the back of the head. Landing. Yurka's head jerked forward, so far his nose almost touched his chest. First he saw stars; then everything really did sort of go dim.

"I'll get you for that!" he whispered, blinking and trying to focus his eyes again. "One more game? Loser does a dare?"

"But what's the dare?"

"When you lose, I'll tell you!"

"Just nothing indecent! And nothing to do with leaders! I'm not going to run around behind Irina with scissors, asking to cut her hair again."

"Fine."

Yurka focused all his will. He knew how to win without any trumps at all by thinking ahead, remembering his opponents' cards, and counting turns. But this time Yurka got lucky: a three, a seven, and an ace. Oh, he'd show them!

And show them he did. Not only was he the first one to get rid of all his cards, he also counted turns and saw that Mikha, Mr. Takeoff-and-Landing himself, would be the one to lose. Which is exactly what happened. Mikha tossed his cards on the towel and edged warily closer to Yurka. "Well?"

"Go to the middle of the beach, kneel, and bow all the way to the ground four times while you shout—" But here Yurka leaned over to Mikha's ear and whispered the words so Vanka wouldn't hear.

"Aw, come on! Four times? Why?" scowled Mikha.

Vanka snorted, amused, and replied before Yurka could: "Because you had four cards left. If you don't like it, we can always count points instead, like in twenty-one . . ."

"Okay, okay," Mikha answered. Downcast, he trudged off to perform his task.

But he didn't go to the middle of the beach, like he'd been commanded to. He only took a few steps, then he stopped right in front of the Pukes. He gave Yurka a questioning look, but Yurka, baffled, was caught stock-still, and it took a few seconds for him to unfreeze and wave his arms frantically: "No, not here, keep going." But it was too late. Vanka watched Mikha fall slowly to his knees and gasped: "Oh, here it comes!" while Yurka stifled a giggle.

Mikha knelt, then repeatedly bowed down and prostrated himself, beating his head on the sand as though trying to break through while yelling loud enough for the whole beach to hear: "Let me into your mine shaft!"

"Hey, Pronin! What are you, crazy?" Ulyana shrieked.

"Get out of here!" scoffed Polina, waving him away.

"Let me into your mine shaft!"

"Misha, that's enough! You got sand all over my dress!" Ksyusha said indignantly.

"Let me into your mine shaft! Let me into your miiiine shaaaaft!"

Yurka was lying on the ground, gasping with laughter. Vanka was clutching his belly with one hand and pounding his towel with the other. The Pukes were pelting Mikha with whatever dresses, skirts, and blouses came to hand and shrieking so loudly that even the whole of Troop Five went quiet. Masha smiled, observing the fracas from her shady spot. Even Lena giggled. But Volodya turned around, annoyed and scowling, to snap harshly at them: "Girls! Quiet down!"

The "girls" only quieted down after Mikha, with a red face, fled the beach in nothing but his swim briefs.

"But why a mine shaft?" asked Vanka, elbowing Yurka.

Yurka smiled and shrugged. "What else is underground? It's the first thing that came to mind."

Soon it grew quiet again—or what passed for quiet at a river beach at a Pioneer camp. Yurka, languishing from the heat, decided to go take a dip. As he got up from his towel, he overheard: "Volodechka's gotten really bad . . ." He turned to look at the girls and saw a frowning Ksyusha talking. "Girls like us are sitting over here in bathing suits, but he pays zero attention, even when that fool Pronin starts carrying on at us." She clicked her tongue in disappointment. "You try your hardest, but all he's got on his mind is kids."

"He just really likes them. Which is a rare quality, by the way." Polina turned over onto her back. "It's cute. He'll make a good dad."

Yurka heard this as he was taking off his shirt and shorts. "Wow, what a model future mother," he scoffed. Fortunately for him, the girls didn't hear anything. They continued their conversation.

"Maybe something happened and now he's worried?" Ulyana said, trying to defend Volodya.

"What is there to worry about? Both the phys ed instructor and the other troop leader are right there," Ksyusha drawled lazily. "No, he's gone all mean somehow. Just you wait, that Pcholkin's gonna get it—"

"No, that's not what I'm talking about!" interrupted Ulyana. "Maybe he has a girlfriend? That second leader there, Lena, for example. Why not? They sleep in rooms right next to each other, so maybe they . . . well, you know. And then they had a fight?"

Polina even sat up. "You might just be right!"

"That's impossible!" said Ksyusha confidently.

"Why's that?"

"Because Volodya wasn't at the dance yesterday, but Lena was, and she danced with Zhenya!"

"That's right!" Polya said, excited. "Everybody goes to the dance, even the leaders of the youngest troops. It's the best part!"

"Whoa there, Pol! Instead of getting all worked up, what about getting Volodya to show up today?" Ksyusha suggested. "Then we can see who he dances with."

"Why does it have to be me?! What's the—"

Polya didn't even have a chance to get good and outraged. Ksyusha interrupted her: "Hey, Konev!" she snapped. "What are you doing standing there? Eavesdropping?"

Yurka was nonplussed at that. Like he really needed to eavesdrop on their stupid blabbering when they were shouting for the whole beach to hear? He could have ignored the outburst, but, to keep up appearances, he grumbled, "I'm standing here because I want to. It's not your private beach."

"Well, it's not yours, either. Beat it!" retorted Ksyusha.

"Whoa, what's gotten into you?" said Yurka, flabbergasted. He'd never heard girls talk like that.

"You're making us look stupid in front of Volodya, that's what's gotten into me! We all heard you put Pronin up to it!"

"Oh? And who drew a picture of me as an idiot in the wall newspaper?" Yurka folded his arms across his chest angrily.

"It's your own fault, you're the one who pulled down those lights. So go on, get out of here! You're blocking our UV rays!"

"Well—no amount of UV rays are gonna help you, you jerk. When you're that stupid, nothing can help you. Any of you!"

He snatched up the shorts he'd tossed on the sand and walked away. He was angry and offended, of course, but he was more perplexed than anything else.

If the three of them got what they wanted from Volodya, what then? Would they divide him in thirds or something? Although they already were dividing him up . . . or rather, not Volodya himself, but the work of . . . of doing what? Seducing him? Conducting an investigation into his personal life?

This was all incredibly dumb to Yurka. After all, he knew the real reason Volodya was so worried. First they'd scared him with drowning victims, now the kids were having water fights. No wonder he was worried to death!

And at that exact moment, a panicked "Heeeelp!" came from the water and the phys ed instructor blew his whistle.

Volodya flinched visibly and jerked forward, about to leap into the water fully dressed. But the thin, girlish voice rang out again, and this time it was tearful, not frightened: "He's shoving me again!"

"Damn these kids!" Yurka read Volodya's lips.

It was a false alarm: nobody was drowning, the kids were just goofing around. The senior campers relaxed. All of them, that is, except Volodya, who swallowed nervously and clenched his fists. At that exact moment, the kids got completely out of hand and an honest-to-goodness fight broke out, with furious poking, shoving, and shouting.

Yurka had no intention of calmly watching Volodya and discussing the situation, like the Pukes. His expression went cold and stern; he swiveled his awesome foreign-import cap so it was on backward and, to be even more imposing, he glared angrily at the little kids. He stomped through the water to Volodya to break up the fight and call the hooligans to order.

After a brief but fierce battle with Pcholkin, who tried to swim away, the two of them managed to drag him by his swim briefs back to dry land. Yurka stood him on the sand and leaned down to him. "Pcholkin, do you want to become a Pioneer?"

"Yes!"

"Did you know that the Pioneers don't take little boys who hit little girls?"

"No! I mean . . . but she started it!"

"Doesn't matter who started it. You can't hurt girls!"

While Yurka lectured the hooligan, Volodya heaved a sigh of palpable relief and headed back into the water to monitor the other children. Yurka left the touchingly chagrined Pcholkin to serve his time onshore and went to help Volodya count his troop's flip-flops, clothing, and heads.

Yurka's efforts were not in vain. He was very pleased to hear not just the whole trinity of Pukes but even Masha—who was usually focused on Volodya—exclaim, "Yurka did such a good job! An honest-to-goodness assistant troop leader!" That proud "good job" was so gratifying that Yurka forgot his hurt feelings for a while, and the words Ira Petrovna had said to him kept reverberating happily in his heart: "I never doubted you, Yura. But now I'm actually proud of you! I'll talk about this at the staff meeting, let them all know what kind of person our Konev is!"

But of all the things people said to him, the sweetest, the absolute nicest and happiest thing of all was Volodya's quiet, exhaled "Thanks," along with the benevolent gleam in his gray-green eyes. That "Thanks" warmed Yurka to the bottom of his heart all that day and night. Because it had been earned, and also because it had been said by him, by Volodya . . . someone who, after that brief half hour together at the beach, Yurka thought he understood better, was closer to. Someone who was maybe even almost a friend.

As it happened, the rambunctious children on the river weren't Volodya's worst problem. That same day, during rehearsal, Olezhka decided to tyrannize the artistic director about getting a big part in the play. He did have a loud voice, and memorized his dialogue quickly, and really got into character . . . but his speech impediment made it hard to tell what he was saying half the time. Volodya didn't want to insult Olezhka, but at the same time he couldn't assign him a big speaking part. In the end, he promised he'd listen to the others, too, and then pick whoever was best. He assured Olezhka he'd get a part no matter what.

Yurka, bored, observed the free-for-all. Watching Masha had stopped being boring and started to become physically painful: in the background she kept pounding out the same old piece, the Moonlight Sonata, which everyone was sick of by now. What was worse, she also played it badly. Yurka tried not to listen, but he heard it anyway, and wished that both Masha and the damned instrument were far, far away.

Music . . . he couldn't imagine himself without music. It had sent its roots deep inside him, become part of him. But now—how long had been trying to rip it out of himself? A year? His whole life? It had been so hard for him to learn to live in silence, but, out of nowhere, here was a piano, and here was Masha, an excellent example of how not to play. And temptation came out of nowhere, too, along with the certainty that Yurka could've played better than her—not now, maybe, but earlier, a whole lifetime ago, back when he still could, when he still knew how. Now he'd forgotten. All he had left was listening to others while he suffocated in his own silence, emptiness, and burning self-hatred.

He watched Masha with gritted teeth. He tried to sneer at the way she cast longing glances at Volodya, but he couldn't sneer. All he could do was get inexplicably angrier and angrier. He wanted to refocus his anger on someone else, like the trinity, but the girls hadn't even shown up to rehearsal.

Yurka barely made it to the end of rehearsal before running off to change for the dance. As he was leaving the cabin, completely immersed in thoughts of the pack of cigarettes in their hiding place behind the fence around the unfinished barracks, someone called his name: "Yurchik!"

Polina grabbed Yurka by the elbow and gave him a conspiratorial look. "Can I talk to you for a second?"

Yurka hesitated for a moment or two, still feeling angry from earlier, but his curiosity won out.

"What do you want?" He turned around and looked at her, half-questioning and half-angry.

"Are you mad at us or something? Don't be mad, Yur. Come on, come over here." Polina pulled him into the girls' room of their cabin. Ulyana and Ksyusha were waiting there. Yurka really didn't like their sarcastic expressions.

"Listen, Yurchik . . ." Polina smiled sweetly and twisted a lock of wheat-gold hair around a finger. "You get along really well with Volodya, right?"

Yurka sighed. So that was what they wanted. The whole trio had a giant crush on the troop leader and now they wanted Yurka to get them together. Fat chance! Although . . . Suddenly he thought of a cunning plan.

"Yes," Yurka answered, letting his gaze pass mysteriously over the three of them. "We talk some. What about it?"

"Does he ever, like, go to the dances, do you know?"

Yurka shrugged.

"I don't know. He's probably busy with the little kids."

Polina perked up and actually bit her lip: "Listen, but what if you could maybe get him to come to the dance somehow?"

Even though he already knew what he was going to do, Yurka pretended he was considering her proposal.

"I can try. No promises. But . . ."

"But what?" Polya smiled even more sweetly than before, but it was such a fake sweetness that Yurka's teeth almost stuck together the way they did when he ate toffees.

"What do I get in exchange?" He smirked impudently.

"What do you want?"

He assumed a thoughtful mien again, going so far as to scratch his chin.

"For Ksyusha to kiss me! On the cheek! Twice, and in front of everybody!"

"What?!" Ksyusha, who'd been sitting calmly on the bed until that point, went red and jumped to her feet. Evidently she disliked Yurka's proposal.

He spread his hands wide. "Either that, or you go get him to come to the dance yourselves!"

The trinity exchanged glances. Ulyana sighed, "Well, at least we tried," while Ksyusha shook her head vigorously in protest.

"Yurchik, wait outside the door for a minute, could you?" asked Polina, shooting a sly look at Ksyusha. "We'll be just a second."

He nodded. He didn't even have a chance to get outside before the girls started whispering furiously behind him. A couple of minutes later, a sullen Ksyusha poked her head out. "Fine. It's a deal."

Yurka nodded solemnly. And when he left the mess hall after dinner, he headed right over to the junior cabins to invite Volodya. A deal was a deal.

CHAPTER FOUR
GOOD NIGHT, BOYS AND GIRLS!

Yura, lost in reminiscence, came back to himself and erased the sad smile from his face. Nostalgia and a painful, sad longing had pierced him to the depths of his soul, especially here inside these walls. He'd wanted so badly to come back here, but to the "here" of twenty years ago, where he could once more hear music, and children's laughter, and Volodya's stern voice. But Yura had to keep going, to find what he'd come to Camp Barn Swallow today to get.

He got up from the squeaky seat, brushed the dust off his trousers, surveyed the stage one last time, and went to the theater exit.

By some miracle, the paved path to the junior cabins had remained intact. The cabins had once been pretty, painted in bright colors and decorated with patterns so they looked like little huts from Russian fairy tales. But now they looked pitiful. The majority had collapsed into heaps of wet, rotten boards that still had traces of old paint on them. Only two of the little cabins—Yura couldn't remember their troop numbers anymore—were more or less intact. In one of them, the roof and the left-hand wall had fallen in, while the other one was almost sound, except that it had settled over time and gone crooked. But it was definitely not worth peeking inside: the porch had sunk more than the rest of the cabin, creating a gap, and the front door had fallen out, leaving a dark, scary, gaping chasm instead of an entrance. The junior troops had always been housed in these cabins, far from the dance floor and movie theater. Yura had lived here in one of his first camp sessions.

As he walked past the playground, Yura winced at a mournful metallic screeching sound. The wind was moving the rusty merry-go-round. It seemed as though the slowly turning disk was still waiting, after all this time, for the little kids to come back so it could bring them joy. But there hadn't been any children here for a long time, and the playground was overgrown by tall weeds.

Yura used to adore this place. The flat lawn around the merry-go-round had been covered by a thick carpet of dandelions that would start out yellow and green, then go pure white, then turn into a fluffy cloud of fuzzy dandelion heads. You could rip up a whole armful of them and run around camp blowing dandelion fuzz into the girls' hair, and they'd get so hilariously mad, and shout at you, and chase after you to get even.

But the dandelions had withered now, with only a few bald little stem ends sticking up here and there from the weeds. Yura bent over to pick one that still had a few little fuzzy parachutes on it. He scoffed bitterly and blew on it, but only a few of the parachutes came off. Unwilling and unwieldy, heavy with damp, they flew all of half a meter before coming to rest on the dark pavement.

Yura tossed the flower to the ground and walked through the thick, wet clusters of weeds to the merry-go-round. Although in disrepair, it was still sturdy. Without understanding why he did it—without even asking himself that question—Yura sat on one of the merry-go-round's seats and pushed off lightly with his feet. It creaked as it started rotating, exactly the same way it had back then, and the sound dragged him down into a whirlpool of memories.

The dandelions that had gone to seed spread over the playground in a thick white blanket. Fuzzy little seeds came off and floated around in the air, tickling his nose. Yurka breathed in a lungful of fresh evening air and turned onto the path to the junior cabins.

It was quiet all around. The children were already asleep, lights out for them having been a little while ago, but no light was coming from the windows of the troop leaders' rooms, either. Yurka pondered: Volodya wouldn't be asleep yet, and troop leaders could stay up even past that if they wanted to—but where would he have gotten off to? Had Volodya really gone to the dance all by himself? Baffled, Yurka looked around, listening to the nighttime silence broken only by the whispering wind and chirring crickets. "If Volodya goes there without me, will that count as me keeping my end of the bargain?" he mused. "Will I get my kiss?"

Suddenly, quick steps sounded among the night's quiet rustlings. Then the porch creaked. Yurka turned toward the cabin and saw a small, tiptoeing figure in pajamas with rockets on them. The stout little boy coming down the stairs of the Troop Five cabin tripped, gasped, and wobbled precariously before catching himself. Yurka recognized the rule breaker as Sasha, the squirming victim he and Volodya had carried to the first aid station the day before.

Yurka flattened himself against the wall of a neighboring cabin. Hiding in the shadows, he cut a wide circle around the little boy, then in two steps came up right behind him. With one hand Yurka touched the boy's shoulder while with the other he covered the boy's mouth, cutting off his yelp of fright.

"What's up with this wandering around after lights out, huh?" Yurka hissed menacingly into the boy's ear.

Sasha ducked his head and squeaked something, getting spit all over Yurka's palm. Yurka frowned and said, "Promise you won't yell if I let you go. Otherwise I'll drag you into the forest and throw you into a nest of black vipers!"

Sasha nodded, and Yurka removed his hand from Sasha's drooly mouth.

"I just—I just wanted some currants," stammered the little boy. "I saw two currant bushes by the first aid station, so . . ."

"Sheesh, Sashka!" Yurka was barely able to keep from laughing. He made his voice stern and said, "How can you want currants in June? Right now, the only berries by the first aid station are on the daphnes, but they're poisonous!"

Sasha scowled: obviously he didn't believe it. Yurka hemmed, musing, then asked, "Why did you go after the currants at night, anyway?"

"Because!" pronounced Sasha firmly. "What am I supposed to do, show everybody where I found the currants? Just you wait,: they'll take them all for themselves!"

"Grandpa Lenin did tell us all to share, Sash!"

Sasha pouted and refused to reply, glowering sullenly.

"How'd you get out of the cabin?" Yurka asked. "Don't they lock the door?"

"Volodya can't get us to sleep. I left while he was trying to convince Kolka to stay in bed."

"Why, you little . . ." Yurka imagined the utter panic that would seize Volodya the instant he saw the empty bed, then increase with each passing minute. "We're heading back. Get going."

He took hold of the squealing Sasha by the ear and dragged him into the cabin, heedless of his complaints.

As soon as Yurka eased open the door to the boys' room, he saw Volodya standing in the light of a dimmed flashlight above an empty bed and staring blindly ahead, eyes perfectly round in horror. He was surrounded by whispering children who obviously had no intention of going to sleep.

"Did you lose this?" asked Yurka softly, dragging Sasha into the room.

Volodya turned around, nonplussed, but his face lit up as soon as he saw the escapee. "I was sure I was done for," he sighed in relief. Then he hissed at Sasha: "Get in bed, you! Right now! What were you trying to do, run away?"

Without a word, Sasha slid under his blanket and rolled onto his side with his back to them.

"He wanted some currants," said Yurka, betraying Sasha. "Listen, what are you doing here so late? Junior lights out was ages ago."

"I can't get these knuckleheads to go to bed! The girls fell asleep quick as a wink—they're well away to slumberland by now—but these guys . . . it's like somebody spiked their dinner with caffeine."

Yurka swiveled his head, surveying the even rows of beds. The boys weren't whispering anymore. Everyone was listening with rapt trepidation not to the adults but to tousle-headed, r-mangling Olezhka, who was intoning in a voice from beyond the grave: "In a dawk, dawk town, in a dawk, dawk house, lived a dawk, dawk—"

"Kitten!" shouted Yurka. The boys convulsed with laughter. "If you're gonna tell scary stories, pick one that's actually scary."

"I know the one with the floating gwavestone, too. That one's the scawy stowy to beat all scawy stowies!"

"Nah, that one's not scary, either. What, can't Volodya tell you stories that are scary for real?"

"No, no. You got it backwawds: he yells at us because we listen to scawy stowies instead of sleeping. But to tell the twuth, we keep telling them anyway . . ."

The troop leader gave a little laugh: "You think I don't know that?" He took a breath to continue but stopped short and frowned as he caught sight of the jokester Pcholkin furtively tucking something under his blanket. In a whisper, Olezhka launched into the tired old story about the toenails in the meat pie.

Yurka listened to Olezhka with half an ear, thinking to himself that he had to extricate Volodya and that, no matter what, he and Volodya had to show up at today's dance. First of all, because Ksyusha'd have to pay her bet: fair's fair! Secondly, because he was looking pretty fair himself, actually, since he'd put on his best—also his only—pair of jeans and his favorite brown polo, the one from East Germany that his uncle had brought him that spring.

His thoughts were interrupted by Volodya suddenly ripping Pcholkin's blanket off and grabbing something small and wooden out from under it. Volodya shouted triumphantly: "Aha! A slingshot! So that's who took out the ceiling light!"

Yurka's thoughts returned to the issue at hand: *What do I do to get Volodya out of here? Make these squirts go to sleep. How do I make these squirts go to sleep?*

It took less than a minute for the answer to come to him.

"So do you all know why Volodya doesn't tell you scary stories? So you sleep better. And he's right. Because Volodya, of all people, knows what happens to anyone who doesn't go to sleep at lights out . . ."

"What happens?" said Sasha, eyes wide.

"Is it bad?" asked another little boy with curly hair who'd frozen where he sat.

Olezhka quaked. "Is it scawy?"

"I won't use my slingshot anymore. Please don't take it," Pcholkin begged.

Just then, from behind the door into the main hallway, they all heard a rush of movement and a girl's stifled giggle.

Volodya bolted for the door to catch the little truant and take her back to the girls' room. From the way Pcholkin groaned, Yurka could tell that the strict troop leader had taken the little boy's slingshot with him.

Yurka took a spot on a free bed and assumed a very serious demeanor: "I'm going to share a big secret with you now. But don't breathe a word to anyone: it's categorically forbidden to tell Little Octoberists about this, since you're supposedly too young for it. So I'll get my you-know-what handed back to me on a platter if anyone finds out . . ."

He was interrupted by a cacophony of voices ardently swearing never to betray him. Yurka cleared his throat and, in a scary voice, began his story: "At night the camp is haunted by a genuine ghost! A long time ago, back before the Great October Revolution, there was a nobleman's estate not far from here where a young count lived with his countess. They were happy together, even though theirs was an arranged marriage—"

"What is that, Yuwka? What kind of mawwiage is that?"

"Don't interrupt, Olezha," Yurka said, and explained as best he could. "An arranged marriage is when two sets of parents agree to have their children marry, and the kids might not only be very young still, they might not even know each other. People did it that way for money."

Volodya came back into the boys' room so pleased, his eyes all but sparkled. He sat down next to Yurka, who continued: "So. The count and the countess really did love each other. They had a large manor, and about a hundred peasants, and a whole lot of friends: counts and countesses, and princes and princesses, and even a grand prince—one of the tsar's relatives—who was like a sort of comrade to the count. But then the Russo-Japanese War started, and the grand prince called on the count to serve in the navy with him. And the count couldn't refuse. So he gave his countess a gorgeous diamond brooch to remember him by and went off to fight. But he never, ever came back . . ."

The little boys had gone silent. As one, they all huddled under their blankets and stared at Yurka, goggle-eyed and bursting from suspense. Volodya was cleaning his glasses with the corner of his shirt while, squinting, he surveyed the boys sternly. Yurka, satisfied with the results he'd produced—the kids were interested—continued in a sibilant whisper: "They say the cruiser he served on was sunk by the Japanese. The countess was informed that her husband had been killed, but she loved him so much that she couldn't believe or accept it. The countess had no children and waited for him, all alone, for many, many years. She never wore her pretty dresses or jewelry again, and she went around dressed all in black. But the one thing she always kept with her—the one thing she always had pinned to her chest or fastened in her hair—was the diamond brooch. The last gift her husband ever gave her. Time passed. The countess was very sad and soon grew sick. She didn't want to see anybody, not even the doctor, and a year later she was dead. They say she was buried in that same black widow's dress, but that the diamond brooch wasn't on her when she went to her grave. The diamond brooch was lost! And ever since, there have been some kind of mysterious goings-on in the manor house. First the furniture would move all by itself . . . then the doors would open and close . . . and then, after the Bolsheviks came to power and made the place into a sanatorium, people who stayed in the old manor house started dying!"

Someone stifled a gasp in the shadowed darkness, and in the nearby bed there was a sudden motion as Sasha pulled the covers up over his head. Volodya elbowed Yurka in the ribs, whispering almost inaudibly directly into his ear: "Yurka, take it easy, they're never going to fall asleep now!"

But Yurka was already letting it rip: "Every night it'd be calm in the mansion. Well, maybe a few dresser drawers would open and close by themselves, but there was no crashing or banging or noise. Yet every morning—uh-oh! Somebody'd end up dead! And this happened every single morning: a person lying dead in their bed. It was terrible: their eyes were all bugged out, and their mouths were frozen wide in a scream, and their tongues were sticking out, and their necks were black-and-blue! Everyone searched and searched for the perpetrator. But whoever did it was never found. And so that sanatorium was abandoned. The villagers who lived nearby, in Horetivka, stole everything out of the manor and stripped it down, not leaving even a single brick. They carried everything away to build their own homes. And now there's nothing there to remind anyone that a count's mansion once stood on that spot, except for this: to this day, hidden deep in a bird cherry thicket, you can find a bas-relief with the countess's profile carved into it. And on her dress is pinned a diamond brooch." Yurka lowered his voice even more. "And now I am going to reveal a big secret to you, but you can't say a word about it to anybody, okay?"

"Okay! Okay! Okay!" came the whispered promise from all sides.

"Are you sure? Do you all swear on your honor as Little Octoberists?"

"Yes!" "We do!" "We swear!" "Just tell us alwedy, Yuwka!"

"Somebody died here, too. They found him right here, in the next cabin over! But only one person died, because after his death the Pioneers found his journal—he'd written about all the weird things that happened at night—and read it and found out everything. The guy who died had been a troop leader . . . a very young one . . . it had been his first year in the camp . . ."

Volodya coughed and raised a skeptical brow.

Yurka shot him a crafty glance, as if to say, *Yes, indeed, this is about you*, and went on: "This is how it happened. The kids in his troop slept really badly. Their leader slept badly right along with them, since he was always walking around, checking everything, worrying . . . and then one night, everyone else had finally fallen asleep, but the troop leader couldn't. His sleep schedule had gotten completely off. He was sitting there with his notebook, writing down everything that had happened that day: where he and the kids had gone, how it had been, how the kids had behaved, that sort of thing. And then in the utter silence he heard a rustle, as though fabric was dragging across the floor. The troop leader grew wary, since it was such a very weird sound: he turned off the light, lay down in the darkness, and held still. At first he couldn't see anything, but as soon as his eyes got used to the dark, as soon as he could discern the outlines of the wardrobe and nightstand, he saw the wardrobe door swing open! All by itself, quick and quiet, as though it hadn't opened just that moment, but had been left open instead. The leader blinked—and suddenly the wardrobe door was closed again, the way it should be! He thought he might've imagined it, so he turned the light on and wrote everything down. The same thing happened the next night: again he heard the rustle of fabric along the floor, again everything got quiet, and again the furniture doors opened all by themselves. And his room was completely empty, with no shadows or sounds. But as soon as he blinked, there it was: the left-hand door of the wardrobe was open . . . and the next time he blinked, the left-hand door was closed, and the right-hand door was open . . . and all this was happening in dead silence . . ."

The exact same kind of silence reigned in the room. The boys were listening so hard they were even breathing slower and quieter. Yurka heard the clacking of someone's teeth chattering, and snorted: at least he wasn't hearing the "pssss" of someone wetting the bed . . .

"So then the troop leader went to Horetivka and talked to the old-timers there, and one old man told him the legend about the countess and the missing brooch. And he realized that the sound he was hearing at night was the swishing of her black dress. He wanted to find out why the wardrobe doors kept opening and closing. But he never did. Because the next morning he was found dead in his bed. Strangled. With bulging eyes—"

"And a bruised neck?" Sasha could barely choke out the words.

"And a bruised neck," Yurka replied, nodding. "The police questioned all the inhabitants of the village. When it was that same old man's turn, he told them the same thing he'd told the troop leader. The policemen thought he'd gone off his rocker and didn't believe his ramblings about some countess . . . about how she'd wandered around her own home first, but then, when it was destroyed, she roamed the camp . . . about how she wanders to this day, looking for the brooch the count gave her . . . and about how, when she doesn't find it, she gets mad and strangles the first person she sees who's awake. Because she thinks whoever's awake is the thief who stole her brooch. After all, he's the only one whose conscience is torturing him so badly, he can't get to sleep."

While Yurka took a breath, Volodya broke in: "And that, guys, is why you have to go to sleep after lights out."

"That's right," said Yurka. "You have to lie there and be quiet so both you and your troop leaders stay safe. Otherwise you'll hear the rustling of the countess's dress and see her opening cupboard and wardrobe doors, looking for her brooch. And that's where she'll get you! And your leaders, by the way, are also awake all night: they're worrying about you, just like the one who died."

The story made an enormous impression on the little boys, who screwed their eyes shut, pulled their covers up to their chins, and lay silent and motionless.

Volodya and Yurka exchanged a look. They both realized that leaving the children now would obviously be a bad idea, so they each sat down in a corner of the boys' room, Volodya by the window and Yurka by the door. They sat in silence, bored.

With nothing better to do in the shadowy room, Yurka started studying Volodya's profile: long, straight nose, high forehead, feathered bangs, sharp chin. *Volodya's actually handsome.* The thought came unbidden to Yurka's mind. *If you take a good look at him . . . if you think about it . . . I mean, probably . . .*

When he'd seen Volodya for the first time, back at the opening assembly, Yurka had thought, objectively, that if it weren't for the glasses, you could even call Volodya classically handsome. That was true without a doubt, Yurka admitted, even feeling a twinge of envy—as well he should, given the way girls melted just looking at Volodya! But now, after peering at Volodya in the dark room, Yurka realized something else: he thought Volodya was handsome subjectively, too. In fact, Yurka felt a strange sense of gratitude. The strange part was that he didn't exactly know who he felt grateful *to*: fate or Volodya's parents. But he did know exactly what he was grateful *for*: the chance to appreciate beauty and experience joy. Because the contemplation of beauty always brings joy. If only Volodya didn't have those glasses, though!

A muffled whisper broke the silence: "Yuwka?"

"What?"

"Awe thewe any doows opening next to you?"

"No."

"And you, Volodya? Any doows opening ovew thewe?"

"No. Everything's fine. Go to sleep."

Everything was quiet for five minutes. Then that same voice, or rather whisper, repeated: "Yuwka? Volodya?"

"What is it?"

"Go to bed. Or the countess will come again and catch you sitting thewe."

"Are you sure you won't talk?" asked Volodya, in what Yurka thought was an overly stern tone.

Very convincing responses rained down from all corners of the room: "We're sure!" "We're sleeping!" "Yes!" "Octobewists' honow!"

Volodya got up and nodded to Yurka, signaling him to follow. As they headed to the door, Sasha reached his hand out from under his blanket and caught Volodya's shorts: "Volodya, can Yura come and tell us scary stories again?"

"I don't see why not, but you'd be better off asking him."

"Yur?"

"On one condition. If you fall asleep this very minute, and if nobody gets up and goes anywhere tonight, then tomorrow I'll come and tell you another one. But if anybody makes as much as a single peep, no dice and no story: you'll have to just sit here staring at your navy blue curtains."

The little boys mumbled their promises and assurances, each in his own way, while Sasha nodded joyfully and wrapped himself in his blanket all the way up to his eyebrows.

"You think they'll go to sleep?" asked Yurka after they walked down the cabin's front steps.

But Volodya didn't respond. He headed briskly to the merry-go-round resting on that same dandelion field directly in front of the cabin. Carefully, so the merry-go-round didn't squeak, he sat down on it and started running the toe of his sneaker along the ground, raising flurries of white fluff. Yura settled down next to him, then asked: "Why are you being so quiet?"

"I asked you not to overdo it, didn't I?" said Volodya accusingly.

"So where do you think I overdid it?"

"What kind of question is that?" With one forefinger, Volodya angrily shoved his glasses back up. "Everywhere, Yura. Now they're so scared, they not only won't go to sleep, they'll probably also wet their beds!"

"Oh, come on! What are they—little guys that can't make it to the toilet?"

"Of course they're little guys! How are they supposed to go to the bathroom when you literally forbade them to open their eyes?"

"Don't exaggerate. I think they're just pretending. Even Sasha is lying there nice and quiet, and he's the most sensitive one of all. But even if I did scare them, so what? There's no drawbacks to peace and quiet!"

"We'll see what drawbacks come up tomorrow morning."

"But what drawbacks? There aren't any! And they liked it, since they asked for another one tomorrow."

Music was playing on the stage in the distance, but the wind was blowing in the wrong direction, garbling the sound, so Yurka couldn't tell what song it was. The alluring sound of happy voices was mixed in with the music.

Giving in to an old habit acquired back when he was still in music school, Yurka started loosening his fingers by tugging on each one in turn and popping his knuckles. Impatience seized him: if only they could just get to the dance already! He'd managed to extract Volodya from his troop cabin; another five minutes and they could be at the dance, where Ksyusha was. But Volodya didn't look like he was going anywhere. Yurka couldn't restrain himself and tried to hurry Volodya along. "So? What are we sitting around for? Let's go to the dance!"

"No," Volodya refused categorically. He nodded at the cabin's dark windows. "I let Lena go to the dance and I'm not going anywhere until she gets back. I can't leave the children here by themselves."

"Ouch, denied! Too bad," said Yurka slowly, disappointed.

"Why is it too bad? Why 'denied'?" asked Volodya, perking up. "What, were you counting on me or something? But we didn't agree on it beforehand, and you know I don't even like dances, anyway. Wait, hold on . . ." Volodya furrowed his brow, then straightened suddenly as he remembered something. "Somebody already invited me today. Ulyana. Yes, that's right, it was Ulyana first, and now you. Tell me what you're up to!"

"Nothing. It's just that the girls were begging and pleading with me to bring you. They just want to, you know, dance with you . . . and everything . . ."

"Wait, what kind of 'everything'?" chuckled Volodya. "What other things would I be doing with them?"

"You know very well what other things," said Yurka with a wink. "What is it? Don't you like them? Not any of them? Not even a little bit? Or are you already going out with someone? Is it Masha?"

"Where'd you come up with that? No, that's got nothing to do with it! I'm a troop leader, and they're Pioneers. So there's your 'other things' for you. Look, why are you sitting here? Nothing's keeping you here. You could go, have fun."

True, Yurka thought, mentally nodding to himself: the music would go on, even without Volodya. For most of the Pioneers, the nightly dances were the most anticipated event of the summer. They were for Yurka, too— usually. But now he was suddenly doubt-stricken. What would he do there? Watch the girls dance with each other as he sat off to the side, too afraid, despite all his outward daring, to ask anyone to dance? And who would he even ask? Last session there'd been Anechka, but this session there was neither her nor anyone else who was even slightly appealing. He'd been planning on getting the promised kiss from Ksyusha, but without his end of the bargain—Volodya—there'd be no deal. So what was there to do at the dance if he wasn't going to dance? Sit over at the edge of the dance floor with Vanka and Mikha, having boring conversations about boring things? Or repeatedly crisscross the dance floor with his buddies? They were fun, sure, but he was tired of them . . .

It turned out there was nothing, and nobody, for Yurka to even go to the dance for. He could've kept trying to convince Volodya, but, to tell the truth, Yurka didn't feel like going to a dance anymore. He'd deliver his part of the bargain some other day. Today he felt just fine right here, under a clear night sky, where not a single cloud hid the stars' bright light or the moon's thin sliver.

"Won't it be a little depressing for you to sit here all by yourself?" he had the inspiration to ask, so as not to sit in silence.

"I was going to read the script, but there's not much light." Volodya patted his shorts pocket and nodded at the single source of light, a dim bulb over the porch. "So yes, it probably won't be much fun."

"Then I'll sit here with you for a while."

"Sure, go ahead," Volodya said indifferently.

"You don't sound very glad about it, even though you were just saying it'll be boring . . ."

"I am glad. I'm glad, of course." Volodya's words were affirmative, but Yurka thought he seemed ill at ease.

The wind changed, bringing the music with it—a wildly popular duet between Alla Pugacheva and Vladimir Kuzmin about the night sky in spring and two falling stars. Although it was summer now, not spring, they still got it right: there were falling stars. Yurka noticed several of them, but he didn't make a wish. He wasn't superstitious, first of all, and secondly, he knew they weren't stars at all, but meteors. There was a whole twinkling vista of real stars, a whole Milky Way of them. As he gazed at the sky, Yurka pondered the paradox of Volodya, who said he was glad but was glad in total silence, without a single emotion on his face. Yet being silent with him wasn't boring, and neither was talking with him.

Volodya sighed, then softly sang a few words of the song, mockingly but perfectly in tune with the music. He broke off and asked, "So, hey, Yur, is that estate far from here?"

"What esta—oh, that estate. There actually isn't any estate." In the dim light it was hard to tell at first, but then Yurka saw how Volodya's face had fallen and asked in surprise: "You actually believed that?"

"You made it all up? All that about the grand prince and the Russo-Japanese War? So many details . . . Neatly done! You're actually not such a knucklehead after all, are you?"

"A knucklehead? Who? Me? Are you saying I'm a knucklehead?!"

"No. That's what I'm saying, is that you're not."

"But then what's with the 'aaaaactuallyyyy'?" Yurka affectedly drew out the word in an imitation of Volodya's Moscow accent. It sounded just like him. "There really is a bas-relief of a woman, though. Down the river, in some wild apple trees."

"Is it far?"

"Half an hour or so by boat. So what about this knucklehead thing?"

"Come on, give it up."

"Is that why you were being all high and mighty before? You think I'm an idiot?"

"I wasn't . . . Fine!" Volodya gave in. "Look, people don't normally expect much from good-for-nothings, right?"

"Now I'm a good-for-nothing, too?!" Yurka feigned outrage. For some reason he felt giddy and happy. He decided to play along, wouldn't leave Volodya alone until he apologized. But an apology was the last thing on Volodya's mind.

"It's your own fault you've got such a reputation."

"It has nothing to do with me! It's just that those stupid troop leaders don't have anything better to do than show up at the worst possible moment, and then they draw their own conclusions without even listening to me. Have you heard about the roof, for instance?"

Volodya's reply was guarded: "Hmm . . . Somebody said something about last year—"

Yurka interrupted him in a squeaky voice, parodying Olga Leonidovna: "'Konev has gotten out of hand! He's jumping around on the roof, breaking tiles, damaging government property, and putting his own health and safety at risk—along with our reputation as educators, comrades! That Konev's a nasty piece of work! A vandal! Riffraff!' And you think so, too, don't you?!"

"Where'd you get that? I never draw hasty conclusions."

"Yeah, right. You went along with 'knucklehead' quick enough." Yurka gave a little laugh. "But it wasn't like that at all, actually. What I was actually doing was helping get a girl's Frisbee for her. I was walking along and I see Anechka—" Yurka broke off at the thought that he was saying the name too tenderly. "Anyway, I see this girl from my troop sitting there crying. So I asked why. Her Frisbee had landed up on the roof and she'd been asking the facilities manager for two days to get it down for her, but he couldn't care less. The Frisbee was a gift from her father, and there was only a day until the end of the whole session! No way in hell she was going to get it back."

"Don't curse," Volodya ordered, more from habit than as an actual reprimand.

Yurka ignored him. "So I went up onto the roof. It wasn't high at all, I just reached up and pulled myself up. No sweat. But that's the exact moment they appeared."

"Didn't the girl explain what was going on?"

"She explained it, but who's going to listen to her? 'You should've asked the facilities manager.' But she already had . . .'"

"So what happened?"

"I got her Frisbee down for her, that's what. Anechka's all happy, beaming, thanking me, but Konev—no, Konev's still just a troublemaker, riffraff."

"Okay, that time you were in the right. But what were you doing, sneaking through that hole in the fence?"

"Getting my smokes." Yurka blurted out the truth before stopping to think.

"You smoke, too?!" cried Volodya, aghast.

"Who, me? No! No, I just—I'm just experimenting. I won't do it anymore!" he fibbed, then changed the topic, just to be safe. "But who told you about the hole? I thought nobody knew about it!"

"Everybody knows about it. Not only do they know about it, they've fixed it."

Yurka snorted. "Fine. It's not like I don't know other ways to get out of camp."

Volodya sat up, alert: "There are other holes? Where?"

"I'm not telling."

"Please, tell me! Yur, what if my little trouble magnets find out? They'll run away!"

"They won't find out, much less run away. It's too far for them, and also they can't use it because they're so short," Yurka assured him. But Volodya continued to huff nervously, so to quell his anxiety, Yurka added, "I guarantee they won't run away!"

"Yura, if anything happens, the senior staff will come down on me like a ton of bricks!"

Yurka picked distractedly at a mosquito bite on his elbow. "Just don't tell anybody, okay? About the hole. Or about the smokes, either."

"I won't tell as long as you show me this other hole. I have to be sure the kids can't get through it. And that it's safe."

Yurka stopped resisting. "It's not a hole in the fence, actually. It's a shallow place in the river. No need to panic. They're not crazy: they're not going to cross a river where the water's up to their necks." Volodya grunted dubiously. Then Yurka remembered: "Tell me this: What story should I tell tomorrow? To the kids? I did promise . . ."

"Come up with something. You were so quick on the draw with the one you just told; another one won't be hard."

"Easy for you to say! There was an inspiration for the brooch story, but that's it. The tank's empty now. What else can I come up with . . . maybe a story about a serial killer?"

"A serial killer?! How'd there be a serial killer way out here?" snorted Volodya.

"I don't know! It's all made-up, anyway." Yurka shrugged.

"No. It has to be more realistic, and there has to be a moral to the story. Maybe we could expand on the topic of the estate instead . . . We could talk about . . . a hidden treasure? That's it! Let's do a hidden treasure."

"Hmm," said Yurka, scratching his chin. "That's an idea. Do you have anything to write on?"

Volodya explored his pockets. From the left pocket he pulled the slingshot, but shoved it back and dug into his right pocket. He extracted a notebook rolled up into a tube, along with a pen.

"Isn't it too dark to write?" he asked as he handed them to Yurka.

"It's fine. I have big handwriting."

"Then go on, maestro, begin!"

"Okay. So the count and the countess were very wealthy. Before he left for the war, the count took a large portion of his fortune, hid it in a chest, and buried it somewhere . . ."

"But what did the countess live on?"

"I said 'a large portion'; he left the rest with her! Where was I . . . And under cover of darkness, on the night of the new moon, he carried the chest out and buried it, marking the location on a map. But even the map wouldn't help find the treasure if you hadn't solved a series of riddles . . . No . . . Wait! The valuables were hidden not by a count but by partisans! Yeah! A cache of weapons!"

Yurka never did make it to the dance that night. For hours past lights out, he and Volodya sat together on the merry-go-round, dreaming up scary stories for the little kids, completely heedless of time racing on.

CHAPTER FIVE

SOME TROOP LEADER SHE IS

After growing closer to Volodya, Yurka began enjoying the theater more, too. Although the place had bored him at first, it became special to him after a couple of rehearsals. It was fun there, and comfortable, and Yurka felt he was a full-fledged member of the team. Even though they hadn't found a part for him yet, Volodya still found ways for Yurka to feel useful, like helping keep an eye on the kids or giving advice on the script and the distribution of parts. And Volodya listened to him. Yurka was flattered.

He had begun to genuinely like Volodya, although Yurka couldn't quite wrap his head around it when he thought about what that word, "like," actually meant. It sounded strange. Because he kept thinking about how it could mean something more like attraction, or being in love, not what he felt for Volodya. Since he had no clue how to explain this feeling to himself, he settled for calling it "a desire to be friends," even "a very strong desire to be friends." Nothing like this had ever happened to Yurka before. This was the first time he'd looked at another boy that way, with special interest, and with a sense of jealous rivalry. Moreover—and this was what was really surprising—his rival wasn't Volodya but the girls. They were his rivals for Volodya's attention.

The process of getting the show up and running was moving slowly, but it was definitely moving. At the third rehearsal they announced who would play the four main parts, but many of the secondary parts were still an open question because there weren't enough actors. For some reason, not that many boys had wanted to be in drama club.

The lead role of Zina Portnova was given to Nastya Milkova, a Pioneer from Troop Two, the second-oldest troop. She read her lines beautifully and even looked like Zina: short, and with the same dark hair and big brown eyes. But unlike Zina, Nastya wasn't brave. Nastya was very nervous when she said her lines, getting so agitated that a red flush spread not only over her face but also down her arms and hands. The part of Galya, Zina's little sister, was to be performed by little redheaded Alyona from Volodya's troop. The part of Ilya Yezavitov ended up going to Olezhka after all. Even though Volodya still had his doubts, there was no way he could get out of it by "picking who was best"; despite Olezhka's problematic *r*'s, he still read the lines far better than anyone else. And he tried really hard. The part of Ilya's brother, Zhenya Yezavitov, was assigned to Vaska Petlitsyn. He was still a little trouble magnet and mischief-maker, but he quickly got into the part and played it very well.

Ulyana secured the part of Fruza Zenkova, leader of the Young Avengers, but from the way Volodya looked at her it was becoming clear he was very dissatisfied with her acting. Polina, on the other hand, was immediately confirmed as the narrator, and her voice-over narration was excellent. The request of the third member of the trinity, Ksyusha, had been heard and granted back at the first rehearsal. She was very proud of her title of costumer, even though she hadn't sewn a costume or even made a pattern yet. Masha, for lack of anyone better, was selected as the pianist—even though, as far as Yurka could tell, she only knew how to play one thing, the Moonlight Sonata. Although the camp had sound equipment, Volodya insisted on "live" accompaniment, pointing out that thirty years ago the show had been accompanied by live music, specifically live piano music.

The actors were still struggling with the script, but for the third rehearsal, it wasn't bad. Even so, Volodya couldn't stop worrying about the parts that weren't yet filled: the Portnova sisters' grandmother, two girls and a boy in the Young Avengers, several Germans, and soldiers and villagers for the group scenes.

"So," Volodya said, lowering his notebook from in front of his face. "Are all the Young Avengers here? Or at least the ones we have so far?"

At his request, Nastya, Alyona, Olezha, and Vaska got into a row onstage. Ulyana sat down at the table onstage.

"Excellent." The artistic director nodded. "Everybody, listen up, especially the Young Avengers. Remember, people, this show isn't just about Zina but about you. You are the main core of the action and the focus will be on you throughout the entire story. I'm going to give you the general outline of the story, so pay attention and don't let us down. All right. You are members of an underground organization. You are heroes. Moreover, you are young heroes, because, as we all know, the Young Avengers weren't much older than Yura, Masha, Ksyusha, and the rest of you. This makes their feat even greater." Upon being relegated to "the rest of you," Polina and Ulyana scowled and muttered to each other. Volodya didn't hear them and went on: "The children of that time weren't like us. Their parents had fought and won the Civil War a generation earlier, and now the kids wanted to fight, too, in their turn, and even found ways to do it. We are frivolous. They weren't. So be aware that I will not tolerate carelessness. Petlitsyn, are you listening to me?"

Volodya gave Vaska such a severe look that the little boy's eyes went wide. "Y-yeees?" he replied hesitantly.

"Are you listening closely?"

"Very!"

"Repeat what I just said," ordered Volodya, continuing to torment him, and with good reason, since last time Vaska had goofed around so much, they'd almost had to stop rehearsal.

Petlitsyn heaved a gloomy sigh, then, with a wry expression, rattled out: "We're partisans! We want to go to war! And you won't tolerate carelessness! And stuff like that . . ."

"Take this more seriously, Petlitsyn! We're not putting on a comedy here."

"All right, fine . . ."

Volodya shook his head ruefully. He obviously wasn't satisfied, but he couldn't waste the whole group's time dealing with just Petlitsyn. So the artistic director got down to business: "Is everyone ready? Hey, Yur, where's the map? Come on, spread it out on the table, quick."

The round table was set a little to the left of center stage. The kids had furnished a space around it with benches and random household items like suitcases, clothes, dishes, and even a samovar—in other words, the items in an average peasant hut. This was the headquarters of the Young Avengers.

"Comrade commander in chief, *sir*! The map is on the table, *sir*!" Yurka reported, then took his seat in the first row of the audience next to Volodya.

Volodya heaved a short sigh of aggravation, then clicked his tongue. "I don't like that peasant hut. Needs more flags and posters."

"More?" Yurka snorted and began counting them off: "We've got DEATH TO FASCIST SWINE; THE MOTHERLAND IS CALLING; WE WON'T SURRENDER OCTOBER'S GAINS . . . Isn't that enough? And it's still early to be thinking about the set . . ."

"No, it's not. This is exactly the time to be thinking about it! If we can't find what we need, we'll have to make it ourselves."

"Look, Volod—that's not logical. They're underground fighters! Your average underground fighter's not going to have all this political-agitational stuff around the hut, much less hang it all over his headquarters! They're on occupied territory, Fascists are everywhere: they can't move without seeing some dumb Fascist fu—uh, sucker . . ."

Volodya exploded to his feet. He hissed furiously, without even giving Yurka a chance to finish his sentence, and drew himself up, ready to either start a screaming match or give Yura a slap in the face—but then chubby little Sashka insinuated himself between the two boys.

"What? How did you get here?!" said Volodya, completely taken aback.

"I walked," squeaked the boy guilelessly. "Volodya, why is Petlitsyn playing Zhenya Yezavitov? I was supposed to be him . . ."

"Because you and your side trips and hooky-playing, Sashka, haven't left me any choice," the artistic director replied sternly.

"Well, can I be Nikolay Alexeyev, then?"

"No. That part's for a boy of around twelve."

"So what am I supposed to do now?"

"You are very good at lying around moaning, Sasha . . ." Volodya said thoughtfully.

Everyone giggled, remembering how Sashka had sprawled on the ground, limbs akimbo, like an empty sack. The artistic director was the only one to remain serious: "You'll play a dying fascist in the part where the Young Avengers blow up the railroad pumping station."

"But—"

"But you'll be the main one, Sash!" Volodya cleared his throat, scratched the bridge of his nose, and pushed his glasses back up with his forefinger.

"Okay, let's move on. The Young Avengers are standing around the table, looking at a map as they plan an act of sabotage. Nastya, go ahead. Start with the line about the enemy troop train on the railroad . . ."

After rehearsal had finished and the children had gone back to their troops, Yurka was finally alone with Volodya. He let out what he'd been thinking about since the very first rehearsal: "I know the 'Moonlight' Sonata's the only thing Masha knows how to play, but it doesn't fit here."

"I wouldn't say that," Volodya objected. "The sonata's excellent for the background."

"No it's not!" Yurka jumped up from his seat and blurted out in a single breath: "Volodya, what romantic lyricism can there be in a patriotic show? Do you know what the Moonlight Sonata even is? It's a nocturne: it's concentrated sadness; there's so much love in it and at the same time so much misery that trying to force it into the background of a show about partisans is just . . . it's just . . . it's not right!"

After delivering this tirade in one unbroken stream, Yurka deflated, falling back into his seat. Volodya stared at him, one brow raised in surprise, but left the emotional tirade without comment. He merely asked: "So what do you suggest?"

"Beethoven's 'Appassionata.' Wait, don't argue. Let me explain. First of all, it's Lenin's favorite piece of music. And secondly—"

"But it's hard. Who can play it?"

"Masha!" Yurka exclaimed. But a moment later he realized Volodya was right: nobody at camp could play the 'Appassionata,' not even Yurka. "Okay, fine. Play the 'Internationale' instead."

"As a tribute to Musya Pinkenzon?"

"Yep," confirmed Yurka, happy they had both thought of the story of the eleven-year-old violinist, who was famous because while the Nazis were preparing to execute him and his family, he'd started boldly playing the Socialist anthem, the "Internationale," and had been shot dead on the spot.

"That's a good idea, I'll suggest it to Masha. But the 'Internationale' is an anthem, after all; it's stirring, triumphant. Doesn't work for background. Let's just stick with the Moonlight Sonata as the background music for now, okay?"

"But that's what I've been saying, is that it doesn't work for that! You don't begin with a nocturne! You don't start out with a theme of eternal rest for the departed!" Yurka drew in a deep breath, preparing to release another machine-gun volley of his thoughts on the Moonlight Sonata, but he was interrupted.

The porch creaked, the door to the movie theater banged open, and an enraged Ira Petrovna appeared in the doorway. Yurka has never seen her like this: her eyes flashed, her mouth was a mean, crooked line, and her cheeks were red-hot.

"Konev! I don't know what you were trying to accomplish here, but you did it. Congratulations!"

Ira was burning with rage. She shouted so loud as she came down the steps toward him that Yurka's heart jumped into his throat. The next emotion he felt after his fright was anger: she was trying to blame him for something again!

"What have I done now?" Yurka took a step toward Ira.

She stopped in the central aisle. Yurka walked up the aisle and stopped in front of her. Staring right into Ira's eyes, Yurka was about to kick one of the seats as hard as he could, to release at least a little of the anger boiling inside him. But Volodya came up out of nowhere to stand beside him and wordlessly lay a hand on his shoulder.

Ira was raging. "Konev, where did you sneak off to all night? Why didn't Masha come back to the troop cabin until it was almost morning? What were you doing to her?"

"But I came back before that!"

At this, Volodya turned to Ira and spoke up. "Ira, let's take it slow and figure things out. What did he do?"

"Why don't you quit poking your nose into other people's business, Volodya! Here you are defending him at staff meetings when he's molesting our girls!"

At hearing this from Ira Petrovna, Yurka's eyebrows shot up and he froze in shock. Volodya croaked out a hoarse whisper: "What?"

Ira remained silent.

As soon as he found his tongue again, Yurka shouted, "I'm so sick of Masha! I wasn't doing anything to her! She's got some nerve, saying stuff like that!" He was about to throw in some curses for good measure but broke off, flabbergasted, as the meaning of what he'd heard finally sank in: "Volodya's defending me?!" Heedless of Ira Petrovna's angry, shouted retort, he stared at Volodya and blinked stupidly. His desire to break something into smithereens evaporated.

But Ira was still in full swing: "The best girl in the troop! She's *this close* to getting into the Komsomol! But as soon as she takes up with you, here we go: her work's sloppy, she sleeps through morning calisthenics, she sneaks out of—"

Volodya interrupted her. "Okay. Stop. Irin, are you trying to tell me that Masha wasn't in her troop cabin last night?"

"Yes!"

"And because Yura wasn't there either, you think he was with her?"

"Yes, exactly!"

"And did anybody see them together?"

"No, but it's obvious!"

The "obvious" was what finally made Yurka lose it. Incapable of swallowing that bitter pill, he kicked at one of the seats. The seat cushion popped off and fell to the floor. Nobody but the troublemaker himself paid any attention.

"What could be obvious to you, though? Yurka was with me!" Volodya was beginning to get mad.

"You're just covering for him again, but he's taking the best girl Pioneer in the troop and—" Then Ira used such a dirty word that Yurka froze in shock.

"I'm telling you again: Konev was with me!" Volodya snapped.

"Don't lie to me! He was not! I know because I walked around your cabin and there were no lights on!" Ira spat triumphantly. "Well now, Volodya! I never expected this from you! Whereas you, Konev: I've taken a lot from you, but this is the limit! Tomorrow I'm going to formally request your expul—"

"Ira. Hold on." Volodya spoke in low tones, trying to bring her back to reason. "Yura really was with me and the boys from my troop. If you need witnesses, we have plenty. And anyway, why are you beginning an inquiry here? Why not at the staff meeting?"

"Because I just now found out!"

"But what the hell was Masha doing staying out all night?" cut in Yurka. "And why are you chewing me out, but not her? Why doesn't she get in trouble for it?"

"Because you . . . because she . . ."

"Because you're used to Yura always being your whipping boy!" exploded Volodya. "And why are you so worried about him, not Masha? Why are you so fixated on him? Are you in love with him or something?!"

Everyone stopped dead in their tracks. Volodya glared malevolently. Yurka sat hard on the seat he'd just broken, barely keeping from falling down. Ira Petrovna pressed her lips together into a thin line as she went pale and started trembling. Anybody with eyes could see the seething rage inside her would burst out any second in a flood of tears—or curses. But the troop leader held herself in check. She pressed her lips together so hard they started turning blue, then she spun on her heel and walked out without a word.

Volodya clenched his hands into fists and sat on the seat next to Yurka, who asked quietly, "So what do you think? Is this it for me?"

Volodya shook his head. "Just let her try saying something at the staff meeting! I'll put her in her place . . . This is beyond the pale! What kind of troop leader is she if she doesn't even know what's going on in her own troop?"

Yurka's heart filled with a sort of inexpressible lightness. "Thank you, Volod," he said, imbuing the words with as much gratitude as he could possibly express.

"Only question is where the hell Masha got off to?" Volodya said slowly, instead of answering.

As they walked from the theater to the mess hall, Yurka's mind shifted far away from Ira and Masha until he was thinking only about his empty, growling stomach. In contrast, Volodya was still grumbling: "Yura, you have to remember to get Irina's permission to leave . . . 'Best girl Pioneer in the troop,' my foot . . . 'Best girl Pioneers' should go to sleep at night, not go traipsing all over camp . . ."

Hearing him, Yurka suddenly remembered: "Volod! While you were running the rehearsal, Petlitsyn tried to get me to get up in the middle of the night and go toothpaste the girls. I said no way, but then he went and talked to Sashka and Sashka nodded. I think they're planning a sneak attack!"

Volodya stopped short: "Petlitsyn? But he's from Troop Two, and Sashka's in Troop Five! What does he care about little kids like Sashka?"

"What do you mean, what's he doing? It's fun to get the little kids involved!"

"Nothing fun about it! It's dangerous!"

"Oh, please, give me a break! Remember what it was like to be Petlitsyn's age! And don't act like you never tried to goad the younger campers into doing that kind of thing!"

"Actually, I didn't, Yura. Nobody dared to play jokes on me, nor did I ever pick on anybody else. What about you? Don't tell me you were some kind of hooligan?"

"A hooligan? Of course not!" lied Yurka without missing a beat. But in reality, oh, what nasty tricks he'd played, what awful things he'd done, whenever he found himself with far too much free time on his hands.

His mother had always told him, "Nature abhors a vacuum," and Yurka had learned the truth of this the hard way. When music disappeared from his life, the vacuum it left behind swallowed up all his emotions, leaving only anxiety and anger. Without music, Yurka felt orphaned. He'd tried to keep himself busy with something, anything, whatever would keep him from thinking about it. He'd collected stamps, made model airplanes, soldered simple electronics, carved wood, set up an aquarium—but he had found it all bland and boring. In search of any diversion that could fill music's joyless absence, Yurka started spending time with the boys from his apartment building who hung out in the courtyard. They were anything but boring. And although they weren't exactly hardened street toughs, they were definitely not the best influence on Yurka. What good did it do him to learn how to do card tricks (and cheat at card games)? Or memorize a bunch of dirty songs and off-color couplets? Or waste time hanging around with his buddies in a building entryway, stealing light bulbs and covering the walls with a whole Talmud of bad words? Or set off several calcium carbide plastic bottle bombs and a couple of smoke bombs at school?

The kids from his building taught him less destructive pranks, too, of course. And last year at camp, in just that one session, Yurka had managed to get almost all the little kids hooked on playing tricks on each other, to the point that something happened in every cabin every morning. In one cabin, a victim would be tied down while still asleep, then be woken up by a gout of cold water he couldn't escape; in another cabin, the perpetrators would sneak up to their sleeping victim and throw a sheet over his head, shouting "The ceiling's caving in!" to make the victim scream like all get-out; in a third cabin, the troublemakers would hide behind the camp washstand, and while their victim was washing his face, they'd tie his shoelaces together so that once the victim tried to walk away, he'd fall flat on his face. And who needs reminding of the "nighttime classics" like toothpasting sleeping campers, or putting cold, wet noodles under people's pillows, or surreptitiously yanking on the curtains while somebody's telling a scary story? The kids were scared out of their wits and had the time of their lives, but Yurka soon grew bored with even the most sophisticated practical jokes.

What had already gotten old for him last year was all the more stale now. And Volodya obviously got no joy from pranks himself. The troop leader's expression was a conflicting jumble of bafflement, worry, and irritation as he said, "Well . . . darn it . . . I sure got stuck with some little scoundrels . . ."

After supper, Volodya fished Yurka out of the mass of pioneers leaving the mess hall.

"Listen, Yur—you are coming tonight, right? I wanted to ask you something."

"What?"

"I keep worrying about that toothpaste. They're still little kids, they don't know it could cause an injury."

Yurka nodded. "That's pretty much true . . . A couple of years ago, some smart aleck toothpasted me right in the eye. It burned so bad, I thought I'd go blind. My eyelid was swollen for a week."

Upon hearing this, Volodya's expression changed so drastically that Yurka immediately regretted his words. To reassure Volodya, he quickly added, "But don't you worry! We know about their dastardly plan, so we can put a stop to it."

"But stopping it won't help. We keep them from playing their trick today, they'll just do it tomorrow. The important thing is that they know never to toothpaste anyone in the eyes, ears, or nose. So I realized we need to tell them a scary story about toothpasting."

"Ah, but yesterday you didn't want me to scare the little squirts."

"Well, Yur, I'd rather my troop pee their beds if it means that nobody chokes on toothpaste. And especially that nobody's eyes get burned!"

Yurka scratched the back of his head. "But what'll we tell them? What's so scary about toothpaste?"

"We've got buckets of time until junior lights out. We'll think of something."

"Pcholkin!" called Volodya in a stage whisper as he leaned down over the boy's bed. "Sit up, you!"

"Why? What now?" the boy grumbled, but sat up obediently.

Volodya felt around under the boy's pillow and pulled out a tube of toothpaste. "This is why." He stood up and surveyed the rows of beds. "Who else has something hidden under their pillow? Sash! You?"

"Hey, why me?" came a squeak from the left-hand row by the wall.

"Because you're always so well-behaved."

Yurka watched all this from his comfortable perch on an empty bed by the window.

"Now, boys," Volodya intoned sententiously, "don't even think of toothpasting anyone! It could be dangerous. Do you understand?"

The response was a couple of listless "Yeahs" and "Sures."

Volodya sighed heavily. Then he took a deep breath and was about to say something else, but suddenly there was a loud shriek from the girls' room, followed by the sounds of trampling feet and a slamming door. And muffled sobs.

"I'll be right back," said Volodya. He jumped up and ran out of the room, flinging "Yur, look after them!" over his shoulder as he left.

"Oh, Yuuuuwaaaa!" Olezhka sang slyly as soon as the door shut.

"Hm?"

"You pwomised us a scawy stowy!" "Yeah, you promised, Yura!" "Tell us another scary story!"

Yurka scoffed and crossed his arms. "Well, now . . . I don't know . . ." he said slowly. "Yesterday, Volodya said I couldn't tell you scary stories anymore, he said you're still too little. And you are still little! You all couldn't even get your toothpasting stunt figured out . . ."

"But how was *I* supposed to know he was going to look under my pillow?!" Pcholkin protested.

"Maybe *some people* shouldn't have blabbed about it loud enough for the whole theater to hear!" Yurka replied, adopting the same defensive tone.

"That wasn't me! That was Sashka!" insisted Pcholkin, scowling.

"I've still got *my* toothpaste, though!" The chubby boy waved the little tube over his head triumphantly.

"Put that away, you!" Yurka shushed him, then continued ominously: "You can't even imagine the kind of horrible things that happen in the Barn Swallow to jokesters who go out toothpasting! And these aren't just stories: I saw them myself . . ."

The room went silent. The only sound was the rustle of Sasha putting the toothpaste back under his pillow.

"So what exactly happens to them, Yuw?" Olezhka stuck his head out from under his blanket and looked at Yura, intrigued.

In a show of bravado, Pcholkin crossed his arms on his chest and asked, "What have you seen?"

Knowing that the boys could see his silhouette backlit against the window, Yurka narrowed his eyes and turned his head to survey the room. "Are you sure you want to know?"

The silence in the cabin held for a good thirty seconds. Finally there was one hesitant "Yes," followed by a few others.

"Okay," Yurka acquiesced grudgingly. "Then I'll share another genuinely scary secret with you . . . The ghost of the countess I told you about yesterday isn't the only one that wanders around Camp Barn Swallow at night. The truth is that—I read this somewhere—this area has an elevated rate of . . . wait, what's the word again? . . . oh, yeah: of anomalous activity! All kinds of supernatural forces and unclean spirits are drawn to this place, especially at night."

In a nearby bed, someone's teeth were chattering.

"What? Is this scary?" asked Yurka.

"Well . . . ," someone in another bed began hesitantly.

"No!" said Sasha boldly.

"Tell us!" urged Pcholkin.

Yura paused for dramatic effect, listening to the utter silence in the room. Then, slowly, he whispered: "Four years ago a girl named Nina came to the Barn Swallow. She was a regular girl, nothing about her was all that memorable—except for her eyes. She had really, really pretty eyes. Big, and a very clear blue, just like the sky."

Olezhka interrupted him. "Did you know hew, Yuwa?"

"Of course I did," Yurka confirmed without hesitation. "We didn't talk or anything, because back then I was just a little older than you all, but she was fifteen, a senior camper, basically a grown-up . . . Anyway, Nina was a very solitary and unsociable girl. She never did make any friends. Some people are just like that,: withdrawn and socially awkward. And because she wasn't able to make any friends and was always by herself wherever she went in camp, everyone started thinking of her as a loner and making fun of her. Everyone teased her and called her names. They even came up with a special nickname for her: the Crusty Old Codger."

The boys giggled. Yurka shushed them.

"One night the girls from Nina's troop decided to toothpaste the boys. This is almost a ritual for the senior troops, you know: if your troop hasn't been toothpasted at least once during your session, the session's is a failure."

The boys perked up. Questions rained down on Yurka from all sides: "Have you ever been toothpasted?" "Has anybody ever toothpasted Volodya?" "Have you ever toothpasted anyone?" This wasn't the time for them, though. Yurka quickly answered a few, then ordered the boys to be quiet and continued. "Anyway, nobody ever asked Nina to go out toothpasting. It hurt her feelings a lot to hear the other girls in her troop giggling and describing the patterns they'd drawn on the boys' faces. And so she was overcome by her hurt feelings, or maybe she wanted revenge, but in any case she used up almost all her toothpaste the next night toothpasting the girls. But because nobody'd ever asked Nina to join them, she didn't know the ground rules. For example, that you never get toothpaste in people's hair, since when it dries it gets hard as concrete and you can't get it out; sometimes you just have to rip the hair out. Sure enough, the next morning two girls couldn't get the toothpaste out of their hair! And revenge, you know . . . revenge is contagious . . . At first the girls thought it was the boys from their troop and were getting ready to get revenge. But then somebody noticed that Nina's toothpaste tube was almost empty and that the Crusty Old Codger herself had gone untouched on the night they were all toothpasted . . . All that day she heard the other girls in her troop whispering and discussing their plans for revenge on the boys, but that night they got their revenge on the completely unsuspecting Nina! She woke up because suddenly she felt this burning sensation all over her face, especially on her eyelids. Still groggy and half-asleep, she opened her eyes and rubbed them, but the burning got so bad that she burst into tears. Trying to clear out her eyes, she rubbed them even harder, but that only made it worse! Nobody lifted a finger to help her. All she heard around her was snickering. So she got up and, unable to see a thing, felt her way out of the cabin and ran away. But the next morning"—Yurka held his breath and let the dramatic pause linger—"the next morning, Troop Three, the first to show up for morning calisthenics, saw Nina in the swimming pool. She was floating face down, in her white pajamas, with her arms stretched wide and her hair gently swaying in the water . . . and she was dead! They pulled Nina out of the pool, rolled her over onto her back, and saw that where her beautiful sky-blue eyes had once been, now there were just red, burned-out sockets!"

"Oh, that's awful!" someone squeaked in the corner of the room. "But how did she end up in the pool?"

"Because she was running with her eyes closed and fell in. And Nina couldn't swim very well, and also her eyes were burning. And so she drowned."

"Yuwa, you saw it youwself, didn't you?"

"But that's not the end of the story!" Yurka announced, interrupting the boys' sudden clamor. "They tried to hush up what happened as fast as they could so word wouldn't spread. They cut the session short and sent everyone home, but the rumors spread like wildfire! And now, any Pioneers or troop leaders who happen to be by the pool late at night, at a specific time—at three seventeen in the morning—see a blue light floating above it. The light hovers there in the air for exactly four minutes, and then, as though blown away by a strong gust of wind, it flies off toward the senior troop cabins. And on the nights it does that, strange things happen there: in the morning, someone always wakes up with toothpaste on their face, on their cheeks and forehead. And it's always just one person, the biggest prankster in the troop, and the smears of toothpaste are sort of weird, as though somebody'd been aiming for the eyes but couldn't quite get it right. And then the pranksters tell about their dreams, which are always about the exact same thing. They hear the splashing of water and they feel someone's fingers touching their faces. And then they hear a girl's soft voice calling to them: 'Let's go play some tricks... I have a full tube of toothpaste...' And nobody has the shadow of a doubt that it's the ghost of the little girl Nina, the Crusty Old Codger, who walks the earth on those nights, searching the camp for someone to play with. People say Nina makes sure to pick the most mischievous kid at camp, because they're the most fun, but also because she wants to get her revenge. So first she calls to them to come out and play, but then she toothpastes them and drowns them! And she wants to toothpaste them right in the eyes, but she can't, because she can't see."

"But Nina only searches for culprits in the senior cabins—right, Yur?" Sasha clarified.

"Where'd you get that idea?" said Yurka indignantly. "I'm thinking she might come and visit us now, since you're all planning on a little mischief. So just be careful with that toothpaste!"

"Can it really burn out your eyes?"

"Why don't you try it, Sash, and then we'll ask Nina to come and check—"

"No way!"

"That's what I thought! Now drill this into your heads, all of you: Never toothpaste anyone in the eyes, nose, ears, or hair. Not at all, not for any reason." Yurka stood up from the bed, cracked his back, and stretched.

"Why not the nose and eaws?" asked Olezha.

"Think about it, Olezh! After you toothpaste somebody, the toothpaste dries and they can't breathe through their nose or get it out of their ears! All right: I'm off to find Volodya, he's disappeared somewhere. Do you all promise to stay quiet in bed and not play tricks?"

"We promise!"

Yurka headed for the door, but paused at Sasha's bed and stuck his hand under the pillow. "I'll just go on and take this anyway," he said, pulling out a tube of toothpaste. "Better safe than sorry."

"Fine, take it. I changed my mind anyway. I'm not going to toothpaste anyone . . . for now . . . ," grumbled the chubby boy.

The narrow hall was pitch-black. Yurka felt his way to the door to the girls' room, opened it carefully, and looked in. The room was silent, all the girls sleeping peacefully, but neither Volodya nor Lena was with them. Yurka turned and tiptoed to the troop leaders' room, which Volodya shared with Zhenya, the handsome physical education instructor.

The room was at the far end of the hall. Yurka couldn't see a thing and groped his way along the wall toward the thin strip of light showing underneath the door. It was always interesting to see how the troop leaders lived, especially Volodya. And now he finally had a reason to go visit the troop leader.

As he approached the door to the Volodya and Zhenya's room, Yurka heard a whisper: "No I didn't! *Lena's* the one who asked *me* to dance!" He recognized Zhenya's voice. He carefully felt for the door in preparation for knocking. But he accidentally bumped the door, which swung slowly and soundlessly open, gradually revealing the troop leaders' room.

The first thing he saw was a neatly made bed, its brown bedspread drawn perfectly taut, a poster for the band Mashina Vremeni—Time Machine—on the wall above it. Next, the nightstand was revealed. Volodya's extremely battered notebook and his glasses case were on it, along with a glass of water and a tiny bottle of valerian extract. But Volodya himself wasn't there. Where was he? Yurka took a step back and turned to leave, but he heard the whispered voice again—"All I did was dance with her!"—and through the open door he saw the phys ed instructor's close-cropped hair and broad back, clad in a blue track suit jacket.

Zhenya was kneeling in front of the other bed, on which, wiping her red eyes, sat none other than Ira Petrovna. Her green circle skirt covered her legs down to the ankle. The red neckerchief over her white turtleneck had gone crooked. Her long hair was loose and messy instead of being pulled back in her usual high, tight ponytail, and her eyes were squeezed shut as though she was trying to decide whether to do something.

Zhenya stood up, leaned close to her, and whispered something in her ear. Ira finally gave in. She reached out to the phys ed instructor, folded her arms around his neck, and kissed him full on the lips.

"Get a load of that!" breathed Yurka, flabbergasted. He groped for the doorknob, thinking to hide the pair from prying eyes—*god forbid any children see this!*—and was pulling the door shut when he banged his elbow loudly on the doorframe. Ira flinched. As the door clicked shut, a commotion ensued behind it.

Some troop leader she is! thought Yurka indignantly as he flew down the hall to the door of the cabin. He'd only seen them by accident, but he still felt awkward and wanted to get out of there as quick as he could. "As if Ira would know what's going on in her troop when she's all wrapped up in her own personal life! Out gallivanting all night herself, devil knows where! How could Volodya allow such outrageous behavior in his own room?"

When Yurka got outside, he finally found Volodya, who was coming back to the cabin, dragging a little girl from his troop behind him. The little girl was sniffling and whimpering. Volodya's lips were pressed in a thin line. The brooding troop leader, immersed again in dark thoughts, didn't even look at Yura but called into the darkness behind the cabin: "Lena! I found her!" In the distance, the second leader of Troop Five said "Thank god!" in a voice shaky from worry.

Yurka had no intention of getting involved in the troop leaders' drama, so he just waved at Volodya in parting. Volodya responded with a silent nod and went into his cabin. Yurka headed off to his own.

But Ira Petrovna still managed to head him off before he got there. She was standing on the ground in front of his cabin's porch, and even in the dim glow of the weak porch light he could see she was blushing as red as the petunias growing in the flower beds by the porch steps.

"Yura, a word," Ira called quietly.

"What?" he said curtly.

Ira Petrovna, usually so forthright, was now at a complete loss: she shifted from foot to foot and kept opening her mouth, then closing it again without saying a word. She was horribly embarrassed. But even though she couldn't talk, Yurka knew what she wanted to tell him.

"I didn't see anything," he announced firmly, poking the little triangles of brick edging the flower bed with the toe of his sneaker.

Ira sighed in relief. "It's good you understand! Of course you saw everything. And you're right, it's not exactly appropriate—this is a camp, there are kids here. But you're a senior camper, you're a grown-up, after all! You see—"

"There's no reason to go into all this, Ira Petrovna," interrupted Yurka, to prevent her from continuing her awkward monologue. "You're the grown-up, and I . . . actually I just want to go to bed. The kids wore me out." And with that, he headed to his bed.

Yurka was well aware that whatever Ira did with the phys ed instructor was none of his business, but it was still very useful for him to have the information. Just let her try to falsely accuse him now!

Nevertheless, as he fell asleep, Yurka again found himself thinking not about Ira but about Volodya. It was too bad they hadn't had a chance to say good night to each other. But it wasn't a big deal; they'd see each other the next day and write another scary story, even better than the first one. *It'll be so great to sit there with Volodya on the merry-go-round, chewing the fat and thinking up stories. If only it were already tomorrow . . .* As he anticipated the coming day, imagining how Volodya, deep in thought, would chew on his pencil, Yurka fell asleep.

It felt like only a second had passed when Vanka suddenly shook his shoulder: "Go out on the porch. Someone's asking for you."

"Ira again?" grumbled Yurka.

It took all his willpower to make himself get up and slowly, listlessly, his eyes still closed, start feeling around for his clothes.

"No. Volodya."

"Volodya?" Yurka's eyes flew open all by themselves.

He went outside and saw Volodya sitting on the bench by the flower bed. He heard the moths flying into the porch light, felt the soft thrum of their wings, saw the flickering shadows they cast. Yurka breathed in deeply through his nose—the fresh night air smelled of damp needles and fragrant flowers—and walked down the porch steps.

"I just stopped by for five minutes." Volodya stood up from the bench and peered through the flickering light, then frowned, concerned, when he saw the rumpled Yurka. "Did I wake you?"

"No, it's fine," said Yurka, stifling a yawn and trying to smooth his tousled hair. "Did something happen?"

"No, no, I just stopped by to say good night, that's all. We didn't get a chance earlier . . ."

"Where were you so long?" Yurka asked as he sat down on the bench.

"I was looking for my little runaway girl."

"A *girl* runaway?"

"Yes, if you can believe it! This little girl Yulya in my troop. It's Troop Five, so this is everyone's first-ever session of camp, but Yulya's having an especially hard time of it; she can't settle in and won't even try . . . She isn't friends with anyone, all she does is ask to be sent back home to her parents, and now she actually went and took off. When I found her, she admitted she'd tried to run away but got lost."

"Why didn't you tell me? I'd have helped you look. We'd have found her in two shakes if we'd both been looking."

"There was nobody else to stay with the boys. But there's no need for you worry about it. First of all, we'll be calling her parents tomorrow, so she can at least hear their voices over the phone. And secondly, it's parents' day soon. Yulya's mother will come and calm her down. Or else take her back home. That'd be the best thing . . ."

"Yeah . . ."

The conversation faltered. It wasn't awkward. They just didn't feel the need to talk. It was too calm and peaceful to talk. The crickets were chirring brightly in the cool of the night. Far away there was a mournful howling, of either a dog or a real live wolf. Yurka didn't know whether this was all actually happening or whether it was some trick of the imagination. He could've sworn he even heard the hooting of an owl. The only thing this night was missing was the crackle of a campfire.

"What do you think? Will the scary story work?" Volodya asked, breaking a long but comfortable silence.

"I don't think so," Yurka admitted frankly. "I'm afraid it'll make them want to experiment and test whether toothpaste really does dry hard as concrete on hair."

"Who cares about hair?" said Volodya, waving his hand dismissively. "As long as they don't do the nose or eyes."

It looked like the sky was resting on the roofs of the little one-story troop cabins. The Milky Way's blanket of colorful stars glittered. Satellites and airplanes blinked their white, red, and green signal lights on and off, looking like flashes of sunlight on water. If Yurka'd had a telescope, he could've made out the galaxies that looked from this distance like tiny, indistinct clouds. He might've even fulfilled his childhood dream of seeing Asteroid B-612 and shaking the Little Prince's hand. Why not? This kind of quiet summer night was the best time for believing in fairy tales . . .

But Yurka didn't have long to enjoy the sky's nearness. After a few minutes, Volodya sighed and stood up. "Well, time to go. I have to get up early tomorrow for the staff meeting, and I can't be late."

Yura stood up, too. While Volodya's right hand grasped his in the customary parting handshake, Volodya reached his left hand up to Yurka's shoulder. Yurka expected Volodya to clap him on the shoulder with it, but instead the troop leader did something that was neither squeezing it or petting it but sort of a combination of both.

"Thanks for everything," Volodya whispered, a bit awkwardly.

"I'll sneak out after lights out tomorrow," Yurka blurted out. "Will you be at the merry-go-round?"

Volodya chuckled and shook his head, but didn't bother rebuking him. "Yes."

It felt like their parting handshake lasted for an eternity. But as soon as Volodya ended it, Yurka's mood plummeted. It hadn't been enough. Yurka had never really thought about the fact that when you're shaking someone's hand, you're holding it. But he thought about it now. And suddenly he realized he wanted to hold Volodya's hand a little longer.

But, drowsy and lulled by the nighttime quiet as Yurka was, he didn't get all worked up thinking about that or trying to get to the bottom of it. He was too sleepy and too ready for it to be tomorrow already.

As he wrapped himself in his thin blanket, Yurka literally plunged into a deep dream, landing not on his hard camp bed, but on soft, fluffy dandelions.

CHAPTER SIX

CONFESSIONS OF THE PERSONAL AND THE PERVERSE

The merry-go-round by the junior cabins became their unofficial meeting place. Yurka would go there after lunch, or when he sneaked out of quiet hour, or at night before the dance started, and after a little while Volodya would turn up, too. Yurka liked sitting on the merry-go-round, slowly spinning this way and that, silently gazing into the emptiness before him and thinking about all kinds of things. He liked it when Volodya sat down wordlessly next to him and gazed off into the distance as well. There was something about sitting like that, side by side, watching the little kids and listening to their shouting, that was somehow special, and unusual, and simple, and close to his heart all at once. It made Yurka feel as cozy as when he played in the courtyard of his grandmother's apartment building back when he was little.

But what he liked best was what they'd been doing the last few evenings when, after rehearsal, Volodya handed Troop Five over to Lena to take care of until lights out, and Volodya and Yurka thought up scary stories for the kids. Once they'd even missed the signal for lights out, the time when they were supposed to go and actually tell the stories they'd been inventing.

The first week of the camp session was over, which Mitka's voice was proclaiming over the loudspeaker as he delivered the morning announcements—as if the Pioneers didn't already know! Yurka remembered that day well. He and Volodya had been sitting on the merry-go-round, and Volodya had gestured at Yurka's face and asked, "How'd you get that scar?"

Stillness reigned over the playground. It was quiet hour, when all campers were supposed to be resting in their cabins. Yurka had slipped away as usual; the ever-responsible Volodya had merely reminded Yurka that as soon as they saw anyone coming down the path to the junior cabins, Yurka had to duck into the bushes. This was because of the occasional check-ins on the troop leaders, making sure they weren't leaving the campers by themselves. But Volodya had nothing to fear, since he and Lena had made an agreement that she'd be on duty during quiet hour, while he'd be on during dances. So she was on duty right now.

Yurka's hand went instinctively to his chin, where the tips of his fingers brushed the old scar under his lower lip. "Oh, well, it's from this one time when some hooligans were giving me a hard time. There were three of them, by the way, and just one of me! And so I . . ." But then he stopped. Yurka told everyone this version of the scar's origin. In it, he was a brave scrapper who got his lip busted fighting some street toughs who'd cornered him. But for some reason he wanted to tell Volodya the truth. "Actually, what really happened is that I went flying off a swing when I was eleven. I'd swung up really high because I was trying to impress the little neighbor girls—they were playing nearby—so I held my hands up, and . . . well, to make a long story short, I did a nice front flip off the swing, plowed a long furrow face-first when I hit the ground, and only stopped moving when I smashed into the sandbox. I busted my lip so bad that I couldn't get it to stop bleeding for, like, fifteen minutes. My dad even had to give me stitches! So that's how."

Yurka was sure that now Volodya thought he was an idiot and a braggart and would laugh at him, but all Volodya did was smile amiably and note, "But at least you experienced a brief moment of free flight!"

Yurka couldn't smother a smile: *Volodya's so weird, though*, he thought. *He's just too nice and understanding.* Yurka would've even made fun of himself for something like that, but not Volodya.

"I didn't actually fly that far," Yurka said. Then he gave the troop leader an appraising glance. "Your turn! Since I shared my secret with you, now you share something with me!"

Volodya raised an eyebrow in surprise, but nodded. "Sure, ask away."

"Why did you really come to be a troop leader at Pioneer camp? Because it's obvious you don't much like dealing with kids."

"Umm . . ." As he considered his answer, Volodya absentmindedly adjusted his glasses, poking his finger at the bridge of his nose. He sighed and rattled off a phrase he'd seemingly memorized: "It's a good way to acquire some useful experience and—don't argue, Yura—to get a good character reference for the Party."

Yurka scoffed. A week ago, at the opening assembly, he'd have believed that Perfectly Perfect Volodya, the ideal Komsomol comrade himself, didn't care about anything but his upstanding reputation, but now . . .

"Here we go again: you and that character reference! But if we're being honest here, is that really the only reason? Just to help your reputation?"

Volodya hesitated. He adjusted his glasses again, even though they were already in place. "Well . . . not exactly. To tell the truth, I've always been really shy. It's hard for me to get along with people, to talk and make friends. But kids . . . My mom works in a day care and she's the one who advised me to come be a troop leader. She said that if I want to learn how to get along with people, it'd be best to start with children, because they draw you out." He went quiet again, and Yurka thought that if Volodya adjusted his glasses one more time, he'd have to reach over and smack Volodya's hand. "You're actually more effective there. I mean, you get along with them better."

Yurka proudly sat up straighter, but then slouched again. "We both deserve credit for it," he said. "I don't really like messing around with the little kids, either. I mean, I don't know how to. But if it helps you, then . . . Oh! I meant to tell you: yesterday after supper I was going to the cabin and I saw Olezhka. He was out on the playground all by himself, crying, so I went up and ask him what happened, and it turns out that this whole time the kids have been teasing him because of his *r*'s, and now that he has one of the main parts, they've really started picking on him. The poor little guy's already insecure, but now he's hearing all this stuff from the kids, like 'How are you going to perform onstage when you can't even say your *r*'s!'"

"They really said that? Who?"

"I don't know. As it is, I only understand every other word Olezhka says, but right then he was crying, too, so I didn't get much of what he said. But, Volod, I thought about it and it's true: he pronounces all those words with *r*'s really badly, like 'partisans,' and 'struggle,' and so forth . . ."

"It's true," Volodya repeated glumly. "It's not the lead, of course, but it's got a lot of lines . . . He asked to do it, though! And I thought it'd give him more confidence in himself, not less. We have to figure something out, but without taking the part away from him, because then he'd be crushed; he really is trying so hard . . . Got any ideas?"

"I do, and that's what I was going to say! Let's take the script now, before he's memorized his lines, and rewrite them so there are as few words with *r* as possible!"

"He doesn't have that many lines, but it's complex, and there's a lot riding on it: it's an important role," Volodya said. "We don't have time for a thoughtful revision, but we'd still have to get it done as fast as we can! Think about it: How many hours will we need? Six or eight, I'd guess, but where will we find them? We can't work during rehearsal, and we definitely can't work while I'm busy with Troop Five . . . There's always quiet hour . . ."

"Yeah, right. Even if they give us the okay on rewriting it, letting me out of quiet hour's another thing entirely," said Yurka bitterly.

"They gave you to me not as an actor, but as a helper. And right now I really need your help. They can't make you do it during the competitions, or during civic duty work, or during the dances. And they also can't make you do the rewriting during rehearsal because I need you then, to help me."

Yurka felt a brief burst of excitement. Not only would he no longer have to sit around, bored to death for two hours, but now he and Volodya would have those two hours all to themselves! But his joy quickly faded as soon as he remembered Olga Leonidovna's stern voice and her constant "Children always have to be kept busy and troop leaders always have to know where their children are." His troop leader was Ira. Not Volodya. Yurka grew dejected. Let Konev the knucklehead out of quiet hour? Yeah, right! It would never happen. Why was Volodya even teasing him with the possibility?

"I don't think it's going to work," Yurka said.

"I'll ask the head troop leader, and I'll also ask Lena to support it. She works with me, after all, she sees everything I do." Volodya had noticed the change in Yurka's mood, of course, and clapped Yurka on the shoulder. "Never hurts to try. Let's see how good a diplomat I am."

So he did. And the next day, as they were walking to the playground after the beginning of quiet hour, Volodya, who usually spoke quietly while they were still by the Troop Five cabin, almost yelled as he told Yurka about it: "Can you believe it, Yur? It took Olga Leonidovna a little while to agree, but it was basically clear she didn't really have anything against it—when she's against something, she lets you know, she comes down on you like a bolt from the blue—but this time she asked what the head troop leader thought, and then as a formality she asked the rest. They all were okay with it, and why not? Makes no difference to them—right?—since I'm the one who has to do the rewriting. But then Irina butts in and starts insisting that it's just the opposite, it'll actually help Olezhka to have to perform the unchanged script in public because it'll make him work harder with the speech therapist! I just about fell off my chair—that's crazy talk, but it's crazy talk that'll hurt Olezhka. I don't even think she really thinks it will help him. She's just trying to put a spoke in my wheel!"

Volodya still hadn't been able to make up with her after the scene in the theater. He'd tried to apologize several times, but Ira would end the conversation without letting him finish. Volodya was upset and admitted to Yurka more than once that he was very worried about the continued rift. But this time, at least, despite what Irina said, Olga Leonidovna ended up being more sensitive to Olezha's problem and granted Volodya permission.

"Really? I'm officially allowed to skip quiet hour?" Yurka couldn't believe it.

As usual, they were at the playground, on the merry-go-round. Yurka was so happy, he kicked off and set the merry-go-round spinning. Until that moment the fluffy white dandelion heads would only occasionally send their downy seeds up past the boys' knees and into their noses. Now, disturbed by the wind, the white fluff flew up into the air in a swirling cloud.

As though on command, both boys simultaneously dug their feet into the ground to stop their spinning. Yurka got a fuzzy dandelion seed in his throat. He started coughing and his eyes started watering. Blinded, he blinked stupidly until he could look around, and when he did, he was struck by the beauty of the place. It was as though he were seeing it for the first time. Fluffy little dandelion seeds were still swirling around and floating slowly to rest in the grass. The small white seeds floating through the air were an echo of larger white things floating through the sky: every day, white planes from a nearby airfield flew past Camp Barn Swallow and paratroopers jumped out of them, opening their white parachutes and drifting down to the ground, practicing their landings. It looked unbelievably gorgeous. How had Yurka not noticed that before?

Once he took a good look, he realized that everything was gorgeous here. And Volodya was really gorgeous. Especially today, right now, after he'd delivered his good news, when he was happy, disheveled and red-cheeked, and bursting into such infectious laughter that Yurka started laughing, too. He'd never seen Volodya so happy. Yurka himself had probably never been so viscerally happy. And from that moment on, they would spend every free minute rewriting the script together.

But it turned out that something always got in the way. They lost almost a whole day because of the girl from Volodya's troop who wanted to go back to her parents so badly. She went into such hysterics that it took both her troop leaders, the educational specialist Olga Leonidovna, and the nurse to calm her down. By that evening Volodya was so exhausted that Yurka let him go to sleep instead of staying up to work.

The second day they lost was parents' day. It added insult to injury that the day was chaotic and went by too fast. Yurka had actually been looking forward to it just as much as the rest of the kids. But it felt like his mom had just had a chance to hug him when the troop concert began. They'd just had a nice stroll around the camp when it was time for lunch. They'd just finished a game of rucheyok—babbling brook—when it was time to eat again. His mom had just gotten a Chinese jump rope contest going—women against girls—when it was time to say goodbye already.

Yurka felt like he'd barely had time to exchange a few words with his mom. The only thing he managed to even talk about was the theater. He wanted to tell her about Volodya, about how fantastic he was and how they'd become such good friends that now he couldn't imagine spending a day without him. His mom would probably be glad to hear it: her son had finally come to his senses and was socializing with a real Komsomol member, not with some kind of riffraff! But once Yurka opened his mouth, he felt abashed, unsure how best to convey his feelings or how to even describe them.

Before she got on the bus to leave, Yurka's mom gave him a kiss and asked carefully, "Have you made friends with any of the girls yet? You didn't introduce me to anyone . . ."

"There's Ksyusha. I'm going to ask her to dance," Yurka replied, awkwardly sticking a finger out toward the girl. He suddenly felt very uncomfortable. His mom had never talked to him about girls before.

Yurka wasn't the only one who was completely exhausted by the end of parents' day. He didn't go to sleep, of course, but he had neither the desire nor the energy to work on the script. So he and Volodya just sat on the merry-go-round and chatted about this and that.

In the time that Yurka and Volodya spent together, they became true friends. Usually, though, they didn't sit around talking but got their notebooks and papers out right away, spread them out on their laps, and bent over them to brainstorm. Or try to.

"Okay. 'Struggle.' 'Struggle . . .'" Volodya chewed on his pencil thoughtfully. He pronounced the sounds slowly, seeming to linger over the *r*. "'Strrrruggle' . . ."

"Battle. Fight." Yurka offered a couple of synonyms and suppressed a monstrous yawn.

They'd been at work for ages. The sun was burning hot. Volodya was sitting on the merry-go-round in the shade of a nearby bird cherry tree, not letting the sun hit so much as the tip of his nose. His handsome nose. Which Yurka kept noticing. Yurka himself hadn't taken off his favorite imported red cap all day. His forehead was sweaty and the buckle of the cap was painfully tight on the back of his head, but he bore the discomfort stoically, rather than run the risk of getting sunstroke even in the shade.

Their work was going well, despite the heat. They'd done more in this quiet hour than they'd done in the previous two combined. But there was still a long way to go. Yurka was tired. He'd been sitting virtually motionless for half an hour and his neck and arms were stiff. He wasn't complaining, though. This was way more important than scary stories. He rolled his neck, stood up from the merry-go-round, and walked around it, stretching out his stiff back.

"Yeah, 'fight' is good," mumbled Volodya, without looking up from his notebook. "'Their fight against the German invaders' . . ."

"'*The* fight . . . um . . . the fight for victory over their attackers'? Hmm . . . sounds kind of dumb . . ."

"And all those words have *r*'s," Volodya pointed out.

Then it dawned on Yurka: "Enemies!" he said, stopping and jabbing his finger up into the air.

"Exactly!" Volodya looked up from his papers and smiled, his glasses glinting. "Oh—no, wait... The next sentence talks about the enemy, and that one has to stay like that."

"Why? Here, let me look at it." Yurka plopped down on the merry-go-round next to him and grabbed the notebook and papers.

Volodya moved over to him and peered down at the pages. He got out his pencil and was about to point at something in the text with it, but Yurka unthinkingly kicked off at just that moment and the merry-go-round started turning. Volodya lurched and fell down on Yurka so hard that the bill of Yurka's baseball cap rammed into Volodya's forehead.

Individual pages slid slowly off the merry-go-round onto the ground, where the gentle breeze sent them scudding in all directions. Both boys turned their heads, following the pages as they fluttered gracefully away. It mesmerized them both. After some time, Volodya looked back down—and blushed. "Oops," he whispered. Then Yurka noticed it too: Volodya had been holding on to Yurka's knee. Volodya quickly let go.

"Sor—sorry," Yurka stammered. He also felt awkward for some reason. He cleared his throat, abashed. Then, pretending to do it casually, for no special reason, he turned his cap around so the bill was in the back.

"That's a strange way to wear it." The comment sounded stupid, as did Volodya's artificially perky tone.

"But I don't wear it that way. I mean, just now I had to... well, so you... it hit you, and I don't want it to... I mean...," he trailed off. Then he changed the subject abruptly: "What, don't you like it?"

"No, no, it looks good on you. Your bangs stick out so funny. It's really a cool cap! And your jeans are really cool, and your polo shirt. I remember how you got dressed up for the dance... that you didn't even end up going to..."

"Well, of course, it's all imported." Yurka was very pleased with himself. He'd never doubted the fact that he had great threads.

"Where'd you get all this bounty?"

"I have relatives in East Germany; they bring it from there. But this cap isn't German, though. It's American, actually."

"Cool!" exclaimed Volodya.

Flattered and gratified, Yurka launched into a detailed narrative of how he got all his prized imported clothes. Although he didn't specify that his jeans weren't actually all that great, since they were made in India, not America.

"You know, over there in Germany, it's not just the clothes that are awesome."

"I know, their technology is, too, and their cars. Once in a magazine I saw this one motorcycle—whew!" Volodya widened his eyes for emphasis.

"In a magazine . . . Yeah, they've got the kind of magazines there that the USSR'll never have."

"Check him out! I'm talking about motorcycles here but he's all about the magazines. That's not like you."

"It's just that you haven't seen 'them, so you don't know what you're talking about. If you'd seen what I've seen . . ." Yurka raised and lowered his eyebrows conspiratorially.

"What? What is it?"

"I'm not telling."

"Yura! Are we in the toddler room at day care or something? Tell me."

"Okay, I'll tell you, but it's a secret, okay?"

"On my honor as a Komsomol member."

Yurka stared at Volodya, eyes narrowed: "Silent as the grave?"

"As the grave."

"This spring my uncle came to visit and brought us all kinds of stuff: clothes, of course, and makeup for my mom, and magazines and other things for my dad. They were regular magazines, just in German, with clothes and housewares and whatnot. So, yeah . . . that night they sent me off to bed but they stayed in the kitchen with the door closed. Pretty soon, my mom left, so my dad and uncle were in there just the two of them. My room happens to be the one closest to the kitchen, so you can hear kitchen conversations pretty well there . . . So the two of them were getting good and boozed up and they'd started talking really loud, so I could hear every word. I just lay there listening, basically. Turns out that my uncle had brought my dad some, ahem, other magazines too. And later when I was at home alone I went and found them."

"What was in them? Was it something anti-Soviet? If it was, then it's dangerous to have magazines like that at home!"

"No, not that! I don't know German well enough yet to read it easily. And there was hardly any text anyway. It was all pictures. Photos." Yurka leaned so close to Volodya that his lips almost touched his ear and lowered his voice to a whisper. "Of women!"

"Ooh . . . Um . . . Well, sure, I know magazines like that exist." Volodya shifted an arm's length away from Yurka, but to no avail: Yurka all but plastered himself to Volodya and whispered hoarsely, directly into his ear, "They were with men . . . You know what I mean? They were with guys . . . They were . . ."

"Enough, Yur. I get it." Volodya slid away again.

"Can you believe that?!" Yurka said in an elated whisper.

"I can. Let's not talk about this anymore, okay? This isn't a Pioneer camp sort of thing . . ."

"Do you really not find this interesting?" said Yurka, disappointed.

"If I say it's completely uninteresting, I'd be lying, but—it's not forbidden for no reason! It's very, very—indecent!"

"Volod, listen, there's something I didn't understand about it." Yurka became animated again. "I saw something unusual . . . You're older, you'll know this. I want to figure this one thing out . . . Were they really taking pictures of it? Or was it maybe, like, a drawing of some kind . . ."

Volodya threw himself at Yurka and hissed into his ear, "Yura! It's called pornography! You are in a Pioneer camp, and I am a troop leader, and a troop leader is telling you that you can't look at stuff like that. It's depraved!"

"But you *don't* look at it. And neither do I. I'm just telling you what was on there. So explain this to me: Was it just wrong? Is that impossible? Or maybe it wasn't real?"

"Dammit, Yura!"

"Come on, Volod . . . are you my friend or what?"

"Of course I'm your friend." Volodya blushed and turned away.

"Then tell me. There was the—the normal way. I get that." Then Yurka, overwrought, blurted out in a rush: "But a few of the photographs showed the guy doing it . . . but in the wrong place . . . He was doing it down where . . . it was where you sit!"

"A chair?" Volodya seemed to be joking, but his expression was not only serious; it was angry.

"Oh, quit it! I just want to know—is it even possible to actually do that? Or not?"

"'Quit it'?" Volodya imitated him with a sneer. "*I'm* supposed to quit it? Yura, you've gone too far. We're done. We're not talking about this anymore. One more word and I'll leave, and Olezhka will 'call on evewyone to stwuggle with the advewsawy,' and I'll tell him it's all because of you!"

Their conversation was cut short by the bugle signaling the end of quiet hour.

"It's time for you to leave anyway," muttered Yurka, hurt.

During snack, he listened with half an ear to everyone's excited chatter about the impending Zarnitsa, "Summer Lightning"—the camp-wide capture-the-flag war game between the troops that most Pioneers looked forward to eagerly. Yurka was preoccupied tormenting himself: he regretted ever asking Volodya about—about *that*. Volodya didn't even look his way, and if his eyes did accidentally fall on Yurka's corner of the mess hall, the expression on the troop leader's face changed from serious to scornful. Or was Yurka just imagining it? He had been imagining all kinds of things—that he and Volodya had become real, genuinely close friends, for one. But now Volodya's reaction, and the ice in his usually warm voice, threw that into doubt. It wasn't as though they'd even had a fight. They'd just had a little tiff, nothing major. But now Yurka was hurt and ashamed by this "nothing major." A strangely sad longing overcame Yurka.

Pensive and morose, Yurka headed to rehearsal, heaping ashes on his own head as he went: "It's your own fault. What an idiot, asking a Komsomol member questions like that! And not just any old member of the Komsomol but one that's so greenhouse-flower perfect. And what was I expecting? I'd be better off asking the guys from my building. They might've laughed at me, but at least they would've been interested!" So maybe it had been dumb of Yurka to talk about it with Volodya, but this kind of subject was, first and foremost, a very personal one, and he had been sharing something personal with Volodya . . . or rather, he'd been trying to . . . But what was he thinking, an ordinary blockhead like him, who hangs out with a bunch of hooligans, trying to be friends with Volodya, a member of the elite like Volodya? Of course Volodya had rebuffed him, and shamed him, and finished him off with that one look, like a final shot to the head. He'd hit Yurka without even aiming and sent him reeling.

Yurka remembered all this and stopped short: "Why'd I ask him, of all people, about this? What was the point? So he'd glare at me, or so he'd understand me? And he says he's my friend! Yeah, right! A liar, that's what he is, not a friend! Friends don't act that way!"

The main square in front of the outdoor stage was packed, as always. Girls from Troop Two were chalking some kind of map on the pavement while redheaded, jug-eared Alyoshka Matveyev hovered around them, making suggestions and proffering chalk.

Yurka hailed him. "What're you up to over there?"

"What do you mean? We're getting ready for Summer Lightning! This is a map we're drawing for Central Command. Olka had this great idea: we'll send scouts to see where each troop is and then mark down here on the map what our scouts find out."

"But there's a dance tonight. Your map will be worn away."

"No big deal. We'll just trace it out again tomorrow. That's faster than drawing it from scratch, right?" chattered Alyoshka. "You want to come be one of our scouts?"

"No, I don't."

Yurka turned away, but he had only taken a couple of steps toward the movie theater when Alyoshka popped back up and grasped his shoulder.

"Konev, come on, just think about it."

"Alyosh, Central Command is the main administration of the whole game; they're the ones who know what all the different troops are doing and keep the game running smoothly. Nobody wants me there. I'm just going to be with my own troop. Why don't you go . . . uh . . . go about your business . . ."

"Why wouldn't they take you in Central Command? They'll take you if you ask. Ask them, Yur! Look at those long legs you've got; you run fast . . ."

Alyoshka trotted stubbornly behind him, panting, huffing, and dancing around, trying to trip Yurka, or tug his elbow, or just get his attention any way he could.

"Alyosha! You're—there's so much *you* everywhere!" groaned Yurka. "Okay, fine, I thought about it."

"You did? What'd you decide?"

"Give me a piece of chalk."

"Here." Alyosha held out the box and Yurka took a piece.

"Thanks. I'm not going to Central Command. I'm going to stay with my troop."

"Then what'd you take the chalk for?"

"I have low calcium levels. I'm going to eat it. Oh, they're calling you, hear that?"

"What? Who? Oh, it's Olya. Well, bye—but still, you think about it!"

Maybe he should've agreed to be a scout? He'd have been able to run around the whole camp and could've found a way to stay with Volodka. As they always did during the epic war game, the troops had dug trenches around their bases, and Volodya would surely be worried that some kids, like chubby Sashka, would fall into a trench and break their arms, and their legs, and the trench itself. Of course, Lena wouldn't leave her fellow Troop Five leader high and dry, but it was obvious that Volodya would need Yurka, too. It was completely and utterly obvious!

"Right, like he needs you!" protested Yurka's pride. "You pester him and dance around him, just like Alyoshka did to you. All he does is sneer and lecture. Hmpf! I wasn't doing all that work with those stupid scary stories and that stupid drama club for myself, but he doesn't care. Well, now he can get by without me! I'm not going anywhere for him anymore. Not anywhere! And definitely not to rehearsal! He'll be sorry he glared at me! Let him mess around with his own dumb show now. I'm not going to help him!" And he didn't. He was already on the porch of the Troop Five cabin, but he turned around and took off back across the dance floor to the tennis courts where Troop One was scheduled to be playing.

There were two tennis courts, not just one, and Ping-Pong tables, too. Except for Masha and the Pukes, all of Troop One was there under Ira Petrovna's supervision. Some of the campers were playing badminton next to the tennis courts, others were cheering them on, and a few were just goofing around inside the box created by the chain-link fence around the tennis courts. Yurka liked to lean back against that fence and bounce his whole body on the little wire rhombuses while watching other people play. But today he had no intention of rooting for other people. Today he intended to defeat everyone and take out his anger on the badminton birdies.

When he was still quite a ways from the courts, Vanka and Mikha caught sight of him and waved him over in unison to be part of their team. Yurka was pretty good at badminton, but these two could neither serve nor return worth a darn, so the only people who joined their team were people who didn't like winning. Yurka did like winning, but he didn't bother asking to get on anyone else's team. Without a word, he snatched a badminton racquet and served. The birdie soared over the net and hit Ira Petrovna right in the forehead.

"Sorry!" Yurka shouted. He expected Ira Petrovna to let him have it right then and there, so he held off from serving again. But his troop leader winked cheerily at him and turned around.

Ira had been avoiding Yurka ever since what happened in Volodya's room. When she and Yurka did have to do something together, she walked on eggshells around him. Yurka wasn't about to tell anybody what he'd seen, of course, but, judging by Ira's angelic behavior, she evidently thought he was capable of that kind of backstabbing and blackmail.

Yurka was privately furious—*Who does she take me for?!*—but didn't utter a peep out loud: after all, this arrangement suited him. The troop leader had quit putting the blame on him and scapegoating him unfairly, and as a result there was peace between the two of them. It was fragile and awkward, but peace nonetheless.

The same could not be said for Ira Petrovna's relationship with Volodya, however. As soon as Yurka remembered that, the scene in the theater came flooding back to him, replaying itself in full color: Ira's white face, her trembling hands, and the tears of fury in her eyes . . . Volodya, standing right in front of her, his eyes narrow and mean: "Do you love him or something?" "Oh, man, Ira Petrovna's never going to forgive him for something like that . . . ," Yurka mused to himself sympathetically. Then he caught himself and spat in disgust: he'd thought about Volodya again!

Volodya was everywhere, even places he couldn't possibly be. Right now Volodya was without a doubt in the movie theater, working with his actors, but Yurka thought he glimpsed Volodya's silhouette over there in the bushes.

The game went on. Yurka slashed his racquet as though he wanted not to hit a birdie but slice the sunbeams to ribbons. The sunbeams remained safe and sound, but the disheveled and sweaty Yurka did kill a great many mosquitoes.

Their team led the count. Vanka and Mikha spent almost the whole game standing in place, but Yurka raced around like man possessed. Before sending the birdie off on its triumphant flight—so lofty it might even hit Ira Petrovna in the forehead again—he turned around and saw Volodya in the bushes again.

This time it was definitely him. Pensively, with a timid smile, Volodya drew nearer to the box of the tennis court but stopped a meter away from the entrance, unable to bring himself to go inside. Instead, he walked around the outside the fence and came to a halt behind Yurka, where he stretched his fingers wide through the chain-link fence and grasped the metal rhombuses.

"Why didn't you come to rehearsal, Yur?" he asked, very quietly.

Yurka still heard him. He batted the birdie away without looking and walked up to the chain-link fence so he could look Volodya defiantly right in the eyes. "I don't have a part, so what am I supposed to do there?"

"What do you mean, 'what'?" Volodya looked at him sadly and shook his head. Then he collected himself and in his habitual troop leader tone, he said: "Olga Leonidovna said that whether you have a part or not, you have to come to every rehearsal. You are helping me and I'm responsible for you."

"So be responsible. What's that got to do with me?"

"So you already want to leave? They'd send you home without batting an eye."

"What can they send me home for? I'm playing with my troop, and with my own troop leader, actually. Ira Petrovna's right here, she'll confirm it."

As he waited for an answer, which didn't come, Yurka bounced his racquet off the toe of his sneakers. Then he looked around and went over to the bench to get a glass of water. Volodya followed him along the fence. "I hurt your feelings," he surmised, casting his eyes down guiltily.

"As if!" scoffed Yurka. "You didn't hurt my feelings. I realized there's not that much I can talk to you about, that's all."

"That's not true! Talk about whatever you want!"

"Yeah. Right." Yurka turned away and started drinking his water.

"What's up with you? I . . . you know what, Yur?" Volodya drew his hand along the chain-link fence and it rattled softly. "I've seen magazines like that too, you know."

"Oh, really? And where'd you get them?" Yurka turned around and fixed Volodya with a mistrustful gaze.

"I'm a student at MGIMO, the Moscow State Institute of International Relations. There are some guys there whose parents are diplomats; sometimes they can scrounge up things like—"

"Wait—where?" Yurka actually shouted. "Where do you go? The Moscow State Institute of—where diplomats are trained?!" Ah, so *that* was how Volodya had known how to get him out of quiet hour!

"Shh. Yes. Just please don't tell anyone about the magazine! Yura, this is serious. If there's even the most absurd little rumor about something like that, I'll get kicked out."

"No way. They wouldn't do that!"

"They absolutely would. They got a guy in my year who had that kind of magazine on him. He was gone less than a month later."

"But if it's so easy to get the boot, how'd you even get in? Family connections?"

"Gee, thanks! You think I couldn't do well enough to get in on my own?"

"It's not about how smart you are, it's just that it's practically impossible to get in. The competition's fierce, and you have to be impeccably ideological, and you have to collect all those approvals from your high school's Komsomol Council and from your regional Komsomol Council and from your regional Party Committee, and you have to go to all the meetings . . ."

Volodya nodded in affirmation as he listened to Yurka, who kept counting off on his fingers all the things you had to do, and what you had to be a member of, and what you had to participate in—and how, and how often—and where you had to go . . . Suddenly Yurka realized: Who else but Volodya would be able to get in to a place as prestigious as MGIMO?

"Well . . . I barely got in, to be honest," said Volodya modestly, smiling, once Yurka deigned to finish counting. "I failed the medical evaluation, if you can believe that. Because of my vision. I fought it tooth and nail. I passed my army physical—I'm fit for military service—but then they wouldn't let me into college . . . Anyway, it's a long, boring story."

"What's it like to go there? Is it hard?"

"I wouldn't call it easy. The main thing is it's interesting. The guys in the dorms have really fun get-togethers. I live at home, of course, but I stop by the dorms almost every day."

"Polite little get-togethers with tea and cookies, right?" Yurka joked, momentarily forgetting that he was mad at Volodya. "Come on, tell me. Are they depraved?"

"Of course not! Come on, we're Komsomol members!" Volodya gave him a stern look but then smiled and whispered, "Just kidding. We have it all: cards, girls, port, samizdat . . ."

"Wait, what? Port? You have alcohol, too?" Yurka was also whispering now. "Where do you get it? When our neighbor got married, they couldn't even get a bottle of vodka for the wedding, they drank ethanol. My dad's a doctor, he got it from work."

"Well, I just *call* it port," explained Volodya. "My classmate Mishka brings it. He lives way outside Moscow, in a little village where they make excellent moonshine. The taste of it reminds some people of brandy, but it reminds me of port. I'm scared for Mishka, though—it's a big risk to bring it in."

Yurka's hurt feelings vanished during this conversation. He forgot them so fast, it was as though they had never existed—not the feelings, or the falling-out, or even the reason they'd argued in the first place. It was like they were talking about what they always talked about, as frankly as they always did, like their behavior and outward appearance was the same as usual: Yurka was tousled and engaged; Volodya was calm and cool and a little bit condescending. There was just one difference: the tall, seemingly sky-high chain-link fence standing taut between them.

"Yur, let's go to rehearsal, huh? Afterwards I'll tell you whatever you want," offered Volodya. His face had cleared; the lines on his forehead had vanished. "Just tell Irina that you're leaving with me."

Yurka nodded. He ran over to Ira and got her permission to leave, glancing as he did so at the handsome phys ed instructor, Zhenya, who was busy nearby. Yurka put his racquet on a bench and left the court.

"So you just abandoned everybody and came out here looking for me?" he inquired as they turned off the main square and walked toward the dance floor.

"I left Masha in charge. She does a good job, of course, but she can't run a rehearsal, and we have to work hard today because we can't work tomorrow."

"That's right—Summer Lightning's tomorrow," said Yurka, disappointed. This meant that after rehearsal today, because they had to get ready for the big mock battle, they wouldn't be able to spend any time together. Like everyone else, Yurka would be busy sewing his fabric shoulder boards onto his uniform shirt. It would take a while, since he wasn't all that great with a needle and thread, but if they were too loose, they'd be too easy for enemy fighters to tear off during "battle." Everyone wore them: one torn-off shoulder board meant you were wounded; two meant you were dead. And after he was done with that, Troop One had planned an evening of parading in formation and singing. And tomorrow all the staff and campers would be completely immersed in the mass game from early morning until late at night.

Yurka should've gone to be a scout for Central Command after all.

CHAPTER SEVEN
EARLY MORNING AWKWARDNESS

A gust of wind made the empty window frame, where not a single bit of glass remained, creak so long and loud that Yura shuddered. The rain had ended a while ago, but fat individual drops were still falling from the roof and plopping loudly onto the broken pavement of the path, making the grass rustle and plinking as they splashed on the broken glass scattered on the ground. Breezy gusts sent the sounds whirling around the dandelion lawn. It felt like nature itself was imitating life, filling the emptiness and trying to deceive him. And Yura would have gladly been deceived. But he couldn't be, because it wasn't just empty here; it was dead. The daily life of Troop Five had been so vibrant, playful, and noisy. Now all that was left of it were the gaping holes where the windows of the boys' room had been and the smaller, narrower window of the tiny troop leaders' room to the left. Once it had been Volodya's room. Once it had been where Volodya had gone to sleep and woken up, even though he was always too busy to get a full night's sleep . . . Yura smiled to himself.

He well remembered how he'd longed to get into Volodya's room. Once he'd even managed a quick look inside, but he'd never actually been invited in.

But why say never? Just because he hadn't been in the past didn't mean he couldn't go there now. Even though Volodya wasn't there to invite him.

Unable to make himself look away from the narrow window, Yura got up from the merry-go-round. He would invite himself into that empty room.

He went to stand in front of the cabin and considered whether he could jump over the hole in the floor of the porch. As he thought it through, deciding whether the rotten wooden boards would hold him when he landed, he heaved a dejected sigh: they wouldn't. But then Yura decided that, since he'd been able to force himself to come back to Camp Barn Swallow after so many years, he was just plain obligated to get inside the troop leaders' room. What if Volodya had left something there to mark his presence, like a funny drawing on the wall, or a word or two scratched into the table, or some gum stuck to the head of the bed frame? Or maybe a candy wrapper in the nightstand? Or a stray bit of thread in the wardrobe? He had to have left something behind, after all! Even as Yura thought this, he knew that Volodya didn't draw on walls, scratch furniture, or chew gum. Still, he desperately wanted to believe that Volodya had somehow guessed Yura would return.

Yura turned left and walked through the trampled flower beds along the cabin towards the boys' room windows.

The Troop Five cabin sat up on top of a broad wooden base that stuck out farther than the walls, creating a narrow ledge that ran all the way around the building. Yura somehow managed to climb up onto it, his rubber-soled shoes slipping on the wet green-painted boards, and work his way over to the troop leader's window. He looked in past the broken glass. The dark, narrow room seemed even smaller than it had before, but the layout of the furniture—indeed, the furniture itself—hadn't changed: a table pushed back against the far side of the room with the door to its right and the wardrobe to its left; two simple nightstands; two narrow beds on either side of the window. Volodya's was the one to the right. Yura was seized by the desire to sit on it, to find out whether it was soft or hard, whether it squeaked, whether it was comfortable.

Wary of cutting himself on the broken glass scattered on the windowsill, Yura cursed himself roundly for not thinking to bring work gloves and brushed the shards away. He took hold of the rickety wood and pulled himself up and into the window.

He paid no attention to the puddles on the floor or to how dusty and dirty everything was. He knelt down and opened Volodya's nightstand. On the single shelf lay the May 1992 issue of *The Peasant Woman*, its pages warped from damp. It had clearly been left there by some troop leader. There was a small book under it. Yura read the title and smiled: The Theory and Methodology of Educational Work with Pioneers . . . Now, that was just like Volodya. There wasn't anything else in the nightstand.

Yura turned his gaze to Volodya's bed. It was a narrow wire-spring frame, more a cot than a bed, its feet bolted to the floor. Given the layer of grime on the bolts, he surmised that it was probably the original bed frame and had never been replaced. So it really had been Volodya's bed. The wide mesh of wire springs was squeaky, bouncy, and rusty. "At least it wasn't rusty back when he slept on it; that's something," said Yura to himself. He smiled. "Just think . . . he slept here!"

Yura pushed down on the network of springs. It groaned piteously in response, the noise underscoring the complete silence that reigned here. The emptiness, too. Apart from the furniture, there was nothing here: no curtains, no bedclothes or cloth of any kind, no books, not even a piece of paper, no torn-off bits of wallpaper or posters on the wall—and Yura remembered once glimpsing a Time Machine poster hanging on the wall; he remembered Volodya liked the group. There wasn't even any trash here, just dust, water, and the dirty slurry on the floor. Plus the broken glass over by the window. Yura walked over to the far corner of the room to stand in front of the only piece of furniture he hadn't investigated yet: the wardrobe. He realized he'd even be glad to find some trash inside it, since that would at least provide the illusion of meaning: that Yura hadn't come here for nothing, that he hadn't climbed through the window into these ruins for nothing, like a sentimental child. Like a complete idiot.

Why had he come in here? Why had he even come back at all? And now that he was here, why was he wandering around the camp, wasting time, instead of heading directly for the place where he was going to do what he'd come to do? But it wasn't so easy to just not look into Volodya's room. And once he'd gone in, it wasn't so easy to just leave.

He threw open the wardrobe door and gazed inside it, transfixed: there lay a heap of wadded-up clothing. His heart went painfully tight when in the back corner, underneath a layer of old shirts and jackets, he found several brown uniform jackets with black shoulder boards boasting the insignia "SA," for "Soviet Army," embroidered in white. His hands shook when, digging through the pile of cloth, he found the only jacket with shiny buttons.

They'd worn costume military uniforms for Summer Lightning. The troop leaders had been given uniform jackets, while the children got uniform shirts. And this particular jacket, the one with the shiny buttons, was still a military jacket, but it was small. It was too big for any of the Pioneers and too small for any of the grown-up Party members. But there was one Komsomol member whom it would have fit just right.

Cynicism, skepticism, and self-irony all vanished in the blink of an eye, discarded somewhere far away, out past Camp Barn Swallow's collapsing fence. All of a sudden it didn't matter how old Yura was; it didn't matter what he'd accomplished, or what he was talented at, or how smart he was, or whether he had the right to be funny . . . all those things had meaning in another life, far away from here, in the present. But here, in the camp where he'd spent his childhood, Yura could be the same way he used to be: not a Pioneer anymore, but not a Komsomol member yet . . . And, funny as it might seem, all this still applied to him. With just one difference: he used to think all this was very important. But now the only thing that continued to be important was the old brown rag he held in his no-longer-young hands. That, and the memory of the person on whose shoulders the black shoulder boards labeled "SA" had rested, on whose chest the golden buttons had shone.

"Greetings, Pioneers! You're listening to the Pioneer radio news program *Pioneer Dawn*," broadcast the loudspeakers as Yurka brushed his teeth. "Be prepared for Summer Lightning as soon as the bugle sounds after breakfast! Pioneer troops will assemble on the camp's main square . . ."

This morning began as usual, with exercises. Yurka wasn't a huge fan of this: he couldn't even get fully awake before he had to run outside to do calisthenics with everyone. Today he'd even gotten there on time, which made him doubly annoyed, since he and the other kids from his troop had to wait on Ira Petrovna when most of the other troop leaders were already there. Volodya, for example, was already doing stretches with his little kids. Yurka wanted to go over and say hello, but reconsidered: the troop leader was busy. Volodya stood with his back to Yurka as he showed his campers how to do the stretches. He was really stretching, too, not just going through the motions. He rotated his neck and rolled his shoulders, then loosened his elbows, wrists, and hands, swinging his arms up and down and to the sides. Yurka listened with half an ear to the girls next to him chattering about last night's dance, but his attention was concentrated on watching Volodya issue commands.

"Feet shoulder-width apart! We're warming up our torso and legs. Now forward bend, and reeeeaach your palms down to the ground." Volodya followed his own instructions. "Sashka! Not so hard, you'll break in two!"

Yurka chuckled to himself, wondering what it was that Sasha was doing. But he didn't even bother trying to spot Sasha to find out. Before Yurka's eyes something far more intriguing was taking place: Volodya slowly and gracefully bent forward and touched the ground. And not with his fingertips, either, but with his palms. His T-shirt slid up, baring his waist, and his red athletic shorts pulled taut around his slim hips, and around his legs, and around the softly rounded place above them . . .

Yurka's thoughts fragmented into a series of interjections, then re-formed into words and sentences again, ranging from *Wow, he's limber* to *Who said people could walk around here in shorts like that, anyway? There are children here! And—and girls!*

Volodya stood straight again and bent over again. The chaos in Yurka's head was replaced by a resounding silence. His body went numb. He couldn't tear his eyes away. It took a few long moments for him to come back to his senses and realize that for something like a minute he'd been frozen in mid-bend, shamelessly ogling those red-clad buttocks.

It was as though he'd been doused with burning-hot water. Blood rushed to his face. Sweat even beaded on his forehead. And it wasn't from the heat, since it was morning and still chilly.

"What on earth are you looking at?!" Yurka howled silently at himself. Everything made him feel awkward: the stupid pose, the fact that he'd blushed, and the fact that he'd stared, and then, to top it all off, there was this strange reaction, this slight, pleasant spasm. Well, no, the reaction itself was normal; he'd felt it before. The strange part here was: Why did he feel it for Volodya? It's not like there was a shortage of slender, pretty girls who were much more interesting than Volodya exercising all around him. But if the girls were "more interesting" than Volodya, why was Yurka looking at Volodya, not them? Maybe it was just that it was still early, and Yurka hadn't had a chance to wake up yet?

There was little chance anyone had noticed his behavior, which hadn't lasted all that long. Still, after yesterday's conversation about the magazines— after his candid and inept questions—Yurka was inordinately ashamed of himself. His painful chagrin and renewed self-flagellation was interrupted when Zhenya appeared on the main square along with Ira and announced: "Good morning, Pioneers! We're starting our calisthenics!"

Yurka was so stunned by what had happened at morning calisthenics an hour ago that he still hadn't managed to regain his composure. He shuffled his way to breakfast as if through a layer of thick fog. Then he went back to his cabin and got ready for the ceremonial opening of the Summer Lightning mock battle, slowly putting on his uniform and tying his Pioneer neckerchief.

He looked at the wall clock: he was running late. Everyone else had already left the cabin. He could hear the distant sounds of the ceremony beginning, Olga Leonidovna's voice enhanced by the loudspeakers. But Yurka stood alone in front of the mirror, trying and failing to get the red rag's knot right. He started losing his temper.

"Why aren't you going to the ceremony?" In the silence that had settled over the room, Volodya's voice rang out so abruptly that Yurka flinched. Volodya had appeared too unexpectedly, and this was absolutely not a good time to have him around.

"I . . . I'll be right there. But what are you doing here? I mean, why'd you come here?"

"Lena took the troop to the ceremony, and I didn't see you on the square, so I came here. My troop is too little to join in the battle, so we're going to stay in Central Command during the game. Are you staying with us?"

Yurka sneaked a glance at Volodya's chin in the mirror but didn't turn around to face him. He didn't want to turn around and look Volodya in the eyes . . . but as soon as he remembered he wouldn't see Volodya all day today, it was as though a weight fell from his shoulders. Good thing he'd fended off Alyoshka Matveyev yesterday and refused to spend the game in Central Command.

"Yura! Hello? Why aren't you talking? Did something happen?"

Yurka yanked the ends of his neckerchief irritably, leaving the knot looking mangled. He turned to Volodya but avoided looking at him, talking off to the side: "I guess I just got up on the wrong side of the bed. And now I'm late, too. You go ahead, I'll catch up." At that moment Yurka genuinely wished, more than anything else in the world, that Volodya would hurry up and leave.

But on the contrary, Volodya took a step closer. He smiled tolerantly and clicked his tongue. "Come on, now, Yur! You've gone through the Pioneers, you're a senior camper already, but you don't even know how to tie your neckerchief?" He reached out with both hands and started deftly retying Yurka's neckerchief.

"I don't—" Yurka choked on his own words. His throat went dry. Heat surged through him.

Volodya knotted the neckerchief so deftly, it was as though he'd spent his whole life doing nothing but that: wrap this end around here, stick that bit through there, give it a tug, and done. As he tucked it into Yurka's collar, Volodya's fingers lightly brushed Yurka's neck. It seemed just an accidental, momentary touch, but it sent an electric shock through Yurka.

"So? You coming with me to Central Command?" asked Volodya again, as though he didn't notice that something was going on with Yurka.

"No, I'm going out into the woods with my troop. At our troop meeting we decided I'd be a spy, try to find out where the other troops' flags are."

"Oh, okay, then . . ." The hopeful light in Volodya's eyes went out and his face fell. Yurka felt a pang of conscience.

"It's just that I promised!" he hastened to explain himself. Although he actually hadn't promised anybody anything. He'd only been thinking of asking to be a spy. Why was he lying—again? And to Volodya!

But there was no more time to ponder the question. Outside, over on the square, Yurka heard that the microphone had gone quiet and the bugle had sounded, calling the Pioneers to fall into formation and head over to their stations for Summer Lightning.

"All right . . . let's go." Volodya went over to the door and waved at Yurka. "Maybe we'll see each other this evening. My kids also asked to go out into the woods, but they're so hard to manage . . . Lena and I haven't figured out how that might work yet."

Yurka grunted his assent and hurried off toward the square, where columns of Pioneers led by the phys ed instructors and troop leaders were going in different directions, each team headed to its own area.

Even though Yurka had eluded Volodya, he couldn't elude his own thoughts. He couldn't stop himself from thinking about everything that had happened and about his reactions. He couldn't not think about Volodya. Even though Yurka did his best to forget about his early morning awkwardness, all his thoughts led back to Volodya anyway. He wondered, for example, how Volodya was doing out there, whether he was able to manage the little kids over in Central Command. And he wondered if Volodya would indeed visit him at his troop's base out in the woods and bring the kids so they could see the tents. And then he revisited yesterday's argument and their conversation. Volodya had looked so guilty yesterday at the chain-link fence around the tennis court! And so sincere, too. So sincere that now Yurka berated himself: How could he ever have doubted Volodya? How could he have possibly called Volodya a liar—even to himself—and failed to believe that Volodya's friendship was sincere?

And then Yurka's thoughts about friendship circled back to what had happened at morning exercises and then in the cabin. Volodya's sincere friendship . . . but was Yurka himself sincere, though? If he was, then why had he been so afraid of an accidental touch?

The fact that it wasn't fear he'd felt was something Yurka really, really, *really* didn't want to admit.

The Summer Lightning mock battle began. Yurka tried to concentrate, but to no avail. He got mad at himself—"How much time can you waste thinking about irrelevant things?"—then hastened to justify himself: "Wait, how's this 'irrelevant'? Is Volodya really 'irrelevant'? No, he's . . . he's very . . ." But he found himself unable to formulate a precise definition of how and in what way Volodya was "very" for him.

At least Ira Petrovna gave him permission to be a spy for his troop. She was even glad for his initiative and convinced he'd be the one to identify an enemy location. Yurka, Vanka, and Mikha had started setting up their tent when Yurka was blindsided by some miserable news: Masha had managed to get assigned as his spying partner. She had begged at great length, apparently. At first Ira hadn't wanted to leave the two of them by themselves, but she'd given in. As he buttoned up his uniform shirt, Yurka looked askance at the rest of his troop as he kept thinking the same question: What in the hell, he'd like to know, was Masha doing asking to be paired up with him?!

Her motive was revealed soon enough. When they got to the middle of the forest, where enemy spies and fighters could've already been on the prowl, Masha hemmed and hawed and finally asked timidly: "Yur . . . you and Volodya are friends, right?"

Yura rolled his eyes and clicked his tongue. So that was it. What else did girls need him for? He was there to be a radio receiver, obviously, broadcasting everything he knew about the Troop Five leader!

"Yur, why doesn't he go to the dances?"

At first Yurka tried to ignore her. He decided that if he just kept demonstratively silent and didn't answer her questions, she'd understand.

She probably did. But that didn't keep her from pestering him. "Yur, come on, it's not like I'm asking you to *do* anything . . . Just tell me! He has a girlfriend, is that it? . . . Yur, does he like Polina? He must have told you . . . The way he was looking at her during the last rehearsal . . ."

After maybe a dozen questions that started to repeat themselves like a broken record, Yurka began to get angry.

"What way?!" Yurka burst out. "He wasn't looking at anybody, any way! He's a troop leader! You do know he has a *job* he's trying to do?"

The outburst surprised Masha so much that she stopped and stared at him, then blinked fearfully. He jerked his chin at her, telling her to keep walking, and added more quietly: "Mash, we're spying out here! Do you understand that? If the enemy sees us and captures us or kills us, our troop will lose a ton of points!"

She quieted down. For maybe twenty minutes.

"Yur . . . has he ever talked about me?"

He was so irritated that the hair on the back of his neck stood up.

"Come on, Yur. What's the matter? Is it hard for you to talk about it? It's just that . . . you know . . ." She blushed and moved closer to him, then reached out and plucked at his sleeve. "The thing is . . . I like Volodya. But he's so hard to figure out. It's like he doesn't notice anyone else—like he's not interested in anybody . . . So you're my only hope of getting closer to him . . ."

"Getting closer to him?! Masha, whatever you do, don't get me involved in your business! I've already gotten into enough trouble because of you. Let it go."

"Come on, Yur, am I really asking all that much? Just ask him about me. It'll be easy. You spend a lot of time together, just the two of you. Late at night, you could . . . or maybe earlier, during quiet hour . . . you could just tell him—I mean, ask him . . ."

"Hold on a second," Yurka ordered, and stopped walking. "How do you know I go find him during quiet hour?"

"Like it's some big secret!" she scoffed. "Everybody knows you do. And that you go see him late at night, too."

"But what about you?! Who are *you* slinking around with?"

Masha stopped in her tracks. "'Slinking around'? You're the one who's slinking around! And it's none of your business anyway!"

"It is my business! Because Ira thought you and I were going off together to fool around. Not only that, she had a fight with Volodya about it. So now your little nighttime strolls are his business, too. Why did Ira think that? Who are you slinking around with? Where do you go? And what's it got to do with me?"

"How should I know?! Ask Irina. And ask about me. Not her, I mean—ask Volodya. Because I can't ask him myself—first of all, it'd be improper, what would he think? And secondly, I never get the chance to talk just to him. You're always there. So help me out, huh? But let's make it worth your while. What if I let you play the piano? Not for the whole show, just for one song. But not the Moonlight Sonata, of course—something easier . . ."

Yurka could've kept himself under control if not for that last thing.

"'Something easier'?" he echoed. "Easier?! Am I hearing things, or did you just say you're better than me?"

"What do you mean? Of course not! I just—"

"That's some imagination you've got there! You don't just think you're better than me, you think you're better than everybody! You think you're the only one worthy of him? You think the earth revolves around you? That Volodya just went and fell head over heels in love with you?!"

"I don't think I'm better than everybody," said Masha, growing angry. "But why not me? Look around! Who else could he fall in love with? You?!" she scoffed.

Yurka rolled his eyes and clapped his palm to his forehead in disgust. "Polina, for instance. You mentioned her."

"So it *is* her!"

"I don't know! But what even makes you think he's fallen in love at all?!" Yurka had gotten so angry and worked up that he didn't notice the tears welling in her eyes. What he did notice were the flashes of yellow back behind Masha, in the bushes: the enemy's shoulder boards.

"Hide!" he hissed, and took off running.

When the enemy spies had passed—Yurka recognized one of them as Vaska Petlitsyn from Troop Two—Yurka searched for the grass they'd trampled to see where to turn off the path toward their base. He found it and headed that way.

Masha, radiating her anger at him with every bone in her body, followed without a word. Around twenty minutes later, Yurka, who'd been relishing the silence, led them to the enemy camp.

Troop Two's base was in an area where the deciduous forest transitioned to a coniferous one. Needles and pine cones littered the sand on which they'd pitched their tents, and there was a smell of resin in the air. Yurka dove into the thick bushes again and watched the enemy camp from a distance. He didn't see anything of much interest, though. They were doing the same things as Yurka's troop. A couple of girls were busy by the campfire. Petlitsyn and his partner were walking through the middle of the camp, evidently headed toward the commander's tent. Semyon, the other phys ed instructor, was doing the kids' physical fitness tests: jumping, squats, push-ups, stretching. Most of the kids were by the yellow flag, standing on the lookout.

Yurka didn't spend too long in his hiding spot. He indicated the enemy's position relative to his own troop's base on his handmade map. Then, after checking his compass, he traced a path between the two. Now he and Masha would have to get back safe and sound to their own camp so they could pass the information on to Ira, their troop commander, and begin their attack.

He felt he'd been squeezed dry, like a lemon. A lemon that was dirty, dusty, and totally fed-up. He and Masha eventually made it back to base, although on the way there they came across three different sets of enemy fighters whose whispered conversations revealed that the rest of his troop's spies had been neutralized. Once he realized that he and Masha were all alone and a whole lot depended on them now, Yurka got truly scared. But the fear that he and Masha would be caught, thus delaying their troop's attack, was a rational, "good" fear. And for the time being it covered up the other fear, the "bad" one, the one that was irrational, profound, shameful: his fear that something was wrong with him.

They got back to their base and gave Ira Petrovna their information. The businesslike troop leader had taken a moment to show off the captain's shoulder boards on her uniform jacket and was now dividing her fighters into three groups: the first would stay in camp to protect their flag; she'd lead the second directly to the Yellow base; and she ordered the third, led by Zhenya, to go the long way around and approach the Yellow base from behind. To Yurka's great delight, Ira took Masha with her but assigned him to Zhenya. Their trek was long and dreary, so all he remembered of it was a jumble of endless forest, his comrades' uniform shirts, lots of whispering back and forth, and his worry that the noise made by a dozen kids would get them found out and captured. But the troops successfully moved into position and stayed there to lie in wait until the other half of their forces approached from the front. Zhenya lay on his stomach under a bush next to Yurka and whispered feverishly: "The Yellows aren't expecting an attack from behind. We have the advantage. We'll get the flag before Irina does." Yurka snorted to himself. He felt like adding, And lay it at her feet!

As soon as they heard the first signal that their fighters had arrived, Yurka and his detachment moved out. But what ensued was a playground scuffle rather than an organized attack: everyone collided with everyone else in a wild free-for-all. Yurka got caught up in the melee like in a centrifuge, then darted in and out of the confusion, somehow managing to tear off two boys' shoulder boards. He wounded Mitka by getting his right shoulder board and killed Petlitsyn by yanking off both his shoulder boards at once.

Thanks to Irina's prayers and Vanka's hands, the Yellow team flag was soon theirs. Yurka's team formed up, started singing army songs, and marched back to home base. Ira was glowing with happiness. Zhenya was out of sorts because one of his fighters had been the first to make it to the flag, not him, so he was trailing along behind, cursing softly. But Yurka was laughing and singing along with everyone else as they belted out the familiar Pioneer song about strong, happy young people working together as a troop to accomplish their collective goals.

Still, no matter how happy he was, he was so exhausted his legs were like wet noodles. He wanted peace and quiet. Once he got back to the victorious hubbub of his troop's base, he quickly ate dinner and hid in his tent, away from the clamor. He stretched out on his stiff mat like a starfish, arms and legs akimbo.

He drew his sleeping bag up over his head and tried to go to sleep. But sleep wouldn't come, prevented not so much by the noise around him as by his own thoughts. Now, no matter how hard he tried, he couldn't drown them out.

Although he'd been able to push them aside during the day, while he was busy, he was no longer able to escape his thoughts now that he was alone.

And what he thought was that he had to find the courage to stop deceiving himself. It was impossible that what had happened at morning exercises was just a little bit of early morning awkwardness. Because his interest in looking at Volodya, his *desire* to look at Volodya, had been so deep and profound that even now he still got a pleasant tingle way down in his chest whenever he thought about it. But what was that? What was he doing? It wasn't right to look at people that way . . . especially not to look at *him* that way. Yurka felt uncomfortable admitting it, but if he quit making excuses and was honest with himself, he didn't want to stop looking at Volodya at all.

He sat up abruptly. He threw off his sleeping bag, rubbed his face with his hands, and violently raked his fingers back and forth over his scalp. Not because his head itched, but because he wanted to rip these shameful thoughts out of his head. He didn't want them! Yurka disgusted himself.

Outside his tent, dusk was falling. He heard the sounds of camp: somebody strumming a guitar, the soft strains of a happy little song, the racket of dozens of Pioneers talking all around him. Yurka even thought he could clearly distinguish the voice of chubby little Sashka somewhere nearby, opining about the buckwheat kasha they'd had for dinner.

"The evening's just getting started, soldier, but you're already going to sleep?" At first Yurka thought he was dreaming Volodya's voice. But Volodya really was standing over him, wearing the exact same uniform jacket as Ira but for two differences: the buttons on Volodya's jacket were shiny, and his shoulder boards didn't have a captain's insignia. Yurka was awfully flustered, but he tried to greet Volodya calmly. Still, he couldn't disguise the nervous tone of his voice as he spoke: "Comrade Lieutenant, sir! Good evening, sir!"

"*First* Lieutenant." Volodya smiled. He turned slightly to display his shoulder boards and pointed at the stars.

"Oh, I see," said Yurka, feigning admiration. He lay back down. "You still alive?"

"Mostly. But they gave it their darndest! Listen to this: I forgot to get my pass, so I went to Central Command to pick it up and my own troop was on watch. But they insisted I show my pass! They grabbed my arms and legs and started pulling in opposite directions and hammering their fists on my back. They don't realize that even though their fists are small, they can still hit pretty hard. So now my whole body hurts! My shoulders, too. Can you stretch them out for me?"

"N-no," stammered Yurka. "I don't know how."

"Too bad . . ." Volodya said, pursing his lips, then lay down next to Yurka on the discarded sleeping bag and heaved a sigh of pleasure. "This feels so good . . ."

Yurka lay still, afraid to move a muscle. Volodya's shoulder with its black SA insignia—Soviet Army—pressed close to his own. Yurka could neither ignore this touch nor move away to end it. Meanwhile, Volodya didn't even notice, apparently. He rolled over onto his side, looked at Yurka, and narrowed his eyes. Yurka looked away.

"What's that you've got there . . ." He stretched his hand toward Yurka's tousled hair, but Yurka shrank away from him. Even as recently as yesterday he wouldn't have done that for anything, but after everything that had happened, he felt Volodya's touch too keenly, as though it were piercing him from head to toe. It scared him.

"Grass?" said Volodya. "Why do you have grass in your hair?"

"'And sawdust in my head,'" joked Yurka awkwardly, quoting the beloved Soviet version of Winnie-the-Pooh. "I was a spy. I spent all day slinking around the forest."

"Well, I spent all day in Central Command being pestered by my kids about coming out here to the forest. As soon as lunch was over, they all started up at once: 'We want to be like the big kids,' 'We want to fight in Summer Lightning, too,' 'We want to sleep out in tents!' Lena was about ready to scream." Volodya folded his hands behind his head. "Sashka and Olezhka kicked up such a fuss that I had no choice but to bring them out here."

Yurka was trying to listen to him, but it wasn't working very well. The meaning of what the troop leader was saying was lost in Yurka's desire to touch him . . . but Yurka turned away emphatically and mumbled, "Ira was saying that just a few kids were coming with you. What about the rest?"

"I told them I'd only take whoever did their best while they were working at Central Command."

"Did many of them do their best?"

"No. I was strict about who I picked. Mostly kids from our drama club. A few got upset, of course, so I had to give them a choice: either a few kids go, or nobody goes at all. Because I wasn't willing to take on that kind of responsibility. And then Lena promised she'd take the rest of them to the movie theater tonight and show them cartoons."

Yurka stood up and looked down at Volodya, who was relaxed and showed not the slightest sign of being tired. It made sense, since Volodya wasn't the one who'd been running around in the bushes and attacking the enemy base; still, the kids could wear you out just as bad . . .

Seeing him stand, Volodya said, "Oh, did you want to go to the campfire? We're going to tell some good stories here in a minute."

"Scary stories again?" grumbled Yurka, grasping for something to pin his mood on.

"Had enough of them, huh?" said Volodya. "Me too. But no, it doesn't have to be scary stories. Although, if they ask, I've got one about the queen of spades."

Volodya smiled warmly. Playful little sparks danced in his eyes. All of a sudden Yurka was filled with a painful longing. "Let's go," he grunted, and shot out of the tent like a bullet. Because it now seemed to him, after that morning, as though there was some kind of subtext to Volodya's behavior, as though it was not weariness that had made him lie down next to Yurka, not curiosity that had made him reach out for Yurka's hair. But that was all just Yurka's own imagination! Volodya couldn't actually know any of what he was thinking. He couldn't! He hadn't seen anything, after all, and as for any improper thoughts of his own . . . well, Yurka would bet his eyeteeth that such thoughts had never troubled Volodya's good, honest Komsomol head.

Volodya came out of the tent after Yurka and gazed after him, puzzled. Olezhka and Sasha immediately swarmed the troop leader and pulled him over to a spot they'd specially prepared for him. Yurka, taking advantage of the momentary separation, sat down at some distance from the campfire.

As they listened to Ira Petrovna, the kids grew so quiet that her soft voice carried all the way out to Yurka: ". . . and the first Pioneer camps appeared in the twenties. They were field camps, meaning that the first Pioneers lived in tents, not cabins. Remember the movie The Bronze Bird, about the Pioneer camp right next to an old manor house?" All the kids nodded. "It was exactly like that. If they could find a building suitable for a camp, the Pioneers would use in it, of course. Anyway, the Pioneers' main task at that time was to help villagers do their work and teach village children to read and write—"

"So they could crank out denunciations and get rewarded with a trip to Artek, the most famous Pioneer camp of all," mumbled Yurka to himself. Ira Petrovna went on: "The main event in Pioneer camps was the campfire assembly, where the Pioneers discussed the results of their day's activity: how many people they'd taught to read and write, how many people they'd helped, what they'd built or repaired. And they made plans for the next day. All by themselves, without any grown-ups, the Pioneers decided who had earned their praise as well as who to reproach, and they did educational work..."

The history of Pioneer camps bored Yurka. Ira told it every single session, because there were always some campers who didn't know it yet. This time Volodya's kids were the primary audience, especially Olezhka, who was so captivated by the story that he just sat there, wide-eyed and open-mouthed. The rest remained politely silent. Yurka did, too. But as he gazed out into the evening darkness, he was glad to listen to a story he was heartily sick of, just so it would drown out the internal voice that was nagging him again.

All of a sudden he clearly heard a soft rustle behind him. He located the source of the sound and tensed. There was some kind of animal rustling around in the bushes just a couple of meters away from him! Without saying a word to anyone, he tiptoed up to the bushes. A very soft peeping noise came from somewhere low down and to the right, almost underneath the bushes. Yurka peered down, mystified. There was movement in the decaying carpet of last year's leaves covering the ground... Yurka's heart fell and a cold shiver ran up the back of his neck. *What if it's snakes?* he thought, horrified. Time seemed to stop. Slowly, trying not to make any sudden movements, he stepped backward away from the bushes.

Yurka had seen those beguiling reptiles more than once and knew to avoid getting anywhere near them. He knew that during the day vipers, which were cold-blooded, liked to warm their bodies in the sun. He also knew that June was their breeding season, so they also liked to collect into big balls in their nests. Phrases he'd heard in school during pre–military training and in biology class flew through his mind: a viper works like a windup mechanism, where the closer you get to it, the tighter it curls up, and then it's like a coiled spring releasing, it jumps up and bites you. And the closer the bite is to your head, the more dangerous it is.

And here was Yurka, the idiot, who'd completely forgotten about snakes and gone traipsing bravely off into the bushes in the middle of the night without telling anyone. He was about to shout to the troop leaders that he might have stumbled into a nest of snakes, and he'd already made his peace with his impending death and prepared himself to be attacked by an enraged viper, when a reddish-brown maple leaf shifted aside and out from underneath it came . . . a little button nose. And then Yurka heard a soft snuffling sound.

"A hedgehog!" Yurka sighed in relief when the prickled round body followed the nose out of the leaves.

Yurka squatted down on his heels and reached his hands out, ready to grab the animal. But, surprisingly, it didn't run away. On the contrary, it came out from under the bushes to him and poked a curious nose into his sneakers. After a greeting like that, Yurka just couldn't leave the little guy under a bush: he was so cute, so brave. Yurka definitely had to show his unexpected guest to the little kids. He chuckled as he took off his jacket, wrapped his new friend in it, and carried him back to the campfire.

The hedgehog was a genuine sensation, for Troop One every bit as much as for Troop Five. The seated kids stopped listening to Ira to jump up and huddle around Yurka. They took the hedgehog out of his jacket and started passing him around, each one trying to tickle or pet him. They loved his funny snuffing and christened him Snuffly. Nobody, not even Snuffly, had any objections to the name.

After the initial surge of excitement waned, they had to decide Snuffly's fate. Ira announced a vote on how to proceed: let him go, or bring him to the camp's Red Corner, a nook devoted to the local flora and fauna, full of books, posters, and live specimens. The vote was unanimous: Feed the hedgehog first, then keep him overnight and bring him to the Red Corner the next day. But when everyone was completely calm again, they realized there was nowhere to keep the hedgehog until morning.

"I saw boxes of canned beef in the field kitchen," Volodya remembered. "I don't think Zinaida Vasilyevna would have anything against us taking one of the boxes."

"A cardboard box? Won't he chew through it?" Ira Petrovna said with exaggerated distrust. Her tone reminded Yurka yet again that she and Volodya still hadn't made peace with each other.

Zhenya interceded: "Even if he does chew through it, nothing bad will happen. He'll just run back into the woods, that's all."

"Zinaida Vasilyevna won't like this!" said Ira, frowning.

"Irina, what do you want us to do?" asked Volodya. "Are we supposed to carry him back to camp? In the middle of the night, through the woods?"

"No. I won't let you go at night. Keep him in your tent."

"I'm not sleeping by myself; I'm with some of the boys."

"Then you think of something," she ground out through gritted teeth.

"What do you want to hear? 'I'll take full responsibility'? Fine. I'll take full responsibility. What an important matter you're making such a fuss about!" said Volodya angrily.

"Guys, not in front of the kids." Zhenya gave each of them a conciliatory clap on the shoulder. The kids who had collected in a circle around them exchanged worried glances. "I can find Zinaida ten fantastic boxes if need be."

Yurka realized he was the underlying cause of the fight: it was because of him, after all, that Volodya had burst out with that "Are you in love with him . . . ?" comment back in the theater. He'd been in a not-great mood already, but seeing this fight threatened to ruin his mood completely. So it was more an announcement than a question when Yurka said, "So does someone need to go get a box, then?" Without waiting for a response, he walked off toward the field kitchen.

"I'm with Konev," Yurka heard behind his back. Volodya quickly caught up with him. He was carrying a flashlight he'd gotten somewhere and lit Yurka's path with it, even though it was a moonlit night and there was no need for electric lights.

"What's wrong with you?" Volodya asked angrily.

"Nothing's wrong with me. And the last thing I need is for you to take out your anger on me," growled Yurka.

"No, no, I wasn't going to take anything out on you. If it sounded that way, I'm sorry. But . . . Yur, I feel like you're avoiding me."

"Not really. I'm just tired."

"Come on, Yura. Don't try to fool me." His voice betrayed his frustration. "I can see something's wrong. Are you mad at me? What for? Did I say something wrong? Or did I do something wrong?" Volodya had now become quite alarmed. He looked Yurka right in the eyes and put his hand on Yurka's shoulder, but physical contact with Volodya was something Yurka didn't want; in fact, it was something Yurka was afraid of. So he shrugged Volodya's hand off. Volodya was now completely baffled: "Is this all still because of the magazines?"

"I'm just—no—I mean, it's just—"

"What is it with you and this 'I'm just . . . ,' 'It's just . . .'? Give it to me straight: What's wrong?"

"Everything's fine. I've been in a terrible mood since I got up this morning. I didn't want to ruin your mood, too."

"Well, you did."

Yurka came to a halt by the field kitchen. "How?" he asked, surprised.

"Because you're avoiding me. I'm worried, you know."

"What? You're what? You're worried?" said Yurka stupidly. Yet deep inside he grew warm. "About me?"

"You're my friend, of course I'm worried about you, and concerned, and . . ." Volodya trailed off and lowered his gaze. He bit his lip, then cleared his throat, and then said carefully, "How about this: if something happened, you have to tell me, because I'm not . . . I'm not a complete stranger to you, after all. And I'm a troop leader, too. I can help you. Okay?"

"Okay. But I really am just tired. Everything's okay, Volod." But Yurka was saying it more to convince himself than Volodya.

"That's settled, then," said Volodya. "Tomorrow, when everybody's still asleep, we're going to go fishing. Want to join us? Or are you too tired? You'll have to get up at five in the morning."

"Whew, five a.m., yikes," Yurka said, hedging. "If I don't get enough sleep, I'll be grumpy and sleepy all day and generally out of sorts . . ."

"You're already out of sorts," grumbled Volodya as they found a box and turned around to bring it back to the campfire. "And I am, too, because of you!

Alyosha told me you'd already told him yesterday you weren't going to HQ, so I thought I'd offended you, so I've been on edge all day. I can't do anything right."

It was simply not possible for Yurka to react to these words with indifference. Volodya was out of sorts without him? On edge? Couldn't do anything right? So that meant he needed Yurka. How nice it felt to be needed. Yurka's alarm about what had happened at morning calisthenics faded; he wanted everything to go back to the way it had been. Yurka smiled. "Fine, okay. I'll get up."

"But don't forget to ask Ira's permission to leave."

"Of course. If it comes up, confirm that I'm going with you. Where are we meeting?"

"I'll wake you up myself."

Yurka was certain that waking up at five a.m. was beyond him. Sure, he'd force himself to, but it wouldn't be so much waking up from sleep as much as coming back from the dead. Even on regular mornings it wasn't exactly the easiest thing for him to wake up, and this time it would be even harder, after such a stressful day . . . But his fears weren't borne out. All he had to do was crawl into his tent for his weariness to make itself felt. The moment he put face to pillow, he fell asleep. But his sleep was troubled: even in slumber, thoughts of Volodya wouldn't leave him in peace. All night Yurka tied Volodya's neckerchiefs, constantly getting the knots wrong. Then he brushed against Volodya's neck. Volodya got goose bumps all over from the timid touch of Yurka's fingers. And then, in real life, Yurka's whole body was suddenly covered in goose bumps too, and he jolted awake in a panic.

He opened his eyes and sat up, breathing heavily and trying to figure out where he was and what time it was. Around him was nothing but pitch blackness and utter silence except for the wind that whistled outside the tent, rustling the treetops.

Yurka crawled out of the tent quietly and carefully, trying not to wake up Vanka and Mikha. The first thing he did was read his watch in the light of the moon. Four fifteen. Yurka sighed. He would've gone back to sleep, but there wasn't a speck of sleep left in him.

The sky was just beginning to brighten. Yura estimated that dawn wouldn't be for another thirty minutes or so, but the beginnings of a pale glow in the sky already signaled the new day.

There was nothing he could do. Yurka headed out to look for a place to wash his face. He found the DIY handwashing station hanging on a tree near the field kitchen and splashed water in his face. A shiver ran down his whole body. He was seized by the urge to go back to his tent, tuck himself tightly back into his sleeping bag, and not go anywhere.

"Fishing? The river? Who needs that? It's totally freezing out here!"

He walked over to the tents. But not to his tent. He'd decided to find Volodya.

The three Troop Five tents were arranged end to end in a triangle. Yurka peeked into each tent in turn. One tent was the girls' tent; the other two were for the boys. But Yurka didn't recognize Volodya at first, since he was wrapped tight in his sleeping bag all the way up to his ears. Next to him lay the snoring Sashka, the wheezing Pcholkin, and Olezhka, whose nose whistled with each breath.

Yurka stepped carefully around the boys and knelt right next to Volodya. The disheveled sleeper looked funny, sillier than Yurka had ever seen him before: evidently he'd been reading his notebook before bed and fallen asleep, since the notebook was lying on his chest, and his flashlight, still on, was on the ground beside him. He hadn't even taken his glasses off. They'd slipped down his nose and were evidently bothering him from the way he frowned and jerked his head as though dreaming of something unpleasant. Yurka couldn't help it and laughed, but as quietly as he could, trying not to wake Volodya.

Volodya opened one eye, blinked, and opened the other. He looked up, blankly at first, then in suspicion, and then in horror: "Did I oversleep?!" He sat up sharply.

"No, just the opposite: still ten minutes to go." Yurka snorted a quiet laugh again.

Volodya adjusted his glasses. Then he put his finger to his mouth to shush Yurka and looked meaningfully first at the sleeping boys, then at the exit from the tent.

Once they were both out of the tent, Volodya asked in a whisper, "Why'd you wake up so early?"

Yurka shrugged. "Don't have the foggiest idea. I just did."

Volodya looked at his watch and said, "Never mind. It's already four thirty anyway. We need to wake the kids. Will you get them up while I go wash my face?"

Yurka nodded and went back into the tent. While he was waking up the kids, Volodya dispatched his lingering sleepiness and collected the fishing gear.

It was Yurka who led their little group to the river: Volodya, as it turned out, didn't know his way around the wooded area very well, while Yurka knew of a great little fishing pier not far from the camp beach. By the time they'd made their way there, it had gotten light out.

"Do you all remember how you need to behave, guys?" Volodya lectured. "I'll remind you. No jumping and no running on the pier. Sit calmly. Fishing isn't a game. Fish like quiet. If you shout, you'll scare them and you won't catch any!"

But the kids seemed to have no intention of misbehaving: they still hadn't really woken up yet and dragged themselves after Yurka, half-asleep and yawning every other minute.

At the river, the reeds rustled and the frogs' croaking was deafening. Yurka took a deep lungful of fresh, damp air and stepped out onto the pier. The boards creaked a little bit under his weight. The rays of the rising sun sliced into the morning mist blanketing the water. Where the pier met the shore, there was a thick rind of pond scum with a nondescript little bird hopping around on it. Yurka was amazed the bird didn't fall through the precarious surface.

He'd never thought in a million years that such idyllic stillness could exist in the same space as the Troop Five boys. But that morning, on the fishing pier in the river, peace and quiet reigned. Neither the rascal Pcholkin nor the reckless Sashka had the slightest intention of getting into trouble. They sat on the wooden planks and held their fishing rods and watched their bobbers like hawks, determined not to miss it if they got a bite.

But the fish weren't biting. So far the only thing biting was Yurka. He was biting the inside of his cheek, trying to stay awake. He gave a huge yawn, then joked, "Are the fish still asleep?" In the past half hour, only Olezhka had gotten a nibble, but he hadn't managed to yank his fishing pole up fast enough. The fish got away, leaving a hook with half a worm on it.

"What a smawt fish!" exclaimed Olezhka, not a bit dismayed. "It bit the wowm but didn't get caught on the fishhook!"

From time to time Yurka would lose track of the world and slip into a doze. His general lack of sleep, on top of yesterday's exhaustion, was making itself known now.

Volodya, sitting right next to him, kept up a quiet murmur of encouragement for the campers: "Don't worry about it. The main thing here isn't the fish—it's the fishing!"

Those were the last words Yurka heard clearly. He didn't realize he was falling asleep. He'd just been watching his bobber, but now his head had fallen to one side, and he'd closed his eyes, and a sweet, delightful contentment spread over his whole body . . .

"I got one! I got one!" Sashka's loud voice burst into his cozy, sleepy little world.

"Pull it out!" squeaked Olezhka.

Yurka opened his eyes and found that his cheek was resting on something hard and warm . . . Volodya's shoulder. Yurka jerked his head up and looking around. His fishing rod was lying on the pier next to him; behind the boys' backs, a few small perch were wiggling in a net. Volodya looked at him without a word.

"Whoops, looks like I, uh . . . fell asleep . . ." said Yurka lamely, looking at the shoulder he'd just been resting on.

"Really? I didn't even notice," said Volodya, feigning surprise. He looked pleased and was barely able to keep from laughing. "You can sleep some more if you want . . . Stripey."

"What?" Yurka asked, confused.

"The fabric was wrinkled and it left stripes on your cheek. Right here." Volodya touched his jaw affectionately and burst into laughter. This was the first time Yurka had been this close to Volodya's face. Volodya had dimples.

CHAPTER EIGHT
KONEV GOES SWIMMING

Dozing off while fishing hadn't solved Yurka's problem: he was still desperately tired. He'd been planning on using quiet hour today to compensate for the hours of sleep he hadn't gotten at night, but Volodya was waiting for him at the cabin. Recognizing the troop leader's tall figure from a distance, Yurka assumed he was going to suggest they go rewrite more of Olezha's lines. Yurka was going to refuse.

"Hi." Yurka gave a demonstratively wide yawn into his fist. "I'm dying here—so tired."

"This is no time for sleeping!" Volodya gave a sly smile, pulled a key ring from his pocket, and shook it, clinking the keys. "You were saying you know where the bas-relief from the scary story is. And I have the keys to the boathouse. You provide the information, I provide the boat! You coming?"

Yurka's sleepiness vanished without a trace. He clapped his hands together in anticipation and joked, "Aha! So being friends with a troop leader has its upsides!"

Volodya chortled. He walked down the cabin steps and nodded at Yurka for him to follow.

"And you won't get in trouble for taking the keys?" Yurka asked ten minutes later as Volodya bent over the locked boathouse door, trying to find the right key,

"What trouble could there be? I mean, I didn't steal them. I signed them out in the little book and got them. The keys are all hanging in the office, any troop leader can take them."

"Just like that, for no reason?" Yurka was surprised.

"What, do you really think troop leaders don't make up reasons to get out of quiet hour?" Volodya winked.

Once they got in the door and through the small building, they saw stretching out before them a dock finished in big concrete pavers. Tires hung along its sides at water level as bumpers. A dozen boats nudged gently against them, each boat secured with heavy chains to its own short metal pile with a little sign displaying the boat's number.

"You know your way around an oar?" Volodya turned and started walking to the end of the dock.

"What do you think? Every summer when we get boat time, I have a little side job of rowing for people. Here, take this one." He indicated the next-to-last boat,. which had a fresh coat of blue paint. "It's got good oars."

Yurka took charge from there. They pulled off the canvas that was fastened over the boat to keep the rain out and got in. Yurka showed Volodya how to maintain his balance as he sat down. Then he took the keys from Volodya, opened the lock, and unwound the chain. It clanked loudly on the concrete. Yurka pushed the boat off the dock and steered it out to the middle of the river.

"The current's strong here," he warned. "I'll row us out and you row us back. Otherwise my arms'll fall off."

"Are you sure you know where to take us?" Volodya asked doubtfully.

"Of course I do! Straight ahead! No intersections or traffic lights here!"

"But if you're being serious . . . ?"

"Like I just said, keep going straight until the river bends. Actually . . . Wait. There's this one place . . ." Yurka got a rapt look on his face, remembering it, and looked at Volodya. "I know you'll like it. We have to go there."

"What is it?"

"Well . . ." Yurka didn't want to say yet. "The troop leaders said we couldn't go there, they say it's dangerous. But I went out there once and it was fine! I got read the riot act afterwards, of course, but . . . Want to go? It's really cool."

Volodya considered it. He adjusted his glasses in his habitual gesture: condescending, holding the glasses by both arms. "The thing is, Yur, I am a troop leader . . . ," he began.

"Even better! You say you allow it and there's no problem."

"Well, I don't know . . . ," said Volodya hesitantly.

"Aw, come on, Volodya!" Yurka exclaimed playfully. "Now, don't be such a... such a Volodya! It's not dangerous there as long as you don't jump out of the boat. I promise!"

"But what if you do? What is it? Sharks? Crocodiles?"

"Pirates! No, just kidding. Just algae. But a lot of it!"

"Does it take a long time to get there?"

Yurka shrugged. "Ten, maybe fifteen minutes."

"In this heat?" said Volodya, frowning. In the cloudless sky, the sun really was baking them mercilessly. On top of that, they'd be on a river that wasn't too deep but was wide, without a single bit of shade. Still... "Okay, fine," he capitulated. "But you'll bear full responsibility!"

"Responsibility's my middle name," said Yurka, chuckling.

The current in that part of the river really was fast and strong, and they were rowing against it. Yurka, out of practice, spent quite a while wheezing and straining until he found his rhythm. After all, it had been a year since the last time he went out in a rowboat.

For a while they moved in complete silence except for the measured splashing of the oars and the whispering of the reeds. To the right the shore sloped gently up, spreading in a green and yellow carpet all the way to the camp fence. To the left a steep bank riddled with barn swallow nests was forbidding with its sheer drops, the tree roots jutting from the sandy cliffs, the muddy sandbars, and the woods looming high over their heads. Still, the trees weren't high enough to cast any real shadow on the river; Yurka, who was not only sitting in the hot sun but working the oars, too, was sweating buckets.

"Hey, Yur... I was going to ask you something...," said Volodya hesitantly, breaking the silence. "Can I?"

"You started, so you may as well finish."

"I heard something about what happened last year. Olga Leonidovna was saying they treated you badly. So basically that's why they decided to let you in this session: because they felt sorry for you. I used to wonder whether I knew the whole story there, but now that I've gotten to know you better, I see I don't know the first thing about it. Will you tell me what happened, and how?"

Yurka drew in a deep breath and let it out slowly. "So there was this one guy, you know, this... creep who was a camper here. He was the one whose dad was in the nomenklatura and had connections, the one who . . . no, I have to tell it all from the beginning. I used to go to a music school attached to a conservatory. My dream was to become a pianist"—Yurka saw Volodya's eyes widen in amazement and hurried to cut off his questions—"but I didn't tell you because I hate even remembering all that. The thing is . . . I really loved the piano, I couldn't live without it . . . No, 'really' isn't the right word. I loved it passionately, for as long as I can remember."

Yurka paused for some time, choosing the right words. He concentrated hard, figuring out how to explain it, how to show Volodya the extent to which music had been important to him. That he had never once imagined his life—imagined himself—without music. Ever since he was little, music had always been with him, the sound keeping his thoughts company. Music comforted, calmed, and cheered him. He heard music in his dreams every night. Music played every moment he was awake. Yurka never grew tired of it. Just the opposite: in moments of silence he became fearful, he couldn't do anything right, he couldn't concentrate. Sometimes he worried he was obsessed, because the piano was the only thing he cared about, the only thing that moved him, and it scared him how alienated he was from most people. It was as though he lived in a different dimension that he was trying to figure out. Was it that the music lived in him, or that he lived in the music? Was the music shining inside him, like a tiny but white-hot star? Or was it he who was inside a gigantic universe, one that only he could feel?

But how was he supposed to explain all this to Volodya? Volodya was a friend, yes, but someone he was still getting to know, and someone who didn't know music at all. And Yurka never talked about all this, anyway. Music was his personal, private experience, one that was delicate and fragile, one that couldn't be formulated using something as primitive as words.

"I didn't go to a regular school but to a special music school run by a conservatory. Have you heard of those?" Volodya shrugged. Yurka explained: "Schools like that teach music along with all the regular school subjects. You attend for ten years, and then when you graduate, you can go directly to the conservatory instead of having to do music academies and auditions like everybody else. So, anyway, I aced the tests after the fourth grade, but starting in the eighth grade everything started going downhill. At the end of eighth grade there's a big test, and in addition to our own teachers the instructors from the conservatory also come, to watch the testing and pick out students in advance to work with after they graduate—" Yurka stopped abruptly.

Volodya, his head tilted slightly, gave him a questioning look. "And?"

Yurka hesitated. He rubbed his forehead and looked away. "I failed. They said I was 'average.'"

"So what? That's not a failing grade!"

"But this is music, Volod! Everything's incredibly serious,: in music you're either a genius or you're nobody. There's no tolerance for 'average' people in music! So I was advised to leave the music school, because once I'd failed the test, there was no way I was going to make it into the conservatory. I'm stubborn. I stayed. But it was a waste of time. For half a year I got nothing but abuse, I got Ds, people said mean things to me . . . so once they'd finally beaten it into me that I'm worthless, I left. I quit, all by myself. I quit music and transferred to a regular school. I haven't touched a piano since."

Volodya was silent. Yurka stared at the river. He was recalling how hard—almost impossible—it had been after that to force the music to be silent and then to learn to live in that silence. To this day he still hit his own hands and squeezed his interlocked fingers together until they hurt—whatever it took for them to unlearn their habit of drumming out his favorite works, or works he'd composed himself, on any available surface. He was even doing it right then, hammering his fingers unconsciously on the oar without recognizing the melody, without even trying to recognize it.

"But why didn't they figure it out until the eighth grade?" Volodya inquired cautiously. "Shouldn't they have caught it earlier?"

"Because I and my talent had absolutely nothing to do with it!" scoffed Yurka.

Volodya looked confused. "What do you mean?"

"What I said! The city executive committee chairman's son was also in the music school. Typical little privileged nomenklatura prick: his daddy's a political boss, so he gets whatever he wants. He was a total mediocrity, always skipping school, but he wanted to go to the conservatory. So they gave him my spot." Yurka took up the oars again. "Isn't it great how it worked out? Konev lives and breathes music, but he's not worthy of being a student because he's 'average,' while Vishnevsky skips school, but it's okay because he's a major talent! Although he has no talent at all! Pretty great, eh?!"

"Yeah . . . ," said Volodya slowly, obviously unsure how to respond. Taken aback, he looked away.

Yurka tried but failed to suppress the eruption of anger that was staining his cheeks red, filling his voice with bile, and making his eyes glitter feverishly. When Yurka pulled the oars, his strokes were even so choppy, they rocked the boat back and forth. He spoke in a strangled voice: "And wasn't it great for me the next summer, either, when I get to camp and see that I'm not only at the same session as that nomenklatura prick, I'm in the same troop as him! That sleazebag, that little shit, that—"

"Hey, take it easy with the name-calling," warned Volodya, but Yurka was so consumed by rage and hurt that he didn't pay Volodya any attention. He put his back into it and started rowing furiously. He'd completely forgotten about the heat, though the sweat was pouring off him. "It's all because of him! He's the reason they threw me out! He's the one who destroyed my life! But my humiliation at school wasn't enough for him, oh no! He decided to pull his shit here, too: he called me a little yid in front of the whole camp! And that's where I couldn't take it anymore. I let him have it, right in his ugly mug, and in front of everybody, too. I got him good, I busted his nose, he was bleeding everywhere . . . I've never hit anybody that hard," Yurka said, grinning bitterly. "I've always protected my hands. My grandma drilled it into me ever since I was little: 'Yura, take care of your hands! Yura, take care of your hands!' But what's the point of taking care of them? What am I preserving them for?"

"Wait, but why 'little yid'? Are you really Jewish?" asked Volodya, obviously trying to draw him toward a less painful topic.

"On my mom's side," said Yurka, without looking at him. "Yeah."

"But how did Vishnevsky find out? There's nothing about you that looks Jewish, just average Russian: your first name, your last name, your face, your hair—there's nothing Jewish there."

"I don't know. He must've seen me in the shower."

"Wait—what?" Volodya said, confused.

Yurka chuckled and gave an airy shrug. "The family tradition . . ."

Then it hit Volodya. He raised an eyebrow and shamelessly looked Yurka up and down. "Oh . . . so that's it . . . Interesting . . ."

Yurka barely kept from blurting out, "Want me to show you?" But he was flustered by Volodya's extravagantly curious, brazen regard and went from bold to timid. He smiled convulsively and went red. He felt hot again.

Meanwhile, Volodya's expression had shifted to flabbergasted. He whistled softly and whispered, "Holy crap! That's awful!"

This made Yurka feel so angry, and outraged, and hurt, that he castigated himself for being overly candid about this ticklish question. Because of Yurka's own wagging tongue, Volodya had accidentally gotten into Yurka's intimate business—but judging by Volodya's intrigued expression, he was in no hurry to get back out. "So Volodya says talking about those magazines is forbidden, but thinking about my private parts is totally fine?" fumed Yurka to himself. Volodya's reaction had cut him deeply. And then his internal voice chimed in, too, reminding him of the incident at yesterday's morning calisthenics and his recent, tingle-inducing dream, so that in addition to the hot sun he now felt such a surge of internal heat that his lungs convulsed in pain.

What he said out loud was a remorseful "It's not like I wanted to!" But seeing Volodya's stunned expression, Yurka got hold of himself and tried his best to continue the conversation: "First of all, nobody asked me. Secondly, I was little, I don't remember anything. And thirdly . . . it's . . . don't go imagining things! It's nobody's business but my own! And it's not 'awful'!"

"No, no—what are you saying?! That's not what I meant!" Volodya shook his head and blushed to the roots of his hair. "There's nothing all that strange about that! It's an old tradition, several thousand years old, it's normal, pretty much . . . But you're not religious, are you?"

"You're not an idiot, are you?"

"Well, no . . . but I mean . . . I was just . . ."

Yurka snorted and looked around. Anything to change the subject. There wasn't a trace of civilization to be seen, neither a hut in the woods nor a roof out on the horizon. He and Volodya gone a good kilometer or two by now. The camp and the boathouse had vanished behind a sharp bend in the river a while ago, and now the boys were in the middle of a pretty but boring landscape: identical patches of sparse woods, identical fields shimmering in the heat haze. There wasn't anything to catch the eye. Except maybe for the high hill coming into view at a distance and the tiny little gazebo on it. But that wasn't where they were headed. Yurka estimated they'd arrive at their destination any minute.

Volodya's soft voice tore him away from his thoughts: "Anyway, I'm really glad you told me about that. About music, I mean. Turns out I don't know you at all."

"Well, I don't know you, either," said Yurka. "Not really. And I didn't tell you about music just because you asked . . . I mean, you *did* ask, but I could've just not talked about it, or found a way to avoid it. But I decided to trust you."

Volodya gave him a grateful look.

"You know," he began quietly, "I could tell you my most dreadful secret, too, but nobody can ever find out about it for any reason whatsoever. Promise not to tell?"

Yurka nodded, puzzled: Had he ever given Volodya a reason to mistrust him? Of course he wouldn't tell a soul, no matter what Volodya revealed.

"You, Yura, refuse to live the way you're told." Volodya leaned closer to him and lowered his voice almost to a whisper, although there was nobody to hear them out in the middle of the river, in the rustling of the reeds. "You say you have relatives in East Germany . . . but have you ever wanted to leave the country yourself?"

This question sounded rhetorical, but Yurka answered it: "Well . . . my grandma tried to go back to Germany. It is her historical homeland, after all. But they wouldn't let her. I have a relative there, but it's just my mom's second cousin, so it's probably not—"

"Well, I want to leave," interrupted Volodya. "Or rather, I don't just want to leave: it's my main goal in life. To go somewhere else and stay there permanently."

Yurka's mouth fell open. "Permanently? But that's illegal, you can be put on trial for that. And you're a Komsomol member, you're so . . . so upstanding, you're Party-minded, you're . . . you're . . ."

"And that's exactly why I am, as you say, 'upstanding' and 'Party-minded'! So I can achieve my goal! The logic is simple, Yur: the only people who are allowed to travel outside the USSR are Communist Party members. 'Proven' Communists can travel even more freely. And that goes without saying for 'proven' Communist diplomats on a diplomatic assignment. And so—"

"And so you applied to MGIMO so you could become a diplomat," Yurka finished for him.

Volodya nodded. Even though there wasn't a soul around for kilometers, Volodya spoke in a subdued voice; his agitated tone, and the way he looked fearfully around, several times, gave Yurka goose bumps. If anyone heard that Volodya was planning on becoming a non-returner, he'd be immediately expelled from the Komsomol in disgrace. His plans, his entire life, would be derailed! And now he'd told Yurka.

"Where do you want to go?" Yurka asked.

"To America."

"To ride a wild mustang through the prairie?" he said, with a nervous laugh.

"A motorcycle. A Harley-Davidson. Heard of them?"

Yurka didn't answer. He hadn't heard of that kind of motorcycle, and he didn't know a thing about diplomats, but now he was scared for Volodya. Just then he remembered Volodya's warning: "It's not as bad now as it was back in Stalin's day, but I could still get in deep trouble . . ."

Yurka almost missed the turn due to his mild state of shock.

"Oh, there it is! It's right there," he exclaimed, pointing at a wall of reeds.

It wasn't deep here, and Yurka's oar hit the riverbed as he turned the boat and headed directly into the reeds.

"What are you doing?" Volodya asked in surprise.

"Everything's fine. Help me. Part the reeds in front of us, just don't cut yourself."

The bottom of the boat scraped in the shallows as they passed through the patch of reeds. A small pool of water opened up before them, thickly carpeted in duckweed and water lilies. The river's current didn't flow into the pool, so the water was still, which allowed the river flora to flourish. Yurka's oars got tangled up in the plants, and he had to stop every so often to pull them in and clean off the chunks of slimy algae clinging to them. But he knew this place, and he knew why he'd brought Volodya here. It was worth it, regardless of the swampy water's particular odor and the clouds of buzzing mosquitoes.

Pond skaters darted along the water's surface. A deafening croaking arose from the reeds. The pond was covered in the usual yellow water lilies. A few especially pushy frogs had taken their seats right on the water lilies' waxy leaves and were observing the boat as it floated past. Yurka scanned the perimeter of the pond with great attention.

"Look! A heron!" he shouted, gesturing toward a part of shore that was thickly covered in reeds.

"Where?" Volodya poked the bridge of his glasses and squinted in the direction Yurka had indicated.

"It's right there. It blends in really well, the little stinker! You can barely tell it apart from the reeds." Yurka took hold of his hand, held it out toward a wall of reddish reeds with a long bill sticking out of it, and ordered, "Point your finger!"

Volodya obediently pointed his index finger, and Yurka took hold of his hand, fine-tuning the direction he was pointing.

"Oh, I see it!" Volodya exclaimed happily. "Would you look at that!"

"What, haven't you seen one before?"

Volodya shook his head. "Nope. What a funny little guy, standing there on one leg! It's pretending it's not even there."

As Volodya watched the heron, Yurka caught himself musing that he was still holding on to Volodya's hand, but he really didn't want to let go of it . . . And come to think of it, Volodya wasn't pulling his hand away, either . . . But eventually Yurka had to let go so he could take up the oars again and guide the boat farther in and closer to shore.

"Here we are," he announced. "Look how pretty it is here." Yurka nodded down at the water. He'd turned the boat so it sat lengthwise in the pool, and now he let go of the oars and relaxed, rolling his shoulders.

Everywhere around them, flowers rocked gently on the water. Instead of the common yellow lilies, these were snow-white; dozens of them, with thick, yellow middles like egg yolks, floating among the dark green burdock-like leaves. Above them, pearly blue dragonflies alternated between hovering motionlessly and darting quickly to and fro. Volodya admired the pond, his gaze first taking in the flowers, then following the dragonflies. Meanwhile, Yurka admired him. Watching the tender smile that played on Volodya's lips, Yurka knew he'd gladly submit to the biting mosquitoes and row here a hundred times, against the current, just to see that same delight on Volodya's face again.

"White water lilies! They're amazing!" Volodya leaned over the edge of the boat and brushed his fingertips against the white petals, as tenderly and reverently as though he were touching something fragile and precious. "There's so many of them . . . they're beautiful. Like the one Thumbelina was born in."

Yurka jumped up from his seat, making the boat rock dangerously under him. "Shall we pick one?" he suggested. He reached toward the flower, grasped the stem right underneath the flower head, and was about to pull, but Volodya slapped his wrist. "Stop that right now! Don't you know those flowers are listed in the Red Book?"

Yurka blinked, startled, and peered at Volodya.

"That's why you had to look for them so long," Volodya continued his lecture. "People just float by and pick them, but it turns out these water lilies are an endangered species! And there's no point picking them anyway, actually: they're lilies, water plants, they wilt as soon as you pull them out of the water. They crumple up and die right in your hand. You can't plant them in a pot, or cut them and put them in a vase like they were roses or something."

"Okay, okay." Yurka stretched his hands out apologetically in front of him, demonstrating that, see, they were empty, they hadn't picked anything or killed anything. "I just wanted to give you one. To remember this by."

"I'm going to remember it anyway. Thank you. It was definitely worth coming out here."

They sat in the boat for a little while longer, admiring the flowers. Yurka listened to the croaking of the frogs and the buzzing of the pearlescent dragonflies and thought about how awfully tired he was of living in silence. Notwithstanding his sad thoughts, it was so calm and easy for him here that he felt like staying until dark, but Volodya looked at his watch and said, with some alarm: "It's already been an hour. We probably won't have time to see the bas-relief today, will we?"

"We could get there okay, but it's a little bit of a hike from the shore to the bas-relief..."

"Too bad." Volodya heaved a sad sigh. "So now what? Turn around and head back?"

"Up to you. The bugle won't be for another half hour."

"Then maybe let's sit in the shade, if only for ten minutes? There's some shade over there by the shore, see?"

"But if we row over there, we'll hurt the lilies...," said Yurka sadly. He wouldn't've minded cooling off, either, since his whole body was burning up inside from the heat.

Yurka expected Volodya to bow to circumstance—or, rather, to the heat—and say they were heading back, but all of a sudden Volodya lit up and exclaimed, his eyes flashing: "Hey, Yur, why don't we take a dip? Is there anywhere around here to get in the water? It's a river; there's got to be someplace..."

Yurka considered it. He thought he remembered a spot out past the bend in the river. Calling it a beach would have been overkill, but it was a place where they could tie up the boat. There was just one problem: he didn't have his swimsuit with him.

"I don't have anything to swim in, Volod. My swimsuit's back in the cabin, and my underwear..." Yurka faltered. Boxers. Swimming in them would result in completely soaked shorts afterward. "I mean... I don't want to go commando after this."

"Don't go commando in your shorts! Go commando in the river!" said Volodya with a wink. He began unbuttoning his shirt in anticipation even though the two of them hadn't begun heading for shore yet. "Why not? There's not a single girl for a kilometer around. Nobody'll see us."

"Makes sense," admitted Yurka. He turned the boat toward the little beach area. Still, he was flustered. Getting undressed... although, no, there wasn't anything weird about it at all. They were both boys. Yurka had gone skinny-dipping a hundred times. And not just that, he'd also been naked while showering or changing in gym and at camp, and he'd never felt self-conscious in front of his comrades before. But comrades were one thing; Volodya was something else entirely. And this was Yurka's first time for this kind of something else.

And, no, it wasn't self-consciousness he was feeling—not at all. Despite all their talk about religious traditions, regardless of Volodya's seemingly improper interest, Yurka wasn't self-conscious. No, he was simply so excited, he was paralyzed.

Still, mindful of the previous day's awkwardness, he turned away as Volodya undressed, and he didn't take off his own clothes until Volodya dove into the water.

Yurka jumped in, submerged himself completely, and bobbed back up. He'd barely had a chance to wipe the water out of his eyes when Volodya took off for the far shore and quickly drew close to it. Volodya's arms hit the surface so powerfully that he sent gouts of water splashing, like a fountain; tiny rainbows winked in and out of existence as the spray sparkled in the sun. *Now, that's a butterfly! Brisk and bold! Wish I could do that!* thought Yurka enviously. His eyes were drawn to Volodya's shoulders. Out of nowhere he had a surge of utterly genuine delight: seems a skinny guy, but then, wow, what strong shoulders . . . !

Yurka just kept standing there in water warm as milk fresh from the cow. He didn't move a muscle as he admired how Volodya swam, how graceful and natural he looked, how free and uninhibited he was. He watched while Volodya paused, took off his glasses, and held them tightly as he dived. And then what Yurka had been admiring yesterday morning showed there above the water for a second, completely bare, uncovered by cloth. It was just a moment, too fast for Yurka to actually see anything, but suddenly his heart was in his throat and a jolt of excitement ran through him. He froze.

The realization of what was happening to him hit home. He stood rooted to the spot. The realization was so plain and simple that it stunned him. How had he not seen this yet? How could he have only now realized the answer to a million questions at once? The answer was so simple! Because who was Volodya to him? A friend. But not just any friend. The kind of friend you think about to sweeten your falling asleep and brighten your waking up. The kind of friend it's so pleasant to look at, the kind you just keep admiring, the kind you can't tear your eyes away from. The handsomest person in the world, the kindest, the smartest—the best in any and all ways. The kind of friend it's even interesting to just sit quietly with. That's the kind of friend

Volodya was to him. A friend whom he *liked*, in that strange, stupid, conventional sense of the word. A friend who was more than.

"No. That can't be!" Yurka didn't believe it. That kind of thing didn't happen between boys. He'd never heard about anything like it, not from anyone. Even the guys from his building didn't joke about this, and they knew everything about everything and joked about everything. Yurka simply did not believe that a friend, who was a guy, could be so drawn to another friend, who was also a guy . . . that they . . . that he . . .

Yurka thought he'd been scared before. After those morning calisthenics, for example. But in hindsight that wasn't actually that big a deal—just apprehension, really. What he felt now was true fear. Why was this happening? What was it? What was it called? Was it called anything? No matter what it was, no matter what it was called, it was unnatural! This kind of thing didn't exist and couldn't be happening to him. Maybe Yurka was the only guy this had ever happened to. Maybe it was some kind of psychological illness? Or just that he was exhausted? In this session of camp, Yurka had worn himself out, drained himself to the last drop; he'd worked his neurons so hard that his brain must've just sputtered and died. He'd go back home, take some time to sit around and do nothing, and everything would be dandy again. Yurka was already eager to go home, except that he really didn't want to say goodbye to Volodya.

What he did want was to share his fear and his discovery with his best friend. Yurka wanted to tell him something private and precious: "I like you. I'm glad you're here." But even imagining saying those words to Volodya was scarier than jumping into icy water from a thirty-meter platform, worse than diving headfirst into the abyss. But what if he actually did it? What if he just threw caution to the wind and told it like it was? What would happen then? In his heart of hearts, Yurka knew exactly what: Volodya would laugh, thinking he was laughing with Yurka, but he'd actually be laughing at him. That's what would happen.

And even if Yurka suddenly discovered a gift for eloquence, even if he was able to explain what "like" and "glad" truly meant, but explain that he wasn't asking Volodya for anything, he was just telling him, out of pure happiness, just so he'd know . . . Even so, Volodya would understand none of this. He'd do whatever he could to try to understand, but he wouldn't, his mind wouldn't process it. Of course not; Yurka's own mind couldn't, either . . .

How could he explain this to Volodya? How could he understand it himself? So far, the only thing Yurka knew for sure now was that he'd never abandon Volodya, he'd never forget him, he'd never leave him. The kilometers would be no obstacle. Yurka would remain his devoted friend, always and everywhere, no matter where his life took him, be it to another continent, or the moon, or Asteroid B-612. Now Yurka would need Volodya even more. When Volodya wasn't near, Yurka would feel the loneliness and emptiness even more. And Yurka would inevitably feel sorrow. He and Volodya would both feel it at some point, but Volodya's sorrow wouldn't be because of the complicated, unreasonable Yurka. It'd be because of some simple, reasonable girl.

Yurka stood stricken. He was afraid to move. He watched Volodya and thought, and thought, and thought some more. His head was spinning, his eyes were dazzled. The water droplets burned in the sun like sparks. The splashing roared in his ears. Stunned, Yurka watched as his best, most special friend snorted and huffed and laughed. But he himself couldn't move a muscle. His whole body had gone numb as he stood up to his waist in the water, hands at his sides.

Volodya soon noticed Yurka's strange behavior and came over. Yurka stared at him fearfully and did a very stupid thing: he covered his groin with his hands. Why did he cover it up? What was he hiding it from? He was in a pond, where nothing could be seen through the cloudy water! But it was instinctive, from a sense of shame. Because it wasn't just his body that would be completely exposed . . .

Volodya's brow furrowed. "Yura, is everything okay?" He touched Yurka's shoulder, which was cold even in the sun. "Is something wrong with your foot?"

What lie could Yurka offer? That he'd cut his foot? No. Volodya would ask to see it, but there was nothing to see. That his head was spinning? Volodya would just send Yurka to sit in the shade, but how would that be any better? What could possibly make anything better for him now?

"It's nothing. It's fine," Yurka mumbled faintly.

"You're all white . . . Did you get a leg cramp? Here, let me help." Volodya came right up close to Yurka and put his hand down into the water, reaching for Yurka's leg.

"No, don't, it'll pass in just a second. It's not a cramp, it's just . . . it's just that I . . . I'm tired, and everything's just off somehow. Like we didn't make it to the bas-relief, for example." Yurka went red. And he did go red: heat singed his cheeks as though somebody'd put a hot water bottle on them.

"Of all the things to worry about . . ." Volodya said dubiously.

A few minutes later they were both dressed and back in the boat, Yurka fervently grateful that his problem had gone away before they were out of the water. Volodya, still unsure what was wrong, tried to reassure Yurka: "We'll make it out there another time. Give me the oars." At this, Yurka just smiled wanly.

The trip back was much faster, since the current itself moved the boat along. Volodya was singing to himself, a song Yurka didn't recognize. He wasn't even trying to listen to it and figure out what song it was; he was looking at the water and thinking about "like."

Suddenly, Volodya exclaimed, "Look at that willow!" He pointed over to the shore. "See it? That huge one there, like a tent—no, like a whole house! I've never seen one like that!"

He was pointing at a place where the riverbank came smoothly down to meet the river. A small sandbank that gave easy access to the water was half covered by a weeping willow, its densely leaved branches bending down all the way to touch the river. "Let's stop, Yur," he said.

"Then we won't make it back in time for the bugle. You said so yourself," replied Yurka quickly. But, seeing the animation in Volodya's eyes, he offered, "Maybe tomorrow?"

"But what if I can't get a boat tomorrow?"

"Then I'll try to remember how to get there on foot along the bank. I guarantee we can get there without the boat." Yurka searched the steep part of the riverbank and then scanned along the top of the cliff. "I know there's got to be a path over there. It starts at the shallows by our beach. The troop leaders don't let the little kids use it, but that makes sense, it's dangerous. The bank is sandy and crumbles out from under you, and falling down a cliff that steep would be pretty bad."

"Let's try to go there tomorrow, then?" Volodya suggested impatiently.

Yurka stopped dead in his tracks. "Since when have you been such a thrill seeker? You looking for adventure?"

Volodya shrugged. "I don't know. I'm just following your example."

Later that day, Yurka went out to find the willow. In an attempt to rid himself of the nagging, alarming thoughts about "like," he memorized every bend in the path, every rise and fall, every ridge and stone. His search for the tree ended up taking some time.

He got back to the movie theater a whole hour after rehearsal started. The actors were performing admirably, and Volodya was completely immersed in the proceedings, so Yurka, bored, wandered around the theater.

The piano was silent for once. Apparently, Volodya had asked Masha for a little time off from her playing, for she now sat scowling in the audience not far from the stage.

Yurka shot a glance at the piano every so often, wishing he'd never brought up that story. Now he was fighting the urge to walk over to it, open the cover, and touch the keys, even just for a second. He didn't want to actually make sounds, he just wanted to feel the cool lacquered wood under his fingertips. While everyone else was busy with their rehearsal in the left half of the stage, Yurka worked up his nerve and approached the piano in the right half. He opened the cover. A gleam of light danced along the keys. Yurka panicked and sprang away.

He bit his lip, eyeing the piano with a hunted look as he unconsciously warmed up his fingers. Out of nowhere a voice thundered at him in his head. Not his own voice. Someone else's. The judge's voice. She'd been a fat old lady with a bad perm. Yurka was surprised he even remembered it. He tried to think about something else, to just ignore the voice, but he couldn't. He didn't want to hear it, but he listened all the same, and it brought him pain: *Do it, Konev. Reach out and touch the piano. It's right there. Play whatever you want, play as much as you want; it won't change anything. You're still worthless, an utter mediocrity, and you have no future in music. Playing will just rub salt in your wounds.* The voice was hers, but the words weren't. They were Yurka's to himself.

"Well hello, schizophrenia ... great ... ," he muttered to himself sardonically, and headed backstage. He wandered aimlessly around the movie theater, bored, until rehearsal was over. He yearned to get into the projection room, but it was locked, as usual. He found just one somewhat interesting place in the whole giant building: a backstage supply closet. He went in and found a box with filmstrips and a projector and showed his discovery to Volodya after rehearsal.

Regardless of the anguish Yurka's frightening discovery had caused, regardless of the bad mood that had tormented him the entire next day, Yurka naturally went to Volodya and his boys after junior lights out. The whole of Troop Five unanimously chose filmstrips instead of scary stories. The boys voted for *The Adventures of Cipollino*, while the girls insisted on *Sleeping Beauty*. After fifteen minutes of heated debate, the young cavaliers agreed to defer to the ladies.

Afterward, as soon as the children had gotten into bed and pretended to be asleep, Yurka and Volodya went out to "their" spot. Yurka was gloomier than ever. He had neither the energy nor the inclination to even talk about anything, much less rewrite the play. Volodya tried again to find out what was really going on, but Yurka was determined not to talk and kept as quiet as a partisan. After a few fruitless attempts, Volodya tried to cheer him up, moaning out the waltz from Tchaikovsky's ballet *Sleeping Beauty*—as off-key as he could—and rocking the merry-go-round back and forth in time to the music. At first, Yurka maintained his silence. Then he grumbled, "Too slow. And now you need to hold it: 'mm-mm.' But then you need to go slower ... ." Eventually he relented and taught Volodya to moo the waltz correctly.

When Yurka went to bed, he dreamed of ballerinas all that night. And for the first time in half a year, he heard music playing in his head. He hadn't had such hard days and sweet dreams in a very long time.

CHAPTER NINE
LIKE TCHAIKOVSKY

Earlier, Yurka had felt pleasantly drawn to Volodya, looking forward to how they'd have fun talking and doing interesting things, but the next morning, after his "Great Discovery," the pull Yurka felt toward Volodya was agonizing.

This condition was utterly new and baffling. Yurka figured that the best and safest thing for him to do would be not to see or spend time with Volodya at all. If he'd been able to, that's what he would've done; he might've even picked a fight with Volodya on purpose. But at just the thought that he wouldn't hear Volodya's pleasant voice and he wouldn't see that special, soft, tender smile—the one Volodya smiled only for him—Yurka's heart seized up in agony. It was as though somebody had opened his rib cage and implanted a magnet that pulled him so strongly and painfully to Volodya that it felt as if it were about to break through his ribs and tear through his muscles. At least, that's what Yurka felt like that entire morning; he barely managed to make it to quiet hour.

Once quiet hour started, he and Volodya went on dry land to find the willow. After walking the entire bank by himself yesterday, finding the path was easy as pie. Walking along it to get to the willow, though, was much harder. The path looped and split and came together again between the trees of the thickly wooded bank, but not a single path led directly to the willow, so they had to break a new path right through the woods, getting caught in the tall weeds, pushing through thick bushes, and picking their way over tree roots sticking out of the ground. And while Yurka, who knew the area, felt as at home there as a fish in water, he had to keep a watchful eye on Volodya. Once, Volodya tripped on some unsteady sandy ground and almost fell off the cliff into the river, and another time he was making his way through a stand of rushes, didn't notice a boggy patch, and nearly got stuck in it.

But no matter how hard it was to get there, it was worth it. In full daylight the willow looked like a living tent, and they very much wanted to get into its shade, away from the awful midday heat. The leafy branches undulated all the way down to the ground, and the trunk of the tree was hidden behind the thick green foliage.

The boys spread the pliant, feathery branches apart with both hands and ducked into the space behind them. They found themselves in a miniature glade, covered with soft grass and delicate fallen leaves as though with a carpet. This carpet was soft and springy and begged for them to lie down and sink into it.

"It's light here, too!" Volodya exclaimed. His voice sounded muffled, absorbed by the green "walls" surrounding them. "I thought the sun wouldn't make it through such thick foliage, but look at those sunbeams there." And sure enough, a handful of sunbeams were slanting onto the grass, seeming preternaturally bright because there were so few of them.

Volodya had brought his radio with him. He turned it on and spent a long time looking for a station. When he found it, the music that came pouring out of the speaker, hissing and cutting in and out, was classical. Vivaldi.

"Let's find another station," suggested Yurka. "Something more fun. And something with better sound; on this one we can't hear anything because of the static."

"No, we're going to listen to classical," insisted Volodya.

"Ah, the hell with that! Try to find Radio Youth instead. That's a good station, it plays your Time Machine sometimes." Volodya shook his head. "Do you really not want to? But you love Time Machine!"

"And you love classical music. Who's your favorite composer?"

"If it's Russian composers, then Tchaikovsky," Yurka began, then interrupted himself. "What difference does it make? What are you doing this for?"

"And why Tchaikovsky, exactly?" asked Volodya brightly, ignoring Yurka's question.

Yurka realized that Volodya hadn't brought the radio along just because. He was trying to get something out of Yurka. But what? Yurka didn't understand. So he got angry.

"Volodya, what is this?!" He frowned and reached for the radio. "Give me the radio."

"I'm not giving it to you!" Volodya hid it behind his back.

"Are you making fun of me? Is that it?" exploded Yurka, sure that Volodya had turned on classical music deliberately. But what for? To torture him?

"Yur, listen, haven't you ever thought that you could try applying to the conservatory anyway? Sure, it'd be later than the others, but what does that matter?"

"No! I told you already,: they won't take me. I'm worthless! I'm not going to even try. So turn it off, now! Why are you taunting me like this?!"

"I'm not taunting you. All I'm doing is looking for a main theme for our show." Volodya looked at Yurka with a disarmingly honest expression.

"So what's with the interrogation about the conservatory, then?" scowled Yurka.

"Well, first of all, it wasn't an interrogation, it was one question. And secondly, it was just—just by the way."

"Oh. Just by the way. Okay, then." Yurka decided to play by Volodya's rules. "So why are you looking for something else if you've already decided to keep the Moonlight Sonata?"

"I didn't decide. I postponed the decision. And right now is the perfect time to look for a new song."

"No way Masha can learn something new in time," scoffed Yurka, unable to conceal his gloating.

"She'll have to, she's got no choice," Volodya said, waving aside Yurka's comment.

"In that case, maybe we should go to the library? It's quicker to find it by looking at the sheet music than by listening."

"What library? No time, Yura! We have very little time left. And if we do it this way, it'll be pleasant as well as productive. But if you'd just stop being mad and help me pick, the 'productive' would be even more pleasant. Help me out here! I don't know the first thing about music, you know. Without you, I'm completely adrift!"

"That's obvious. Who, given all the symphonies to choose from, picks the Moonlight Sonata?" But Yurka relented. "Oh, fine. If you're really completely adrift, then fine."

"I am, completely," said Volodya.

They settled in behind the green wall of branches hanging all the way down to the ground. They got out Volodya's notebook and pencil, to finish altering the script for Olezhka, but they kept getting distracted.

"'Air' from Orchestral Suite No. 3," proclaimed Yurka, without waiting for the radio announcer. Yurka recognized all the melodies from the first few notes. "Bach."

"No, it doesn't fit the show," Volodya mumbled listlessly. None of the pieces they had heard yet were a fit.

"And it won't work anyway unless you happen to have a symphony orchestra lying around somewhere," noted Yurka just as listlessly.

After "Air" from Orchestral Suite No. 3 ended, Yurka spoke up again. "Pachelbel's Canon. It sounds stupendous on the piano, by the way. But we can't use it, either. It's too happy."

"Really?" said Volodya, perking up. "Wish I could hear it . . . Would you maybe play it for me?" Yurka shot him a baleful look and Volodya quickly assured him, "Joking! Joking! Although . . . I would be interested in watching Mr. Yurka Konev in a suit, hair combed, back straight, sitting at a piano and playing diligently." Volodya chortled.

"So this is it, huh? And now you're never going to stop making fun of me?"

"Nope." Volodya smiled, but saw that Yurka was starting to brood again, so he went back to rewriting the text. "Okay, so we need a synonym of 'store.' They're storing the weapon in a hole, in a hollow log."

"'Stick it in the hole'? Hey, that works!"

Volodya laughed. "We'd better go with something like 'hide.'"

Two sentences and thirty minutes later, Yurka took the pencil from Volodya and sat down on the grass. He chewed on the pencil, lost in thought about yet another synonym. Volodya lay down wearily on his back next to Yurka, then closed his eyes and folded his hands behind his head, yawning. "I'm so tired, it's bonkers." Then he stretched so luxuriously that Yurka was infected with tiredness, too, his eyelids growing heavy, his body relaxing . . . A little more and he'd fall asleep himself . . .

But he resisted. He shook his head and lifted his eyebrows high to open his eyes. "So I wore myself out yesterday running around the woods, and then I didn't get enough sleep, but what made you so tired?"

"Oh, right, you probably think the troop leaders get to relax at camp just like the children, is that it? And that they don't get tired?"

"Well . . . okay, maybe not just like the children—obviously troop leaders aren't children—but I don't believe for a second that you all don't relax just as much as they do. Because you do nothing but give commands and order people around, then you lie around under a willow, kicking back while other people do all the work." Yurka smiled. "What, am I wrong?"

"You of all people know how exhausting children are! My nerves are all shot to hell because of them. And so if we troop leaders are going to get enough sleep and maintain our energy, we need extra time, sleep, and food. Especially food!" Volodya raised his index finger. "And this applies to all troop leaders, by the way, whether they're experienced or not. So whenever you see a troop leader, even the most seasoned one ever, know that he's hungry. And sleepy."

"I've never seen you suffer from a lack of energy."

"That's because I'm usually angry, and I'm energetic when I'm angry."

Yurka thought this conversation was hilarious. He laughed and said, "So go ahead and sleep, you angry old troop leader. Now you've got the chance."

"No, we haven't done our daily quota yet . . ."

"I'll do it. Sleep."

Volodya didn't take much convincing. He closed his eyes without taking off his glasses and immediately started breathing heavily. Seemed like he really was super-tired, seeing as how he'd fallen asleep instantaneously.

The radio was on. Mozart's Symphony No. 40 was rounding out the World Symphony Hour radio program. Rachmaninoff's Piano Concerto No. 2 opened the next program, the Russian Piano Music Hour. The sun sank to rest on the distant treetops during the concerto's tender second movement. One especially bright ray flashed as it pierced the willow's leaves and crawled slowly along Volodya's cheek toward his eyes. Yurka saw this and sat a little farther to the left so his shadow would cover Volodya's face. As he scribbled on the script, he remained almost motionless, trying not to move and accidentally let the sun bother Volodya or wake him up. He glanced at Volodya every so often to see whether he'd woken up.

A warm breeze gusted and blew up the edge of Volodya's shirt, revealing his belly button. Yurka stared at his concave stomach, at the pale skin as soft and delicate as a girl's. Yurka's was nothing like that. He put his hand under his own T-shirt, touched his stomach, and confirmed it: his skin was rough. Wouldn't it be nice to touch Volodya's . . . It was a passing thought, but it made it hard for Yurka to breathe, and heat burned his cheeks. Yurka wanted to turn away and keep working on the script, but he was frozen; he couldn't even move enough to look away . . .

The heat moved from his cheeks to his jawbones. His jaw throbbed. Yurka now felt a hunger to touch Volodya, not just a desire. But at the same time he was afraid: What if Volodya woke up?

Unable to control himself, without acknowledging what he was doing, Yurka stretched out a slow, tentative hand. Volodya sighed and turned his head to one side. He was still asleep. *He's so defenseless*, Yurka thought, bending over Volodya, arm extended. Yurka's fingers hovered just above Volodya's belly button. He grasped the edge of Volodya's shirt, and the thought came to him unbidden: *Am I brave enough?*

He wasn't. He sighed and pulled the fabric down over Volodya's bare skin. He turned away.

Flustered, he sat there without moving a muscle for so long, his feet fell asleep. On the radio, Rachmaninoff's Piano Concerto No. 2 was ending. It was at the last minute now, the best minute, Yurka's favorite part; it was so innocent and good. Unlike Yurka.

He flexed his back and shoulders and tried to get up, but—now, this was a fine pickle—when he stood up, he found that it wasn't just his back and shoulders that were stiff. Again! Prickly cold needles of alarm ran across his whole body. Yurka was unable to grasp how this could be happening. He was tormented by a nagging question: "What is wrong with me?"

"All done?" came Volodya's voice suddenly.

Yurka jumped. "Who, me? No, I was just over here . . . uh . . ." He hastily pulled his T-shirt down past his waist.

"What do you mean?" Volodya was confused. "You didn't finish rewriting it?"

"No," Yurka said warily. He leaped to his feet and whirled away from Volodya. He was too ashamed to look at him. Yurka tried to do some breathing exercises to calm down. A deep breath in and a slow breath out. In . . . out . . . in . . . out . . . It didn't help.

Volodya didn't speak.

Yurka was beset by thoughts, each one worse than the last: *Not this again! Why? What if he noticed? But he couldn't have; he didn't open his eyes. But what if he did anyway? What then? I'll say I remembered those magazines. It won't look good but at least he'll understand,* Yurka decided. But then he grew angry again. *But I didn't even do anything. All I did was think. I'm pretty sure I have the right to think what I want!* Then he started trying to calm himself down. *Volodya couldn't have seen, he couldn't have found out.* Still, calm eluded him.

What was it he'd heard from the guys from his building? He needed a cold shower? Yurka spat in frustration and started getting undressed. Volodya, meanwhile, sat up and looked at him skeptically. "Yur, what's up?"

"I'm hot," Yurka tossed back over his shoulder, falling over himself in his hurry to jump into the water.

They listened to the radio as they made their silent, leisurely way back to camp. One piece had ended and the next one had begun, and from the very first notes it jarred all thoughts out of Yurka's head. He could feel that he knew it, not in his brain, but in his body, and that he knew no other music the way he knew this. It was as though he heard not a piano, but a beloved, half-forgotten voice. His heart went so tight it was painful to breathe and his face drained of color. He stopped short. Volodya, who had kept walking for a few steps, turned around but didn't say anything.

"Do you hear?" whispered Yurka. His voice was hoarse and even a little frightened.

"Hear who? We're by ourselves."

"Not who, what—the music. This is it, Volodya! Just listen to how gorgeous it is."

Volodya held the radio up high until all the static was gone and stayed that way. He didn't move a muscle. The boys listened intently, afraid to breathe. Yurka smiled sadly as he looked down at his feet. Spots of red on both cheeks replaced his momentary pallor. Yurka saw Volodya notice this out of the corner of his eye, but he wasn't paying enough attention to process how strange and piercing Volodya's gaze was. Yurka wasn't paying attention to anything at all. He was entirely absorbed in the sounds, first delighting in them, then tormented by them, being warmed and scorched in turn.

"That really was gorgeous. Calm, harmonious . . . ," said Volodya once the composition had ended. "What was it?"

"Peetch," whispered Yurka grandly. He hadn't looked up yet. He couldn't even make himself lift his head, much less move from the spot.

"Peach?"

"Peetch—Pyotr Ilich Tchaikovsky. His 'Lullaby,' the second of his eighteen pieces for piano." Yurka spoke like a robot, without a single emotion.

Volodya, on the other hand, grew animated: "You know what—that 'Lullaby' is perfect for us. You were right when you said no nocturnes! This is just what we need! And it's a good thing it's Tchaikovsky. His music's guaranteed to be in the library. We have to go look right away . . ."

I hated it so much, and loved it so much . . . , thought Yurka, still deeply shaken. It was the one, his competition piece, the piece that had destroyed everything. But it wasn't the reminder of his failure that was tormenting him. What was suffocating him now was his memory of how happy he had been when music was part of his life, when it was the most important, most integral part. But what hurt even more was the reminder that it would never be that way again. Without music, there wouldn't be anything at all. There would be no "future." What awaited Yurka without music was merely "tomorrow."

"Okaaaay," Volodya said, in such a strained voice that Yurka looked up. "Yura, here's the thing: I'm sick of pretending I don't notice what's going on." Yurka choked: What had Volodya noticed? What?! But Volodya didn't beat around the bush, continuing, in a worried tone: "The day before yesterday you ran away from me through the forest, yesterday you went around pale as can be, today your breathing is labored and your face has this unhealthy flush . . . Since you're not going to tell me what's happening to you yourself, I won't ask anymore. I just want to suggest that maybe we go see Larisa Sergeyevna?"

"No, no, we don't need to. I'm fine, I just got some dust in my eye. I've got allergies. Didn't you know that?" Yurka spoke without thinking—anything to change the subject.

"But allergies don't manifest that way . . . ," Volodya tried to object.

"I'm especially sensitive. Come on," said Yurka, then turned and rushed ahead. Volodya followed him.

They were more than halfway along the winding path when Volodya mumbled hesitantly that he was afraid the battery wouldn't last long and turned the radio off. A heavy silence descended. Even the birds had gone quiet. Volodya kept opening his mouth and then closing it again without saying a word, as though he were trying to ask about something but couldn't work up the nerve. As they approached the dock he finally managed it. "So about that 'Lullaby' . . . is there maybe some important way it's connected to you? Don't take this the wrong way, but . . . going white like that because of music . . . it's strange."

"Volodya, I already told you everything about myself. There's nothing else. Why are you harping on secrets so much? It's like you have a whole cupboard full of them!"

"You know all my big secrets now, too. But I have others, of course. Just like everybody else."

"Then tell me the worst one!"

Volodya paused. After a moment he said hesitantly, "I've never had a friend like you before, and I probably never will again. And also, lately I've been seeing myself in you, so . . . Well, like I was saying, I avoid people. There's a reason for that, of course . . ."

And he went quiet. Clearly, he wanted to tell Yurka something that was genuinely important. Yurka could not only hear it in his tone of voice but read it in his tense posture and his clenched fists. His burning curiosity began to eclipse the alarm and sadness that had been brought on by hearing the 'Lullaby,' and the longer Volodya remained silent, the more his curiosity overshadowed them.

"Well?" Yurka, tired of waiting, couldn't stand it anymore.

"I'm like Tchaikovsky!" Volodya flung out.

"Like Tchaikovsky? How?"

Volodya turned and looked Yurka right in the eye. So directly that it made Yurka uncomfortable, so he blinked. But then Volodya's pensive mood seemed to evaporate all at once. He turned back into his businesslike, condescending troop leader self and announced firmly, "I like music."

"Well, duh, of course you do. Gee, thanks for the revelation!"

"Yur, come on, be serious: Do you really not know?" Volodya laughed. But his laugh was strange, hysterical.

"Know what?"

"About Tchaikovsky..."

"What don't I know? I know everything: where he was born, where he lived, how much he wrote, what he wrote... Oh! Here's something interesting: his last piece, Symphony No. Six, is called the Pathétique. 'Pathétique' means full of deep emotion, about life and death," he explained, unsure why he was still talking. "He wrote it, and he directed it, and then nine days after the premiere, he died!"

"Oh, well, that's good."

"What? What's good about that?"

"It doesn't matter."

"Tell me!"

Volodya's mysterious behavior was irritating Yurka. He started circling Volodya, begging him, "Tell me! Come on, tell me!" But Volodya just smiled awkwardly and shook his head no.

Yurka was frustrated. "I'm not leaving until you tell me!"

Volodya looked at the boathouse visible on the opposite shore and gave in. "I read his diary. It was translated into English, but it was complete."

"His actual diary? The thing he wrote with his own hand? Not his autobiography but his actual *diary* diary?" asked Yurka, stunned.

"You got it," replied Volodya, with a sly smile. His entire face had "Finally I know even just a teeny bit more about music than you do!" written all over it. He clearly enjoyed making this big of an impression on Yurka.

"I didn't know there was anything like that... but... So what's it say? And why isn't it in Russian? Is it really not in Russian?"

"It is, but the versions published in the USSR have been edited. They've had bits taken out."

"What do you mean, 'taken out'? Why? That makes no sense: Why should Americans get to know more than Russians? He's our composer!"

"But there's stuff there, in those diaries, that's... gratuitous."

"What?" Yurka's eyes lit up. He grabbed Volodya by the arm and shook him. "What is it? Tell me! What is it? Did it say what he was like? How he composed?"

"He was quite capricious. He suffered from bouts of rage. He drank. He drank a lot. He played cards. He had a mania for it, for cards..."

Yurka's face fell. "Well, then, it's a good thing that that's not in the Russian diaries. Let the Americans go on digging up all kinds of dirt about great Russians. We don't need that! Why would we need to know anything bad about Tchaikovsky? Why remember that? And anyway... But wait: Why are you bringing this up?"

"You asked. I answered. And I'm talking about all this not to sully his name but just to prove he was a normal person. Do you know anything about Tchaikovsky's personal life? That he was married but that he separated from his wife after a few days? You could even say he was never married at all."

"Married or not, what difference does it make? I have no interest in that. I'd rather you tell me how he composed!"

Volodya shot Yurka a look, then nodded. "Of course you're not interested in that. Rightly so. How he composed? On a schedule, every day. If he didn't write anything that day, he'd be upset, but he still composed every day. He listened to other people's compositions. Good ones, to take as examples. Popular ones, so he'd be in the know. Bad ones, so he could learn from other people's mistakes and avoid making them himself."

"Was he often dissatisfied with what he'd written?"

"Very often."

"And did he hear the music? I mean, while he was composing, did the music play in his head? Or before he wrote it down? I mean..."

"I understand. It did. But again, not always."

As they conversed about Tchaikovsky, they walked down to the river and crossed the shallows. They were so engaged that when they heard the bugle, they both flinched in unison from surprise. Only then did they come to their senses and hurry off to where the troops assembled. They ran into Masha, who was sitting out of breath on a bench by the athletic fields. They were so engrossed in conversation that they didn't reply to her muted "Hi."

Once he rejoined his troop, Yurka got into formation like the rest of them. But unlike the rest of them, he didn't listen to Ira Petrovna. He was thinking about how Volodya was right: even a great composer was, first and foremost, a human being. The same kind of human being as Yurka. And if a musical career was in store for someone Tchaikovsky's age, who chose music instead of a boring civil service desk job when he was already twenty-five years old—which, Yurka felt, was basically just plain "old"—then maybe all wasn't yet lost for Yurka, either? This thought, as unlikely as it was, cheered him. Somewhere deep inside him, desire sparked to life: the desire to sit down at the piano and play something lively and happy. Maybe Pachelbel's Canon?

After snack, Yurka was so loaded down with civic duty work that he was in danger of not finishing it until late at night. He tried asking Ira Petrovna's permission to get out of it, explaining that the script had to be finished today. But Ira was adamant.

"Come on, Ira Petrovna, let me out of it," he whined. "I really need to finish writing the script. Why don't you have me sit down and rewrite it right here next to you so you can see I'm not just trying to get out of work, I'm doing something!"

But his begging and persuasion had no effect on the troop leader: "Not a chance, Yura. These beds aren't going to make themselves. And don't get all mopey; together you and I will be done in no time."

"Together? That's unexpected . . ." Yurka was surprised, but glad at the same time. Being alone with Ira Petrovna meant the chance to ask a couple of important questions and try to get her to make peace with Volodya. Lately, this was all Yurka could think about every time he saw her.

It really did go quickly when they worked together. Yurka swept the floor while Ira Petrovna watered the flowers and wiped the windowsills. They checked that the beds in the boys' room were made and went over to the girls' room to check there as well. As they did, Yurka said, "They sent me to hang the strings of lights because I'm the tallest Pioneer, to haul mattresses with Mitka because I'm the strongest, to direct the show because I'm the most grown-up . . . But why am I fluffing pillows? Because I'm the laziest?"

"Because you haven't had this duty shift yet," Ira replied, offended. "Quit it. You imagine hidden motives everywhere you go."

"But what if I'm not imagining it? What if there really is one?"

"What are you getting at?" asked Ira stiffly. "Is this about Zhenya—"

But Yurka interrupted her: "No. Masha. Why did you think I was off with her that time?" He'd switched to the informal form of the word "you" in his eagerness.

"Don't pay any attention to that. I just thought that's what had happened."

"Fine, but why?"

"You two were the only ones out of the whole troop who were gone. And you and Masha are the most grown-up, so you're both probably already interested in . . . dating. It's nothing, Yur, it doesn't matter now."

"It matters a lot! You and Volodya got into a fight because of it!"

Ira shrugged and turned away. Yurka leaped into the fray. "Ira, forgive him, please! So he went a little crazy and said something stupid. He didn't do it to be mean. Volodya doesn't have a mean bone in his body. You're a troop leader yourself, you must know how hard a troop leader's first session is . . ."

Ira gave him a look of astonishment. She set a freshly fluffed pillow on the bed, corner up—a "sail"—and threw up her hands. "Well, now! Yury Ilych and I are so close, he tells me what I do and don't know and even addresses me informally! What an honor!"

"I mean it. You could at least hear him out."

Heedless of his troop leader's explanations and her obvious objection to the idea, Yurka kept defending Volodya until their shift was done and Ira began to give in.

"You're a stubborn one. But why are you speaking for him? If he wants to say he's sorry, he can come himself, not send his mediators."

"But he tried, though, didn't he? Today after breakfast, yesterday after the campfire . . ."

"Well . . ." Ira faltered. Instead, she gave the girls' room one last look. "Hey, see that? Ulya has more flowers. Not half a session in and she's already swimming in admirers."

But Yurka kept pressing her: "Volodya didn't send me. I came myself. This is his first session as a troop leader. You're the professional here, but he . . . Come on, please forgive him. He was tired, exhausted . . ."

"Okay, okay. Just tell him he has to come say he's sorry himself and then I'll forgi—" She broke off and corrected herself: "Then we'll see." She smoothed a blanket, surveyed the room again, and smiled in satisfaction. "We did a good job. You are free to go, Yury Ilych."

Yurka was proud of himself. As he walked out of the cabin, he decided to hold off on the script; instead of working on it, he'd go to his secret hiding place to celebrate his win with a victory smoke.

The year before, Yurka had made a hole for himself in the fence around the unfinished barracks. At the time, there was only a flat spot ready for construction, but now a hulking four-story building loomed there, like the ones in the big sanatoriums. In the spring, during active construction on the site, Yurka's hole in the fence was filled in, but even so, the site of the new building, surrounded on all sides by a tall fence, was the emptiest spot in the whole camp and still offered tons of hiding places. So Yurka found a place in a pile of broken concrete pavers to hide his cigarettes.

His whole body vibrated from the rush of adrenaline as he pulled the prized little package out from under a paver. He didn't even like smoking that much. It was the secrecy that made it attractive: getting the pack in the first place, and then, so his hands wouldn't smell, finding a slender twig, breaking it almost all the way in half, setting the cigarette in the middle, and lighting it. He didn't even have to smoke it, just light it and look around to see whether anybody might have seen him. And then, if anybody had, he'd take off so fast that even if they had seen him for sure, they'd never be able to catch him.

He stuck his hand under the paver and pulled out the pack, already anticipating his "sacrament." He found a twig, bent it in the prescribed manner, inserted the cigarette, and was getting ready to light it when he saw Pcholkin digging around in a pile of construction debris by the path leading from the unfinished barracks to the Avenue of Pioneer Heroes.

"Hey!" Yurka shouted, then froze, but too late: the cigarette was still in the twig, and the twig was still in his hand.

"Aha! I'm gonna tell everybody you smoke!" Pcholkin crowed.

"And I'll tell everybody you go poking around in the unfinished barracks. What are you doing here?"

"I'm looking for treasure! But you're here smoking!" Pcholkin stuck out his tongue.

"I'm not smoking. I'm just holding it. I mean, it's not even lit," replied Yurka as he thrust the cigarette in his pocket.

"I'm telling anyway! Or, wait—if you sing me a song with cusswords in it, I won't tell anybody." Pcholkin had stooped to blackmail.

"You aren't big enough for cusswords yet. I'll sing you whatever else you want," said Yurka, knowing that if the little boy told on him, he'd get into so much trouble at home that being kicked out of camp and separated from Volodya would seem like trifles in comparison.

Without condescending to respond, Pcholkin took off down the Avenue of Pioneer Heroes, shouting at the top of his lungs: "Yurka's a dummy, his cigarette is crummy, he smokes and steals and sneaks around, he flunks and fails and sleeps on the ground."

Yurka raced after him. Pcholkin turned toward the tennis courts. Using his short height to his advantage, he didn't run around the swings, steps, and athletic equipment; he just ran right underneath, easily darting through or behind them. But Yurka had to go around. If it hadn't been for that, he'd have caught Pcholkin right away, but as it was, he just shouted helplessly, "Stop! You'd better stop!" In reply he heard, "Yurka's a dummy!"

"Yura! Petya!" He heard the names, but his mind didn't process them. He ran and ran until at last Pcholkin was no more than half a meter away. All he had to do was stretch out his arm and grab him. But then a terrible voice thundered right in his ear: "Konev! Pcholkin! Attention!"

Both Pcholkin and Konev stopped dead in their tracks, giving in to their automatic, unconscious reaction of *You hear an order, you obey it!* Volodya walked briskly toward them across the tennis court. His face was pale, his fists were clenched, and he was glaring at Pcholkin as though he could strangle him just by looking at him.

"What's the meaning of this, Petya?! Where have you been?"

Pcholkin looked questioningly at Yurka, a mischievous grin spreading his lips. Yurka sighed. "Fine, I'll sing you one. But not that one."

"The one about the graveyard, then."

"Fine. The one about the graveyard."

"Deal!"

"What are you conspiring about?" interjected Volodya. "What are you planning? Yura?"

As soon as Yurka looked at Volodya's face, he understood the difference between an angry Volodya and a furious Volodya. So he hastened to, if not calm down the troop leader, at least distract him: "We aren't planning anything. I saw Petya on the path to the unfinished barracks. He was digging in the trash pile from the construction—"

"What for?!" interrupted Volodya, fixing Pcholkin with a hard stare. "Any injuries?"

"I was looking for treasure," squeaked Pcholkin as he displayed his healthy and uninjured knees, elbows, and palms to the troop leader.

"Petya, there is no treasure in the camp," Volodya ground out through gritted teeth. Yurka could tell that he was trying to calm down. But it wasn't working very well.

"But Yurka told us about it himself." Pcholkin gave an offended sniff.

"That treasure's made-up. Yura will confirm it."

Having assured himself the child was uninjured and was in fact standing live and well right there in front of him, covered in dirt from head to toe as one would expect, Volodya got himself under control. His voice became even, his breath grew calm, the gleam of his glasses was no longer fierce, and his eyes weren't shooting out bolts of lightning.

"Volodya's telling the truth. There's no treasure," said Yurka, confirming Volodya's words.

"Yes there is! Maybe it's not gold or jewels, but there is a treasure. And I was looking for it."

"Petya, I forbid you from going to the unfinished barracks. It's dangerous there. If you so much as poke your nose out there again, I won't let you go to the river for the rest of session. Is that clear?"

"You're the ones who tricked us, but now I can't go to the river. That's not fair!" said Pcholkin, offended.

"You can still go to the river. I'll let you off this one time. But don't you go near the unfinished barracks again," ordered Volodya. Then he turned sharply on Yurka and asked suspiciously, "But what were *you* doing there?"

"Just hanging around," he mumbled. The unlit cigarette was burning a hole in his pocket. Pcholkin smiled knowingly.

Yurka's conscience started bothering him. What kind of example was he giving Pcholkin? If he didn't tell Volodya the truth, then he'd be lying.

"I was smoking," he admitted. He saw Volodya set his finger on the bridge of his glasses and adjust them. He ducked his head. "Here it comes..." But contrary to Yurka's expectations, Volodya didn't start reading him the riot act. All he did was throw up his hands in frustration and mumble, exhausted, "Et tu Brute . . . Come on, Yura, how could you do that? You're in camp. Aren't you ashamed to do that in front of the children?"

"I am ashamed. I won't do it again. Pioneer's honor."

Yurka could tell that if it hadn't been for Pcholkin, the troop leader would've cursed him up one side and down the other, but as it was, it looked like he was going to get off easy. Volodya was bawling him out, but it seemed to be for show: "You're not foisting your 'Pioneer's honor' off on me. Give me your own word, on your own honor."

"I give you my word, on my honor." Yurka nodded, chastened.

"Okay, then," said Volodya, although he was still frowning. "Okay, Konev. But don't even try breaking my trust. Pcholkin, what do you have to say for yourself?"

"Octoberist's honor, I won't go to the unfinished barracks anymore."

Volodya shook his head and scoffed gently. "Oh, you two. What will I do with you?"

Yurka remembered that he wanted to tell Volodya about the chance for him and Ira Petrovna to make up, but just then the three Pukes bustled over. "What are *you* doing here? Did you come over to say the costumes are ready?" Yurka asked maliciously, while ignoring Pcholkin, who was pulling at his arm, clearly impatient for Yurka to sing the promised song.

Polina said hesitantly, "Um . . . yeah . . ." as she shot a look at Volodya.

"Well, not exactly," Ulyana admitted.

"No," Ksyusha summarized.

Just then the camp director walked over. "Ahem," he apologized.

"Hello, Pal Palych!" they all greeted him in unison. After he called Volodya away, Pcholkin began nagging Yurka: "Come on, Yura, come on, let's have it. You promised, so come on!"

Without answering him, Yurka began glumly:

> *"The Ivanov graveyard is sleeping,*
> *An icy mist blankets its ground;*
> *But the dear little dead in its keeping*
> *Woke up and are walking around."*

The next part was a little more fun:

"Come see me in my grave, come see me in my home,
Just come and see me, dear, we'll have a singalong,
Just come and see me, dear, we'll rot away together,
And the wiggly ol' worms will love us forever."

And then glum again:

"You'll press your yellowed bones close,
You'll kiss my skull tenderly . . ."

"That's not the right one!" protested Pcholkin indignantly. "It's the one about 'The cold wind howls in the graveyard, something something forty below, an old man sits in the graveyard, something something down below . . .' You know it! And then the gravedigger gets diarrhea, and the corpse crawls up out of his coffin and yells at him!"

Yurka sighed. "Fine." And he began reciting it.

Yurka knew the poem, of course. And Pcholkin knew it. Everybody knew it. And everybody was pretty darn tired of it. It's just that Pcholkin was obviously getting a kick out of seeing a grown-up recite it.

Once Petya had heard his fill and stopped pestering him, Yurka saw that the camp director had let Volodya go. Volodya was standing there looking around for someone. Yurka ran over to him to tell him about Ira, but first he inquired, "What did Palych want?"

"He wanted to apologize. He couldn't do it in front of everyone. It seems he's the quiet type when he's not yelling profanity in your face."

"He cussed you out?" Yurka figure he must've misheard. It wasn't possible that Pal Palych, the camp director, was capable of something like that. But evidently he was.

"He did. Piled it on, an hour ago, in front of the kids. Great pedagogy there, huh? What kids are going to listen to a troop leader after the director yells at him in front of them?"

"Well, he's just a—"

"Watch your mouth! There are children here!" barked Volodya angrily. But now Yurka knew why he was so irritable and didn't take it personally.

And there were indeed four girls from Troop Five next to them, shouting a tongue-twister at the top of their lungs: "ONCE THERE WERE THREE HANDSOME BROTHERS: YAK..."

Yurka frowned. "Why was he yelling at you?"

"... YAK-TSEEDRAK, AND YAK-TSEEDRAK-TSEEDRAK-TSEEDRONY..."

"Because of the show. Camp Barn Swallow Day is on Friday, but we don't have a single thing ready for it. It wasn't so much about a thing as about a person, though..."

"... ONCE THERE WERE THREE LOVELY SISTERS..."

"Was it me?" asked Yurka, horrified.

"Not you... another inmate..."

"Who?"

"Guess."

"... TSEEPA, TSEEPA-DREEPA, AND TSEEPA-DREEPA-DREEPAMPONI..."

"Pcholkin?"

"You got it."

"What a pest. So what's up, is there just no way to keep him under control?"

"He's the director's nephew. Any other questions?"

"... THEN ALL THREE BOYS WED ALL THREE GIRLS: YAK AND TSEEPA, YAK-TSEEDRAK AND TSEEPA-DREEPA, YAK-TSEEDRAK-TSEEDRAK-TSEEDRONY AND TSEEPA-DREEPA-DREEPAMPONI..."

"Can we step away?" begged Volodya.

They moved off a little to where it was more calm and quiet. The girls shouting their tongue-twister had made Yurka forget what it was he'd been waiting to tell Volodya. As he tried to remember it, he blurted out the first thing he could think of: "Why doesn't that Pcholkin come to drama club?"

"He's busy then. That's when he's in the model airplane club breaking model planes."

"A future construction engineer?"

"A current destruction engineer."

"Oh, just like Alyosha Matveyev! Except Matveyev's not the one who broke the lights. It was me. If it had been him, they'd have given him a reprimand! But I get threats!"

"Learn to do evil with an innocent smile on your face."

"Good advice. Hard to believe it came from a Komsomol member."

Volodya winked and said, "Okay, all joking aside: Palych warned me that tomorrow he and Olga Leonidovna are coming to rehearsal to see how the show is coming along. So, Yura, we've got to get that script finished today, even if it kills us. I've got a million things to do. Can you rewrite it without me? Does that work?"

"Sure. Sure I can," said Yurka slowly.

"Then you should get away from this oral folk art over here." Volodya indicated the girls, who were already re-wedding Yak and Tseepa, Yak-Tseedrak and Tseepa-Dreepa, and so on. Soon, Yurka knew, all the couples would start having children. "Go somewhere calmer, like your cabin. You'll get more done where it's quiet."

"Okay, sounds good," Yurka replied quickly.

"Yura, you're a man among men! Thank you! You're excused from rehearsal," Volodya said, then turned and headed off, calling back over his shoulder, "Meet me at the merry-go-round this evening if you need anything . . ."

"Volod! Hey, Volod!" Yurka caught up with him. "Wait. I just remembered: I convinced Ira to have a talk with you. Go find her today and make up with her, okay?"

"She didn't think it was weird for you to be the one to ask her about it?" Volodya clearly didn't like that. Although Volodya might have said thank you, instead of turning up his nose . . .

"All I asked was for her not to avoid talking to you," said Yurka, offended.

"Well . . . okay . . . ," said Volodya, preoccupied. He looked around as though searching for Ira but found Masha instead. "Oh, Masha! Masha, hi! If you're not busy, could you come over here?"

Masha raced over, smiling so happily, it was as though she'd been waiting all day for the invitation. She said eagerly, "Yes, yes, I'm not busy!" but then, self-conscious, blushed. Volodya nodded to Yurka, and he and Masha walked over to Lena so Volodya could transfer responsibility for the children to her for a while. Everything would have been fine except for one gesture Volodya made that caught Yurka's eye: as soon as Masha had run up to him, Volodya touched her shoulder in a way that was a little too friendly. The gesture was seemingly innocent and didn't mean anything special, but still, Yurka thought with distaste, *All he has to do is whistle and she comes running, perky as can be.* In the meantime he, Yurka, had been tasked with rewriting the text all by himself, as though his presence would somehow bother Volodya. All this made Yurka a little unsettled. But as soon as he got to his cabin, Yurka sat down to get some work done, and his vague misgivings dissipated immediately: he really did work very well in the quiet. How had Volodya put it? Oh, right: he'd get more done.

CHAPTER TEN
AN EVENING OF KISSES

Yurka surprised himself by finishing the edits to Olezhka's lines so quickly that he not only managed to make it to rehearsal, he arrived a few minutes early. Just knowing the script was now finished made him happy. He ran into the movie theater.

It was almost empty inside. There were only two people in the whole place, Masha and Volodya, because the rest of the cast was still spread all over camp with their shovels, brooms, and dustrags, doing their civic duty work. Waving the pages of the script over his head, Yurka ran up to the stage. Since he was concentrating on making sure he didn't trip and send all 175 centimeters of him plummeting to the ground, he didn't immediately realize that something in the movie theater had changed.

But then he stopped short, took a good look at the stage, and recoiled, stung by an unfamiliar sensation. Masha was onstage playing the piano while Volodya bent over her, listening. It was as though Yurka were waking up from a deep sleep. He listened for a moment, then all but dropped the script: Masha wasn't playing the Moonlight Sonata. She was playing another melody, one that was far more beautiful, a melody Yurka loved very much but hated even more. The unfamiliar feeling grew even more painful as he recognized Tchaikovsky's "Lullaby" through Masha's labored, stiff rendering. The very song he and Volodya had discussed. The song Yurka had failed his exam with.

Masha was playing it wrong. Masha was playing hideously, as though she wasn't even looking at the sheet music: first she'd go too fast in places where she should slow down; then she'd play too slow, and sometimes she'd just plain hit the wrong notes. The sounds went back and forth from blending in harmony to convulsing in cacophony. Yurka's head started pounding immediately from the caterwauling. But Volodya seemed to like it. He stood relaxed, elbows propped on the top of the piano, nodding in time with the music. Masha was very pleased with herself, occasionally tearing her eyes away from the keyboard to look at Volodya with lovelorn eyes and smile.

"Not bad, but you do need a little more practice," said the artistic director gently when she finished. "We don't have much time left. Do you think you can do it?"

Masha nodded. "I'll start practicing right now, while you're all busy rehearsing. Is that okay?"

"Of course," replied Volodya.

"Ah-hem!" coughed Yurka as loudly as possible, to signal that he was present.

Volodya stood up straight as soon as he saw Yurka. "Oh, hello! Is the script ready? Did you bring it?"

"Yes," replied Yurka coolly.

"Excellent. Oh, and I found a part for you."

"Where'd you come up with it?"

"It was always there. You just didn't bother to read the script all the way to the end." And Volodya was right about that. Yurka, focused as he was on Olezhka's lines, had completely forgotten about all the other parts. "The Gestapo officer Krause. It's a supporting role, but an important one. You don't have a lot of lines, but tomorrow you need to have them memorized so well you can rattle them off in your sleep. Do you think you can do it?" he said, echoing the exact words he'd said to Masha. Yurka squirmed.

He didn't want to. It didn't feel good to play a German, even one that ended up getting killed off later. Deep down, it felt to Yurka a little bit like a betrayal, even though he knew that was a big exaggeration. His grandmother had lost her husband to the Nazis; his mom, her father. Yurka himself had never seen his grandfather, not even a picture of him. But if he were going to refuse to play this part, he'd have to explain why. It was all his friends and family could talk about whenever they saw each other, every time they got together on holidays, to the extent that, in spite of everything, Yurka started to be ashamed of it. Yurka didn't want to have to talk about what he dismissively called his "dreary" family history, especially not in front of Masha.

He thought it was too banal, too Jewish, too similar to the stories of a thousand other families who'd lived in Germany, or in other occupied countries, during that time. His grandmother had told the story of how she lost her husband, and how she looked for him afterward, to everyone she met, as well as to Yurka himself. Yurka knew the tale by heart: how hard his grandfather had worked to get his pregnant grandmother out of Germany and into the USSR as the Holocaust escalated, trying and failing several times before he succeeded just before it would have become impossible. How his grandfather had intended to follow her but vanished, and how she had waited for him, and how she had searched for him later, obsessively, with the help of those of her relatives in Europe who had miraculously survived, and how she had traced him all the way to Dachau, and how, against all common sense, she had believed until the day she died that Yurka's grandfather might have escaped from the concentration camp . . .

His grandmother had died, so this story had stopped being told, but evidently it was now Yurka's turn to tell it. He was capable of sharing something like this with Volodya, but with Masha? No. Not for anything, not ever.

"Fine," Yurka mumbled listlessly, reaching out to take the piece of paper on which Volodya had copied out Yurka's lines by hand. In a monotone, Yurka read, "'My brave Fräulein, I am aware that your parents remain in Leningrad. And I am also aware that your beloved city has fallen. A new flag flies above it. But I assure you that all you have to do is agree to a small compromise and share a few bits of information with Hitler's army command, and—'"

"No, not now," Volodya interrupted him. "Memorize it first. We'll rehearse it later. Right now we'd just bother you, though, so you can . . . you're free to go."

"Come again?" Yurka's mouth fell open. He was flabbergasted. "What are you doing, kicking me out?"

"No, no!" Volodya hastened to explain. "I'm just giving you your day off. You've earned it. You can learn your lines, or you can just relax—you've worked a lot already. But, anyway, just do what you want."

Yurka stayed, of course. All his previous enthusiasm had evaporated. His mood hadn't just fallen a little, it had collapsed in a heap. Even when

Olezhka showed up and Volodya presented him ceremoniously with his new lines, and Olezhka thanked them both and began practicing them, it didn't make Yurka feel the least bit better.

Once the entire cast had arrived, the kids started running through individual scenes from the show. Volodya capably instructed the young performers while Polina and Ksyusha, eyes alight, whispered about something, but the crestfallen Yurka sat in his usual spot in the front row, fighting the urge to put his fingers in his ears: Masha was plinking the piano keys as she worked on the music, and Yurka couldn't listen to someone else performing his competition piece.

He had played the "Lullaby" so many times in his life that he felt like he hadn't just performed it, he'd composed it. He had spent so many hours hearing it in his head, he had spent so many hours sitting at the piano, memorizing it, experimenting with it, looking for the ideal sound and trying to figure out how Tchaikovsky himself had imagined the piece. Yura had spent so much energy on the "Lullaby" that it felt like it belonged to him. But now somebody else was playing it!

Masha. She was trying to run through it in her head, trying to get to know it, trying to adjust her heartbeat to fit its tempo and rhythm and make it the music of her soul. But the worst of it was that she was only playing the "Lullaby" to please Volodya. To make him like her. And it was working! Every so often he'd step away from rehearsal and go over to Masha and nod in satisfaction as he murmured something. It looked to Yurka like he was praising her.

Apparently, Yurka was the only person who knew Masha wasn't playing it right; that she was playing badly, playing it totally wrong! He knew he could play it way better and that Volodya would like it way more. But making himself even walk up to the keyboard was worse than death.

Masha just kept on playing and playing. She'd finish and then begin all over again, then finish again and begin again. Finally, Yurka couldn't take it anymore.

He leaped up onto the stage and was barely able to restrain himself from slamming the cover down on Masha's fingers and flattening them. "Stop it!" he shouted. "That's enough, I'm telling you!"

Masha snatched her hands back from the keyboard and stared at Yurka, frightened. A tense silence hung in the air. Everyone who was there froze in the middle of whatever they were doing: Olezhka, looking through the tube of his rolled-up script as if it were a spyglass; Volodya, caught in midair as he was sitting down in his seat in the audience; Polina and Ksyusha, covering their open mouths with their palms. They all turned their heads and were now watching Yurka closely. But he didn't care. He had lost control of himself.

"Masha, that's nauseating!" he exclaimed. "You're playing the 'Lullaby' like it's some kind of polka! Where's your accompaniment racing off to? Why is it drowning out the main motif? And why so loud so soon? Right here," he said, stabbing his finger into the sheet music, "it has to be more tender. And why aren't you stepping on the pedal? Can you not feel the music at all? Do you not understand in the slightest how this piece has to sound?!" He caught his breath. Then he went on, more quietly but far more angrily, grinding the words through gritted teeth: "Masha, you're utterly worthless!"

For a couple of seconds, Masha was still as a statue, processing what she'd heard. Then her lips began trembling. Yurka saw that she was trying to say "Look who's talking," but she was gasping so hard for air that she couldn't speak. Then she burst into quiet tears.

"Bawl all you want! It won't change anything!" announced Yurka. Immediately he felt someone grabbing him by the elbow and pulling him away.

"We're going to step out now," Volodya hissed in his ear, pulling him off the stage and toward the exit.

They went all the way to the far side of the outdoor stage, where nobody who was inside the movie theater could hear them through the open windows.

"Yura, what was that?!" Volodya exploded. "What do you think you're doing?!"

But Yurka scowled and wouldn't talk.

"For crying out loud, Yura . . . Don't you think you went a little too far?" asked Volodya, a little calmer now. He leaned back against the wall with a sigh and closed his eyes wearily. But Yurka felt so hollowed-out inside that he didn't even have the strength to raise his voice.

"Quit lecturing me," he groaned. "Is that why you asked me to leave? Because you knew I'd shout at her?"

"Yes," Volodya replied simply.

"Am I really that predictable?" This idea made Yurka even more dejected: Was he really so simple that even reactions as deeply personal as these could be seen coming a mile away?

"No," said Volodya without pause. "It's just that I care about what you say."

Yurka, surprised, lifted his head to look at Volodya, but he must've anticipated this reaction, too, because he wasn't looking back. An awkward silence dragged on.

Yurka didn't know what to say, or whether he needed to say anything at all. He did know one thing: he didn't want Volodya to leave yet.

"Do you at least see that you did something cruel?" Volodya finally deigned to look at Yurka directly—right in the eyes—and more sternly than ever before.

"Cruel?" Yurka scoffed. "Masha's the one who's being cruel. She doesn't have a clue about what she's playing, Volod! This is classical music, it's difficult, it's impossible to understand in ten minutes! You can't just pick up the music, look at it, and play. You have to feel it. You have to immerse yourself in the music, put yourself into it, let it flow through you. My ears bleed listening to Masha's tedious struggling! Tchaikovsky would roll over in his grave if he heard that!"

Volodya listened to him, alternately raising and then lowering his brows.

"Do you understand?" Yurka had wound down and was now completely played out. "You don't understand anything. You have to live and breathe music, the way I did, to understand . . ."

"I understand the gist," Volodya said. "Maybe not as well as you, but still . . . You're going through a hard time, but that doesn't change the fact that you treated Masha badly. Look, Yur—I'm the only one who really knows about your musical past. And Masha had nothing to do with all this. When the parts were being distributed, she was designated to play the piano, so what am I supposed to do now—" he broke off. "I'm not going to kick her out of the show!"

"I'm not asking you to! But don't let her play the 'Lullaby,' it's impossible to listen to that!"

"How about you don't tell me don't? And if it's so hard for you to listen to her, play it yourself! You know the piece, you know how to play it better—"

"No!" Yurka cut him off sharply. "Don't even think about it.'

"But why?"

"Because I said so! I can't, and that's that!"

"So what do you suggest? You don't like how Masha plays, but you don't want to play yourself—"

"I'm fine with Masha playing, just not that!"

"But it fits the show perfectly! And Masha fits. But you—"

"I can't stand to listen to the 'Lullaby' being played like that!" Yurka burst out, interrupting Volodya. "Don't you understand? That's my piece, the one I flunked out of music school with!"

Volodya's face changed. "Oh, so that's it," he said. "Yurka, why didn't you tell me earlier?"

"I don't know! It's embarrassing, okay? And now here's Masha, playing it every which way, and I—"

"And you still have to say you're sorry," Volodya said. "You need to ask her to forgive you."

"Yeah, right! I'm not asking anybody for anything! Ever!"

Volodya rolled his eyes. Then he shook his head and smiled in that patronizing way he sometimes did. "So you are a child after all."

"You're the child! I'm not afraid of apologizing. It's just Masha; she—she drives me crazy!"

Volodya scoffed and gave a shrug. "Girls are always driving you crazy, everywhere you look."

"That's not true!" shouted Yurka, although he was horrified to realize Volodya was right. To cover it up, he admitted, "I liked one girl. Anya. She was here last year but didn't come this year."

"Oh . . . so that's it." Volodya's smile went from condescending to artificial. "What about this session? Nobody at all?"

"Well . . . I don't think so." Yurka paused; then, succumbing to a sudden reckless impulse instead of rational thought, he all but gave himself away: "I mean . . . there is somebody . . . but for hi—for *her* I don't exist."

He'd just cut off his oxygen with his own words. His head started spinning, and he felt sick to his stomach, and a clammy fear constricted his throat. A thought pounded in his head: *Now! Tell him now. You won't get another chance like this!* But he couldn't bring himself to do it. He stared directly at Volodya, face-to-face, without a word.

The remnants of Volodya's smile fell away. He was looking Yurka right in the eyes, just as directly, but where Yurka's gaze was soft and questioning, Volodya's was demanding.

"Who is it?" he asked seriously.

"A girl from my apartment building back home," Yurka said. Even as he did, though, he thought, what if he took the risk and told him? What would happen then? It wouldn't hurt anybody. And after all, whatever Yurka's older comrade said in reply might be useful for Yurka in the future. Because, to tell the truth, Yurka didn't have any close friends, just "guys from my building," and all they were good for was a few laughs, nothing personal or honest. This might be his only chance to tell anyone about this.

"You just like her? Or . . . or is it more than that?" Volodya's voice had turned cold and hoarse; his voice was so foreign, so rude in tone, that Yurka didn't even recognize it.

That tone didn't fit. It didn't fit either Volodya's face or the situation. Although the situation seemed unreal to Yurka, too—a Pioneer camp, Pioneers, summer, the heat—inside he was cold. It was like Yurka wasn't here but in some gloomy November, looking at himself and Volodya from the outside. It was like he was watching two movies at the same time, the sound from one and the picture from the other.

"It's more than that," Yurka sighed. He turned away, unable to bear Volodya's bleak gaze.

"Ah. That's good," replied Volodya.

"That's good?!" Yurka was astonished. "Nothing good about it! I think I . . . I'm in love, probably . . . I don't know. I'm not sure. It's just that nothing like this has ever happened to me before. And there's nothing good about it! It's hard for me, I don't know what's going on."

"But what makes you say you don't exist for her? Have you told her?" Volodya shuffled his sneaker back and forth along the pavement, examining the bushes, so he saw neither Yurka's face nor Yurka's pose.

"No. It's useless," whispered Yurka sadly. "She's not . . . uh, she, uh, moves in different circles. She's never liked people like me, and she never will. She just doesn't even notice me like that. She looks at me but doesn't see me. For her, it's like I don't even exist in that way. But there's nothing to actually blame her for here. Or me either, probably. That's just the way things are."

"Neither of you are to blame, for anything. But you know, for some reason I don't believe she just doesn't notice someone who's such a troublemaker." Volodya's tone had changed, gotten warmer.

That warmth, and his words, and the knowledge that Volodya genuinely wanted to support him, all lent Yurka courage. So Yurka dared to ask the crucial question: "What if you were in my position? What would you do? Would you say anything, being a thousand percent certain there's no chance of it being mutual?"

"But what would you lose if you said something?"

"Everything."

"Come on, don't be so dramatic about it."

"I'm not being dramatic. That's how it is. If she finds out, her attitude toward me will change and nothing will be like it was before. And that means I'll lose what I have now. And what we have now is the best we're ever going to get."

"Is it really that hopeless?"

"Absolutely." Yurka nodded and repeated, "So? What would you do?"

Volodya sighed and cracked his knuckles. Yurka looked up and saw Volodya adjust his glasses. But not by the arms, like always; he did it the way he did when he was agitated about something, awkwardly shoving the bridge of the glasses up his nose with one finger.

Volodya, sensing he was being looked at, turned away from Yurka and said harshly, without thinking: "If I'm in love with someone, then I have an interest in making sure that person is *happy*." Volodya emphasized the last word. "And I have a greater interest in that person's happiness than anyone else does, even the person themself. And so I will only do what's good for the person. And if that requires me to stay away from the person, then I'll stay away. In fact, if it'd be better for that person to be with somebody else, then I'll not only step aside, I'll push the person to be with that somebody else."

"But how are you yourself supposed to go on, then?"

"You just keep going the way you've been going." Volodya shrugged.

"Doing everything for the sake of another person? Sacrificing yourself? That's crazy talk . . . ," scoffed Yurka. Evidently Volodya was too grown-up after all, and Yurka was still just a child, because he didn't understand Volodya. Not in the least. Or did he not want to understand? Or was he afraid of sharing the same fate?

Volodya replied harshly: "What makes you think 'sacrificing' is the right word? A sacrifice is voluntary. You don't have to make it. But this is entirely different: you don't have a choice. And there's no other way out of it, either. Think about it, Yura: if you have everything you want, and you're completely happy, but she's unhappy, how will you feel? Nothing else will matter if you find out the person you love is suffering!" Volodya's words were forceful, stony, each one louder than the last. "Yur, listen: if you find yourself worrying about what *you'll* get when you do something for the person you love, then you're an egotist. And if that's the case, then I've got good news for you: it's not love. Because there's no egotism in love."

Yura was listening closely but couldn't find anything to say in reply. One thing was clear, though: if Yurka had Volodya's brains, he'd have already understood by now that what he was feeling wasn't some kind of "love." What he was feeling was childish nonsense. It was so logical, so simple, so self-evident!

A wave of relief washed over Yurka. His feelings for Volodya would pass. And that meant everything was fine. And everything was definitely temporary. And he'd definitely make peace with himself again, if he could just be patient.

But that would be later. Right now, though, Yurka had to find something to say to Volodya, if for no other reason than to keep their conversation from ending on such an unpleasant note.

Barely able to restrain a smile, Yurka murmured the first thing that came into his head, regretting it the minute he said it: "You talk as though you . . . as though you know what unrequited love is. You didn't just come up with that out of thin air, though, right? You've gone through something like that yourself?"

"I have," Volodya answered, not looking at Yurka. After a short pause he crossed his arms and croaked angrily, "And I still am."

An avalanche of ambiguous feelings plowed into Yurka. He was overjoyed that Volodya had trusted him, overjoyed that he'd uncovered a new side of Volodya that was hidden from other people. But at the same time he burned with raging jealousy that he wasn't the girl Volodya was talking about.

Yurka wilted. "Why aren't you with her?" he mumbled lamely.

"Because it's best that way."

"But where did you get the idea that the girl you love will be better off with someone else than with you?"

"I didn't 'get the idea.' I know."

"But won't she be better off with someone who's willing to do anything for her? Someone who loves her so much?"

"With another person like that, yes. But not with me."

"But why?"

"Because I'm no saint, Yura! Don't try to get me to prove anything to you. You can't make me."

"Fine. Have it your way." Yurka floundered, then remembered and woodenly repeated Volodya's question: "Who is she?"

"I'm not telling. It's too personal," Volodya shot back.

"Don't trust me? And you call yourself a friend . . ."

"Think what you want. I'm not telling."

"At least tell me her name, because we'll have to refer to her somehow when we talk about her ag—"

"We won't be talking about her again."

Yurka wanted to be offended by this, but didn't have the heart. He, of all people, knew exactly what it was to be afraid to reveal even a name. But, on the other hand, Volodya's response, "I'm not telling," was worded in such a way that Yurka couldn't stop thinking about it. Because Volodya could've fobbed him off with something vague, like Yurka did: "a girl from my building." Or "a classmate." Or he could've just said any random name. But no! What he'd said was "I'm not telling," as though any information, even a name or brief description, could point to a specific person. So why the secrecy? Was she famous or something? Or . . . maybe Yurka knew her? Maybe she was someone at camp?

Volodya interrupted Yurka's musings. "Enough about me. What about you? You don't want to even look at anybody else? There are lots of pretty girls around."

"Nobody like her, though. And what difference does it make? Even if I liked one of them, they don't like me." He shrugged. "I'm not you. Every last one of them has fallen head over heels for you."

"Yeah, right. 'Every last one of them,'" Volodya scoffed.

"Most of them. And our group—it's not the drama club, it's your fan club! It's the Vladimir Davydov harem!"

Volodya snorted. Encouraged by the smile that had flashed across Volodya's face, Yurka continued in that vein: "I told you how the girls harassed me, trying to get me to bring you to the dance . . ."

"Yeah, I remember that," replied Volodya, a little less somber now.

"Ksyusha was going to have to kiss me in front of everybody for that . . . on the cheek . . . twice!"

"Oho!" said Volodya, and clicked his tongue.

"I know! I'd kind of forgotten about that, actually . . ."

"Do you want her to?"

"Well, duh!"

Volodya considered this for a moment.

"So listen," he said softly, making up his mind about something. "Since this is important, want me to go to the dance? I'll go today."

"Of course I do!" Yurka could already see how shocked Ksyusha would look when he informed her he'd done his part of the bargain and was waiting for her to do hers.

"Done! As soon as we finish, I'll go get Lena to switch with me. And for now let's get back to rehearsal. We've still got half an hour left."

"You go on," said Yurka, waving his hand dismissively. "First of all, I'm taking a day off today, and second of all, you don't need me anyway. I'll go on a walk and get some air before the dance. We'll meet by your cabin on the merry-go-round."

Volodya nodded and headed over to the theater. Yurka raced over to his hiding place on the construction site of the unfinished barracks. He needed to get the cigarettes Pcholkin had caught him with and move them to a different hiding place. There was probably a reason Pcholkin kept talking about some kind of hidden treasure: What if he meant Yurka's smokes? Yurka hadn't dared revisit the scene of the crime earlier, but now was the perfect time.

Once he had the incriminating evidence in hand, he returned to the movie theater, walked around to the back of the building, and clambered through the bushes there to his second hiding place. It didn't hold a candle to his first hiding place, being small and narrow; a small chunk of mortar near the bottom of the wall had come loose, revealing a small crack where he could fit his cigarettes, then cover them up by replacing the chunk of mortar. But Yurka wasn't ready to part with them yet.

Club hour was about to end. Yurka took advantage of the fact that for the moment, all the Pioneers were busy with clubs, either inside a building or on the athletic fields, so nobody was out where they could see him. He took out the pack of filtered Javas and a box of matches, struck a match, lit the cigarette, and inhaled with pleasure. Even though he'd promised Volodya he wouldn't smoke anymore, he just had to calm his nerves now, after such an emotional upheaval. He wanted to take a moment to settle himself... and also to try and figure out who this mysterious stranger of Volodya's was. Maybe she wasn't even a stranger at all?

Apart from the girl campers, there were only two other girls at Camp Barn Swallow, both of them troop leaders: Lena and Ira Petrovna. Yura refused to even consider that it might be the unashamedly plain Lena. He knew it wasn't okay to think like that, and he was embarrassed of his opinion, but he couldn't help himself. They didn't go together at all, not even in the slightest. Also, Volodya was always all business anytime he interacted with Lena. Yurka knew he couldn't definitively exclude her as a possibility, but in spite of himself his thoughts turned to Ira, who was more attractive—to him, at least.

But his theory about Ira also fell apart immediately, because Volodya was so gallant, he would never have hurt her like that if he had feelings for her. Still, Yurka remembered Volodya's comment about how he'd be capable of pushing the girl he loved away if it was for her own good, so Yurka couldn't rule out that Volodya had said that for a reason. Maybe Ira could be Volodya's secret passion after all.

Yurka's imagination painted a vivid picture of Volodya going to have a tryst with Ira Petrovna late at night when everyone else was asleep. In the dark, in the quiet, his mask of calm would fall away and then it would be a completely different Volodya, one who was sincere, ardent, and flustered, whispering to Ira about his feelings. Maybe he'd even kiss her, ask her to hold him . . .

Yurka scoffed in disgust. He clenched his fists in a sudden fit of anger that fell on him out of nowhere. He was barely able to restrain himself from hitting the wall of the movie theater, instead using a fist just to scratch his nose.

Still, on the other hand, what did they have to hide? Yurka knew from camp gossip that neither Ira nor Lena were married. So was it because of Zhenya? But what would be keeping Ira from just breaking up with Zhenya, then? The answer was obvious: Volodya himself was keeping them together. He'd just said that his beloved would be better off with another person.

But what didn't make sense was why it was a big deal. She was a troop leader, he was a troop leader . . . As long as they didn't start parading themselves around in front of everybody's faces, nobody would even think to judge them for it. Volodya couldn't just be afraid of gossip, could he? Even if he were, he, of all people, would know Yurka could keep a secret. Volodya had shared the kind of secrets that could mean expulsion from the Komsomol; even just the thing about wanting to go to America—! An affair with a troop leader was nowhere near as bad as that. Whatever it was, it couldn't be worse than what Volodya had already entrusted to Yurka.

That meant that it couldn't be a troop leader, then. So who was it? One of the girl Pioneers? That would be really bad. Being kicked out of the Komsomol was punishment enough for a lot of things, but not for an affair with a Pioneer. Volodya might well ruin his own reputation—and, worse, hers—for decades to come. People didn't joke about that kind of thing; people didn't betray that kind of secret, not even under torture, especially if their beloved's happiness, which was precisely what Volodya cared about, would be put at risk . . . If Yurka were him, Yurka would've kept quiet, too. He was keeping quiet about himself.

But still—who was she? If it really was one of the girl Pioneers, then which one?

As he clamped the cigarette in his teeth, the smoke blew back into his right eye, making him squint. He tucked the pack into the crack, replaced the chunk of mortar, and pushed his way back out of the bushes. His gaze chanced to fall on a window through which he could clearly see the entire stage and audience. What he saw happening there made his eye, already teary from the smoke, start twitching spasmodically.

It was like Yurka was watching a silent movie. The cast members filed out of the movie theater, leaving those same two people inside: Masha and Volodya. She still hadn't calmed down yet. She was hunched in a seat in the first row of the audience, face buried in her hands, shaking. Once the door closed behind the last actor, Volodya sat down beside her. He whispered something in her ear. Yurka expected him to then get up and leave, but the troop leader kept sitting beside her. He kept talking to her and rubbed her back and stroked her hair. It looked... romantic. Too romantic. It actually looked intimate, as though they were... together.

What if they really are *together?* thought Yurka, and the strange stinging sensation shot through him more painfully than ever. The pain surged from a tiny speck in the pit of his stomach and flooded his belly and chest. It swelled, burning and pulsing, like a boil. Physically unable to keep looking at them, Yurka angrily stamped out his cigarette and fled back to his troop cabin.

He walked into the boys' room, collapsed on his bed, stared at the ceiling, and tried to make himself calm down. Then he remembered something that brought him relief: these feelings would soon pass. And he felt better. He was an egotist after all, which meant that his feelings weren't actually real. It was just a delusion. Yurka probably just missed Anechka so much this session that he'd unknowingly transferred all his attention to the only person who was close to him, who he enjoyed being with: Volodya. Who would've thought? And that's how the troop leader became the object of Yurka's strong but purely friendly affections. That was it. Just Volodya instead of Anya. Pretty awkward.

The Troop One boys all came bursting into the boys' room and raised a racket as they retold a story about Alyosha Matveyev almost pulling down the basketball hoop. As he laughed along with the others, Yurka could feel his anger and hurt feelings draining away by the minute as his mood began returning to normal. It wasn't what you'd call a good mood yet, since traces of despair were still echoing inside him, but Yurka had an idea of what would raise it to that level. He went over to the girls' room right after dinner to tell Ksyusha that today he'd finally be bringing Volodya to the dance.

The girls' room was noisy with arguing and shouting. All the girls in the room, even Masha, were squeezed into the corners or flattened against the walls, leaving the space in the middle for the Pukes, who were on the verge of a fistfight.

"Why did you throw my hairspray away?!" shrieked the enraged Ksyusha.

"There wasn't any left!" Ulyana shouted in her own defense, white as a sheet. Her friend's reaction had obviously surprised her.

"Yes there was! There was a little left at the very bottom, it would've been just enough for my bangs!" Ksyusha's bangs, which were sticking straight out in front of her, were trembling as much as her chin. "You go get it back out of the trash!"

"Girls, I looked in our trash. It's not there," Polina interjected, trying to calm her friends down. "Ul, maybe the dumpster hasn't been emptied yet? Why don't you look there?"

"Why don't you go digging around in the dumpster!" said Ulyana, outraged. She was pale not from fear, as Yurka had thought at first, but from anger.

Yurka's mood brightened instantly when he realized how viciously the Pukes were fighting.

Polya tried to calm them down again. "Come on, girls, don't fight, okay? I asked my mom and she's bringing hairspray, two cans of it! She's definitely bringing it!"

"And when is that?" Ksyusha was almost crying. "Camp Barn Swallow Day isn't until Friday! What am I supposed to do until then?"

"When I tease my bangs, they stay up just fine without any spray at all!" Polya the peacemaker assured them.

"Oh, Ksyuuushaaa!" sang Yurka, poking his head in the doorway. "I've got news for you. There's good news and bad news. What do you want first?"

"What is it?!" all three Pukes asked in unison. The rest of Yurka's girl troopmates stared at him, eyes narrowed inquisitively.

"Fine, I'll start with the good news. Guess who's coming to the dance tonight?"

"What?!" Ksyusha actually fell to a seat on her bed. Her shaggy bangs fell in a clump onto her face. Apparently this good news was bad news to her. "Oh come *on*! Who does this, Konev? Why today? Why not yesterday, or on Camp Barn Swallow Day, or literally any other day when I have hairspray?!"

"You don't need to thank me," Yurka said magnanimously. "But you do owe me something instead of thanks, remember? And that's the bad news."

"What kind of person *are* you, Konev?!" she cried again. "I remember already! I remember!"

"And it has to be twice, not just once! You remember, right?" Yurka was unable to restrain himself any longer and broke into a broad, malicious grin.

All the girls except the Pukes turned their heads to stare first at Yurka, then at Ksyusha. Brazen, she didn't even turn red. But Yurka did. Not from embarrassment, though. From barely suppressed laughter. Her anguish was hilarious to watch.

"I said yes, didn't I?! Oh, Ulya! Why, oh, why did you throw away my hairspray?!"

The apple trees around the dance floor had been decorated with strings of lights. They flashed and sparkled, embellishing the evening's deep blue with their yellows and reds. Music poured from the speakers. San Sanych, the facilities manager, was working the sound and light equipment that had been set up on the stage. The on-duty troop leaders, armbands in place, were patrolling the dance floor as the Pioneers danced their hearts out.

Familiar faces from the older troops appeared here and there. The boys—each and every one of them all dressed up, hair painstakingly combed, and smelling of cologne—were casting searching glances this way and that. The girls—each and every one of them all made up, painstakingly dressed in the latest trend, and flaunting teased bangs—were hanging around in languorous expectation, flirting, making eyes at the boys, and trying out shy little dance moves.

For ten minutes or so, Volodya and Yurka stood around under the apple trees, out of the limelight, watching the others. But as soon as the troop leader came around the row of chairs on the far side of the dance floor and joined the dancers under the roving rays cast by the light equipment, it was like a wind blew through the crowd. The first to notice them was Katya from Troop Two. She pointed at Volodya and leaned over to whisper in the ear of first one friend, then another, and the news flew with the speed of sound. Not a minute had passed before Volodya was surrounded by the twittering Pukes, and Masha, and another pair of the bravest girls. Yurka actually felt a little sorry for him, seeing the expression of obvious despair on Volodya's face.

After a minute of this, Volodya somehow extracted himself from the bevy of clingy girls. He grabbed Yurka by the shoulder and pulled him to one side. He sat down on a chair and caught his breath.

"What's up?" Yurka asked him. "Aren't you going to dance?"

"Why?" replied Volodya, surprised.

"What do you mean, 'Why?'? Because we're at a dance, that's why! People dance at dances! It's fun!"

"Not really, not when you can't dance," said Volodya deprecatingly.

"Well, let's just go lurch around to the music. Look at Matveyev busting a move over there!"

Alyosha Matveyev considered himself an avant-garde kind of guy, so he was dancing in a strange way that looked contrived and jerky. First he waved both his hands around up in the air, something like a broken marionette, or maybe a working robot. Then he plopped down onto the asphalt and waved his feet around the same way. Alyosha had once explained to Yurka that it wasn't actually convulsions; it was a dance: "It's really hot right now in Moscow, Leningrad, and the Baltics! It's called 'breakdance.' It's so cool! But yikes—what a hard dance." Yurka decided that when he got a minute, he'd find out from Volodya whether kids in the capital knew about it. But when he saw the undisguised skepticism on Volodya's face, he decided to ask some other time.

"No, thanks. I'm definitely not going to do any 'lurching around,'" scoffed Volodya.

"Aw, come on! Are you not going to dance at all? Not even a slow dance?"

"With who?" said Volodya, blushing.

Yurka snorted. "You mean with which one?! Look how many candidates there are! Every girl here is yearning for you to ask her."

It was true. Yurka looked around and noticed girl after girl gazing hopefully in their direction. Most of them were looking at Volodya pleadingly. Half of them were probably thinking, *Well, why not? What if I'm the one he asks?*

But Volodya shook his head. "It won't look right if I dance with just one of the girls. What if the others get mad at her? So . . . and besides, I didn't come here to dance, but to see Ksyusha kiss you. Go get her. She's over there." He gestured to where the Pukes were standing. "I'm here, so you've fulfilled your part of the bargain. Time for her to pay up." Volodya was clearly in a good mood, chuckling as he talked.

Yurka smirked and walked over to the Pukes. He was bursting with confidence. With impudence, too.

"Hey, Ksyukha!" he called loudly. "Here I am!"

All three of them stared at Yurka in surprise.

"A deal's a deal! I brought him, so keep your promise."

"Promises are made to be broken!" squeaked Ksyusha, who clearly didn't want to keep her word.

"Now, now, girls, that wasn't our agreement. If you don't kiss me right now, Ksyusha, I'll make Volodya leave. Yeah! How do you like that, eh? But on the other hand"—Yurka let a pause hang dramatically in the air—"if he stays, maybe he'll ask one of you to dance!"

Yurka knew that wasn't going to happen, but Polya's and Ulyana's eyes glittered with curiosity. Ksyusha was the only one who wasn't burning with enthusiasm. But Ulyana stepped in, grabbing Ksyusha by the elbow and dragging her over to Yurka.

"Go on," Ulyana whispered, nodding at him.

"Nuh-uh!" Yurka stopped them. "You promised to do it in front of everyone. We're going to the middle of the dance floor." He held his hand out to Ksyusha. "Shall we dance?"

She sighed and trudged gloomily after him.

A silly little song by a group that was popular at first but had now started getting on everyone's nerves was pouring out of the speakers:

Your eyes are the color of morning skies,
Your hair's as golden as fields of wheat.
Flowers bloom in my heart from your smile . . .

"It's like the song's about you," said Yurka, magnanimously complimenting Ksyusha. A disconcerted smile flashed across her lips.

It would've been hard to call their awkward shuffling "dancing." The only thing Ksyusha allowed him to do was put his hands on her shoulders in comradely Pioneer fashion while they both tapped their feet in time to the music, holding each other at arm's length.

"Why do you hate me so much?" Yurka asked her.

"I don't hate you, but it's your fault, anyway. You shouldn't have jumped on Vishnevsky like that," she mumbled angrily. "It's your fault he didn't come, you know."

Yurka hadn't known she cared whether or not Vishnevsky came to camp. "It isn't, actually. He spent the whole session last year bragging about how his dad got him a vacation voucher to Bulgaria for an entire summer this year," replied Yurka dryly.

It was like a dam burst. Ksyusha flooded him with questions. Apparently she cared an awful lot. But Yurka wasn't listening. He was looking out the corner of his eye at Volodya, who was sitting at the far edge of the dance floor, leaning back in a chair, arms folded on his chest, smiling and watching the two dancers. He also caught other campers looking at him enviously. Vanka and Mikha all but applauded when they caught his gaze.

The song ended, but Ksyusha was in no hurry to either leave or kiss him.

"Come on, let's go," Yurka urged her. "What are you waiting for? Two times!"

"You don't happen to have Vishnevsky's address, do you?" Ksyusha asked, blushing.

"No. Kisses!"

Ksyusha rolled her eyes, sighed, and moved closer. Yurka gallantly turned his side toward her and offered her his cheek, so she could reach it if she stood on her tiptoes. She held her breath and gave him a quick peck on the cheek. Yurka squinted his eyes shut in satisfaction as he felt that first soft little touch on his cheek, then a pause, and then a second one, which was even nicer. He liked it very much.

When he opened his eyes, all he saw of Ksyusha was her back as she rushed away to rejoin her friends.

Vanka and Mikha, flabbergasted, were waving their arms like crazy, beckoning him over. He obeyed.

"How?!" exclaimed Vanka. "How did you do that?!"

"Aw, man, why are you so lucky?" whined Mikha, who was green with envy.

"What's the big deal, guys?" asked Yurka, faking surprise.

"That's Ksyusha! She's as mean as a dragon! But don't tell her I said that, okay?" Mikha said, catching himself. "Me she snaps with a towel, but you . . . She kissed you!" he pointed out, as though Yurka didn't already know.

"Yeah," agreed Vanka. "It's the kind of thing we can only dream of . . ."

"Oh, come on, like she's so super-gorgeous," said Yurka dismissively. "We've seen better."

"That's right! That's the way to be," said Mikha, energetically demonstrating his indifference. But immediately he added again, in a frightened whisper, "Just don't tell her I said that, okay?"

"But still—how? It's some kind of trick, right?" persisted Vanka, stumped.

Yurka shook his head. "Nope. I earned it," he said with a proud jut of his chin, then turned and hustled back to Volodya.

But Volodya wasn't on his chair anymore. Yurka looked around, lost.

"Maybe he went over to the outdoor stage to make up with Ira? He'd hardly have gone back to his cabin without telling me." Sure that Volodya was here somewhere, it was just a question of finding him, Yurka went to the far corner of the dance floor and climbed his apple tree—the same one he'd been hanging the string of lights on at the beginning of the session. Carefully, though, this time. He pulled himself up and stood with his feet on either side of the forked trunk. He felt like a pirate in a crow's nest as he started examining the area.

The crowd below started moving. Some boys were asking girls to dance, and Yurka was a little envious of them—what an adrenaline rush! Other campers were having fun without any partner at all, while a few, like Mitka, were standing hesitantly in place, lonely and nervous.

The announcer who read Camp Barn Swallow's *Pioneer Dawn* was standing under a tree decorated with a string of red blinking lights and watching Ulyanka. He kept turning red as a piglet and then, as the string of lights blinked out, returning to being as white as chalk.

"And now we'll take a little break . . ." The camp director's voice interrupted both Yurka's observation of Mitka and the dance music. The Pioneers hollered in protest. "... so Olga Leonidovna can announce the results of our Summer Lightning campaign! And then we'll have our ladies' choice dance!"

Olga Leonidovna stepped out onto the stage for precisely one minute and without preamble announced loudly into the microphone that ultimately the winner of the Summer Lightning campaign of session two of the Pioneer Hero Zina Portnova Barn Swallow Pioneer Camp for 1986 was ... friendship!

A smattering of tepid applause followed. But as soon as the first notes of "Ferryman," the smash hit of the summer, started playing, a whisper of excitement passed through the boys, and all the girls started looking around at once. They were urgently trying to find someone.

"The leader of Troop Five," guessed Yurka. And following the direction in which most of the glances were pointed, he did indeed locate Volodya.

The troop leader was standing near the stage behind a tall speaker, which was why Yurka hadn't noticed him right away. As expected, Volodya was talking with Ira Petrovna. From a distance it was impossible to hear their voices or tell what emotions played on the troop leader's face, but Yurka could see Masha walking slowly and hesitantly toward them. She stopped and said something to them as she wrung her hands behind her back and shifted from foot to foot. Volodya nodded to Masha. Ira clapped Volodya on the shoulder, smiled, and walked away. Volodya bent slightly toward Masha and extended his hand gallantly.

Time stretched like syrupy fruit kissel dripping from a spoon. Yurka, frozen in an awkward position, saw Volodya leading Masha slowly, oh, so slowly into the middle of the dance floor ... he saw the girls looking enviously at them ... he saw Volodya carefully place his hand on Masha's waist, keeping her at arm's distance ... and a hot wave of hurt and anger rose inside Yurka again.

The Pioneers made a wide circle around Volodya and Masha, who swirled around the dance floor alone. Yurka observed them, flustered. His imagination added details, putting the dancing pair in a spotlight among dozens of lights, and all the stars were out, and the moon shone only for them, singling them out ...

"You're jealous," whispered his subconscious helpfully, naming the feeling that burned inside him. That was it, that was the same terrible sensation Yurka had felt today while spying on them through the window of the movie theater. It was jealousy, and the sting of it was far worse, far more painful, than ever before.

"Traitor! Liar!" raged Yurka. "He said he wouldn't dance with anyone, but he betrayed me! And that's not even dancing: he's just pressing up against her! Masha, of all people! That stupid little ditz Masha! A friend, he says! Look what kind of friend he is!"

Meanwhile, the speakers were pouring out Alla Pugachova's languid and—in Yurka's opinion—dreary voice as she sang "Ferryman," about pairs of lovers stuck on opposite banks of a river. The song was coming to the end, where she just kept repeating the phrase about how the ferryman would never be able to unite so many separated lovers, since there were so many of them but just one of him . . .

"And there's just one of me, too, hanging around by myself in this tree like a—a macaque! Like an idiot!" Yurka finally lost it. He grabbed hold of an apple growing on a nearby branch and yanked it free. He threw it at Volodya without aiming. He was sure he'd miss and the apple would hit the ground and explode, spraying them both with juice. But it traced an almost perfect arc through the air and hit Volodya smack in the shoulder.

What happened next took just a few seconds.

Yurka realized that he absolutely had to get out of the apple tree, because if they found him there, they'd throw him the hell out of camp! He'd never climbed down from a tree so fast. He dove down to the ground as nimbly as a circus acrobat and escaped the dance as fast as an Olympic runner.

But Yurka only thought he'd escaped. A few minutes later, red as a lobster, he stopped and looked around. There was a little windowless shed nearby. Yurka ducked around the corner of the shed and leaned back against the whitewashed wall to catch his breath. Only then did he sense the sweet smell of lilac and hear the humming of electricity. The power shed.

"Yura!" came a nearby call. "I know you're here! I saw you go this way."

How on earth did he catch me? thought Yurka, despondent, but decided it didn't make any sense to try running again. Even if he evaded Volodya today, he'd still have to deal with him tomorrow.

"I'm here! Over here!" he called out.

Volodya walked up to him. Yurka assumed a very guilty mien and ducked his head low. But Volodya didn't look angry; more like confused. He rubbed his bruised shoulder and looked at Yurka, perplexed. "Why did you throw an apple at me?"

"I'm sorry," Yurka said sincerely. "I didn't mean to, honest. I didn't think I'd hit you. Did it hurt bad?"

"Well . . . I felt it," chided Volodya. "Why were you in the apple tree?"

"I was looking for you, and I could see better up there."

"And . . . ?" prompted Volodya, expecting further explanation.

"Masha was driving me mad," Yurka admitted truthfully. "She invited you to dance, and you accepted."

"So?"

"You said you wouldn't dance with anyone! But then who did you dance with but her, even though you know how much she irritates me!"

"Yura, I don't understand what the issue is." Volodya rubbed his eyes wearily. "Explain so it makes sense."

"The issue is that I saw you in the movie theater today! I saw you comforting her!"

"You were spying on us?"

"Yes! I was spying on you!"

"What for?"

"What difference does it make? First you hug her and stroke her hair, and now you're dancing with her . . . What next? Do you like her?"

"No," Volodya replied firmly. "And anyway, what do you care what Masha and I—"

"But you said we were friends!"

"Of course we're friends. But what's that got to do with this? Yura, for the last three days something's been up with you. I've been asking, but you won't talk. And now you're out to get Masha. But what you did just now—that's too much!"

Yes, Yurka was aware his behavior was extremely odd. Rationally, he was aware of it. And Volodya's relationship with Masha shouldn't have provoked such a hurricane of emotion in him. But it did. His heart was spasming and breaking all at once. His chest felt both tight and hot. His cheeks burned, but chills raised goose bumps on his skin. His fingers trembled.

Volodya was calm. He stood with his arms crossed on his chest. Yurka approached him and, without breaking eye contact, said: "I want to be the only person in your life!"

"You are. You're my only friend," Volodya said softly, even affectionately. "Yura, if you like Masha, just tell me. I'll back off."

"'Just tell me'?! Maybe *you're* the one who'd better tell *me*!"

"What is it I'm supposed to be telling you?"

"The truth. About her. Because it's her, isn't it! Why didn't you admit it was her from the start?! Why are you hiding it? And what are you even hiding, anyway? That you can barely wait a year for her? Just wait, and you'll get everything you want! But I won't ever get anything!"

"A year? I don't understand." Volodya really did look baffled now. He even let his hands fall to his sides. "But hold on . . . wait . . ." He thought furiously for a second, then clapped his hand to his forehead. "No, I was right a minute ago! That's why you're so strange, that's why you're avoiding me and picking on Masha: you like her, but she likes me!" Volodya burst out laughing.

As Yurka watched this travesty of his own making unfold, he instantly became furious. Suddenly everything around him was too intense, as though all his senses had sharpened at once. The hum of the power shed sounded deafening; the smell of the lilac felt cloying; even the dim light of the moon and stars was blinding him. In that light, Volodya's face became paler and his gray-green eyes shone like emeralds. And maybe Yurka only imagined this, but along with the fake happiness there was something else in them, too. As though Volodya understood more than he should; as though he knew what was happening to Yurka even better than Yurka himself did. But Volodya was lying and putting on this clown show anyway.

"Your 'girl from my building' is Masha? Yur, I'm more than happy to . . . to . . . I won't get in your way! Be bold, and you'll get everything you want!"

"What are you even saying?!"

Yurka no longer knew what he was saying or doing. Time slowed down for the second time that evening. The humming in his ears was joined by the thundering of his heart. Yurka filled his lungs with air and tried to shout over the din: "It's not Masha who I won't have! It's you!" Then he turned away.

"Wait! What?!" Volodya grabbed Yurka by the arm and turned him around. He furrowed his brows, gazing directly into Yurka's eyes. "What did you say? Say it again!"

"How am I supposed to explain this to you?" croaked Yurka hoarsely. He took hold of Volodya's shoulders, pulled him close, and paused for a heartbeat, then pressed his lips to Volodya's.

Volodya gave a muffled gasp and his eyes widened in surprise. But Yurka simply lost all sense of self, all sense of self-awareness. All that existed was the way Volodya smelled . . . like apples . . . and also, just a little bit, the warmth of Volodya's skin.

This lasted a couple of seconds, and then Yurka felt one more thing: Volodya's hands on his shoulders. But before he could be glad, Volodya gently but insistently pushed him away.

Volodya, flustered, stared for a few more seconds at Yurka's burning face. Then, keeping his hands in place so he held Yurka at arm's length, Volodya said sternly, "You quit that."

CHAPTER ELEVEN
THERE WILL BE MUSIC HERE

Yura used the uniform jacket to sweep the shards of glass off the windowsill, then he climbed out of the troop leaders' room. The dandelion field looked very sad indeed, so he left it behind without regret and went to where the athletic fields and tennis courts used to be. They'd looked so huge when he was young, but now they were pitiful little patches overgrown with weeds.

Everything looks bigger and more meaningful when you're a kid, he thought as he walked a circle around the courts. He sighed and shook his head, which was stubbornly beset with the thought of how inexorably time passes, how pitiless it is to everything, like a plague that kills everything it touches.

Wary of tripping on the chunks of asphalt hiding in the wet grass, Yura was looking down at his feet, so he spotted the torn, rusted chain-link fence lying flat as though it had grown into the ground. At one time that fence had enclosed the court, and at one time Volodya had clung to it desperately, apologizing for the thing with the magazines and telling him about MGIMO.

"I wonder if he ever graduated?"

His gaze landed on a dark mass in some tall weeds by the side of the mess hall. Yura approached it. Long, thin rectangles lay scattered among chunks of broken brick and clumps of fallen leaves. The black ones were smaller, the white ones bigger. Piano keys. The entire instrument was here, smashed in, the panels ripped off and the lid broken. The piece of wood that had once been the front panel still bore the gold letters reading "Elegy." The hammers were scattered around and broken wires jutted from the piano's innards.

It was almost physically painful for Yura to see that the instrument he'd played when he was young was now in such a state. "How did it get here? The movie theater's not nearby . . ." It must have been some village guys from Horetivka, when Horetivka still existed.

The Elegy . . . he remembered that make of piano. It had been one of the most popular uprights in the entire USSR. All day cares, schools, and other institutions tended to have that exact model. The Barn Swallow Pioneer Camp had been no exception. The very same kind, in brown, had been in the movie theater and had been used at all the rehearsals. It was the one Masha had played.

Yura reached down and touched the scattered keys. He remembered them not the way they were now, but clean and shiny. New. If they had the capacity of memory, they wouldn't have remembered his hands, either. Back then his hands had been different. Young. Yura was spellbound by the melancholy picture of his aging hands on the timeworn keys. How alike they were.

Scenes from his memory, flat and indistinct, flickered in his mind's eye. It was as though time had turned and raced backward, and the keys turned white right before his eyes, and now his fingers on them were young and inexperienced.

The scene came to life and became crystal clear, just as though it were real, with details, full of sounds and smells . . . the movie theater, at night, in the summer of 1986, and him, a teenager, in the movie theater, in summer.

"Yur, wake up! Come on, Konev, get up already! If even one person's late to morning calisthenics, that's it: no best troop title for us."

Morning calisthenics. Breakfast. Assembly. Civic duty work. Drama club. Volodya would be everywhere. There was no place to hide from him. Yurka had told him everything, and Volodya knew his hiding spots. Volodya would find him and ask, *Why did you do that?*

Don't get up. Today of all days.

"Yur! Come on, Yura, wake up, let's go," whined Mikha, pulling Yurka's blanket off. "Why are you dressed?" he asked, surprised, but Yurka didn't reply.

Yurka had already known the day before that Volodya would look for him after he ran away, so he'd gone right to the place the troop leader would look last: his own cabin. He'd jumped into bed without undressing. If Volodya had shown up, it was after everyone was asleep, and he didn't risk waking him.

Yurka didn't know whether he'd been asleep when Volodya was there. Basically, Yurka had no idea what he'd done all night. He'd closed his eyes, but had he slept?

He got out of bed, changed clothes wordlessly, and trudged out to morning calisthenics.

Turned out to be easy to walk in a column: no need to lift your gaze off the ground. You drag yourself along, looking down at the feet of the person walking in front of you, and you're a hundred percent sure the column will take you somewhere. And it did. It took him to the athletic fields, where the entire camp gathered to do morning calisthenics. Including Volodya. If only he could get out of there!

How easy it was to just observe the shadow of the person in front of him and copy the motions. Yurka was physically incapable of lifting his head, even though he got yelled at to pull his chin up and keep his back straight. But Yurka couldn't do it. Volodya was everywhere. They would meet; their eyes would definitely meet; it was inevitable, unavoidable. Yurka wouldn't drop dead on the spot, of course, but he wouldn't be able to just stand there. Maybe his feet would be rooted to the ground, maybe his whole body would be frozen, but he'd still find a way to do something. He'd take it out on himself, all the anger and hate . . . he could bite his tongue off, but his tongue wasn't his enemy. It wasn't something he'd said that Yurka could hate himself for; it was something he'd done. Why had he gone and done that?!

Assembly. Troop One traditionally stood facing Troop Five. Yurka and Volodya were the tallest out of everyone there, and, like everyone there, they had to look straight ahead. But Yurka didn't obey the rule, because he could feel Volodya's gaze. This gaze didn't freeze him, nor did it burn him; it smothered him, so much that he felt his face was about to turn gray.

Pioneer anthem. Flag. He had to lift his hand in the Pioneer salute. Looking up high was allowed. This was good. It was okay because it wasn't straight ahead.

They assigned everyone's duties. Yurka was detailed to the mess hall. On his way there, he noted that the Avenue of Pioneer Heroes was paved with excellent asphalt. It was smooth, and gray, and patterned by the shadows of the birch trees along its length, and it glimmered with spots of sunlight that pierced the foliage. But the weird thing was that these little bits of light kept changing, first running together into little blotches, then spreading and diffusing like ink drops in water. Or maybe the problem wasn't the asphalt;

maybe Yurka's eyes were the problem? No. Yurka himself was the problem. Why had he gone and done that?

While he set out chairs in the mess hall, he tried to come to terms with the idea that he and Volodya had no future together, and that after what he'd done yesterday, all he'd have from then on would be the past: their brief friendship and all else that was good, including Yurka's leniency toward himself, his self-respect, his self-esteem, were trapped in yesterdays. And his confusing feelings for Volodya had to remain there too.

While he spread the tablecloth, Yurka decided he had to forget these feelings, whatever they were, as soon as possible. No matter what he did, any recollection of Volodya would inevitably be tainted with the memory of his own shameful act. And then he'd remember the response: "You quit that." No, this feeling would not let Yurka live in peace. But live he would!

Yurka knew that somewhere, out there past the camp fence, was a vast, alluring terra incognita where he would undoubtedly find freedom from all of this: the memories and the shame. It would be so great if he could escape, to get out past the horizon. No—not *if*. *When*. He had to escape!

Yurka moved his spoon around his bowl. He ate slowly and mechanically, with no idea what he was eating. He wasn't paying attention. There was a big pat of butter in his bowl, a yellow splotch on top of a pale, flavorless blob. He knew a piece of bread was disintegrating into crumbs in his left hand, and he knew there was a hot drink by his bowl, but he had no idea what was going cold in it, tea or hot cocoa. When somebody sitting across from him drank, Yurka drank. When they ate, Yurka ate. Not because he wanted to, but because somebody said he had to.

He got up only when all of Troop Five, headed by both troop leaders, had left the mess hall. While the other campers with kitchen duty cleared and wiped off the tables, Yurka hauled trays of dirty dishes and thought about what to do next.

Morning calisthenics, assembly, civic duty work ... he'd survive all that. He'd survived last night somehow, hadn't he? But the play—his role was so small, anybody could handle it. Really, he wasn't needed at rehearsal at all. Maybe Volodya would even take pity on him and kick him out of drama club. Then there'd be fewer encounters, after all; fewer words, fewer regrets. Maybe

Yurka could even figure out how to live in a way that kept him completely away from Volodya. Maybe he could get used to not being around Volodya. It was easier because it wouldn't be Volodya anyway—not the Volodya who'd been with Yurka up until last night, the one who was good, and kind, and interesting, the one he felt close to. But sooner or later Yurka would've had to endure this separation anyway. Sooner or later Yurka would've had to learn not to love him.

The girls tasked Yurka with putting the chairs on the tables so they could mop the floor. The chairs weren't made of anything heavy, just the thin, almost plywood seats and aluminum legs, but he was surprised by how heavy they felt. He soon tired, but stubbornly kept on lifting chairs, one after another. This kind of boring work was very conducive to thinking.

He and Volodya would eventually run into each other, and what would he do when Volodya asked, *Why did you do that?* Because he would ask, obviously. He was Volodya.

Yurka let out a prayer, without knowing who it was to: "Let him never talk to me again! Let him not even come close to me, let him act like I don't exist, let him not even look in my direction—just don't let him ask me about anything!" Yes, it would be awful. But Yurka was strong. He could stand both contempt and hate. He and Volodya would be comrades in that contempt and hate, actually. Let them have that, at least, as the last thing they'd share. Let the worst happen, in the worst possible way, as long as Volodya didn't ask!

Yurka walked to the middle of the mess hall, where the girls had already mopped, to set out the chairs again. He was reaching up for a chair but flinched when a soft, but painfully familiar voice said behind him: "Yura?"

He was here! Yurka locked his eyes straight ahead and his heart fell. The large, spacious mess hall, with its tiled floor and simple, white, weightless furniture, was as bright and clean as an operating room, but in a heartbeat it transformed into a dark tomb. Cracks shot through the black walls, which shifted and then slowly fell down on top of him.

"Yura, what's going on?"

Despondent, bereft of speech, Yurka couldn't so much as peep, or breathe, or move a muscle.

"Let's go. We need to talk." Volodya put his hand on Yurka's shoulder, then shook it gently, but all Yurka did was silently duck his head. The Pukes were also on duty in the mess hall that day and they gathered around the boys. Volodya, who didn't let go of Yurka's shoulder, talked with them and even looked like he was smiling, but Yurka could feel Volodya's hand on his shoulder trembling.

Volodya somehow extricated them from the girls and hissed through his teeth right into Yurka's ear: "Yura, I said we're going!" The floor seemed to tremble from the cold in his voice. Without waiting for any kind of reaction, he seized Volodya's arm and dragged him from the mess hall.

Yurka didn't know how he ended up outside. The white entrance hall, the creaking door, and the gray stairs raced past, a series of film stills in rapid succession—the way Yurka's entire life was racing by, actually. The humid morning air touched his cheeks. Yurka found himself on a bench. Volodya had sat him down and was now looming over him, a giant grim shadow.

"Explain what happened yesterday! What's it all mean?"

"I kissed you. Because I fell in love with you, apparently." This is what Yurka tried to say, mentally repeating "I fell in love with you" as though he were seeing how it tasted. He didn't like the taste. It was flavorless, fake. But he couldn't come up with another explanation. So he tried to reply, "I like you," but the words got stuck in his throat. The only thing he could actually force out was "I don't know."

"How can you not know? Was it a joke or something?"

Yurka flinched involuntarily. He couldn't raise his eyes to look at Volodya. But it wasn't just his eyes: his whole head felt so heavy, he couldn't understand how it hadn't broken his neck. Yurka searched obstinately for words, he strove with all his might to find an answer, his gaze combed the gray asphalt—maybe if the answer wasn't inside him, he'd discover it out there?

Volodya waited, pacing back and forth, shuffling his sneakers along the asphalt and breathing loudly with impatience. But Yurka still had no idea how to answer him, so he just let his eyes wander over his own hands and feet as he sniffled, barely audibly. Apparently the silence was beginning to drive Volodya crazy, since he started shuffling louder and breathing more angrily, then took to cracking his knuckles. Suddenly he crouched down on his heels in front of Yurka, looked into his eyes, and said, in a painstakingly civil voice, "Please, tell me what's going on with you. At least now, while we're still friends, I'll hear you, I promise. If you say you were joking, or that you were making fun of me, or even that you were getting back at me, I'll understand. If you say it was an accident, or that you didn't mean to, I'll believe you."

Yurka's mouth twisted in pain: Volodya was giving their friendship a chance, naïvely trying to preserve at least some of it. Yurka realized this, but instead of playing along with Volodya's lie, he threw caution to the wind, gathered up his courage, and sighed out the truth: "I meant to."

"What?" said Volodya, looking stunned. "You meant to? What do you mean, you meant to?"

Volodya had indeed been giving them a chance, but Yurka didn't think for even a second that there was any point. You can't bring back the past. The good, pure spark that had flickered to life between them would go out now. All they'd have left would be embarrassment, hypocrisy, and tension. And it was all Yurka's fault.

"But you can't do that, Yura!" Volodya was, it seemed, completely on the same page. "That kind of thing is—is very dangerous! Don't even think about it!"

Volodya stood abruptly and turned away. He stood there motionless for a minute and then resumed his pacing back and forth. Yurka felt his world crashing down around him as his eyes tracked Volodya's shadow moving to and fro.

He scraped together the last dregs of self-control. Without putting much hope in it, he mumbled in a dead voice, so low it was husky, "But you said you'd understand. That we were still friends."

"But what kind of friends can we be after that?!"

Everything went still, inside and out. The wind vanished; all sound ceased. But all of a sudden, off in the distance, as though it came from another universe, came the sound of a child screaming. Not happy shrieks, as was usually the case, but cries of terror.

Volodya stopped in his tracks and ordered, "Wait for me here."

But as soon as he'd taken a couple of steps, Yurka lurched to run away. Quick as a flash, Volodya grabbed his wrist and made him sit down on the bench. He didn't let go of Yurka. "I'm not done yet."

"But we're not friends anymore. And that's that!"

"No it's not. I've told you a hundred times, the games you're playing are stupid and dangerous. But this—!" His voice broke. Volodya was barely able to keep himself under control. To keep from yelling, he strangled his voice down to a whisper: "Never tell anyone anything about what happened. Don't even hint at it. In fact, you'd better forget about it all like a bad dream. And from now on, don't you dare let yourself even think about things like that!"

His hand tightened painfully around Yurka's wrist. Yurka winced but didn't make a sound.

"Volodya!" called a girl in a shrill voice. Yurka didn't recognize who it was. Right now he wasn't in any condition to recognize anyone or anything. "Volodya, come quick!"

For the first time since Yurka had known him, Volodya acted against his own nature. Instead of automatically running off to answer whenever and wherever he was called, Volodya stayed where he was and shouted, "Can't you see I'm busy?!"

"Volodya, it's Pcholkin again. He made Sashka fall down!"

Volodya growled out, "Be right there!" Then he bent over Yurka and said through gritted teeth, "Wait for me here. And don't you move a muscle!"

"Volodya!" the girl sobbed. Only then did Yurka recognize who it was: Alyona from Troop Five, who played Galya Portnova in the show. "Voloooodyaaaa! Pcholkin spun the merry-go-round toooo faaaast! Sashka's nose is bleeeeding! The whole playground's covered in bloooood!"

Volodya blanched and finally managed to let go of Yurka's hand. Gently, he pushed Yurka down. He hissed, "Son of a bitch!!" through his teeth and ran off to where Alyona was pointing. Yurka was left by himself.

Yurka was ashamed. He'd ruined everything. He wanted to vanish from the face of the earth, disappear, be lost, so Volodya would never see him again; to be wiped from Volodya's memory, so Volodya wouldn't even remember him.

They weren't friends anymore. Volodya might sit Yurka down like that again once or twice and start asking questions. Without meaning to, he'd torture Yurka. But the biggest torture was that Yurka had destroyed their friendship. It was true, now, that they were nothing to each other. And now he was going to have to spend a whole week close to Volodya, trying not to look at him, making sure to stay out of his way, so as not to remind either of them of that humiliating kiss. But how? How was he supposed to be able to look at Volodya now? How was he supposed to speak with Volodya only at rehearsal, and only about rehearsal, without the slightest hope of hearing even a single kind word about himself? All he could do was mess things up. He longed to hear something kind, something reassuring, but what he'd get would be something else entirely: he'd get the cold shoulder from the person who in just two weeks had become closer to him than anyone else who'd ever shown him even the least bit of caring or affection. It was inevitable that Yurka would go crazy: he already was!

What use was camp to him without Volodya? Why should he torture himself living right here next to Volodya but not having Volodya? What good would it do him to suffer from pangs of conscience and burn up inside from shame? After all, Yurka hadn't liked it here anyway, from the very first day of session.

The thought that had been running through his head all morning came to him again, insistently, blaring out louder than ever: *I have to get out of here!*

He got up, ripped off his on-duty armband and threw it on the ground, and ran away from that damned bench. He ran heedlessly down the path toward the Avenue of Pioneer Heroes, thinking of just one thing and motivated by just one goal: he had to get out of this camp—hopefully for good!

He only stopped once he realized he was standing in front of the bust of Marat Kazey. He flinched when he saw the face of the Pioneer Hero, for even that plaster boy was condemning him. "Paranoia," scoffed Yurka to himself. He looked to the left, where the avenue led to the main square at the very center of camp. Straight ahead was the path to the unfinished barracks, where he'd made the secret hiding place for his smokes. To the right was the gate, the camp exit. To the right was freedom! And, through some stroke of luck, both on-duty Pioneers and the watchman were gone. *They probably ran over to the commotion Pcholkin was causing*, thought Yurka. *Well, they're gonna get it after this!* He raced to the exit.

The heavy gate creaked, opening up onto a path through thick, dark forest, much denser than the woods in camp. It even smelled different there. It was cleaner, and breathing was easier. That was freedom for you: at first the smell of it made your head spin, and only later did it reach your brain. It reached Yurka's brain with the thought *There's no Volodya here, so we won't run into each other!*

He ducked into the thicket. He went through the trees on purpose, since he was afraid the campers on watch duty had only stepped briefly away and might see him leaving. As he made his way along the road leading from camp to the highway, where cars and buses drove past, he hid, ducking from tree to tree. He was planning his escape. He had a long way to go and time enough to think.

The first question was when to make a break for it. Not now, for sure: he didn't have any clothes, or money, or the keys to get in once he got home. It'd be better to try at night while everyone was asleep. No, it'd be better in the early hours before dawn. He'd have to hide somewhere near the camp and wait for the first bus. He didn't know where to wait, since Volodya knew all his hiding places. He'd have to find a new one. Maybe out here, in this forest? Yurka decided that right now he'd walk all the way out to the bus stop, memorize the path, and look at the bus schedule. Did they run regularly out here? One of them, at least, would have to go all the way to the city bus station. And from there he could get home.

All of a sudden he remembered the smell of home. The kitchen: slightly stuffy and sweet. The sitting room: dust and paper, because of the big library filling the bookcases lining one wall. Then the smell of his room burst into his memory: the piano's aroma of wood and lacquer. It was so quiet and peaceful there, so good. And Yurka used to think it was boring.

His next thought was alarming: nobody would be expecting Yurka at home. But he'd show up there. He'd just say it: *I ran away from camp. Let me in.* His mom would shriek and maybe even start crying, while his dad would start playing on Yurka's conscience: he'd go all quiet and just look at his son with an expression of complete disappointment. That look was worse than everything else.

For a second Yurka thought about running not home but to his grandma's, the one on his dad's side. She loved Yurka no matter how he behaved, and she wouldn't even say a word about it; quite the opposite, she'd secretly be happy and wouldn't betray him to anyone. The idea was very appealing, but Yurka shook himself: *Hide behind Grandma's back? Be a coward? That's just what I need! As though just the shame of it weren't enough. My parents will go crazy when they hear their only and dearly beloved child has vanished. How will Mom take it? And what about Dad? He'll stay mute the rest of his life!*

Yurka dragged himself slowly along. A kilometer away from camp the forest was completely wild. In some places he had to fight through bushes or climb over fallen trunks. The path turned out to be a hard one. One time Yurka even fell into some wet, crumbly earth and got stuck, as though the camp didn't want to let him go and was insisting he come back. But what Yurka wanted to do was cry. Like a pitiful baby. Because no matter how he distracted himself by planning his escape, no matter how he suppressed his hurt, his sad longing, his painful thoughts about Volodya, they kept bubbling up. Volodya had spoken in that nervous voice, and when he'd crouched down in front of Yurka, he'd looked at Yurka that way, the same way his dad did: a look of disappointment and sadness. "No. Don't think about that. Better to think about escape. Better to think about crime and about punishment."

What would Yurka's parents do to him for this? Well, what *could* they do? Lock him up at home? Hardly: Yurka was too old for punishments like that. Take away his pocket money? That would hurt, but it wasn't fatal; usually Yurka didn't even have enough small change in his pocket to jingle. So he was used to that. Maybe they'd send him to work at his grandmother's day care? Actually, that version sounded likeliest; his mother had already warned him he'd spend all summer working at the day care if he fought with anyone at camp again. Yurka had acted as though the threat cowed him, but the truth was that didn't scare him a bit. He had his little friends at the day care, like Fedka Kochkin and "Celluloid" Kolka. Just like last year, the three of them would wander around the village at night, keeping watch and catching hooligans and hedgehogs. And there was a neighbor boy, too: Vova, who was Volodya's age and just as judgmental... Volodya! Reminders of him were everywhere. Why was everyone named Vladimir? Well, what do you expect if the leader of the world proletariat's named Vladimir; of course half the country will be named after him. All those Vovas, Vovochkas, Vovchiks... Volodyas... Volodenkas...

Just then Yurka tripped over a scraggly stump and just about fell flat on his face. He had to admit he'd miss Volodya terribly. He'd regret destroying everything they'd had. He'd never see Volodya again. Never. Period. And Yurka wouldn't even have a photo to remember him by, since troop pictures weren't printed until right before the end of the session.

He glimpsed the highway between two tree trunks. A couple of hundred meters farther out was the bus stop. It was gray as concrete and massive, monolithic, as though it'd been chiseled out of stone; it was also very pretty, with the pointed edge of its sky-blue roof sticking up and out like a wing, although he couldn't tell whether it was the wing of a plane or a barn swallow. And right up under the peak of the roof, in fat metal letters with occasional spots of rust, were the words PIONEER CAMP.

Crossing the highway was easy. So was memorizing the bus schedule. There was only one bus that came all the way out here: the 410. Yurka was amazed. This was the first time in his life he'd seen a three-digit bus number. The first bus left the depot a little after six in the morning and got to this stop at seven ten. Yurka memorized that and nodded. He peered at the schedule one last time for good measure. It was very old, and in the part where the bus number was written, there was a wide crack, so maybe it wasn't 410 after all. But that didn't matter. The main thing was that the end station was in the city.

Now that he'd collected the information he needed to plan his escape, he looked around and surprised himself by calming down. There was such a pervasive sense of peace here. The deserted highway, the forest whispering all around, and the cool inside the old bus stop composed an idyllic scene, completed by the clear blue sky in which the airy white domes of a dozen parachutes floated weightlessly down to the ground like white dandelion seeds. Yurka smiled. How nice it felt out here, away from his troubles. He sat down on the bus stop bench in the shade and one last time repeated to himself what he'd decided on and confirmed. His plan was this: break the fence around the unfinished barracks at night and make a hole he could get through, like last year. Then get his stuff together and escape early in the morning while everyone was still asleep. Get to the bus stop and sit there waiting for the bus. Then home. Get the tongue-lashing from his mom and await the divine retribution from his dad. And then would come the sad longing for Volodya, strong enough to make Yurka howl, sob into his pillow, and writhe and moan until he turned himself inside out. Why, oh, why had he gone and done that?!

Yurka buried his face in his hands. Why??! And how was he supposed to stand being all alone now with this confusing, bittersweet feeling? Guilty and alone, being eaten alive by his conscience?

When the thirst that had been torturing him for at least an hour finally became intolerable, Yurka stood up, spit a thick wad of saliva, and turned back toward camp. As he trudged through the woods, a new set of doubts tore at him: was he really capable of this? Of not seeing Volodya? Of burning all his bridges without leaving even the slightest chance for reconciliation, of going away without saying goodbye? Without asking for forgiveness? But then, how could he forgive Volodya for pushing him away? He kept remembering Volodya's reaction, there in the lilacs behind the power shed, the scene looping on repeat: Volodya telling him to quit it.

Yurka kept trudging along. It seemed like he'd never make it. In general, the way back from somewhere was usually faster than the way there, but not for Yurka. Not today. For him it was the opposite.

Burning rays of bright June sun pierced through the thick foliage of the dense wild woods and prickled his skin awfully. And everything inside Yurka complained and screeched, too. He felt like a dusty abandoned piano that nobody had played in a long time, that people used as a place to put random stuff. The taut wires inside had gone slack, and water had gotten on some of them and they'd gotten rusty, and a pedal was broken and hanging loose, unconnected ... And then he'd open the lid, which would also creak and be hard to move, and he'd lightly rest his fingers on the keys, yellow with age ... but instead of tender, touching sounds, he'd elicit a horrible din, because the piano had been out of tune for ages, after all, and the hammers were bent ... You play a B but get a little B-flat in there, you play the C above middle C but it doesn't even make a sound ...

His friendship with Volodya seemed to be saturated with music. Music was always playing: the Pioneer anthem when he saw Volodya on the square, Pachelbel's Canon on the radio during their first meeting in the theater,

Masha playing the piano during rehearsal . . . They heard the music from the dance floor during their nighttime sessions on the merry-go-round . . . the music coming from the radio while they were under the willow . . . His feelings for Volodya were always resonating with music, because wherever Volodya was, there was always music.

Yurka pulled the creaky gate shut behind him, ignored the duty guards' questions, and wandered off in no particular direction. Children were running around. On their faces, there wasn't even a trace of the alarm they'd felt earlier during the episode with Pcholkin. Just like there wasn't even a trace left of his and Volodya's friendship. So he'd figured out his escape plan, but other things were making themselves known now, too: uncertainty, exhaustion, and hunger. He had missed snack running around the woods. There was a long way to go until dinner, and there was no sense going to the mess hall, since they wouldn't even give him a crust of bread. No surprise there: Zinaida Vasilyevna never let him have anything extra during her shift. He could go to the tennis courts, but he had neither energy to play himself nor interest in watching others play. He could go to some other club, but there'd be nothing for him to do there. He could go to the river, but he'd see Volodya. No. Seeing him now would be the worst thing possible.

But Yurka wanted to see him this very minute.

"I have no idea what's going on!" Yurka whispered while his feet headed to the theater of their own accord.

On the main square, girls were playing Chinese jump rope while the boys were making matchstick guns out of stolen clothespins. Yurka wandered around so lost in thought that he didn't notice anything around him, though he did tuck his arm behind his back instinctively whenever a small, noisy person ran by him too close and too fast. Yurka thought of the movie theater. There definitely wouldn't be anyone there yet, and the piano was there, and all of a sudden Yurka wanted badly to sit down at it, open the cover, put his hands on the keyboard, and, without daring to breathe, run his fingers across them weightlessly, just to feel them. Maybe he could even play something. But what? What would he like to hear right now? Immersed in his ponderings about music, Yurka realized that only at his beloved instrument could he figure himself out—only there, and nowhere else. And nothing else besides music was capable of calming him down. Only music could get through to him, settle into his very soul, put it in order, and extract from its deepest depths an understanding of what was happening to him. Only it could reason with his feelings, let him make peace with himself, explain everything.

But to force himself to touch the piano, Yurka had to conquer a fear that had seemed unconquerable. Although what was that sharp, prickly fear compared to this, the leaden, aching dread Yurka had been feeling all night last night and all day today? What's more, he'd been afraid for so long. Like skin that gradually coarsens and loses sensitivity, Yurka's heart had grown coarse; his emotions had grown numb. He'd stopped caring. Did that mean he'd finally be able to play now?

Inside the movie theater, it was cool and dark. The navy blue curtains were drawn, so all the theater's interior spaces were lit only by the sparse sunbeams coming in around the edges of the thick cloth. It was like the theater was sleeping in peace and quiet. But it wasn't empty. Olezhka was walking back and forth across the stage, whispering to himself, his nose buried in a thick stack of papers.

"Aren't you all at the river?" asked Yurka, a little overly loud because he was so surprised.

Olezhka winced and came to a halt. "Oh! Yuwka! We'we done, we'we back alweady."

"I see. But what about— Where's Volodya?" Yurka grew alarmed: What if he was here somewhere?

"He's busy. Petka Pcholkin committed sabotage. He made a cawbide wocket to send Sashka to the moon, because ouw Sashka's the one who wants to wowk at the Baikonuw Cosmodwome. But Petka's wocket didn't wowk. The space capsule blew up."

"Cawbide?" repeated Yurka, not understanding. But then he worked it out. "Oh, carbide!" he said, then thought it through aloud: "The same stuff I used to use for my cherry bombs. So that's what Pcholkin was looking for in that construction debris! That's why he was digging around in the rocks. And the girls' hair spray didn't just vanish for no reason! 'There was just a little bit left at the bottom.' Yes, that's it—just a little left, and so the rocket exploded faster than he thought. You have to make your rockets out of *empty* spray cans."

"Yeah, yeah, yeah! It made this huuuuge explosion! The giwls hid in the bushes, and the boys hid in the bushes, and then they busted Sashka's nose, and it was pouwing blood evewywhewe, thewe was blood all ovew the main squawe. Lena was squealing like cwazy. Boy, was it scawy! So Volodya mawched him off to the diwectow. They've been in thewe evew since. But why didn't you come to swim?"

"I was just . . . doing something."

"Will you come tomowwow?" Olezhka asked hopefully. "And why'd you come now? Awe you doing something now too?"

"I . . . I want to play the piano. But don't tell anybody, okay? I don't play very well and I'm embarrassed. That's why I was able to do it now, when nobody's around."

"Oh, okay, I get it. Well, go ahead and play. I'm going. I also have to . . . do something." Olezhka grinned and skipped away so swiftly that Yurka didn't have a chance to shout goodbye after him.

And so here he was, all alone, except for the upright piano. There was one just like it in Yurka's room at home, with one difference: his piano had a layer of dust and was covered with clothes, toys, and books piled so high the lid wasn't visible. But this piano was clean, and gleaming, and beautiful.

Yurka was at the piano before he could think about it. He reached out and turned on the lamp. As soon as he saw the keys, illuminated by the warm yellow light, panic seized him again.

"This fear is nothing compared to the horror you went through yesterday. And this feeling of your own worthlessness is nothing compared to the humiliation of Volodya pushing you away," he encouraged himself. It was a strange sort of encouragement, but it worked. He moved closer to the piano.

He sat down, lifted his hand, and placed it carefully on the keyboard. Anticipation of a low, deep C shot from his fingers to his chest like an electrical shock. It might seem such a little thing, calling forth just a single solitary sound, but what an effort it took to make himself do it. His heart fluttered with joy: he could do it! The C burst forth, pealing through the theater.

Yurka was transported by joy and delight. His fingers, stiff from lack of conditioning, didn't strike the keys; rather, they immersed themselves in the keyboard, pressing out other notes as he tried to remember something simple and play it.

"How did that go again?" he mumbled to himself. "F-sharp, A-sharp... F or A? Not A. F. F, F-sharp. Or was it G? How does it go?!"

Yurka tried to remember the melody he'd composed himself. At the time it had seemed so simple; he'd played it with his eyes closed, delighting his parents and especially his grandma on his mom's side, the one who'd dreamed her grandson would become a pianist. After a year without music, Yurka had forgotten the melody so thoroughly that now he could only remember it with great effort. And the other problem was that his fingers were stiff.

Yurka started stretching them and trying to recall the melody visually. "F-sharp and A-sharp two above middle C, then up another octave to F natural and F-sharp... F natural, back down to A-sharp, F-sharp, A-sharp... Yes! That's it! I remember!"

At that moment, all his miseries faded into the background; at that moment, all his problems became insignificant. He had remembered! He was playing! He was finally playing; he was bending the keyboard to his will; he was eliciting beautiful sounds; he felt like he could do anything! He knew there were no heights he couldn't attain! His rapture carried him out of this world into another one, comfortable, warm, and sonorous. It was as though Yurka had been launched into outer space and was floating there, enchanted by the yellow and white sparkling of stars. Except that in his outer space the stars were sounds.

The door to the movie theater creaked softly, but Yurka didn't turn around. "F-sharp, A-sharp, F, F-sharp. F, A-sharp, F-sharp, A-sharp...," he whispered, playing the same phrase over and over, shifting his hand up and down the keys, remembering the forgotten motions.

Suddenly he heard furious footsteps. "Not a junior camper," concluded Yurka. "A heavy tread." But he was playing the piano and, turning back to the piece, he forgot about them immediately. Completely immersed in his music, he was no longer paying attention to anything else: he didn't look around; he didn't listen to anything but the music.

The footsteps froze abruptly. Then individual steps, drowned out by the piano notes, quietly approached him one by one. The sneakers of the uninvited guest squeaked a little on the lacquered parquet floor; hands pulled out a hanky to clean a pair of glasses; the hanky rustled—but none of this mattered to Yurka.

F-sharp, A-sharp, up to F, F-sharp, F, back down to A-sharp, F-sharp, A-sharp...

"Never do that again," Volodya requested, his voice trembling.

Yurka froze: Was he imagining it? No. So the footsteps had, in fact, been Volodya's. Yurka turned around. Volodya, breathing hard, was standing in a circle of light next to the stage. As he stared at the ground, he slowly drew in a deep breath. The moment he put his glasses back on, he became completely calm, as though by magic.

"There he is. He came," said Yurka's internal voice. "He came himself. He came to me. Again. But what for?"

"What exactly shouldn't I do?" asked Yurka gingerly.

"Don't disappear. You were gone for five hours!"

"Okay" was all Yurka could mumble in response as he watched Volodya sit down cautiously beside him on the piano bench.

"I thought I'd kill you once I found you," snorted Volodya ruefully. "And I was looking for you. At first just me, then I sent out kids to help find you. If it hadn't been for Olezhka, I wouldn't have known what happened to you until this evening. I don't know what I would've done."

Yurka found his voice. "It's good you're trying to act like nothing happened. I want to act that way, too, but it's not working." His hands started trembling. Again a maelstrom of thoughts and emotions burst into his head. And again Yurka placed his fingers on the keys and started walking himself through the second part of the melody. That was the only way he could retain his self-control. "F, F-flat. Dammit, no, that's not it. F, F-sharp. Or flat? Dammit!"

Volodya ignored his outburst, continuing: "I'm not trying to act like nothing happened. Just the opposite... So basically, this is why I'm here—besides finding out whether you're okay, of course..." He cleared his throat awkwardly. "I had a lot of time to think about what happened. I tried all night to decide what to do. All night—but it was no good: I kept going off in the wrong direction! Because it never even occurred to me that you might have been serious. I mean, it occurred to me, of course, but I drove the thought out of my mind. It was too fantastical. And then it turns out that it was just the opposite, it was real. And I panicked. I didn't say what I should've said. Or what I actually wanted to say. But while I was looking for you those five hours"—he emphasized those last words—"I thought through it all again. But this time I got it right. So . . . well, I came here. To tell you what I decided."

"F, F-sharp . . ." Stop. "What difference does it make? We're not friends anymore, after all."

"Of course we're not. What kind of friends can we be after that?"

They remained silent. Volodya sat with his hands clutched together in his lap and looked at Yurka's reflection in the piano's lacquered front panel. Yurka was watching Volodya out of the corner of his eye himself. He didn't want to watch Volodya, but he did. He didn't want to sit so close to Volodya on the small bench, but he did.

"F-sharp, A-sharp, up to F, F-sharp . . . F, down to A-sharp, F-sharp . . . ," Yurka said hesitantly.

"Yura, aren't you even a little bit afraid?"

"What am I supposed to be afraid of?"

"Of what you did!"

Of course he was afraid. And he was also confused. And very hurt. But how much more frightening and painful it was to realize he had lost Volodya because of what he'd done. He'd just ruined everything, in one fell swoop.

"You're acting like such a child," sighed Volodya, not waiting for Yurka's response. "But I'm actually a bit jealous of you."

Yurka remained silent.

"Your recklessness really does make me jealous. You break the rules so easily; you shrug and act without giving a thought to the consequences . . . I'd like to do that too. Even just once, just one time, do not what I *should* do but what I *want to* do. If only you know how sick I am of constantly thinking about the correctness of everything I do! Sometimes I get so fixated on monitoring myself—on tracking what I do, and say, and how I behave—that it crosses over into paranoia and panic attacks. At times like that I'm physically incapable of calmly evaluating what's going on, you understand? And what you did felt like a total catastrophe. But . . . but maybe it's not all so bad? Maybe I'm exaggerating?"

Yurka didn't understand what Volodya was getting at. He was afraid to interrupt Volodya's monologue because all he was capable of now, really, was just getting it all out, just saying what he felt without thinking about it beforehand,

and he didn't want to make both himself and Volodya uncomfortable, to take a thing that was already ruined and smash it to pieces. So he remained silent. All the more so since, for a long time now, he'd had a thick lump in his throat that kept him not just from talking but from even breathing.

But Volodya stared expectantly at their reflection in the lacquered panel. His gaze wandered tentatively around Yurka's face, pausing to focus on Yurka's eyes, as though he were searching them for an answer. Then he abruptly cleared his throat again and said: "Listen, Yur, I was thinking about something, and I want to know what you think of it. There is such a thing as very close friends, who . . . I mean very close friends. Special friends. For example, in school, or at my institute, I saw guys walking arm in arm or even just sitting with their arms around each other."

"Okay. And?" Yurka finally swallowed the lump in his throat and spoke. "Okay, so they walk around that way. Let them. That's what people who are close do. They can do stuff like that. But we can't."

"What do you think . . . Do they kiss?"

"Are you making fun of me or something? How would I know? I've never had 'special' friends!"

"What about me?" Volodya said, sounding a little pathetic.

"Go find Masha. I'm sure she's fed up waiting for you."

"Come on, Yur. Quit it. Masha's just here on vacation, she's just like everybody else."

"'She's just like everybody else . . . ,'" parroted Yurka mockingly. At the mention of her name, he started banging on the keys so the notes would be louder, so he wouldn't hear his internal voice, the monologues that would reawaken his jealousy.

Yurka wasn't aware of the fact that he was playing ever more confidently, that he was now playing from memory, without looking.

He couldn't take his eyes off of Volodya's reflection. Volodya was pale and still, stealing shy glances at Yurka and biting his lip. Then he said, "I don't want to think that what happened was bad. But no matter how hard I try not to, I do. Maybe I'm just getting panicky and paranoid again and I'm just making a mountain out of a molehill, but I'm really scared. Yura, tell me: What do you think?"

"About what, exactly?"

Volodya scooted even closer. Yurka played even louder.

"Did you do that because . . ." Volodya hesitated, wiping the sweat off his brow with his palm. "Would you . . . be that? I mean . . . do you want to be not a regular friend to me but a special friend?"

Yurka banged the keys as hard as he could. "F-sharp, A-sharp, up to F, F-sharp, F, down to A-sharp, F-sharp, A-sharp! F, G-sharp, up to F, G-sharp, F, down to G-sharp, F, G-sharp!"

"That's enough! I can't shout over this!"

"F-F-F-F . . ." All of Yurka's insides were trembling.

Volodya grabbed his hand and pressed it down on the piano keys. Everything stopped: the music, and his breathing, and his heart. Yurka turned toward Volodya. Volodya's face was a couple of centimeters away. He could feel Volodya's breath on his cheeks again. Volodya was so close to him that he stopped thinking at all. A shiver ran down his spine. Volodya's cold fingers trembled as they pressed Yurka's hand, and his eyes glittered feverishly behind the lenses of his glasses.

Volodya swallowed slowly and with difficulty, then whispered: "Maybe there's really nothing wrong with kissing a . . . a special friend?"

And then it finally hit Yurka: this was what Volodya had been trying to tell him for the past ten minutes. It didn't just hit him; it crashed down on him like a ton of bricks. But on his heart, not his head; his heart took the blow, and Yurka actually reeled from it.

"Volodya . . . what is this?" Yurka asked, the stupidest question in the world, but purely to make sure he hadn't misheard. "What are you saying? Who are you trying to fool? Me, or yourself?"

"Nobody."

"But I mean . . . are you sure this isn't . . . you're not deceiving yourself?"

Volodya shook his head and licked his dry lips. "No. Are you?"

Yurka, eyes bulging, was in turmoil, barely breathing. He blinked. He squeezed Volodya's fingers. Heart beating fit to burst, Yurka croaked, "No."

Yurka couldn't believe what was happening. Volodya of his own accord bent his head down and moved closer. His pupils were huge as he gazed urgently at Yurka, holding Yurka's hand. Volodya was holding Yurka's hand! Not like always, but tenderly, reverentially, his fingers stroking Yurka's. Volodya's lips were close, and he smelled nice.

But what was he, Yurka, supposed to do now? Purse his lips? He hadn't even thought about this back by the power shed. But that had been yesterday. That had happened a very, very long time ago, and to someone else. And right now the main thing for Yurka was to neither suffocate from joy nor go deaf from the hammering of his heart. He closed his eyes and turned toward Volodya. He felt Volodya's breath—not on his cheek now . . . lower . . .

And then the porch of the movie theater creaked.

"The tram flies by, its brakes a-squeal, its headlight shines across the mud! The tram ran over an Octoberist and left him in a pool of blood!" recited Sashka outside the door.

Yurka jerked away, clumsily, his face scraping against Volodya's glasses, and leaped to his feet. Volodya's shaking hands flew up reflexively, then fell back down with a clang onto the piano keyboard. A *blyanngggg* thundered out, spreading cacophony—aural and otherwise—through the entire theater.

"Eww! That's such a gwoss poem!" Olezhka scolded Sashka.

The door opened, revealing all the little kids from the drama club. The senior campers weren't there yet. Yurka was heaving for breath as though he'd just run a race. Volodya was sitting at the piano, blinking, his gaze roving uncomprehendingly between the keyboard and the incoming children.

"You're so early today . . . Your shift of civic duty work hasn't ended yet . . . ," he mumbled hoarsely.

Mentally, Yurka shouted, "Thank goodness the porch creaks!" but didn't risk saying anything out loud.

CHAPTER TWELVE

FROM LYRICS TO PHYSICS

During rehearsal, Volodya tried to act as though nothing hugely momentous had almost just happened between them a couple of minutes ago. Yurka, though, sought out every opportunity to be near Volodya, even for just a second, and spent the whole rehearsal on pins and needles. He paced nervously between the rows of seats because he was simply unable to sit still in one place. Every so often he looked over at Volodya and caught Volodya looking at him. The always stern artistic director had lost his edge and was looking a little distracted.

The rehearsal was in full swing when the porch steps creaked and two more people came into the theater. Olezhka was the first to notice them: he'd been gazing dramatically into the distance as he recited a bombastic monologue, but he broke off in the middle of a word.

"Ahem," Pal Palych greeted them.

"Good afternoon, Pavel Pavlovich," replied the children, without stopping what they were doing.

Olga Leonidovna followed the director into the auditorium, jotting something down in her notebook and whispering soundlessly to herself as she walked: "Fix steps." Only then did she greet everyone out loud: "Good afternoon, children!"

Everyone greeted her in unison, too. The educational specialist made a beeline for Volodya, and Yurka joined them immediately.

"I just came over to check in and see how things are going for you out here. Camp Barn Swallow Day is the day after tomorrow, so the show has to be completely ready."

Volodya grew pensive. "I'm not sure it will be, actually," he replied apologetically. "We're doing our best, but there's a lot to get through and not much time. And the set, too . . ."

"Ahem!" said Pal Palych indignantly.

"Volodya!" said Olga Leonidovna, interrupting Pal Palych. "I am not *asking* you if it will be ready. I am *telling* you it will be ready. But all right, show me what you've got. We'll see."

They began their run-through. Olga Leonidovna observed the actors with a cold, calculating gaze, writing things down in her notebook without a word and occasionally rolling her eyes. Yurka, following her reactions, realized to his chagrin that they were in a pretty bad position. He had been at all their rehearsals and was keeping track of how the show was progressing. It seemed like the younger kids had already learned their lines, and Masha was playing slowly but with confidence—although she didn't touch the "Lullaby"—and the Pukes were working hard on their end, too, but everything was just still too rough around the edges. There were a few scenes they'd only run through a couple of times at most. But the set! Sure, there wasn't supposed to be a big, complicated set for the show, but some of the stage decorations had to be built and painted from scratch, and they hadn't even gotten past sketching them yet.

So Olga Leonidovna and Pal Palych weren't happy. Of course. Yurka had known both of them for six sessions now and, as hard as he tried, he couldn't remember them ever being happy with anything. But the worst thing was that Olga Leonidovna wasn't happy with their Zina Portnova.

"Nastyona. You do know the story of your character, right?"

"Ahem . . . what kind of question is that, Olga Leonidovna?" interjected the director. "There's no way she doesn't know it." Every camper knew every Pioneer Hero's story by heart.

"Of course I do," confirmed Nastya. "My classroom's even named after her."

"Then you should remember that up until the war, Zina was an ordinary little Soviet girl. But you're playing her as though she were some knight of ancient Rus, even though she was a real person and some of her relatives are still alive today. Zina wasn't born a hero, she became one, and your task is to show that becoming, not immediately announce, 'I'm a hero, and that's that—I don't cry and I'm not afraid.'"

"Olga Leonidovna, should we take another look at the script?" interjected Volodya, seeing that poor Nastya was already trembling. "You point out the lines you don't like and Konev and I will rewrite them."

"The script is fine. It's Nastya's acting that's the problem."

Nastya went pale and her eyes brimmed with tears. Olga Leonidovna noticed and changed her fury to benevolence.

"Nastyona, don't worry, everything will be fine. All you have to do is imagine yourself in those circumstances. Like this: you're Zina, you're a tad bit older than you are now, you're fifteen. You're kind, and upbeat, you're a good student, but like all children the thing you like most is playing and having fun. You and your girlfriends think up interesting things to do together: you write up a wall newspaper, or you organize a dance group—because you dance beautifully, you know—or you do a puppet show for the little kids..."

At this point Yurka heartily clapped the woebegone Nastya on the shoulder, man-to-man style—she almost fell down—and proclaimed, "That's how Nastya really is."

Nastya gave a big fake smile. Olga Leonidovna didn't budge, going on as though she hadn't heard or seen anything: "You live in Leningrad and your friends are there, and your family, and your school, but you and your little sister, Galya, have gone to your grandmother's little village near the town of Obol, in the Byelorussian SSR, to spend the summer at grandma's."

"And that's when the war started!" interjected Sashka, who was covered with Band-Aids like a telephone pole covered with flyers and ads. He jumped up onstage and started running around, gesticulating wildly. "Attack! Pow! Pew-pew-pew, rat-a-tat-a-tat!"

The educational specialist put her hands on her hips. "You think this is funny, Shamov?"

"N-no..." Eyes bulging, Sashka shrank back a step.

"Joking about the great suffering of not only the Soviet people, but the whole world—!"

"Sasha had no intention of joking!" Volodya interceded. "Olga Leonidovna, in peacetime it all seems so distant, it seems like all this has nothing to do with us. But that's how it should be..."

Then the camp director chimed in. "Ahem... but people didn't know there'd be a war back then, either. And they wouldn't have believed it if you'd told them the war would begin tomorrow. Children were on vacation, in villages or... ahem... in Pioneer camps, like we are now."

"That's right!" agreed Olga Leonidovna. "And actually the first strategic facility the fascist air force destroyed wasn't a train station or a factory but a Pioneer camp!"

Yurka could no longer stand idly by and listen to the kids, who were working hard, being lectured in this way. He liked absolutely none of this: the conversation was idiotic, it was insulting to the kids, and it was boring.

"So what did they bomb the camp for?" he interjected, shooting a challenging look at Olga Leonidovna. "It's just a waste of ammunition, after all. They should've hit airports, transportation centers . . ."

"The camp was in the little town of Palanga, right on the border between the Lithuanian SSR on one side and Nazi-occupied Poland on the other. The fascists attacked in the very early hours of June 22, 1941. They shelled the camp directly, capturing it all on film. Read Mykolas Sluckis if you're interested, Konev; he wrote about it. But we've gotten off-subject. Where were we . . . ? Zina and her sister are spending their summer with their grandma in a little village near Obol. The war begins. Out of nowhere, all of a sudden. Their village, in the northern part of the Byelorussian SSR, is immediately occupied by German soldiers. And so she—that is, you, Nastya, just the same way you are now, good and kind—you start seeing nothing but blood and death all around you. A year later you join the ranks of the Young Avengers, a troop of local children. You learn to shoot, to throw grenades . . ."

Dried-up old fish, Yurka thought furiously to himself as the educational specialist's flood of words finally abated. She shook her head solemnly, then insisted that Yurka read his lines.

After she listened to him, she declared: "No, Konev. You're also doing it wrong."

"Really . . . ?" Yurka said slowly, dripping with sarcasm. Fortunately for him, Olga Leonidovna didn't catch his tone.

"Yes. Your character's coming off as too human. But he's a monster, not a person! All the Germans were monsters!"

"Really . . . ?" Yurka said slowly, again, but this time he was genuinely surprised by her vehemence. Still, he recovered quickly and fell into line: "Okay, what should I do, then?"

"Well, I don't know, make some kind of monstrous face."

"Like this?" Yurka beamed a wide, self-satisfied smile.

The cast snickered. The educational specialist blinked stupidly, then burst out laughing herself. "Don't be ridiculous, not that."

But she didn't smile again. She listened to everyone else stony-faced, with pursed lips. Then, frowning so hard you could've used her forehead for a washboard, she pronounced her verdict: "No. This is completely unsuitable for the Pioneer Hero Zina Portnova Barn Swallow Pioneer Camp. This is absolutely unfit for offering to the public and disgraces our name. Volodya, I expected much more from you!"

"Ahem . . . yes . . . ," agreed the camp director.

At first Volodya just blinked, flustered. Then he ground his teeth so hard that the tendons stood out in his cheeks. Her words clearly cut him deeply. They couldn't have done otherwise: Volodya was devoted heart and soul to preserving his reputation, and now there'd be a black mark on it. A small one, but still. This one wasn't directly from Pal Palych, and there wasn't any cussing involved, but it was in front of everyone. Again.

"But, Olga Leonidovna, the script is genuinely very difficult, and the topic is serious," he said, trying to justify himself.

"I know, Volodya! But I was counting on you and thought you could handle it!"

"I *can* handle it! We can *all* handle it! But we need more actors! We're just not getting enough boys, even after I asked them to come join us—this is what I've been telling you, yesterday and the day before . . ."

The educational specialist pondered for a moment, then nodded. "Then we're postponing the premiere! We'll do the show the very last day, before the final campfire."

"But that'll mess up our original plan: we wanted to do it on Camp Barn Swallow Day, so we specifically picked an old script, and chose music for it . . ." Volodya shot Yurka such a guilty, pleading look that Yurka felt he'd been splashed with boiling water.

"Either the last day or not at all," proclaimed Leonidovna.

"All right," said Volodya, surrendering. There was nothing he could do, anyway. "But what about the boys? Help us bring in some more actors, Olga Leonidovna. Everyone in the whole drama club has already gone out and tried to all but drag people in, but they're still not coming. All we need them for is the crowd scenes, they don't have to say a single word."

"I'll help," the dried-up old fish said, nodding and jotting something in her notebook. "But in that case it has to be even better than I expected." She nodded again and jotted something else in her notebook. She gave a couple more instructions, glanced at her watch, and left.

There was almost an hour of rehearsal remaining, but the actors, all riled up from the harsh critique, had no idea where to start or what to do. The cast wandered aimlessly around the movie theater until Volodya's thunderous roar "Over here, everyone!" drew all the boys and girls to one place.

Yurka thought the artistic director was going to start sending them all over the stage in a frenzy, making them push themselves to the limit, but all he did was say, "All right, guys, did you hear that? Olga Leonidovna is absolutely not happy with what we've done. But fortunately for us, she's allowing us to postpone the premiere to the last day of camp."

A murmur ran through the gathered cast. The kids had been hoping to perform on Camp Barn Swallow Day, the special celebration held each session to honor their beloved camp. A few of them even had their parents coming. As he surveyed the downcast faces and listened to the pitiful sniffling, Yurka felt very bad for the actors. Volodya was also hurting, to judge by his guilty face and downcast eyes. An awkward silence lingered.

"It's my fault," squeaked Olezhka. "It's because I can't say my *r*'s wight . . ."

"It's *all* our faults!" Yurka interrupted. "But nothing bad actually happened. It's fine, guys, let them postpone the show."

Volodya chimed in. "Let's think positive. We just got a little more time, plus we're getting actors for the crowd scenes. But the main thing is that we've been given a big honor: performing for the official closing of session!" He smiled. Olezhka sniffed again, but his face brightened. "They're paying attention to us now! That means they'll help us and the show will turn out way better than it is now. Guys, I'm expecting you to do your absolute best!"

To get the kids a little more excited, Yurka also added in a scary voice, "And if you don't do your best, and we're a flop, then every night for the rest of your lives you'll be visited by the vengeful spirit of an artistic director who killed himself, and the spirit will haunt you, and keep you from sleeping . . ."

"What is this crap?" said Polya indignantly.

"What kind of spiwit is it, Yuwka?" said Olezhka, perking up. "Tell us!"

Yurka paused to think. "Okay, I will. But not tonight. And not even tomorrow. I'll tell you if for the next three days you work hard at rehearsal and then do a great job in performance! Deal?"

"Deal!" chorused the kids, while the Pukes scoffed and rolled their eyes simultaneously.

Yurka caught Volodya's eye: he nodded to Yurka and soundlessly whispered, "Thanks." And that's when the jitters hit Yurka for real. He kept looking at the wall clock, but its minute hand was apparently taunting him, going so slow that Yurka sometimes thought it was just standing still. How he longed for rehearsal to be over! For everyone to leave the movie theater, so he could . . . Yurka didn't know what, exactly. But he felt a sharp need to be alone with Volodya.

The step by the entryway creaked yet again, and once more a strained silence descended over the theater. Yurka turned to look at who'd come in. The person standing on the threshold was Ira.

She threw up both hands apologetically. "Keep going, I don't want to distract you. I'm just looking for . . ." Then her voice turned harsh all of a sudden, and unconcealed anger rang out in it: "Konev! Get over here! Come on!"

Yurka instinctively ducked his head into his shoulders. He knew a tone like that did not bode well. While he was slowly trudging up the center aisle toward the main exit, he racked his brain, trying to remember where he'd managed to botch it. And it turned out there were a lot of places: he'd skipped out from mess duty, he'd run away from camp, he'd wandered around nobody knew where for five whole hours, if not more . . . And it was unlikely his disappearance had gone unnoticed, of course. In comparison to everything that had happened since he got back to camp, Yurka's flight now seemed insignificant, unimportant, not the kind of thing worth worrying about. But he was apparently the only one who thought that. And now he was going to get it, and how.

But to his great surprise, Ira Petrovna looked more worried than angry, and she just asked in irritation, "How can you disappear for so long, Yur? We were worried!"

"What was there to worry about?"

"You just went and abandoned your mess duty and disappeared! How long were you gone? Why didn't you tell anyone beforehand? How can you just run off like that? Did you even think about anybody else? Volodya was beside himself when he came to me and said you'd vanished!"

Yurka swallowed nervously. He hadn't actually thought about what would happen here at camp while he was wandering around in the forest, looking for the bus stop and figuring himself out. Nor had he thought about how Volodya would feel... because once Yurka had come back, Volodya hadn't yelled at him, instead blindsiding him with completely different words and actions...

Ira went on: "You only think about yourself, but other people suffer because of you! I've never seen Volodya like that! He was running around looking everywhere, you know! He crawled all over the unfinished barracks, and even went out onto the river! The duty phys ed guys told him over and over they hadn't seen you, but he combed the whole beach anyway, and even took a boat and went out somewhere! He's always so calm, you know, so levelheaded, but it was like someone else had taken over his body—and it was all your fault, Konev! Yura?! Hey, Yura! Are you even listening to me?!"

Yurka was listening. Ira was asking him a lot of questions, but he wasn't coming up with answers quick enough, and he doubted he even needed to answer them at all. But now, just thinking about what Ira Petrovna was telling him, thinking about how Volodya had felt when he found out Yurka wasn't in camp, Yurka felt the hair on the back of his neck start to rise. Suddenly it hit him: Volodya had looked for him! He'd gone down to the river. Had he tried to go to the willow? Had he taken the boat to get to it? And another thing: Volodya hadn't gone immediately to tell the educational specialist. Neither had Ira! But that kind of negligent attitude toward the job, *and* the loss of a Pioneer—that would mean getting fired on the spot, if not being hauled into court.

What had Yurka almost done?

"Why didn't you report it to Olga Leonidovna?" he asked, head bowed guiltily.

"If you'd been missing any longer, we would have! I was on the verge of going to the office, but you can thank Olezhik for telling us right away that you were here in the movie theater. And Volodya had asked me not to tell anybody yet. It would've meant a reprimand for us, but you would've been kicked out of camp. And then also"—she hesitated for a few seconds—"you kept my secret..."

Yurka nodded and said softly, "I'm sorry, Ir..."

"What good is your 'Sorry' to me, Yur? You can see yourself that I'm not even angry. I just really want you to understand the full gravity of your actions. Yura, you're already grown, but you're acting like such a child. Grow up already!"

Yurka winced. Acting like a child—the same thing Volodya had said to him an hour ago, word for word!

"Take responsibility for your actions! Remember they can have consequences for people other than yourself!"

"I will, Ir. I'll do my best," Yurka said hurriedly, so that Ira would let him go and stop lecturing him.

She reached over, squeezed his shoulder, and said, more affectionately now, "I get it, it's been hard for you after what happened..."

Yurka's guts turned to ice. What was she talking about?

"It's all very unpleasant and hurtful, but, Yura, it's not Volodya's fault either. There's nothing else he can do..."

"Wh-what?" fumbled Yurka.

"I know everything. He told me. I get it."

He told her? Was that even possible? Would Volodya really go and reveal something like that to Irina? Yurka felt frantic.

"Is this... what are you talking about?" he asked, his voice trembling.

"About Masha, of course. About how Volodya assigned her your competition piece. I know how much music means to you, I remember how much you suffered for it. But, Yura, that's no excuse for doing something so stupid! And it gives you no right to drag other people into your own personal problems!"

Yurka let out a breath. Ira thought Yurka was acting out because of Masha and the music. She didn't know the real reason!

"I'm sorry, Ir. Really, I'm sorry." Now he was being sincere, and way more direct. "I really wasn't thinking of the consequences. I... I'm an idiot!"

She took her hand off his shoulder.

"You're no idiot, Yur. Not at all. You just need to grow up a little."

Yurka nodded again, not knowing what to say to that. Sometimes he didn't understand Ira. She supported him so often, and protected him, and was affectionate with him, even though his behavior was sometimes pretty darn awful.

He made up his mind to ask her something he'd long been wondering. "Ir . . ."

She'd already turned away to leave but looked back at him over her shoulder, eyebrows raised.

"Why is your relationship with Zhenya a secret? What's the big deal?"

Ira forced a smile. "Do you really not know? I thought the whole camp was talking about it."

"No. I don't listen to gossip."

"Fine, I'll tell you. You'll find out anyway. Zhenya's married. I mean, he's going to get a divorce, but it takes time . . . Don't tell anyone, okay? I don't want rumors to spread. It's fine if people know that about him, but if people start talking about me, saying I'm wrecking someone's family . . . It's just something that happens in life, but it could end up making me look pretty bad. We're in a Pioneer camp, with kids, where we're all promoting family-oriented values, but what kind of example am I setting?"

Yurka was stunned by Ira's candid admission but decided to mull this information over sometime later.

Ira sighed and concluded, "Okay, get back to rehearsal now. The call to dinner will be sounding soon. Promise me you'll shape up."

"I will."

As she walked away, she added, "And apologize to Volodya."

Yurka returned to the movie theater determined to talk to Volodya immediately and to apologize first thing. But when he saw how the artistic director was darting around the stage, shaking the script at people, when he heard Volodya's voice trembling with tension and exhaustion, Yurka realized that this was not the time. He remembered what Ira had just told him a few minutes ago and decided to act like a grown-up.

The sound of the bugle calling them to dinner caught the whole drama club by surprise. Volodya and the actors scattered to find their troops and get in line for the mess hall, but not before agreeing that everyone whose acting had displeased Olga Leonidovna would come back to the theater after dinner to rehearse some more.

As they were leaving the theater, Yurka poked Volodya in the ribs and smiled, letting him know he was there and interested in talking. Volodya also smiled, but it was forced and awkward.

That smile completely took the wind out of Yurka's sails. Volodya had almost kissed him! Why did he seem so awkward toward him now? Maybe he didn't want to after all? Maybe he'd just done it out of pity? But do people really kiss people out of pity? Well—*almost* kiss them? He had to mull all this over, digest it, wrap his mind around it . . .

On his way to the mess hall, Yurka realized he had absolutely no appetite, even though he hadn't eaten anything since breakfast. That fake smile was making everything even more muddled. There were so many questions buzzing around in Yurka's head, so many thoughts, suspicions, and doubts, that he felt completely exhausted. And the last thing he wanted now was to be stuck in a mess hall in the middle of a raucous crowd of people and see Volodya nearby—again—but not be able to work up the courage to go talk to him, and just be left asking himself even more questions.

Yurka grabbed a quick bite and then returned to the empty movie theater. At first he was going to sit down at the piano once more and try playing something, but then he saw a notebook on a seat in the front row of the audience. He immediately recognized the bent cover with writing all over it: Volodya's notebook. Had he forgotten it as he was rushing out to dinner?

Yurka picked up the notebook and started leafing through it. He saw a bunch of notes penciled in the margins. They were mostly technical: "Ulya overacting," "stage decor: forest," "costume for grandma?" and so forth. It was interesting for Yurka to look through these notes, even though he already knew most of them, since Volodya went through them with everyone at rehearsal. He read the script almost all the way to the end and got to the scene with the German. Above it he saw a note of just one word: "Yurochka." His heart skipped a beat and he couldn't breathe for a second. Volodya had written his name here when he decided to give him the role, but *how* he'd written it! Could it actually be that Volodya privately thought of him that affectionately? Yurochka . . . He never called Yurka that out loud!

While the rest of the camp was finishing dinner, Yurka studied his lines. There weren't many, but they were hard. The evil Gestapo officer Krause was a negative character, but that was hard to reconcile with the tender penciled note above his lines.

Still, Yurka was determined to surprise Volodya, so he settled in to rehearse. He paced around the stage, reading his lines to the empty auditorium and imagining that he was sitting at a table, interrogating Zina, sitting across from him . . . Yurka thought he wasn't doing half bad. But then that step creaked and the actors came piling back in.

It wasn't a small group: joining Yurka were all three Pukes, Nastya, and Sashka. Olezhka also joined the outsiders, even though everyone had been happy with his acting. Masha had also really wanted to come, but Ira Petrovna had dragged her back to the cabin to rehearse the accompaniment for the Troop One dance number for the concert celebrating Camp Barn Swallow Day. Masha resisted but had to go. Yurka was glad he'd spend the evening without her dismal piano plunking.

Yurka, the Pukes, and Volodya all sat in the back row of the audience while the little kids warmed up for the scene with the fascists. The Pukes weren't saying anything, but their presence was bothering Yurka anyway. With them around, he had to act like nothing special had happened or was happening, although inside him the sirens had been blaring and the steam trains had been shrieking for an hour already, everything smoking and shaking: "Grab Volodya and get out of here!"

"Olga Leonidovna was right about some things," the potential kidnap victim mused aloud. "The partisans were under constant suspicion. There were two thousand German soldiers in Obol, a whole convoy of executioners. Torture and death were assured for any partisan who fell into their hands . . . and here we are depicting these heroes as though they didn't even feel fear!"

"What she wants is professional actors!" said Yurka indignantly. "The moral of the show is to demonstrate that anyone can be a hero," he said, repeating the educational specialist's words. "You know what, though? Kids like us today wouldn't be able to fight like those kids did during the war, much less win. But here she is, asking us to portray them."

"Yikes, shut it, Konev. You'll jinx us. We can do it . . . ," Ksyusha said gloomily.

"I told you we should've done something modern," Ulyana protested, and in a soft, pleasant voice, started the poignant duet from *Athena and Venture*: "You'll wak with the dawn's first ray . . ."

Polina stared dully at the floor.

Volodya ignored the protest. He glanced at Yurka and shrugged. "Yes we would. It's war. They'll kill you anyway. Your only choice here is to either surrender or get revenge for the ones they already killed. But enough lyricism. Time to get to work."

A tense atmosphere settled over the auditorium. Volodya already turned into a stereotypical demanding artistic director whenever he stepped inside the theater, but now he was utterly pitiless, ignoring everything around him to focus solely on rehearsal. He blew his top, and yelled at the actors, and scolded the little kids, even though they were already sitting as quiet as mice.

But Yurka didn't hide his boredom. There was a long way to go until his scene as Krause, and it was by no means certain Volodya was even going to rehearse it. So what was he supposed to do with himself? Sit around languishing until rehearsal was over and then hope Volodya would be in the mood to talk? No way. Yurka was tired of all the waiting and hoping. The last three hours had felt like an eternity.

There was an incident with Ulyana during rehearsal. She was overacting badly, and after yet another repetition of her monologue, Volodya's patience snapped. He cut her off in the middle of a word, shouting: "Can you really not hear yourself, how terrible you are?! Do you not understand you're an avenger? You're a partisan, Ulya! Why are you reciting your lines in a sing-song like a four-year-old at a preschool parents' day?!"

Yurka cringed, squeezing his eyes shut: on top of the general tension and Olga Leonidovna's criticism, Volodya had gone too far. It was no wonder that Ulyana burst into tears. And Volodya immediately regretted his words, of course, and rushed to console her. He put one arm around her awkwardly, and she seized the opportunity to bury her face in his shoulder, getting tears, snot, and mascara all over his sleeve.

"Ulyana, I'm sorry, I didn't mean to . . . What I said was stupid . . . Come on, now . . . don't cry . . ."

But Ulyana just sighed and pressed even closer to Volodya.

Yurka was boiling with rage and jealousy: here was another one, just like Masha, turning on the waterworks to make Volodya grovel. And it was working! Conscientious, kindhearted Volodya was there on the double with his apologies, demeaning himself in front of her. *Well, aren't you just so sympathetic!* thought Yurka indignantly. *Dancing with random Mashas because you feel sorry for them . . . Did you feel sorry for me, too, and that's why you wanted to kiss me?!*

He stomped angrily to a far corner of the theater, then sat down in a seat at the end of a row that was obscured in the darkness of the closed curtain. Scowling, he fixed his eyes on the bust of Lenin gathering dust in a corner. He remembered how a couple of days ago Volodya had made him carry the incredibly heavy bust off the stage like he was some kind of porter. Yurka snorted and frowned even harder. He sneaked a look around and saw that nobody was paying the least attention to his travails. Only Vladimir Ilych gazed morosely at him with his blank plaster eyes.

"What are you looking at?" mumbled Yurka. Nobody heard him. Onstage, Ulyana was still convulsed with sobs and Volodya was still murmuring apologetically to her.

Lenin, obviously, didn't answer Yurka's question.

Yurka stood up and walked up to the bust. On its pedestal, it was about as tall as he was. "Nobody needs me," Yurka complained. He reached out to Lenin's forehead and ran his hand over the rough plaster of the leader's bald head. He heaved a sigh. "You and me, we're the same, huh? Nobody needs you either, you're standing over here in the corner too, gathering dust . . . Eh, Vladimir Ilych, you're the only one who understands me." He grasped the head of the plaster statue in both hands, leaned forward, and kissed Lenin right in the forehead. "Thank you for listening to me . . . I actually feel better now . . ."

"Yura!" hissed Volodya behind him. "What on earth are you doing?!" Judging by his tone, he was furious.

Yurka turned around and looked at the artistic director. Indeed, Volodya was furious, no doubt about it: his eyes flashed lightning.

"What? I'm rehearsing!" protested Yurka, and began reading his lines, whispering them into Lenin's ear: My brave Fräulein, deep in the heart of this small mechanism"—he stuck out two fingers to make a pistol and poked it into Lenin's temple—"lies one single solitary round. It is not large. But it is deadly. All my finger has to do is twitch, completely by accident, and there will no longer be any need for long, drawn-out conversations. Ponder this, my brave Fräulein. Your life is priceless, but it would be so easy to simply end it with one careless move . . ."

"Yura, what's with the anti-Soviet antics?!"

Yurka turned around and looked at him, nonplussed.

Volodya closed the distance between them and said right in Yurka's ear, "You do get how that looks from the outside, right? You're insulting the memory of the leader of the revolution."

Yurka scoffed. "Oh, to hell with that revolution! To hell with Leonidovna and her partisans and fascists! That's all she and Palych ever do: paint some people as all evil and some people as all good . . ."

"What? You're complaining because they're calling *fascism* evil?! Have you lost your mind? Have you gotten so into your part that fascism isn't automatically evil now?"

"I'm not saying that! But what about the opposite? Maybe Communism isn't automatically good. Think about it! Volodya, have you really never wondered why they only ever talk about the same things when it comes to fascist Germany? The war, the annihilation, the concentration camps . . . But what about the social structure, the political system? Why don't we get anything about them? Could it be because at that time in the USSR everything was exactly the same way? Just instead of Jews in the camps, it was dissenters, and instead of Aryans, it was Party members? The Germans even had their own version of Pioneers!"

Volodya frowned. "What are you getting at?"

Yurka didn't know. There he went again, talking utter nonsense just so people would pay attention to him, like a little kid. Yurka didn't like it. He disgusted himself. But he couldn't stop. He couldn't let Volodya go back to Ulyana.

"I'm saying that Germans are people too, like us. They're not all scum."

Volodya scoffed. "But how do you know if they're scum or not? Because you have an uncle who lives there? So what? *Now* they're okay, but back then the whole country had become murderers!"

"Not all of them!" exclaimed Yurka.

"Well, *obviously* not all of them! But, Yura—" Volodya paused. He exhaled in frustration. "Look, you have to have better judgment! I know you want to think and speak your mind freely, and you can, but just not here! You have to adjust your behavior to fit the situation, and if you can't, then you need to learn to lie! Nobody should even *think* the things you're saying aloud!"

"Seems like I've heard this somewhere before," growled Yurka through gritted teeth. "But I'm talking about something else, Volodya. Our honored Communist Leonidovna is only demanding our patriotism so she can check a box. Our quasi-Komsomol girls here are nodding their heads, but then they go cry their eyes out when you're mad at them. Just look around: nobody gives a crap about the heroes! These girls are only here because of you!"

"And you have some other reason?" Volodya's eyes flashed. He turned around to leave.

Yurka was also here because of Volodya, actually. But Volodya . . . Volodya was doing the show not to check a box, not to attract somebody's attention: he legitimately wanted to showcase the Pioneer Heroes' feat for people, to let people know about it. He was the only one who was genuine about any of it, and he probably felt very lonely.

"Yes! I do care!" In any case, Yurka decided to correct his mistakes later; right now all he wanted was for Volodya not to have the last word.

Time stretched out longer and longer, as though it weren't half an hour but half a day. The clock's second hand seemed to be making fun of Yurka, crawling slowly and stumbling at every tick, so much that it felt like there should have already been five more each time the hand finally moved.

Finally Volodya clapped loudly, stood up, and said, "That's it for today, folks." Yurka noted that the time was only eight fifty by the clock, even though finishing early was completely out of character for the artistic director, especially now, when every minute counted. "Go take a break. Polya, Ulya, and Ksyusha, your task is to rehearse the Avengers' dialogue a few more times, just among yourselves. Especially you, Ulya. Have the girls help you. You're still overacting a bit. And you, Sashka, are a dead fascist, so remember that and stop snoring when you're lying onstage! Dead! Not asleep! Got it?"

Everyone he addressed nodded.

"You're dismissed."

The little kids scattered. The girls, whispering to each other, also proceeded languorously to the exit. The last person to leave the stage was Ksyusha. Yurka happened to be at the other end of the auditorium at that moment and saw her walk up to Volodya, but he didn't hear what she asked him. Volodya shook his head no.

After Ksyusha left, Yurka demanded, with a twinge of jealousy in his voice, "What did she want?"

"She was asking me to come to the dance."

"And?"

"No go." Volodya shrugged nonchalantly. "We still have a bunch of work to do here. Speaking of which, come on, I wanted to talk to you about the set."

He got onto the stage and called Yurka to follow him. Yurka's brows shot up—"What, he seriously wants to talk about the set now?!"—but he trudged along anyway.

"Look," said Volodya, gesturing toward the back left corner of the stage. "This is where we'll arrange the HQ set: desk, chairs, the propaganda posters up there—a base, basically. And over here"—Volodya walked over to the right side of the stage—"we won't open the whole curtain, and this will be where we do the outdoor scenes. We'll have the hollow log here, their hiding place. We still need to think of a way to hide the rifles so they're not visible from the audience, though: our log isn't actually hollow like theirs was, ours is a regular one."

Yurka was only listening with half an ear. Normally he would've wanted to get into the details, but he couldn't get himself to focus on anything but the fact that he and Volodya were finally all by themselves in the empty movie theater.

"Well, but maybe we could actually put the log right up next to the curtain and then stick the rifles under the curtain . . ." Volodya ducked behind the curtain and gave the heavy fabric a sharp tug. A cloud of dust enveloped him. "Ugh! Crap, now we'll have to beat the curtain, too . . ."

Yurka couldn't stand it anymore. He strode quickly up to Volodya and shoved him so that Volodya fell back against the wall, pinning the curtain to the wall behind him. Yurka grabbed the edges of the curtain and wrapped the dusty fabric around them both, hiding them from the empty auditorium.

"What are you doing?" asked Volodya, somewhere between indignant and surprised.

"I'm picking up where we left off."

Volodya shook his head: "Not here I won't. What if somebody comes . . ."

"But nobody can see us!"

"Yes . . . that's right . . . ," whispered Volodya, and put his hands on Yurka's shoulders.

Yurka screwed his eyes shut and lunged for Volodya's lips. Their lips touched and Yurka just stood there like that, holding his breath and keeping his eyes shut tight, afraid the same thing would happen now as at the power shed and Volodya would push him away. But Volodya didn't push him away. Volodya's hands tightened on Yurka's shoulders and he pulled Yurka in. That innocent touching of lips to lips called forth such a storm of feeling in Yurka that he felt as if both a tender, romantic Viennese waltz and the nimble, surging "Ride of the Valkyries" had started playing at the same time inside him. It caught him in a whirl and tossed him up into the very sky, almost like what the music had done to him a couple of hours ago. But until now, he'd been clueless about the fact that playing music was hardly the only thing that could make him soar. And that heaven started not way up in the sky but somewhere about a hundred and seventy centimeters from the ground, at the level of Volodya's lips. And also that, from now on, everything would be different, everything inside him would change—and everything outside him, too: the nights would now be bright, the winters warm.

Suddenly Volodya tensed, his back going tight as a bowstring as he turned his face away, although he pressed Yurka even closer, clutching him almost painfully tight. Yurka had no time to react before he went deaf: Volodya sneezed so loudly that Yurka's ears rang. Then he sneezed again. And again. As they fought their way out of the dusty curtain, they were both laughing, Yurka with his head thrown back, but Volodya bent double, from sneezing, or guffawing, or both.

They both continued giggling stupidly as they made their way back to the Troop Five cabin. And Yurka also got the hiccups.

That night the little boys didn't run riot. They didn't even ask for a scary story. Volodya had probably worked them too hard. This was the first time Yurka wasn't glad they fell asleep so quickly, because it meant Yurka had to leave.

Their goodbye handshake was a little awkward. All night Yurka been dying to ask Volodya one burning question, but he just couldn't muster the courage. Now, as they stood in silence, right hands clasped, Volodya wouldn't let go, as though he were waiting for something. When Volodya finally released his hand and softly said, "Bye," Yurka had no choice. He had no more strength to wait until tomorrow. He panicked: "No! Wait! I want to talk to you. I have something to ask you."

"What?"

"I don't get it. You were talking about there's a girl you like, and—"

"Is that really what I said?" Volodya interrupted. Yurka stared at Volodya, confused. "I didn't say 'girl.' I said 'person.'"

"But then who is it?"

"It's a long story. Forget about it," urged Volodya. Out of nowhere he hugged Yurka, then just as suddenly released him. "And then I'll forget about the 'girl from my building,' too."

"It's hard to forget something like that," grumbled Yurka.

Volodya snorted mirthlessly. "Tell me about it." He took both of Yurka's hands in his own and said regretfully, "Yur, we can't keep dragging this goodbye out. Irina's going to notice. And it really is time to get some sleep. Right now the main thing's to make it to tomorrow, right?"

"Wrong. I'm coming to you today," said Yurka firmly. "Tonight, late, after everyone's asleep. At midnight, or maybe a little later."

"No. We can't risk it, especially not after this afternoon."

"I'm not asking you. I'm telling you. I'm coming. I'll tap on the window."

"Don't . . ."

"Even if you don't wait up for me, I'm still coming."

"Well . . . okay, then. I won't be able to get to sleep anyway, after today. Just be careful and stay out of trouble."

Waiting until the little kids fell asleep was no problem, but it was a long time until the senior troops went quiet. As soon as Yurka lay down in bed, all the day's accumulated tiredness hit him like a ton of bricks. He kept drifting off, but with a supreme effort of will he caught himself every time and made himself wake up. He wanted to see Volodya again too badly to let himself doze off.

Once the camp had gone not only quiet but dark—some of the outside lights were turned off after lights out—Yurka knew it was time. He got up, dressed, and left the cabin.

This was the first time he'd seen the camp so quiet and empty. His imagination ran wild, fed by the lack of sleep and the day's trepidations: Had the enemies of the Soviet Union gone ahead and hit the place with an atomic bomb, killing everything around? He couldn't hear any owls hooting or any barking from the dogs over in Horetivka; only the crickets gave themselves away with their violently loud chirping. Yurka had even heard that some insects, like cockroaches, were capable of surviving a nuclear war.

All the windows of all the cabins were completely dark. At last he reached the Troop Five cabin, which was just as dark and quiet as the rest.

Yurka instantly found the window he needed. He stepped up onto the small ledge formed by the base of the cabin and knocked. A few seconds later, a pale face with glasses appeared out of the darkness. Yurka pointed back behind himself at the bushes and whispered soundlessly that he'd wait for Volodya there.

Volodya came out dressed all in black a couple of minutes later, but even that brief wait felt like an eternity to Yurka. He rushed out to meet Volodya and grabbed his hands, but Volodya jerked back: "What are you doing, they'll see! Not here."

"Fine," grunted Yurka sullenly. He held tight to Volodya's wrist and dragged him through the bushes toward the athletic fields.

"What kind of Pandora's box have I opened here?" hissed Volodya, running behind Yurka.

They went by the tennis and basketball courts to end up by the pool. The only thing past the pool was dense woods. Right now it was petrifyingly dark out here. The water rippling in the pool looked black, and the moonlight cast shadows onto it from the tall trees. At the far side of the pool, past the row of starting blocks, statues of swimming Pioneers stood with their backs to the woods. Two white plaster silhouettes, of a girl in a swimsuit with an oar and a boy getting ready to dive, glowed like ghosts against the background of the dark, gloomy woods. But Yurka couldn't have cared less about how scary it all looked. He barely registered it. Instead, he dragged Volodya on, skirting the pool to hide behind the pedestal of a statue.

He took a step toward Volodya, wanting to embrace him, but Volodya pushed him away: "Wait, people can see us. Let's get down."

Volodya sat on his knees on the grass right next to the pedestal and pulled Yurka down. Yurka submitted, but he was horribly offended. "If you push me away just one more time, I'll disappear out of your life for good. I'll—I'll run away for real!"

"Fine," said Volodya. In the dark, it was hard to tell which emotions were playing across his face. "I'm sorry. You know why I do that . . . But I won't do it anymore." Then he paused. "So you did mean to run away earlier? Where were you?"

"Over there." Yurka gestured in the general direction of the road. "I went out to the bus stop."

Volodya took a deep breath and let it out slowly, as though he were trying to get himself under control and calm down.

"For five hours?! Yura, I just about lost it looking for you!" Volodya whispered hotly. "I ran around the camp like a crazy person. I checked every room in the unfinished barracks, every single one! And there's forty of them in there! But you weren't anywhere. And I was afraid to ask about you, in case anyone figured out that you were up to who-knows-what again and told Leonidovna. You know how fast rumors spread here, and if she found out, that's it: Consider yourself already kicked out of camp. And that was if I could find you! But what if I couldn't?!" Now Volodya was doing his best to yell at Yurka in a whisper.

"Oh, simmer down! What could happen to me? This isn't my first time here; I already know every—"

"Who knows what could happen? Something could! Do you have any idea what kind of things I was imagining?"

"Like what? That I went to drown myself?" Yurka chortled.

"And you think that's funny? Want to see how it felt to be in my shoes? Because I can do that for you. I can do that for you right now!" It was clear that Volodya was barely holding himself back from shouting at the top of his lungs: he was breathing heavily, and his hands were shaking—possibly his whole body, too.

"Okay, okay, calm down. I'm here, nothing happened, everything's fine."

"I thought I'd strangle you as soon as I saw you!"

"Don't worry so much. It's just me. I mean, I understand that you are responsible for me—"

"What the hell does responsibility have to do with it! You're a living human being and you're my . . . my friend. And especially after everything that happened yesterday . . ."

"Then strangle me, if you want! Just quit freaking out."

Yurka faltered to a halt in mid-sentence. He was flustered. Volodya had suddenly put his arms around him.

"I'm not angry anymore," he said quietly. "I stopped being angry as soon as I saw you play."

He released Yurka from his embrace, making Yurka almost groan aloud in despair. Yurka wanted it to keep going; he wanted their embrace to be permanent; he didn't want to let Volodya go at all. Yurka, still on his knees, shuffled closer to Volodya and took his shaking hands in his own.

"If you had just heard me play instead of seeing me, you would've kept wanting to throttle me," Yurka said half-jokingly.

"Don't talk nonsense. You play really well," said Volodya. Tenderly and very, very slowly, as though he were trying to sense the warmth of Yurka's hand with every cell of his skin, he ran his fingers along Yurka's palms and whispered, "Yura, take care of your hands. They really are delicate." He lifted Yurka's hands, then bent down his head and kissed them tenderly.

Yurka was terribly embarrassed. His face started flaming and he could feel himself going red all the way up to the crown of his head. His cheeks were burning—but forget his cheeks: his fingers spasmed and then turned to stone, so he couldn't straighten them. That was what made him good and truly self-conscious. Yurka cast about frantically for something to say and seized on the first thing that came to mind. It was also the stupidest thing. "Yours are too! I mean, I like your hands a lot too. They're so soft . . . as if you . . . as if you moisturize them."

"No," chuckled Volodya. It looked like he'd finally been able to relax. "I don't do anything special to them."

Yurka's vision was going blurry from how close he was to Volodya. He desperately wanted to kiss him but was too shy to ask. He shifted in his seat, moving carefully closer to Volodya, and lamely mumbled something without even knowing what he was saying. "Nothing at all?"

The main thing was to talk, to distract Volodya with conversation—didn't matter about what—and keep nudging closer.

"No," said Volodya slowly, flustered. "Well, maybe I wash them in really hot water sometimes . . ."

Yurka was willing to swear he'd seen Volodya raise his eyebrows, even in the dark. Now Volodya was very close, just a couple of centimeters away, but kept making no move to kiss Yurka. It was as though he were waiting for something. Maybe the thing to do was just ask directly?

But Yurka, in his impatience, whispered something completely different—"Really, really hot water?"—and edged just a teeny bit closer.

Volodya was sitting in the exact same place in the exact same position, stroking Yurka's hand and looking at Yurka with flashing eyes. "Almost boiling." He smiled. "Why?"

"Maybe I should, too?" Volodya was already too close. Yurka couldn't breathe.

"No, it would hurt you," Volodya said seriously. Then he laughed. "Yura, what are we even talking about?"

"I don't know . . ." Yurka exhaled heavily, decided to hell with his shyness, and pressed his lips to Volodya's.

Suffocating from nerves and rapture, Yurka was afraid Volodya would push him away again. But that didn't happen. The kiss was innocent and very long. But even if it had lasted an eternity, it wouldn't have been enough for Yurka.

Suddenly, Volodya reached out and touched a lock of Yurka's shaggy bangs and said, "I've wanted to do that for a long time." He smoothed the lock of hair, then stroked Yurka's ear and temple tenderly. It was ticklish, but felt so good that Yurka moved his head, pressing his temple up under Volodya's fingers. It was like he was a cat asking to be petted.

Volodya chuckled quietly. He took Yurka's hands in his own again. Without speaking, he ran his nose along Yurka's cheek. There was more pleasure and tenderness in that gesture than in all their kisses combined, making something inside Yurka burst open.

They stayed there, hiding behind the statue, kneeling in front of each other and holding hands, until the sky went from black to inky blue. Volodya started and looked around at every sound, even though it was always obvious that it wasn't footsteps but the wind, or pine cones falling in the woods, or someone rattling their shutters far, far away. But no matter how dangerous and scary it was, he probably wanted to stay just as much as Yurka did.

Afterward, Yurka couldn't get to sleep for a long time. His wildly joyous thoughts made his heart do a frenzied tap dance. As if it were possible to fall asleep when everything was rumbling and rattling inside him, and his internal voice was refusing to shut up, and on top of that it wasn't whispering, or burbling, but shrieking with happiness! When his hands just itched to open the window, and his feet ached to carry him to the troop leaders' room, and he wanted to wrap himself, legs and arms and all, around Volodya and never let him go. Although—no, it would be better to steal him away, to drag him off into a dark corner and then wrap himself around him. But, actually, it didn't matter where they twined themselves together: Let them do it in the middle of the main square, as long as nobody bothered them! Yurka never managed to figure out the best way to turn into twining ivy and wrap around Volodya, since he finally fell asleep. His dreams were just as confused.

Yura blinked a few times and looked around. It had started raining again, and the wind had picked up a little and was blowing cold droplets into his face. The cracked asphalt led farther, to the athletic fields, where the morning calisthenics had been held. The fields hadn't fared much better than the rest of the camp. But one thing that had been preserved amazingly well was the big banner stretched out over the podium where the phys ed instructors had stood to demonstrate the exercises. The banner was sheltered from the wind and rain underneath a long awning, so on the faded cloth it was still possible to discern athletes crossing the finish line, as well as the slogan ALL WORLD RECORDS MUST BE OURS!

The twenty-five-meter pool had been on the other side of the athletic fields. There were lots of swim races. Yurka remembered the splashing, the shrill whistle blasts, and the troop leaders' shouting as if had been yesterday. But now all that was left of the pool was a great big pit whose far edge was crumbling in. The little tiles had come off the walls and rainwater had collected at the bottom and gone all green and swampy. Only the starting blocks, with their barely legible lane numbers, could indicate to the random passerby that this had once been a pool.

But the weathered, broken statues of swimming pioneers, covered in a layer of green, still stood on their pedestals. The woods behind them had grown considerably thinner. Yura heard the rumble of excavators and the whine of chain saws coming from out past the trees. He walked a little way into the trees and saw large clearings in the middle of what had once been a thick coniferous forest. The trees were coming down fast here, and out in the distance he could see a construction site. Out past that bristled the triangular roofs of completed homes.

Yura sighed and returned to the statues of pioneers. He walked up close to the pedestal and stood at the exact place where that evening, twenty years ago, he and Volodya had spent half the night kneeling face-to-face, holding hands, unable to let each other go. Yura chuckled, remembering how badly his legs and back had hurt afterward. But his smile evaporated immediately: this exact place was soon to be wiped from the face of the earth. Yura's childhood, his happiest memories, were going to be destroyed irreplaceably, by progress as well as by time. Of course, nobody needed an abandoned Pioneer camp anymore. It was just taking up space. Yura imagined the "new" stepping on Camp Barn Swallow like a giant's enormous foot, crushing it. Soon, nothing would be left. Nothing left of what had been so precious to him.

He stood by the base of the statue and looked down at the ground. This was where they had sat, where Volodya had held his hand, and embraced him tightly, and promised he'd never push him away again. Yura smiled to himself. His memories warmed him from the inside. How naïve he'd been then. Just a dumb kid who had no idea how serious the thing that was happening to them was. At the time, everything had been pure emotion for Yurka: the rapture of first love, the joy of it being requited, the sweetness of reciprocation... Maybe it was good that Yurka had been such an absolute child. Because thanks to his innocent, childlike view of things, he hadn't punished himself the way Volodya had. He hadn't hated himself; he hadn't hurt himself; and—this was the main thing—he hadn't made the terrible mistake that Volodya would go on to make, in the very near future, just a few years after working at Camp Barn Swallow.

CHAPTER THIRTEEN
LULLABY FOR A TROOP LEADER

The next morning Yurka was playing pioneerball with Troop Two on the beach. It was packed. The girls from Troop Two who were in the play were also here: Nastya, who was playing Portnova; Katya, who was Zina Luzgina; and Yulya, who was the village traitor. They greeted Yurka in unison. It made Yurka feel really good.

Troop One was ahead, but, as was the rule at camp, friendship came out the winner anyway.

Yurka grumbled to Ksyusha, the only Puke who was playing: "Next time we have to call our team 'Friendship' so we win for sure."

"Perfect!" replied Ksyusha happily. She even smiled at him. Yurka was stupefied. Ksyusha?! Smiling at *him*?!

After the game was over, Yurka, who was dying from the heat, went over to the water to swim—or, rather, to help Vanya dunk Mikha. They'd promised to be ready as soon as the final score was announced, but they got held up back on the beach. Yurka got tired of waiting and got into the water on his own, but he'd only just started swimming around, relaxing and cooling off, when Olga Leonidovna and Volodya appeared on the beach.

The educational specialist was assiduously explaining something to the artistic director, who was himself assiduously looking around, searching for someone. Yurka guessed who that was. He stuck two fingers in his mouth and whistled loudly. Volodya saw him, squared his shoulders, waved, and smiled, glasses flashing. And then Yurka remembered what had happened yesterday. He hadn't forgotten, of course, but now he remembered it even more clearly—so clearly that he felt Volodya's breath, Volodya's smell, on his lips. A warm feeling spread through his chest, and Yurka went still, a stupid expression on his face. He relaxed so much that he almost went underwater, but he came back to his senses and started moving his arms again.

Olga Leonidovna yanked Volodya's sleeve—just like Yurka, Volodya had stopped, transfixed, to gaze at him—and dragged the troop leader over to the Troop Two boys, who were sitting in a circle on their towels. Then she dragged him over to a little group of boys from Yurka's troop: Pasha, Mitka, and Vanya. After the boys nodded, scared, Olga Leonidovna grabbed Volodya's arm and they went away.

The whole visit didn't take very long. Yurka hadn't even had time to get out of the water. He shouted to Mikha and Vanka, who raced over to him, kicking sand on whoever was sitting on the beach and splashing water on whoever was playing in the river.

"What did she want?" Yurka asked.

"She was asking us to be extras in the big crowd scene," replied Vanka. "Well, not really asking. She told us we had to, and that was that."

"Ooooh," said Yurka.

"'Ooooh,'" Mikha mimicked him mockingly. "Hey, Yurets, listen: that artistic director of yours, I heard he's, like, harsh. He's mean! But don't tell him I said that, okay?"

"Volodya?" laughed Yurka, remembering the way that last night into the early morning the usually stern eyes under their glasses had come right up to his face, and then closed, and hadn't opened again until the end of that long, warm kiss. Yurka burst into a sweat even though he was in cool water. "Oh . . . uh . . . if something goes wrong, Mikh, Olga Leonidovna's the one who'll tear your head off, not Volodya."

"Oh no, we're done for!"

"Come on, Mikh, it's no big deal," said Vanka. "Petlytsin over there's the one who got hit with a speaking part. All you and I have to do is stand there without saying anything and we'll be fine."

"No you won't!" said Yurka indignantly. "You have to do what Volodya says, guys! Just you try goofing off . . ."

"We won't!" Mikha assured him.

"We get it!" confirmed Vanka. "So can we swim now, or what? We're gonna freeze if we stand around any longer."

"Race you!" shouted Yurka, and leaped forward.

When they got back to the beach, Yurka dried himself off slowly as he gazed at the opposite shore, hoping to see the willow, and mused, "So Petlitsyn was given a speaking part, huh? Must be Yezavitov. That's too bad. Volodya didn't want that. Mitya'd be better, that voice of his is pretty darn big."

"Where is Mitya, anyway?" asked Vanka, who had stretched out lazily on the hot sand.

The answer followed promptly.

"Greetings, Pioneers! You're listening to the Pioneer radio newspaper *Pioneer Dawn*," said Mitka himself, his voice booming from the speaker. "Tomorrow is the long-awaited celebration for our beloved Barn Swallow Pioneer Camp! There will be two important events today in preparation for it. First is the dry run of the talent show, which begins after snack. Performers from Troop One must be at the main square at sixteen hundred hours. Performers from Troop Two—at sixteen thirty . . ."

As Mitka dictated the rehearsal times for the rest of the troops, the girl tryhards from Troops One and Two copied them down intently. Olga Leonidovna had decided to have at least some kind of event to replace the play and ordered them to put together a little variety show, just an hour long, full of easy, simple songs so the performers wouldn't need more than a day to get ready. Yurka wasn't participating in it. All he knew was that the girls were going to do some kind of dance.

Mitka finished reciting the information for the first event and moved immediately to the second one, which was far more important and involved all the campers: "Today the whole camp has to do weigh-ins at the first aid station to confirm that everyone has become healthier and gained weight. Weigh-ins are mandatory. Larisa Sergeyevna will only see Pioneers when they come with their troops. She will not see individual Pioneers. Your troop leaders will inform you of your weigh-in times."

Not half an hour later, Mitka himself appeared, informing Yurka of some important news as he approached: he had been drafted to participate in the play, too. But Olga Leonidovna had given him a job that required some of the heaviest lifting in the whole show: raising and lowering the curtain. Yurka felt bad that the charismatic Mitka hadn't been given a speaking part, but in the end he was still grateful; at least now he wouldn't be the one who had to deal with the curtain.

As usual, they marched back to their cabin in formation. Yurka traditionally walked in front, next to Vanka, followed by Polina and Ksyusha, the next tallest pioneers in their troop. The girls were whispering loudly. Suddenly, Ulyana, who was right behind them, broke into their conversation excitedly: "Girls, get this: somebody left me a note on the beach. I was getting dressed and saw that something had fallen on the ground, a little piece of paper . . ."

"What's it say?" Ksyusha interrupted rudely.

"Let me read it! Come on, hand it over!" said Polina, perking up.

"Hey, Van, will our competition with the troop leaders be before the talent show tomorrow? First the assembly, then the competition, troop leaders versus campers, and then the talent show, right?" asked Yurka, looking for something—anything—to keep himself occupied. He already knew he had listed the events in the right order; he was just hoping that Vanka might know something more. But Vanka kept quiet. He was eavesdropping on the girls.

"'I like you!' Oooohhh! That's great, Ul! 'I like you!'" cried Polina happily. "Who's it from, do you know?"

"Hey, Yur! Konev!" Ksyusha called out. Yurka flinched. What did he have to do with any of this?

"Hm?"

"Did you happen to see if anybody came over to where our things were while we were out swimming?"

"Of course I didn't. Like I need to keep track of your things!"

"Maybe it was you! Maybe you're the one who left the note, huh, Yurchik?" giggled Ulyana.

Yurka sensed a jealous look from Mitka, who walking nearby, but Yurka just clicked his tongue and rolled his eyes.

Yurka wasn't able to go see Volodya until quiet hour. When he did, he could tell that Volodya had wanted to see him just as much, if not more. Volodya tilted his head down just a little bit and looked at Yurka directly but tenderly. He didn't say anything, but Yurka didn't need any words. He knew he didn't have any, either—none that were capable of expressing, even privately, the joy of being near Volodya. He caught his breath at the realization that they had that same closeness, and how much it permeated them both, and how tightly it bound them together. Yurka yearned for just one thing: to kiss Volodya as soon as possible.

It seemed as though Volodya wanted the same thing: without a word, Volodya nodded toward the river, and, without needing to discuss it, they headed toward the willow.

Once they were both underneath its branches, Yurka decided that this must be what absolute happiness was like: to forget himself, to stop sensing himself entirely as he touched his cheek to Volodya's, nuzzled him, pressed his lips to him. Listening to his breathing, inhaling his smell, seeing the way his eyelashes fluttered behind his glasses . . . "This is a dream," Yurka assured himself. But it wasn't him dreaming; it was the rest of the world. Some folks call sleep the "little death," and, indeed, everything around them really did seem to have died away. The breeze touched their skin and, with its gentle, warm gusts, set the willow branches swaying, and as they moved they let the sunbeams come flashing and dancing in.

Volodya was sleepy. He kept rubbing his tired eyes and was constantly yawning, but he bluntly rejected Yurka's offer to let him sleep awhile: "We've got too little time left. And we've still got a lot to do."

Yurka caught his breath. "And what is that, exactly?"

"Let's run these lines."

Yurka hadn't had any specific ideas in mind. Afraid of his own thoughts, he hadn't even dared to imagine what might be. But right now, right here, when they were finally alone with each other, they were going to run lines . . . ?!

"Why not?" he said, forcing a smile. He began, affecting a strong German accent: "My braffe Fräulein, I am affare zet your parents remain in Leningrad. And I am also affare zet your beloffed city hass fallen. A new flag flies above it. But I assure you zet all you haffe to do is agree to a small compromise, and . . ."

Yurka's parody of an accent was funny enough that he and Volodya ended up laughing themselves silly, distracting Yurka from his very disappointed thoughts. Volodya took the script from Yurka and started reading it himself, but he "zee'd" and "eff'd," as Yurka put it, too artificially. "Volod, you're overdoing it. Don't go to extremes. It has to be harmonious, like music. Listen—"

But Volodya cut him off. "Yur, you know something? You're really handsome when you're playing . . ."

"Handsome . . . handsome . . . handsome . . ." The echo reverberated through his mind. Yurka's vision started to swim. Any thoughts of Germans, "zees" and "effs," and all the rest of it simply vanished. He sat and looked at Volodya, abashed. In a quiet, affectionate voice, Volodya said, "You get such an interesting look on your face. You're inspired, but intense. You probably don't even notice that you don't just sit still, you rock back and forth, and sometimes you sing along under your breath, and sometimes you bite your lip. When I look at you, it's like you're somewhere far away. It makes me want to guess where you are. You should practice more often . . . I like it a lot . . ."

Volodya trailed off, blushing shyly. Refusing him when he was so good, so affectionate, when he was so dear to Yurka, was absolutely out of the question. But so was saying anything in response; the words simply lodged fast in Yurka's throat.

Volodya lay down on the grass, rested his head on Yurka's lap, and looked up at him with such a tender look that everything in Yurka's chest started melting. Forget talking—even breathing became impossible. Yurka put down the script and turned on the radio to keep the silence between them from growing heavy.

The radio station was playing its Russian classical music program again, and when the sounds of Tchaikovsky came from the speaker once more, Yurka was unable to restrain the storm of emotions inside him. In a voice trembling from joy, he said not the words that were surging up inside him but other words, about music: "Do you hear how it immerses you? It's like you're sinking into it: the bass envelops you, the air grows thick, everything goes still, and we go still, and we descend slowly, as if through honey, until we settle on the very bottom . . ."

"If I'd heard that two weeks ago, there's no way I'd have believed that Yurka Konev was the one saying it." Volodya smiled, but then turned serious. "You have to be the one to play the 'Lullaby' for the show!"

"But I've completely forgotten how to play it."

"Then remember! It has to be you, Yura. Please, I'm asking you. Play it."

His face was radiant, and the furrows in his brow were smoothed away, and the ever-present weariness that had by now become just another feature of his face was gone. Yurka gazed at Volodya, lost in admiration, and couldn't help asking if he could stroke Volodya's hair.

Volodya nodded. Yurka brushed his fingers along Volodya's temples and twined dark locks of Volodya's hair around his fingers. He bent over closer.

Feeling awfully shy, he asked in a whisper: "And could I take off your glasses, too? I've never really seen you without them . . ."

What an intimate act that turned out to be, taking Volodya's glasses off! It was so thrilling, so stirring, that his fingers shook, as though even more of Volodya was going to be revealed than if he'd been naked. Volodya's glasses turned out to be surprisingly heavy, and his face without them looked peculiarly sleepy and tired. There were dark circles under his eyes, and on top of that he squinted in a funny way.

Then those eyes opened wider as he remembered: "Oh, that reminds me: I have a present for you!"

He sat up and carefully extracted a large white mass the size of an apple from his shirt pocket. "Here. I picked it yesterday but forgot to give it to you. You wanted one, to remember that moment. Take it." He opened the hand that was stretched out to Yurka and revealed a wilted white water lily.

"You went all the way to the pond?" whispered Yurka as he held the lily in the palm of his hand. It was light as paper and even more fragile. "And you picked one anyway, even though you were the one who was all 'Don't, the Red Book, the Red Book' . . ."

Volodya shrugged pensively. "It felt like it was important to you. And it . . . well, it has to die anyway, sooner or later."

"It wasn't all that important at the time, but now . . . now, it actually is important, yes. Thank you. I'll keep it."

They remained silent for a time. Yurka was disappointed that Volodya didn't lie back down with his head on Yurka's lap but stayed sitting up. Volodya watched the river, lost in his own thoughts for a while. Then, as though he'd just remembered, he shot out in a single breath: "Yura, when did you realize that you had special feelings for me? Was it back then, in the pond, when I suggested that we go swimming? When I . . . got undressed?"

Yurka was terribly disconcerted at the question. He turned red and said, quietly and hesitantly: "Maybe I realized it then, but it all started before that."

"Before that?" Volodya sighed with relief and looked Yurka right in the eyes. "When exactly? What did I do? Was it when I let you sleep on my shoulder?"

"No, it was before that. On the merry-go-round, probably."

"Was it when I touched your knee?"

"'Was it when I did this? Was it when I did that?'" said Yurka, irritated. "It happened all by itself. You didn't do anything!"

"Are you absolutely sure about that?" Volodya bit his lip in consternation, and his gaze turned pleading.

"I'm absolutely sure," said Yurka.

"Good," said Volodya, finally lying back down and putting his head back on Yurka's lap. "That's good."

Yurka didn't want to restrain himself any longer and risked reaching out again to touch Volodya's forehead. Volodya finally closed his eyes. Yurka started stroking his hair, and he felt his whole being go peaceful for several long, sweet minutes.

"Should I turn the radio off? Maybe you could go ahead and get some sleep?" Yurka asked after a moment.

"I wouldn't be able to, anyway."

"Are you worried about the play?"

"That's not it, it's just that when you don't sleep for a long time, it gets harder and harder to fall asleep, and I haven't slept for two nights now."

"If you can't sleep at night, then sleep during the day. Right now. I'll guard you."

"Why do I need a guard?" Volodya smiled. "I'm not going anywhere."

"I'll make sure nobody comes and finds us. And I'll also study my lines," said Yurka, smirking.

Volodya laughed and nodded. "Let's give it a try."

Yurka stopped stroking Volodya's hair, picked up the notebook, and was holding it in both hands when Volodya, without looking, took Yurka's left hand again and put it back on his head. Yurka chuckled. There wasn't a trace of emotion on Volodya's face.

Yurka tried to study his lines, but he was unable to concentrate on the words. He kept looking down at Volodya's face, admiring it, watching how his cheeks and eyelashes twitched. Yurka was consumed by both admiration and apprehension at the same time.

"Not happening?" Yurka asked quietly.

"No," sighed Volodya.

"Should I sing you a lullaby?" laughed Yurka.

"Yes. But it'd be better if you played it. At the play. I really want to see the most extraordinary Yurka, the very best Yurka in the whole world, sitting at the piano, and I want to hear the 'Lullaby.' You love it so much, and I . . . I want to watch you so much. I want to admire you. Play it—for me."

Yurka would sooner have gnawed the willow down with his teeth than refuse Volodya now. After hearing that, he felt like the best person on the whole planet. How could he not feel that way? How could he not become the very best Yurka of all? So he did.

"I'll play it. For you."

He returned to camp after quiet hour, drew a piano keyboard on a long piece of paper, and started training his visual memory. He also got some blank sheet music, copied the "Lullaby" onto it from the library copy, and kept it in his pocket so he always had it and could go over it anytime he had a free moment.

But that night he didn't have a chance to practice, because Olga Leonidovna drowned him in errands. Once he finished one, she piled on even more, as though she were mocking him. Evidently she had decided that Konev the knucklehead was the cause of Volodya's failure to have the show ready on time, so the dried-up old fish was going to work him as hard as she could in punishment.

Volodya, for his part, was completely drowning in troop leader business. Troop Five was now preparing a sketch for the camp's special show, and Yurka had neither the time nor the opportunity to help him or even see him. From sheer longing, they managed to steal ten minutes to be together in the evening. Yurka was tempted by the idea of them getting together late at night, but knowing that Volodya hadn't slept in two days, he didn't even think of suggesting it. Yurka knew that he needed the rest, because the things he hadn't paid adequate attention to earlier were obvious now: the dark circles under Volodya's eyes, Volodya's generally pale and subdued air. No matter how much Yurka wanted to spend every minute with Volodya, he didn't have the right to demand that Volodya not sleep at all.

The next day, Camp Barn Swallow Day, Yurka knew it would be hard to find even half an hour before the celebration when he and Volodya could be alone. But it turned out far worse: they couldn't manage even a single minute. Starting first thing in the morning, Yurka was tasked with a gazillion chores, like digging to the center of the earth, completing five Five-Year Plans in three years, building a couple of Baikal–Amur railroads, and moving the piano. The piano was the one that made him most indignant: it would fall out of tune!

"Faster, higher, stronger!" came the phys ed instructor Semyon's voice from the athletic fields. He must've been shouting himself blue in the face if they could hear him all the way out on the main square.

For the first time in his life, Yurka was missing morning calisthenics. With Olga Leonidovna's approval, though, he was headed to the stage to decorate it for the talent show. He listened to the phys ed instructor as he walked, expecting the trees to splinter from the impact of that thunderous voice, and thought about how he, Yurka, was already faster, higher, and stronger than he ever had been, but he was even more than that: he was just plain miraculous. There was no other way to explain it; how else could such fairy-tale wonders be happening to him, Konev the knucklehead? Volodya, that very same Komsomol Goody Two-shoes—handsome, smart Volodya—had kissed him and held his hand and told him, "You're so handsome when you play." "If I had my way," Volodya had told him last night, "I'd never let you go."

Moving the piano turned out not to be that hard: Yurka had both the jug-eared Alyosha and the facilities manager, San Sanych, to help him, and the piano had wheels, and both the movie theater and the stage had ramps. But he still felt sorry for the instrument. The whole time they were moving it, Yurka muttered futilely to himself: "They couldn't be happy with just a tape recorder, oh no. What if it rains?" Once they'd gotten the piano in place, they tested the sound, and he cursed. Sure enough, it was out of tune now, and the B didn't even make a sound.

"So who's going to tune it?"

"There's more handymen around here than you can shake a stick at, Yurok. We'll find somebody." The facilities manager marched off to the administration building.

"Don't you know how?" asked Alyosha naively.

"No. I did try once; I hated it when it didn't sound quite right, but I didn't have the patience to wait for a tuner, so I fiddled around with it myself. Then a wire snapped and I just about bit the dust," Yurka recalled, not without some pride. "See that scar on my chin?"

"Isn't that something! You sure are brave, Yurka. You know what? People said all kinds of things about you, but I didn't believe them. I told them Konev's a good guy. And that's right! You are!"

"Oh? And what kinds of things did they say?"

"Oh, different things: some people said you're a knucklehead, others said the opposite, that you're aiming for assistant troop leader. Don't pay any attention. Let 'em say what they want."

"Who says that?" asked Yurka, thinking of Ksyusha.

"Well . . . just don't tell anybody I told you, okay?"

"I'll keep quiet as a partisan. They'll never drag it out of me."

"Masha Sidorova complained to Olga Leonidovna about you, saying you're keeping the artistic director from doing his job, but there you are tuning the pia—"

"Masha?!" shrieked Yurka, furious. Then he added, more quietly, "Just you wait, Masha . . . I'll get you for this!"

"Hey, but keep it a secret! You promised!"

"I'll keep it a secret, Alyosh. It'll be secret."

It was time for breakfast. The first thing Yurka did was run and look for Masha so he could grill her about why she was tattling on him. But she was nowhere to be found. There were only two Pukes at breakfast; Ksyusha was missing. Yurka went over to them and asked, "Do you know where Masha is?"

Ulyana smiled flirtatiously. "Why do you want to know?"

"I just wanted to inform her that she's no longer participating in the show. I'll be doing the accompaniment!"

"Uh-oh . . . ," said Ulya slowly. "Go look in the club building. She and Ksyusha are making the wall newspaper for the celebration."

Yurka was suddenly hit by an idea, one he liked so much that he decided not to go looking for Masha at all. He knew the news about her being kicked out of the play would travel through the grapevine quickly and that Sidorova would come find him herself.

After having some breakfast, Yurka went back to the main square. Troop Three and their troop leader were also there, rehearsing.

The June heat baked them as they listlessly intoned the theme song from a popular TV miniseries:

> "There's something that's changing my everyday life,
> It's the voice of the bright future calling,
> I stand: I've decided to walk out and meet it,
> The horizon beckons, enthralling . . ."

Yurka and Alyoshka were hanging the heavy navy curtains to that listless accompaniment. They were both getting tired and frustrated: some of the thin loops kept falling off the curtain hooks, while others kept tearing and had to be sewn back together then and there, with the heavy curtains pulling on them. The musical director didn't want to release his charges, so they continued singing their sad children's song about a bright future.

Every so often, Yurka caught himself listening to it. He didn't especially like the television miniseries it was from; he thought it was too dull, and while it might've been interesting to watch the first time, the second time was already boring. But he'd seen all five episodes, repeatedly, and he was sick of it. Last year, after it premiered, it went on to play constantly on all the TV channels. He almost had the thing memorized. He knew this song, too, but he'd never paid attention to the words. Now, though, he listened to them and grew sad: the song reminded him that time was flying, that this session of camp would be over soon, and that he and Volodya would have to part.

The kids kept on repeating the last stanza:

> "I promise I won't let down my friends,
> I'll strive to be a better person.
> I hear the call to leave my past behind,
> I stride enthralled to the horizon."

Even the shade was melting from the insanely hot sun, but still a shiver ran down Yurka's back: "I hear the call to leave my past behind . . . I stride enthralled to the horizon . . . ," he repeated to himself. All of a sudden he realized that the song was ghastly! It wasn't about some bright future at all, the way it was supposed to be in the show. It was about losing a good and meaningful present time: the time of childhood. Yurka was already overworked, he was reeling from hunger, and then his imagination started churning out fantastic images: he saw a broad gray path, and himself, and Volodya, and everyone who was here. They were walking up ahead, not realizing that they were headed somewhere they could never come back from—that they weren't walking of their own accord; they were being pulled by the black hole of the future drawing them into the unknown, which would inevitably consume them all—him, and Volodya, and all those children.

He shook his head and tried to focus on something else: "We only have one more panel to hang."

When the bugle finally called everyone to lunch, Yurka had no appetite but ate anyway, staring at Volodya over on the other side of the mess hall. Volodya was standing with his back to Yurka, in his usual shorts, white shirt, and red neckerchief. All of a sudden it occurred to Yurka that after a very short time Volodya wouldn't be wearing them anymore. Volodya would change. And Yurka would change, too. They'd both inevitably grow up. He realized that he didn't want to grow up; he didn't want to go into that "bright future." Not only that—he was actually afraid of it.

They would be parting in less than a week. Maybe not forever, maybe only even until next year, but still parting. And what would Volodya be like when Yurka saw him next summer? Would Volodya get taller and more broad-shouldered? Would he smile more often or less? Would his gaze be more strict, or more weary, than it was now? Or maybe the opposite—softer and kinder? So many questions that no one could answer.

Lunch ended. Dessert—a sweet sukharik with raisins—helped his mood a little. He decided he'd use dessert to improve his mood from neutral to good, to that end sneaking a second one, but then he took one look at Volodya, half-starved since the kids had started acting up again and were keeping him from having a decent meal, and decided to give it to him instead.

They met at the exit to the mess hall. Volodya refused to take the sukharik, insisting that Yurka eat it himself, but Yurka was adamant. Volodya thanked him and promised that as soon as he got control of his horde of urchins, he'd meet Yurka at the stage, if he could do it before the beginning of the ceremonial assembly.

Yurka walked away from the mess hall, thinking: *As if this was big news, the end of session. Of course session's ending. Everything ends, and this is ending, too. But why does it have to be so soon?* He had thought this would all last forever.

At camp, where each day is worth two, a lot of people thought that. Yurka couldn't believe that in less than a week his entire life would change: there'd be no more forest, no more camp, no more friends, no more theater, no more Volodya. And there'd be no more of the old Yurka Konev, the one his mom had put on the camp bus. Because he'd already changed. As recently as a month ago he wouldn't have been able to conceive of himself doing what he was doing now: helping, maybe even being a bit of a tryhard. But most of all that he'd be playing the piano again. It would make his mom so happy when he cleared all the stuff off his instrument. But would he be happy, after he went back to his cramped room in his damp apartment in his outdated building, one of a thousand identical buildings in his dusty old city?

That same sad longing took hold of Yurka again. To ward it off, he headed for the glorious instrument that helped him forget whatever he needed to.

Alyosha and the other people decorating the main square ran off to their cabins. It was almost quiet hour and silence reigned throughout the camp. The only people making any noise were the camp cook, Zinaida Vasilyevna, clanging the pots and pans as she hauled them from storage out to the kitchen, and the two phys ed instructors, Zhenya and Semyon, who were sitting on a bench in the shade of an apple tree, doing a crossword puzzle. Yurka got up onto the empty stage and checked that the piano had been tuned. He nodded in satisfaction, pulled the rumpled piece of paper with the music for the "Lullaby" on it out of his pocket, sat down at the piano, and put the piece of paper on the stand.

The tender melody began trickling through the overheated air like honey. Yurka bent in concentration over the keyboard. His fingers hovered over the keys and held still, barely touching them. The dark G-flat and A-flat octaves alternated with lower Cs and B naturals, after which his fingers floated delicately back up to the lighter Fs and Cs. But Yurka was dissatisfied. It was a complex composition, and after his long hiatus it was coming back to him with difficulty. He wasn't getting anything right. Every so often he'd play a wrong note and jerk his head in irritation. As he repeated it over and over, running his fingers up and down the keys, Yurka began to think that maybe, back in school, that one judge had been right. Maybe he really was worthless?

Suddenly everything went dark: somebody had sneaked up behind him and covered his eyes with their hands.

"Can you play it like this?" murmured Volodya. Yurka could hear in his voice that he was smiling.

"Hey, let go!" said Yurka, feigning indignation.

"Nope!" Then, without taking away his hands, Volodya began, "So tell me, Yur: Are you satisfied with your progress? Our show is in three days. Come on, practice hard so you're ready in time."

"I will be, just not this very minute. I'm not in the right mood. Come on, Volodya, let go! Or how about this: I'll play with one eye shut."

"Nice try! What do you take me for, an idiot? No. Both eyes shut."

"Not a chance!"

"Okay, then what about like this?" He spread his fingers apart a tiny bit. Yurka could see the keyboard.

"There we go! That's more like it!" Yurka laughed. He looked around to make sure that the dance floor was completely deserted, then leaned his head back and rested his head on Volodya's stomach. He looked up at him and smiled. Volodya was smiling, too.

They played that way until Volodya suddenly jerked his hands down and lurched away. Yurka flinched in surprise, opened his eyes, and watched him go. At the edge of the stage, a pale Masha was clutching a broom and staring at them, her eyes wide.

It made Yurka uncomfortable. But he took one look at the frightened Volodya and that fear passed to Yurka, too.

"Where're you flying off to?" blurted Yurka, trying to relieve the tension and turn it all into a joke.

"What?" replied Masha angrily.

"On your broom," explained Yurka. "You're standing here pretending you're sweeping a completely clean square."

"You think this is funny, Konev? Do you want to tell me what this is all about?"

"What do you mean? The fact that you're a witch? Or the fact that you're a *snitch*?!"

"Quit it, Yura!" intervened Volodya. "You too, Masha! I already told you he was joking. Yura's going to play just the 'Lullaby,' not the accompaniment for the whole show."

"Then why did he tell the girls he was—"

They were interrupted by the bugle signaling the end of quiet hour. If they hadn't been, Yurka would've started tearing into Masha, he was so mad at her.

Soon Mitka's voice over the loudspeaker announced it was time for the ceremonial assembly.

The day flew by. First came the assembly: the flag, the Pioneer salute, singing the Pioneer anthem. Then everyone ran over to the athletic fields for the competitions. There were sack races, a tug-of-war, relay races—Yurka actually beat one of the Troop Three leaders—and a ball game called lapta. Then all the senior boys, including Volodya, were called over to play soccer. Yurka focused solely on the soccer ball and the goal, promising himself he'd beat the troop leaders' team even if he had to do it all by himself, but it came out a tie.

The last part of the celebration, the talent show, was the part Yurka was least excited about. Partly because performing was always more interesting than just watching, but also because in this case there wasn't even anything worth watching. The only thing that caught his attention and made him laugh was the Troop Five piece, when the kids did a skit about a rocket launch from the Baikonur Cosmodrome. Sashka was pilot and spaceship all rolled into one. He'd been encased in a gray cardboard tube from head to toe and proudly surveyed the audience from a round hole cut in the tube for his face while he waggled the tip of the gray cardboard cone perched atop his head. Pcholkin stood at the control booth mashing his finger into a red button, also made of cardboard. At Sashka's signal—"Fshoom!"—he was launched into space, where little girls, the stars, ran circles around him and all the rest of the boys from Troop Five sang a song about the Earth seen through a spaceship window.

Yurka didn't have the foggiest idea what this had to do with celebrating Camp Barn Swallow Day, but it was funny.

The next troop's performance was boring. Yurka started shifting in his seat, looking around to find Volodya. It didn't take him long: Volodya was sitting two rows back, his head bent, his eyes either lowered or closed. He looked exactly the way he sometimes looked at rehearsal: as though he were reading a notebook on his lap. But this wasn't rehearsal, and he had no notebook in his lap. Troop Two's skit ended, and everyone clapped, and Volodya's head fell heavily, then he shook himself, then he jerked his head up. From the way he was blinking, Yurka could tell the troop leader had fallen asleep. He hadn't been able to fall asleep in the quiet underneath the weeping willow with his head in Yurka's lap, but he could here, at a noisy performance, sitting right next to Olga Leonidovna.

There was no way she wouldn't notice that, of course. And she did. She immediately gave Volodya a look of concern and asked him something, but once she heard the answer, she didn't start chiding him, as Yurka had expected. Just the opposite: she called Lena over, whispered something in her ear, and nodded toward Volodya. He stood up immediately and walked off. Yurka guessed where he was going: to sleep.

And it's a good thing, too, thought Yurka. He resigned himself to listening yet again to the sad, listless children's song about the glorious yonder.

Yurka longed for evening like it was manna from heaven.

Once the celebratory dance party started that night, he ran straight for the Troop Five cabin. Once inside, he took only a couple of steps into the dark hallway when he jumped out of his skin: somebody had run into his stomach and then squeaked from surprise.

"Sasha? Why aren't you in the boys' room, sleeping? Are you going hunting for currants again?"

"No, it's not that," puffed Sashka, trying to catch his breath. "Volodya's sleeping, so Zhenya's sitting with us, telling scary stories. I went out to pee."

Yurka smirked. "What, are they that scary?"

"No, it's not that," repeated Sashka listlessly, clearly having missed the joke. "It's just the opposite. He's telling the one about DSC. It's so boring! Save us, Yura!"

Torn between his desire to go to Volodya's room—all the more so since Volodya was there alone—and his duty to help the slumbering troop leader get the kids to bed, Yurka wavered. Ultimately, he came back to himself when he realized he was at the door to the boys' room. He didn't realize right away that Sashka was no longer next to him.

It was dark in the boys' room. Zhenya was sitting on a chair by the door, holding a flashlight and intoning, in a spooky voice, "The car was labeled DSC, for Death to Soviet Children! It stopped next to the little boy, and a man came out. He walked up to the little boy and started telling him to get into the car, promising him a puppy, and candy, and toys. But the little boy wouldn't do it. He got scared and ran away, but the car drove off after him—"

"Yuwka!" screeched Olezhka happily.

The phys ed instructor jumped. The little boys babbled excitedly: "Come sit with us!" "Tell us a scawy stowy!" "Are there really cars like that?"

"Now, let's all listen to Zhenya," suggested Yurka as he sat down on Sashka's empty bed, frantically sorting through his options for what to do now. Yurka wasn't thrilled at the possibility of spending the bit of the day that was left until lights out with the boys, then spending the night all alone.

Zhenya continued in a voice from beyond the grave: "The little boy was able to hide in an abandoned building and avoid the spies, but if they'd caught him—"

The boys' room door was flung open, which kept Zhenya from finishing the story. In the doorway stood a sleepy, tousled, and disheveled Volodya with a self-satisfied Sashka bobbing around behind him.

Yurka, unable to suppress the joy that suffused him, automatically moved toward Volodya and seized his hand. Volodya gripped his hand back, pretending that it was just a regular handshake of greeting. The boys were triumphant: "Now we'll get a good scary story!" Even Zhenya was glad to see the troop leader, rolling his eyes and groaning, "Finally! Can I go now?"

"You can go now," said the sleepy Volodya through a yawn. "Thanks for covering for me."

"And now will you tell a scary story?" squeaked Sashka, his eyes narrowed calculatingly.

At that point Yurka realized the troop leader had had some help waking up. Then it hit him that Volodya would also doubtless be hungry, and he started fretting in earnest: Where could he go and what could he do to get Volodya something to eat?

Meanwhile, Volodya plopped down clumsily on the edge of an unoccupied bed and tried to smooth his tousled hair, but he ended up just making it stick out even more. Baffled, he whispered in Yurka's ear: "What do I tell them? We haven't thought anything up in a long time."

"So think of something!" Yurka whispered back. He nuzzled Volodya's ear with his nose, as if accidentally.

"My brain's not working at all right now," grumbled Volodya.

Suddenly, Yurka had a revelation: almost every child's parents sent care packages from home, meaning that the boys had food! Yurka said excitedly, "I'm giving you a five-minute head start. Come up with something." Yurka moved to the middle of the room and started issuing orders: "Listen up, everyone! If our troop leader's brain is going to be able to think, it needs fuel. That is, food. Dig deep into your grain bins, scrape every last kernel out of your corncribs! We have to feed our troop leader!"

"What's a corncrib?" someone queried from the right side of the room by the window.

"And a grain bin," came a question from the left side of the room by the door.

"Your care packages," Yurka explained. "Is there anything left from your care packages, or did you already go through it all? Sash, I know for a fact that you've got cookies under your pillow." He stabbed his finger toward Sashka's bed. "I'll trade you half a pack of cookies for one first-rate scary story."

"How do you know I've got cookies?" scowled the chubby boy.

"Because I check your beds every morning," Volodya chimed in, confirming Yurka's guess.

For a wonder, Sashka did not try to argue; he just pulled out the package of Jubilee cookies and clutched it to his chest, asking doubtfully, "Are you sure the scary story will be first-rate?"

"Depends on the cookies," said Yurka, crossing his arms on his chest.

"But the main thing is that it's new and based on real events!" Volodya said, indicating to Yurka that he'd had an idea for a story.

"Great!" said Sasha, nodding in approval, but his hand still wavered when he held the package of cookies out to Volodya. "But if the scary story's no good, I get my cookies back!"

Volodya nodded and snatched the package of cookies. Crunching ensued.

"No, not all chewed—" began Sashka indignantly, but Volodya, his mouth still full of cookies, began the story: "So this was literally the day before yesterday, in the early hours of morning. Imagine this: I wake up from some kind of strange noise in the troop leaders' room. I open one eye and look down at the floor, and there's some kind of strange black blur crawling across the floor. It's shapeless, but it has these scary pointed parts on it! It crawls straight up to Zhenya's bed, making this terrifying rustling noise, like—" and he crunched into another cookie. "But Zhenya's just sleeping like nothing's happening. I'm paralyzed with horror: I have no idea what this thing is or what it's capable of. But then, all of a sudden, the black blur stops. And it starts moving around, turning in circles, and then it turns around and heads away from Zhenya's bed and toward me! But I'm too scared to move. I can't even reach out to feel for my glasses on the nightstand. So I end up catching hold of a book instead, and I crawl over to the edge of the bed, and I prepare to attack . . . It's headed toward Zhenya again, so I take advantage of the situation to jump out of bed and go over to it, but as soon as I raise my hand to hit it, the blur rushes toward my feet! I shout and jump away. Then Zhenya wakes up and has no idea what's happening. I poke him, but then he sees it and lets out a stream of curses! Then he picks the blanket up off his bed and throws it right on top of the blur. And he says to me, 'Volodya, put your glasses on!' So I go over to my nightstand and plop on my glasses, and meanwhile Zhenya is gathering the blanket up into a bundle and holding the bundle in both hands. I look at it, and what do I see sticking out of it but . . . a little pink nose! And the thing is snuffling! So fess up: Which of you took Snuffly from the Red Corner and brought him in here? You just about gave a troop leader a heart attack!"

Yurka couldn't help it and burst into loud laughter. The boys started laughing, too.

"That's not a scawy stowy at all!" squeaked Olezhka happily. "That's a funny stowy!"

"Right! A funny story, not a scary story, because you get what you pay for with your so-so cookies. You were warned!" announced Yurka. Imitating Volodya's managerial tone of voice, he ordered, "That's it. And now time for bed."

"Blankets to chins. And no talking," chimed in Volodya.

It took them half an hour before they could get the kids to bed. Once they'd left the cabin and taken a lungful of fresh, still-warm air, Volodya asked Yurka merrily, "How are you? How was your day?" Then he surprised Yurka by shaking his hand even though they'd already shaken hands hello that day.

"I missed you!" Yurka burst out.

As though he'd heard his own words from the outside, Yurka immediately blushed and his throat closed up tight. He'd just blurted something very candid indeed. He cleared his throat and patted the merry-go-round, inviting Volodya to sit down next to him. Volodya, for his part, seemed to like what he'd heard. He smiled, then adjusted his glasses and began, "And I also—"

He was cut off by the desperate shrieks of twenty voices coming from the girls' room. Volodya rushed onto the porch and tried to open the door, but it was locked from the inside. Yurka ran over to the window and hopped up to peer in. He saw "ghosts" in bedsheets with flashlights flying around the room. "Volod! Everything's all right. It's not sabotage. It's ghosts who flew in to visit the girls," he informed Volodya, laughing.

Volodya ran over to him and looked in the window, too. Yurka felt Volodya casually put his arm around his waist. "Six ghosts!" exclaimed the troop leader, as though nothing all that special were going on—as though saying, *So I put my arm around him. That's totally normal.* "Let's get 'em!"

He withdrew his arm from around Yurka and with a ferocious grin he raced over to the other door, which was unlocked. Yurka stood underneath the window and watched as, a few seconds later, Volodya jubilantly cried, "Aha!" and burst into the room with the terrified girls, moved the disheveled, flustered Lena to one side, and caught the first ghost. The others were scared and rushed to flee out the cabin door, but Yurka was waiting for them in the doorway.

They didn't leave the cabin until all the ghosts had been neutralized, delivered back to their own room, and put back in bed.

"So what's gotten you so cheerful?" said Yurka, amazed. It used to be that Volodya got upset when people didn't follow the rules, while Yurka was amused, but now it was the other way around. He hadn't even noticed when they'd switched places.

"Firstly, I've finally slept, and secondly, I realized that if I don't learn to have a sense of humor about pranks, I'm going to end up killing these little squirts," chuckled Volodya. "Clearly the scary story really was bad this time. It didn't work."

Then Volodya took Yurka's hand and pulled him into the thicket. Yurka couldn't tell what the bushes were in the dark: either lilacs or some other sort of tall shrub. There was a large clump of them at a small distance from the cabin. Inside, it was quiet and dark. It felt like they could hide from everyone here, even from ghosts with flashlights, and the best part was that Volodya and Yurka could see the whole wide-open yard.

But they were no longer watching over, or waiting for, or looking for anybody. Now that they were finally alone, they had eyes only for each other. Tremulously, they embraced and whispered in eager conversation about nothing at all.

Not half an hour later came the sound of someone's footsteps walking along the path to the Troop Five cabin. Yurka heard it first and pulled away from Volodya. "You hear that?"

Volodya put his finger to his lips, pulled a branch down a little to make a small gap in the bushes, and peeked out. So did Yurka. The person coming down the path was Masha.

She peered into the window of the girls' room for a long time, apparently looking for someone in the dim space lit only by a night-light. Yurka could tell who she was looking for: Volodya. When Masha didn't find him there, she went over to the other window, the one to the boys' room. She looked in, listening and waiting. Once she was convinced he wasn't in there, she walked through the flower bed to the third window.

"My room," whispered Volodya.

That room was completely dark, so Masha quickly went back up on to the porch. The door gave a quiet creak as she carefully went inside the cabin. Volodya tensed visibly.

"Where does she think she's going? Is she crazy?" He moved sharply, about to leap to his feet, but Yurka grabbed his arm.

"Wait, hold on. Is there anything wrong in there? I mean, any blackmail material, stuff like that?"

"Well, no, actually," said Volodya, after some thought.

"So sit tight, then. What's she going to think when she sees you lurking around in the bushes?"

"Like hell I'm going to sit here and hide when somebody's digging around in my room!"

Volodya emerged from the bushes just in time. Masha was coming out of the cabin and ran into Volodya in the doorway. It was too late for Yurka to sneak away. His alarm grew with every passing moment. A terrible realization was driving him to distraction: Was the lovelorn Masha so far gone that she was actually stalking Volodya now?

Yurka was trying to fight down an insane urge to run over to her and tell her off. Then he froze in his tracks, realizing he was a hopeless idiot. The porch was too far away. Not only could he not hear what they were saying, he couldn't even read their lips because the swarming bugs were making the dim light from the weak bulb flicker and it was impossible to see anything. But one thing was clear: Whatever Masha was telling Volodya was making his indignation melt away.

They finished their conversation. Masha moved calmly down the porch steps to the path and walked away. When she was out of sight, Yurka burst out of the bushes and ran over to Volodya.

"So? What did she say?!" he exploded, panting from agitation.

"She was looking for you," replied Volodya. He sounded worried. "She said Irina was looking for you, and since you weren't in the theater, Masha thought you might be with me. It's not necessarily so strange. You're both in the same troop, and she helps Irina a lot, so nothing's out of the ordinary here, but . . . I wasn't expecting it."

"Not so fast. This is way out of the ordinary! You know what? I've heard Masha is saying stuff about me. And she's basically just acting really suspicious. Have you noticed? She winds up around us too often . . ."

"Are you sure you're not exaggerating?"

Yurka saw Volodya's somewhat patronizing smile and faltered. Volodya doubtless thought Yurka was still jealous of the time he danced with Masha and was willing to accuse Masha of anything as a result. And if that really was what Volodya was thinking, well, he was right! Yurka's passionate urge to leap out of the bushes and catch the spy red-handed was indeed motivated by jealousy. But Yurka thought of other arguments in support of his theory, too, and he said them aloud: "This isn't the first time she's gone wandering around at night. Remember that time Ira came to the theater and jumped on me, asking what I was doing with Masha and where I'd been? And you know what else? No matter where we are, she's always there. Volod! We have to report that she's out at night!"

"Well, why don't you start with Irina?"

Yurka's mood was already ruined, and Volodya was getting paranoid again: he kept holding still to listen and look around, and he wouldn't let Yurka even touch his hand. And the evening was coming to an end, anyway.

He quickly said goodbye to Volodya, returned to his cabin, and found his troop leader. Expecting her to glare up at him and start shouting the moment he appeared at her door, he'd already prepared his mumbled excuses, but Ira just stared at him in surprise and said, "No, I wasn't looking for you, actually." Yurka was picking his jaw back up off the floor when Ira seemed to realize what he'd said. "But hold on: Where were you?"

"With Volodya."

"Do you have any idea what time it is? Yura, if you need to be out after lights out, you have to let me know!"

Yurka struggled to calm his swirling, fearful feelings as he fell asleep. There were always a lot of girls buzzing around Volodya, but it seemed to Yurka that Masha was among them too often. He was probably just jealous. And he'd evidently been infected by Volodya's paranoia, too . . .

CHAPTER FOURTEEN
"I SWEAR: NEVER AGAIN"

Time had run out. The cast—Volodya especially—was scared out of their wits once they realized that the premiere of their show was the day after tomorrow.

Yurka skipped morning calisthenics to rush to the theater and immerse himself in practicing the "Lullaby." He stayed there all day, so Volodya's nerves didn't affect him much. The same couldn't be said for the rest of the drama club, who had a pretty rough time of it. Volodya was incensed at the loss of the entire previous day due to the Camp Barn Swallow Day festivities, so starting first thing in the morning, he spent the whole day pulling actors in threes, twos, and even one at a time out of their activities and civic duty work to run tirelessly through their individual scenes.

Two clubs were mobilized to help with the show, the sewing club, and the art club. But while the tailors, armed with Ksyusha's sketches, were working as hard as they could, the artists were just goofing off. At least, according to Volodya. They weren't able to make as many set decorations as the show required, so Volodya took a few of the sketches from them and set to work painting decorations himself with the help of actors and volunteers like Alyosha.

As for Yurka, while he was worried, he was completely calm when it came to the show. If they kept working at this rate, he was sure they'd be ready in time. That wasn't what was tormenting him. The problem was that time was running out not only for the actors, but for him and Volodya.

Volodya understood this, too, and took action. He managed to find moments even in that chock-full schedule to run over to visit Yurka in the movie theater, pecking him on the cheek and tousling his hair.

Yurka was sad nevertheless. His sadness made the "Lullaby" sound magnificent, but even that wasn't enough to reverse his mood. The only thing that made him really happy was that the time they spent alone together was exclusively theirs. And even though the moments they did steal and the tender, lightning-quick glances they did share all filled his soul with joy, Yurka waited in agony for the hundred and twenty minutes of quiet hour. They'd finally be able to really be together! They'd be alone. They could forget about the rehearsals, and the set decorations, and all the rest of it. They would live as fully as they could, breathe as deeply as they could, so they'd remember each other, so they'd remember this summer, the most magical time of both their lives.

"We can't seem to make it out to that bas-relief from your scary story," said Volodya when quiet hour rolled around, jingling the keys from the boathouse in his pocket. "What do you think: Should we try again? Last time we were on a boat we didn't even try to get out there."

Yurka was about to argue that the day had gotten overcast and it looked like it was going to rain buckets, but he changed his mind. Was getting all wet really that big a problem?

They went down the path to the dock, got into a boat, and started out in the same direction as before. This time Yurka set Volodya to the oars: his turn to row against the current. Volodya didn't complain, but halfway there Yurka could tell he got tired and switched with him. It was a lot farther to row to the bas-relief than to the lily pond.

Yurka called the place with the bas-relief the "ruins." It was an uneven patch of ground overgrown with weeds and surrounded by sparse pines. It was unclear whether it was a church or a manor house that used to be here, but either way, the remains of walls and the little hillocks of the foundation testified that something had definitely been there. All it took was a close look to see the shapes sticking up out of the tall weeds.

But their path took them farther, to a little space bordered by spreading vines forming a lush living fence, sprinkled with little white flowers like the sky with stars. A regular old moss-covered wall peered out from behind the vines. Yurka walked up to it, looked at the confused Volodya, pulled the vines aside, and grinned: "This wall here is our bas-relief."

"It's very old, I'll give you that, but it's obviously not a . . . Wait a minute!"

Volodya squinted. He exclaimed softly when he made out the barely visible figure that stood out from the rest of the wall, but he didn't have a chance to utter a word before Yurka got on his knees and started tearing away the vines and moss.

"Careful! Those vines are clematis. It's poisonous!"

"How do you know all that? Are you a botanist or something?"

"No, it's just that my grandma was really good at growing flowers," said Volodya, shrugging. He extracted the notebook he always carried with him from his shorts pocket and tore out a couple of sheets. Equipped with the paper as makeshift gloves, the boys started clearing the bas-relief of the vines and moss. Soon a woman's profile emerged from the living velvet, followed by a neck and chest, and then the silhouette of the baby the woman was holding close.

"She's posed like the Virgin Mary," said Volodya, amazed. "That's interesting . . . but this is a secular woman. Is she the lady of the estate?"

"She's my ghostly countess. See these buds?" Yurka pointed at the little pointy-leafed, star-like flowers. "When I found it, the clematis was still blooming, and right here"—Yurka pointed at the woman's collarbone—"there was a big white flower, like a brooch. That's how I came up with the idea for the scary story. I've never heard of there actually being an estate here, though."

"Is it maybe a gravestone?"

"Doesn't look like it. But who knows . . ."

The bas-relief and the living fence surrounding it were beautiful in a mysterious, Gothic way, but apart from looking at it there was nothing else to do here. By Yurka's calculations, they still had quite a bit of time left.

"So tell me something: How long until we have to be back in camp?" he said calculatingly. He had a way better idea.

"An hour and change . . . almost an hour and a half," Volodya estimated.

"Great!" Yurka said excitedly. "I know this one place . . ."

"How do you know all this? All these places!"

"Well, I am a deadbeat and a good-for-nothing," said Yurka, smirking. "I'm always wandering around where I shouldn't and poking my nose where I shouldn't, and that's how I find all kinds of cool stuff."

"Whatever you say." Volodya smiled. "Okay. Let's go."

"We don't have to go far to get to the path, but then it's a long way up, waaaay up there." Yurka pointed at the cone-shaped wooded hill looming to the east.

"What's up there? Seems like all there is over there is forest."

"See that spire? There's a tiny little gazebo up there at the very top."

"Are you sure there's a way to get up there?"

"It's okay, there's a path. It's true that you have to scramble in places, but—"

"Are there any snakes up there?" interjected Volodya.

"—there aren't any snakes up there," finished Yurka, in sync with him.

As they went up the steep incline, they had to help themselves at times by pulling on some roots that were sticking out of the ground. Once, something happened that made Yurka's heart leap into his throat: a gnarled dry root he was holding on to broke off underneath his weight, so he almost went tumbling downhill like a stone. But the rest of their journey was without incident, and soon they came upon some steps cut into the ground that led directly to the little gazebo.

The rickety little edifice wasn't especially attractive: a plain wooden hut, its green paint peeling in places. Inside was a small table surrounded by uncomfortable, narrow benches. Everything was plain and mediocre. What made the little gazebo unique wasn't its construction, but the fact that it was covered with writing on every possible surface: walls, beams, benches, table, floor . . . The writing was everywhere, outside and in. *Seryozha and Natasha, Session One, 1975. Dima + Galya, Fourth Session, 1982. Sveta and Artur were here: Camp Barn Swallow, Session One, 1979.* A great multitude of names, dates, and numbers, written in different handwriting, in different colors, with different paints, pencils, and pens. Many had been cut into the wood. Many others had hearts around them.

Yurka walked over to the far corner of the gazebo and called Volodya over. He leaned over the edge and pointed out into the distance. "This is what I wanted to show you. Look."

It was as though the hut was clinging onto the very edge of the precipice: a steep overhang of bare earth that fell for many meters until it met a thickly forested area that also fell steeply away, all the way back down to the water. Out past that, stretching for many kilometers, all the way to the horizon, was the steppe, cut here and there by the ribbon of a meandering river. The water, reflecting the overcast sky, was gray and white, but here and there, where the sun pierced through the clouds, the water sparkled and flashed with reflected rays. The grass, all dried up from the summer heat, was plastered flat in a yellow carpet as far as the eye could see, except for occasional spots with hints of green.

From here they could see the place they'd just been: the glade with the bas-relief, and the pool where they'd gone to see the lilies, and, of course, the camp.

Yurka sneaked a look at Volodya to see his reaction. He was gazing out into the distance, enchanted, breathing slowly and deeply, his face showing utter tranquility.

"It's beautiful, isn't it?" asked Yurka, moving toward the little table in the middle of the space.

"Very. But how did you find out about this place?"

"Strange you've never heard about it. You are a troop leader, right?" Yurka leaned back against the table and hefted himself up to sit on it. He kicked his feet back and forth as he told the tale: "This is called the lovers' bower. Some girls from the senior troops told me about it two years ago, and all the troop leaders know about it—at least, the ones who aren't at Camp Barn Swallow for the first time. It's always been sort of like a tradition for camp couples to come here before the end of the session and write their names . . . I've never understood it, but I came out here one time just out of curiosity, to see it with my own eyes."

"What didn't you understand?" asked Volodya, moving close to him. "It's all very symbolic. You look at these names and you really can feel the romance—all these lovers. Can you imagine how much feeling has been concentrated here over the course of many years? How many tender words have been said?"

Yurka was on the verge of giggling at Volodya's sentimentality, but he met Volodya's eyes and went still. Volodya was looking at him so earnestly, so longingly, that it was as though . . . as though Volodya was talking about them? Volodya leaned over, braced his hands on the table on either side of Yurka, and pressed the tip of his nose to Yurka's. He closed his eyes and breathed out . . . then breathed in, slowly and deeply . . . and at that, Yurka's heart started thundering so frantically that it seemed about to pound right through his chest. He brought the space between them to a minimum and stole a quick kiss. "Want us to leave our names here, too?" he whispered.

Volodya shook his head. He rubbed the end of his nose on Yurka's again and murmured quietly, "Don't. Wouldn't be good if somebody from our session saw it. I'll remember it anyway, Yur, without writing anything at all."

Yurka put his arms all the way around Volodya and pressed his lips to Volodya's neck, when suddenly Volodya shuddered and dropped his hands from Yurka. Yurka flinched, looked down, and saw that Volodya's arms were covered in goose bumps. Both of them, completely covered, all the way up and down. Volodya looked away. To keep from making Volodya feel even worse, Yurka pretended he hadn't noticed anything. And Yurka decided that to make sure Volodya didn't feel as uncomfortable as that ever again, he'd never do that again—never touch Volodya's neck.

They went back to camp the same way they had come. Although Yurka knew an easier way, the boys had left the boat onshore, and it had to be returned.

By the time they got as far as the river, the wind had picked up, covering the water in little ripples. The sky to the east went dark.

"It's going to rain soon," said Volodya, looking up. "We need to get back quick."

"We'll get back quickly now that we're going with the current," Yurka said, hoping to calm him.

He got into the boat and took the oars. Volodya pushed off from shore and hopped in.

They did get back quickly. Yurka put his back into the oars, the boat flew along, and it wasn't fifteen minutes until they were tying up at the dock.

The wind had gotten stronger. The first raindrops plopped down from the gray sky.

"It's going to come down any minute now!" said Volodya, raising his voice. "We probably won't make it to camp. Let's get under cover here at the boathouse!"

"You tie up the boat, I'll go get some canvas." By now, Yurka had to shout to be heard over the wind.

Yurka raced off the dock and flung open the door to the boathouse. He grabbed the canvas, and before stepping back toward the dock he glanced out to the window facing the beach. There was someone out there.

He ducked down, then poked just his head back up and took a better look. The person was approaching the boathouse. It was Masha.

"Fucking hell!" he whispered through gritted teeth. "This is all we need!"

He raced back down the dock. Masha wouldn't be able to see him until she went through the building and came out on this side. When he reached Volodya, Yurka acted without thinking. He grabbed his elbow: "Lie down in the boat, quick!"

"What?"

"Masha's coming!"

"But we haven't done anything. Why do we need to hide?"

"Lie down, I'm telling you!" ordered Yurka. "I'll cover us up with the canvas."

Volodya was flustered, but quickly hopped into the boat and lay down. Yurka followed him.

As he settled into the boat, he became aware that Volodya was correct: until they'd hidden in the boat, there wasn't anything they could be caught doing. But now, since they'd hidden, there must be something they needed to hide. And if Masha saw them climbing, disheveled and wrinkled, out of a boat that had been covered in canvas, then who knew what the hell she would think. There would be no end of questions and inquiries. Yurka cursed quietly. He was the one who'd gotten them into this, who'd made them lie there without moving a muscle.

"How'd she get it into her head to come here?" he moaned quietly.

"No idea," replied Volodya. "She didn't exactly pick a great time to go for a walk."

"That's what I'm saying! She's stalking you!"

Yurka peeked carefully out of the boat. He didn't have a very good view. All he could see was a small area of the dock. But he was able to see Masha's feet in her little black shoes and white anklets. She walked back and forth a couple of times. Then she walked over to their boat and stopped. Yurka's heart did a somersault. She stood there for a second . . . then she took a step toward the boat . . . and then there was a deafening crack of thunder and the rain came sheeting down. The heavy drops drummed on the canvas. Masha yelped loudly and ran back to the boathouse.

"Is she gone?" asked Volodya anxiously.

"Yes. But I thought she'd seen something, dang it."

"Will you be able to see her leave from here?"

"Of course not. She's in the boathouse. How am I supposed to see her up there?" asked Yurka, irritated. "Maybe just in the window. But only if I'm lucky."

Volodya paused, then murmured, "I see. So we'll have to lie around here until the bugle."

Only now did Yurka realize how tight it was there for the two of them. Moving extremely slowly and carefully, so as not to rock the boat, he turned onto his side so he was face-to-face with Volodya. His eyes still hadn't gotten used to the dark, and if he hadn't poked Volodya's forehead with his nose, he wouldn't have even known what position Volodya was in or where he was facing. Yurka slithered down a bit lower, and once his eyes adjusted, he was able to discern the outlines of Volodya's glasses.

The rain was beating down on the canvas, and a cold, wet breeze was coming in around its edges, but Yurka was hot because Volodya was too close. Yurka wanted to touch him, not lay there unmoving like a little toy soldier. Yurka felt around, found Volodya's hand, and gave it a hesitant squeeze. He felt how dry and warm it was. Volodya breathed out a faltering sigh and gave Yurka's fingers an answering squeeze.

"Yur," he said hoarsely.

"What?"

"Kiss me."

Yurka's heart skipped a beat. A wave of sweetness washed over his body. Everything around him smelled of water—rainwater and river water—and that's exactly what Yurka would always remember when he remembered his first real kiss.

Volodya let him do more than usual: not just give Volodya's lips a quick, innocent peck with his own but press his lips to Volodya's and keep them pressed tight. This kiss lasted either several seconds or a whole eternity and was accompanied by the ferocious hammering of a heart, although it was unclear whose, Yurka's or Volodya's. And then Volodya parted his lips. Yurka was about to pull away, thinking this was the signal for the end, but he felt an even softer and wetter touch.

Yurka didn't know how to kiss for real. He'd never done it. Volodya knew how, though. His lips caught up Yurka's, pulling him into a kiss that was grown-up, and tender, and dizzying.

The rain had slowed and calmed, but Yurka had absolutely no desire to grow calm himself. He didn't want to let go of Volodya's hands and lips. He forgot about everything, about his irregular breathing, about the heat and languor filling his entire body, he didn't want to stop, to break out of this moment. If he could've stayed next to Volodya forever, in that boat, underneath that canvas, Yurka would've done so without a second thought.

Volodya didn't want it to end, either. He let go of Yurka's hand and put his arm around Yurka, pressing him close, so close Yurka could tell that he wasn't the only one who was burning hot. Without knowing why, Yurka put his hand on Volodya's waist and ran his fingers underneath Volodya's shirt to touch his skin. It was as though an electric current were running through his hand. Volodya shivered. Their kiss became rough and ravenous.

When the distant bugle came, signaling the end of quiet hour, it seemed deafening to Yurka. He tried to act like he hadn't heard anything, but Volodya tore himself away and sighed, then said, "It's time, Yura. We have to go."

As though he were grasping at straws, Yurka asked, "Do you think Masha's left yet?"

"The rain stopped and she heard the bugle . . . Let me check."

He sat up a little and, just like Yurka had done earlier, lifted up the corner of the canvas. At that moment Yurka very much wanted Volodya to see Masha's feet out there and come back here, to him. He wanted to be able to hold Volodya and kiss him, even for just another minute.

"There's nobody there," said Volodya. He sat all the way up and threw the canvas off the boat.

The bright midday light blinded Yurka. Everything around them was damp and dripping, but the sky had gotten lighter, and in the distance the sun was poking through the clouds.

Volodya climbed out of the boat. Yurka followed him. While they were fastening the canvas back down, Yurka fought the desire to walk up to Volodya, embrace him from behind, and stand still, just like that, for a long, long time.

"That's it. Good job, everyone. You can go," announced Volodya, ending the rehearsal. The actors, pale from exhaustion, applauded. It had taken them until the fifth try for the cast to finally run through the entire play from start to finish and get it to where it was more or less bearable.

And while the actors were so worn-out after that day that they were literally falling down from fatigue as they left, the artistic director was so spent that Yurka didn't know how he was still able to stand. Volodya was working himself to death, without hearing or seeing or noticing anything around him. His neckerchief had even gotten twisted around with the knot to the back, so it hung on his neck like a noose.

Yurka noticed that and snorted. He got up from the piano, went over to the artistic director, and reached out to fix the errant scrap of cloth.

"I wish they'd huwwy up and give me my vewy own neckewchief!"

Yurka actually jumped from surprise. He'd been certain all the actors had left the movie theater. But the spry little Olezhka had popped out from behind the bust of Lenin like the proverbial devil from a snuffbox.

Volodya lurched away from Yurka and adjusted his neckerchief himself. Then, with a forced smile, he explained, "Our little Olezhka here dreams of having the honor of being the first in his class, or even in his whole school, to be accepted into the Pioneers."

"Aaaahhhh," said Yurka slowly. He turned to Olezhka. "So have you already memorized the oath?"

"Suwe have!" Olezhka blushed, stood at attention, and began reciting expressively: "I, Wyleyev, Oleg Womanovich, as I entew the wanks of the Vladimiw Ilych Lenin All-Union Pioneew Owganization, in the pwesence of my comwades do solemnly pwomise: to fewvently love my Mothewland and to live, study, and stwuggle, as the gweat Lenin instwucted, and as the Comm—" Olezhka broke off and sucked in a huge breath. "—unist Pawty teaches, and to hold inviolate the pwecepts of the Pioneews of the Soviet Union!"

"Well done!" Volodya praised him. "And how do you give the Pioneer salute? Do you know that?"

"I do! Want to see?"

Yurka clicked his tongue. Volodya and Olezhka had to pick this exact time for a lesson! Without hiding his boredom, Yurka sat down on the edge of the stage, dangled his feet, and started snoring demonstratively. Volodya ignored him.

"Show me," said the troop leader. He shouted out the call: "For the struggle for the good of the Communist Party: Be prepared!"

Olezhka barked the response—"Always pwepawed!"—and threw his hand up in the Pioneer salute.

Volodya adjusted Olezhka's hand so it was higher than his forehead, not at the level of his nose. "You need to hold your hand higher than your head. That means that you will hold the interests of the Pioneer organization higher than your own. And also, during the oath ceremony, the person who ties your neckerchief for you will ask tricky questions."

"Oh deaw!" said Olezhka, scared. "Awe they hawd questions? Have you asked questions like that?"

"I have. I asked a future Pioneer how much a Pioneer neckerchief is worth."

Yurka, who had recovered somewhat, called out, "Fifty-five kopeks!," enunciating each word.

"Yur, come on, you know very well that's the wrong answer. Why are you messing with him?" asked Volodya, irritated. "A Pioneer neckerchief is priceless, because it's part of the red banner. Can you remember that, Olezh?"

"Yes, I'll wemembew that!" nodded Olezhka. "Okay, bye. I'm going to pwactice the oath some mowe befowe bed!"

"You'd be better off practicing your lines!"

"I'll pwactice my lines, too!"

Olezhka ran off. Yurka started thinking about how it was too bad that Volodya was deceiving the little guy. After all, that was precisely what a Pioneer neckerchief was worth: fifty-five kopeks. No more. Because in the end it was just a dyed rag. By Yurka's age, everyone believed this firmly. As if they were mocking their neckerchiefs, they wore them every which way: torn, or wrinkled, or drawn on, or covered with souvenir pins and badges, or backward like a cowboy bandana—the way Volodya's had just been.

Maybe ten or twenty years ago the neckerchief had still meant something, had symbolized values and ideals. But now all that had vanished into the past. And when Yurka failed his piano exam, that was the point when he had begun to suspect nobody had any ideals or values left. Soon enough, something would happen to Olezhka, and he'd learn the same thing. Yurka felt preemptively sorry for Olezhka, for what a cruel disappointment was in store for a little guy who was so inspired, so full of dreams.

Yurka wanted to share his thoughts with Volodya, but before he could, the movie theater door opened again and the guys from the art club carried in several panels of stage decorations.

"Here's the pumping station and steam engine," said Misha Lukovenko, the head of the drawing section. "Like you said, we drew the outlines, but you'll fill everything in."

"Oh, thank you so much!" said Volodya gratefully. "Did you bring the paint?"

"Yes, it's right here." Misha handed him a big box with jars and brushes and reminded him, "I'll pick it back up tomorrow."

As soon as the artists left, Volodya turned to Yurka and asked, "Well? Shall we get to painting?"

Yurka groaned in despair. "Now? But, Volod, you're exhausted, worn-out, and I'm tired too . . ."

"The clock is ticking! There's two days' worth of work here, at least—we have to paint it, then it has to dry . . . and then we'll have to touch some things up, too."

"Maybe it could still wait until tomorrow?" asked Yurka, with no real hope of success.

"Nope! But if you're tired, I can do it myself." There was no accusation in his voice. Yurka knew Volodya's enthusiasm was such that he could spend all night in the theater to get everything done himself. But could Yurka really allow him to do something like that?

So they both stayed there to paint the stage decorations. They laid the giant panels out right on the stage floor and crawled around on them like partisans in the field, wielding their brushes. The work wasn't hard, but it took a long time and there were some tricky bits here and there. It had gotten dark long ago, and it had been at least an hour since the bugle had sounded lights out, but they were still painting away.

It was past midnight when Yurka looked at all their work, estimated they'd done about half, and surrendered. He tossed down his brush and lay spread-eagle on the floor.

"That's it. I'm tired. Volod, let's wrap it up, we're working like draft horses here."

But Volodya kept moving his brush like a windup toy. "No, we have to finish it today. You heard them: tomorrow we have to give the paint back."

"Have to this, have to that . . . ," grumbled Yurka. All of a sudden he leaped to his feet, stomped over to Volodya, and tore the brush from his hand. "No, we don't have to!"

Volodya glared at him angrily and tried to grab the brush back, but Yurka skipped away and hid his hands behind his back.

"Look at that! You're painting outside the lines! You're tired!"

"We have to—"

"We've still got a whole day and a half to go!"

"We only have a day and a half left!"

"Your stage decorations aren't going anywhere! They're fine!"

Yurka angrily threw the brush away and took three steps toward Volodya, so he and Volodya were nose to nose. He looked Volodya right in the eyes and said, in a much quieter voice, "But we are going somewhere. Do I have to remind you what's happening the day after tomorrow? Apart from the show?"

Volodya frowned and looked away. But he immediately lifted his eyes back to Yurka's, and in them Yurka saw both understanding and regret simultaneously.

"I remember," Volodya replied sadly. "You're right."

Yurka put his hands on Volodya's shoulders and rubbed them. Then Volodya's neck. Then he ran his fingers through the hair on the back of Volodya's head. Volodya responded by embracing him, wrapping his arms around Yurka's waist and holding Yurka tight, reaching for Yurka's lips. But he didn't kiss Yurka the way Yurka was expecting.

"No, kiss me like you did in the boat," Yurka asked, pressing Volodya even more tightly to himself.

"It's no use," responded Volodya gravely. He paused for a moment, lost in thought, then added, "Yur . . . Yura, do you think we're maybe doing this all for nothing?"

"For nothing? What do you mean? Don't you want to anymore?" Yurka was expecting Volodya to hasten to assure him of the opposite, but Volodya just shrugged silently. Then Yurka started worrying in earnest. "But I don't want to stop doing this, Volodya! I like it! Are you really saying you don't like it anymore?"

Volodya turned away. He looked up at the ceiling, and then he looked down at the floor, and then he finally answered, "I like it."

"Then why do you say it's for nothing?"

"What if I let myself get out of hand again? And this is strange, you know. It is. It's against nature. It's not right. It's disgusting."

"You think this is . . . disgusting?" said Yurka, flabbergasted.

He thought about it. Okay, maybe from the outside they really did look strange. But that was only from the outside. Being "inside" their relationship, their friendship, maybe even their love, felt completely natural and wonderful to Yurka. Nothing was better than—nothing could be better than—kissing Volodya, holding him, waiting to see him again.

"I don't think so," said Volodya dejectedly. "But other people do. But that's not even the point. I feel like I'm leading you down the wrong path with all this, Yur."

Yurka got mad. "Remind me again: Who kissed who back by the power shed?!" He crossed his arms and scowled.

The corners of Volodya's lips started to turn up, but he held back his smile. After a pause, he asked, serious again: "Well, what do you think about this, Yur?"

"I try not to think," answered Yurka, equally seriously. "What's the point? Neither you nor I can stop ourselves. And us kissing isn't hurting anybody."

"Except ourselves."

"Ourselves? I'm having a hard time seeing how I'm suffering here. Quite the opposite. It makes me feel good and I like it. What about you?"

Volodya smiled awkwardly. "You know the answer to that already."

Yurka didn't bother with asking or arguing anymore. He just seized the initiative. This was their second real, grown-up kiss. And it was nothing at all like their first one. Back then, in the boat, it had been hot and nerve-wracking, the boat melting away under the beating of their hearts and the pounding of the rain, but now it was quiet. Completely quiet. Outside the windows was nothing but night; inside the enormous auditorium was emptiness. It was as though everything had frozen, was holding its breath, and there was only the two of them, rediscovering each other lingeringly, slowly, softly, through the movements of their lips.

But then there was a loud crash in the doorway, and something clattered and rolled. The boys leaped apart so fast it was as though a bolt of lightning had struck, throwing them in different directions. A small flashlight was rolling down the steps of the auditorium one by one. And in the doorway, her eyes round, stood Masha, reeling.

Yurka's first reaction was panic. Next came paralyzing horror. It felt as though the entire earth had fallen out from under his feet, as though the stage were breaking apart, as though everything around him were turning upside down. Then he was struck by confusion and disbelief: Maybe it was just his imagination playing tricks on him? Because where on earth could Masha have come from, showing up here at almost one in the morning?

But there she was. Living and breathing. And getting ready to get out of there as fast as she could: she was already feeling around behind her for the door handle.

"Hold on!" shouted Volodya, the first of them to recover from his shock.

Masha froze. He ran down from the stage and took the stairs up several at a time until he was next to her. "Don't run away. Please."

Masha couldn't utter a word. She was opening and closing her mouth, gasping for air like a fish tossed up onshore.

"Mash?" Volodya reached out to her, but she jerked away from him as though he had the plague. All she could manage to do was choke out a squeaky, "Don't touch me!"

"Okay, okay . . ." Volodya let out a shaky breath. He was trying to speak calmly, but his strained nerves were evident in every word. "Whatever you do, don't panic. Come down here, please. I'll explain everything."

"What?! What will you explain?! You—you—what are you even doing . . . It's disgusting!"

It was like Yurka's mind just shut down. He couldn't figure anything out or make any decisions. He couldn't even feel his hands. And his legs were made of cotton wool and wouldn't hold him up. But there was no time to waste. And so, with an unbelievable effort of will, Yurka forced himself to walk over to them. Masha stared at him, her gaze even more wild and terrified than the look she had given Volodya.

"Mash," said Yurka, forming the words with difficulty. "Now, don't go jumping to conclusions."

"You're abnormal! You're sick!"

"No. We're normal. We're just—"

"Why are you doing that? That's just not right! That doesn't happen . . . People don't do that . . . That's completely . . . it's just completely . . ."

Masha started trembling and whimpering. Yurka realized that she was a hairbreadth away from hysterics. Right there, right then, she was going to go and wake everyone up and—

Yurka didn't finish what he was thinking. He was starting to feel feverish himself. Everything started swimming before his eyes. It felt like he was about to faint, and then he'd just keep going and be swallowed up by the earth. He managed to preserve some semblance of at least external calm, although internally he couldn't stop replaying the terrifying images that kept parading through his imagination,: images of the shame and condemnation that would await him and Volodya as soon as Masha told everyone. They would become outcasts; they would be punished, a punishment it was terrible to even contemplate!

"We were just fooling around, you see?" chortled Volodya nervously. "Getting into mischief from boredom, from having nothing to do. And it's no big deal, there's nothing going on here. You're right, this doesn't happen. There's nothing happening between us here."

"What, are there not enough girls around for you? What is he giving you that we can't?!"

"Of course that's not it! Think about it: nature itself dictates that boys like girls, that men like women, and that's the way it is. Mashenka, he's not giving me anything, and I don't want anything from him. We're . . . Yura and I are . . . we're just . . . we don't mean anything to each other. We're going our separate ways after Camp Barn Swallow and we'll forget each other. And you forget about this. Because this is just nonsense; it's not worth it . . . it's meaningless, just a delusion . . ."

Yurka heard him, but the words were muffled. Unable to breathe calmly, he shut his heavy eyelids and winced in pain. The pain burned his entire being without focusing on one particular spot; it flowed through him, seeming to even reach out past his physical body. Because Volodya could have said they'd done it for a bet. He could've said anything at all, even that they were "practicing" kissing. She might've believed it, wouldn't she? But when Yurka opened his eyes and looked at her, he could read his answer in her face: *No*. Masha couldn't be tricked with excuses, jokes, or promises. If she was going to believe them, she needed the truth. Maybe even just a grain of truth, but still the truth. And there was truth in Volodya's words: the laws of nature, and their separation. And "Yura and I were just . . ."

Yurka stared at Volodya, seeking an answer to the terrible question that had just occurred to him: that there might not have been a drop of lies in anything Volodya was saying. It was painful for him to hear all this, but even more painful to realize that saying exactly this was their only way out.

"Masha, please, don't tell anyone about this. If anybody finds out about something like this . . . it's a black mark against us, for our whole lives. It'll ruin our futures . . . Do you understand me?" continued Volodya. Yurka continued to stand there dumbstruck.

"Okay . . . okay . . . ," sniffled Masha. "Swear you'll never do that again . . ."

Volodya took in a deep breath, as though he were gathering his thoughts. "I swear. I'll never do it again."

"You too." Masha turned to Yurka. Her eyes went from beseeching to cruel. "Now you!"

Yurka caught Volodya's eyes for a moment, seeing pure and absolute despair in them.

"I swear. Never again," Yurka choked out.

CHAPTER FIFTEEN
THE BITTER TRUTH

"Swear you'll never do that again..." Masha's voice was still ringing in Yurka's ears. As was Volodya's answer, and his own oath... "Never again, never again, never again..." How could they promise something like that? Was that even possible? But Masha had left them no choice. That damned Masha! He and Volodya didn't have much time left anyway, and now even those little crumbs had been stolen from them!

Only one day had passed, but to Yurka, tormented by loneliness, that one day felt like a month. Several times he was on the verge of deciding to hell with Masha and with whatever she might say about them, because there was such a storm raging in his chest that if he didn't release it, it'd tear him apart. Yurka was drawn to Volodya... Yurka wanted to see him, hear him, touch him... but he stopped himself. He knew that giving in to that urge, even once, could cost both of them too much.

Of course, they saw each other in the theater. They were spending hours finishing the stage decorations and rehearsing. Olga Leonidovna had officially released the drama club from all activities and all work so the kids could concentrate completely on their premiere. So naturally Volodya was right next to him all the time, and Yurka heard him, and saw him, and could touch him if he just reached out his hand. But he couldn't. They couldn't even allow themselves to look at each other any more than necessary. Masha was always lurking around somewhere nearby, like a guard dog, never taking her eyes off them. All Yurka had to do was think about it, hope there might be a chance, for him to be pierced by Masha's suspicious glare.

Yurka felt like he'd had one of his vital organs removed. He was apparently still living, still doing whatever was asked of him, following instructions, walking, eating, talking. Still breathing. But he couldn't get enough air. There wasn't enough air to get. It was like part of the oxygen had been shut off, or that some kind of poisonous gas had been added. And every hour without Volodya was poisoning his existence. It felt to him as though the entire world had descended into twilight; colors were blurring; shadows were shifting and melting. It was getting to be unbearable, living all alone in that gloomy, empty world. But even more unbearable was seeing how much all this was hurting Volodya.

Volodya was trying to hide it. He ran rehearsal as usual—shouting at people, ordering the actors around, and giving the actors notes—but there was none of his former enthusiasm. It was as though Volodya had been snuffed out inside. He was acting like a programmed robot again. He didn't worry anymore. He wasn't panicking. It seemed like he didn't even care whether the show would be a success, because his only emotion seemed to be sadness. There was so much of that sadness in his eyes, so much that it could already fill half a lifetime . . .

Even as he was falling asleep, Yurka saw Volodya's downcast face, tortured by sad longing, and he himself realized, with sad longing of his own, that a whole day, one they could've spent together, had disappeared. A whole evening, gone. A whole night, gone.

The task Yurka faced the next morning was overcoming his aversion to doing anything and eating his breakfast. He poked with his spoon at the clump of cold wheat glue that was being passed off as oatmeal. Usually it smelled good, but this morning all food was off-putting to Yurka, even the vatrushki. Those, now, those were excellent: fluffy, bursting with jam filling, fried perfectly brown on both sides. But he didn't want the oatmeal at all. In general, there was a lot that Yurka didn't want at all, but mainly he didn't want to be in the same camp, inhabit the same plane, be subject to the same geometry, as Masha. And in point of fact, it was clear from her expression that nothing tasted sweet or good to her today, either.

Yurka felt as though somebody had sprinkled sand in his eyes: blinking hurt, but so did looking. But he couldn't not look. At least, he couldn't not look at the Troop Five table.

The kids were acting up again. Sasha was waving his hands around, while Pcholkin was all abuzz, whispering in the ear of the little girl next to him until she shrieked and leaped to her feet. Today it was Volodya's turn to keep an eye on them during breakfast—that is, to not eat breakfast. Lena was sitting nearby and also looking at them every so often, but she wasn't getting up from her chair for any reason whatsoever. So it was Volodya who got up and went over to sort things out. He looked sleepy, pale, faded. In a tired voice he asked the little girl what Pcholkin had done to her.

While Yurka was pushing his oatmeal around with his spoon, and while Volodya was sorting out the young hooligan, and while Masha was watching them both, the blockhead Sashka finished eating and gathered his dishes, putting his glass on top of his bowl, and began to carry them all to the kitchen. One of the other little boys in the troop stopped him, pulling on his sleeve, so Sashka stopped right behind Volodya. Sashka leaned over, murmured something in his little friend's ear, and burst into laughter at his own joke. Yurka knew that now Sasha would gesture with his hands and that the glass would tilt, then fall off the bowl it was balanced on, and then it would land on Volodya's bowl, which was at the very edge of the table. So Yurka opened his mouth to shout, but it was too late: Sashka's glass had already tipped over. It fell against the edge of Volodya's bowl and sent it, and the oatmeal on it, flying. It knocked into Volodya's glass of tea with the vatrushka sitting on top, sending them both crashing onto the floor. Volodya looked wordlessly on as half his breakfast was smashed to bits and the other half was smeared all over the gray tiles.

Yurka expected Volodya to start shouting, but all he did was turn his completely helpless gaze to Sashka and sigh wearily. He didn't even say a word. It was obvious he hadn't gotten enough sleep and was so tired he just didn't have the energy to be angry. "And now he's going to walk around hungry for hours," muttered Yurka to himself. Sure, there was still oatmeal left in the kitchen, but the vatrushki were all gone; Yurka had already asked, hoping he could nab one more. But Volodya's being hungry wasn't the worst thing; he knew Volodya was used to not getting enough to eat. The worst thing was how sad and detached Volodya was. He hadn't been that bad the day before. Yurka felt so sorry for Volodya that the last ghost of his own appetite fled.

While Lena scolded Sashka and got the troop into formation for exiting the mess hall, Volodya called over the campers who were on kitchen duty to clear away the mess. Meanwhile, Yurka wrapped his own vatrushka in a napkin and walked over to Volodya. He pushed through the cluster of kids and held it out to him, saying, "Here."

"Thanks, but you should have it yourself. You like them so much."

"I don't want it. I'm full," insisted Yurka stubbornly, shoving the vatrushka at Volodya.

"I got enough, too."

"Take it! It's for you!" Yurka wanted to say more. He was hoping all the kids would leave and he could say, "Everything's for you: the vatrushka is for you, and I'll even get you some compote. Everything is for you, as long as you smile." But behind his back he heard Masha's "Ahem."

"What do you want?" Yurka asked gloomily.

"Nothing. I'm just waiting for you."

"For me? Why?"

"Just because."

"What the hell do you want from me?!" Yurka was beginning to get mad.

"You promised not to see each other and not to do that anymore!" squealed Masha.

Volodya flinched and mumbled without breathing: "Masha, we're not doing anything. But we can't just not see each other." He spread his hands wide. "It's camp."

"What is this? Are you going to forbid us from talking to each other, too?!" interjected Yurka.

"Yura, don't start," Volodya requested warily. "Please. Don't get in a fight. That'd be just what we need . . ." He shook his head nervously, blinked hard, turned on his heel, and strode quickly to the kitchen.

Yurka peered up balefully at Masha as he helped the camper on kitchen duty pick the bigger shards up off the floor. Masha stood there, arms akimbo, until Ksyusha grabbed her by the elbow and dragged her over to join the Pukes.

Yurka took advantage of the situation to follow Volodya.

It was quiet in the kitchen. The only sound was the bubbling of the water being brought to a boil to wash the breakfast dishes. Yurka dumped his shards into the trash and went farther into the kitchen, looking for Volodya. Volodya was standing at the stove over an enormous vat as big as a cauldron.

Yurka couldn't see his face in the clouds of steam rising from the vat of water. Volodya was still as a statue, holding his right hand so low over the boiling water that the skin was turning red.

"Hey, what are you doing? That's hot!" Yurka hurried over to him in consternation.

Volodya swiveled around abruptly. His face was contorted, as though by a spasm, and his glasses were fogged over. Yurka's confusion gave way to alarm. Whatever Volodya was doing, it was very strange! And then came a wave of fear: "What's he doing? What's he doing that for?"

The steam had fogged up the lenses of Volodya's glasses, so Yurka couldn't see Volodya's eyes. It was like Yurka himself was floating in a fog, he was so confused and scared by the unreality of what was happening. For a split second he even thought that the steam might be cold, and so, to test it, Yurka held his own hand out to the vat of boiling liquid, lowering it almost all the way to the water. "Ow!"

"Move your hand! You'll burn it!" Volodya swatted Yurka's hand away from the heat. "I'm—it's okay for me. I'm . . . tempering my hand."

His harsh voice brought Yurka back down to earth immediately, even though what he was saying made no sense. People tempered their children with cold water, not hot. A moment later Volodya's glasses cleared up, the fog evaporated from the lenses, and Yurka could see his surprisingly calm, even slightly detached expression.

"But tempering's cold. Do people really temper themselves with boiling water—" began Yurka doubtfully. He didn't get a chance to finish.

"I've been doing this for a long time, but you aren't used to it. You'll hurt yourself," warned Volodya, settling into his usual supercilious troop leader routine. Yurka actually sighed in relief at the familiarity. But then Volodya carefully took hold of Yurka's wrist, brought Yurka's hand to his lips, squeezed Yurka's hand, and blew on it, whispering, "Take care of—"

"Your hands," Yurka finished, rolling his eyes.

"—yourself." Volodya smiled and quickly kissed Yurka's thumb.

Yurka was so abashed that he didn't know what else to do other than turn it into a joke: "Oh, but, see, I love myself too much to—"

"So do I," Volodya interrupted him.

But Yurka didn't have a chance to process the meaning of those words.

"What are you doing in here?!" came an indignant screech. Masha was standing in the middle of the kitchen, so angry that the steam could've been boiling out of her, not out of the vats of water.

Yurka was just readying himself to vent his rage on her when he felt a brief but very warm touch on his forearm. Volodya quickly squeezed him and let go.

"That's enough. Don't get into it again," Volodya said quietly. It seemed like he was about to say something else, too, but Yurka left without waiting for Volodya to finish. Yurka's rage was roiling inside him even more furiously than the water boiling in the giant vats, but since Volodya had asked him to, he would find a way to stop. Yurka would do anything for him. He would sacrifice everything for Volodya, give Volodya everything. The best of everything. He'd give Volodya everything that was tastiest; he'd give him the sky, the air. All the music would be for Volodya. All of Yurka would be for Volodya. Everything that Yurka had, or had ever had, or would ever have. Everything that was in Yurka, everything that was useful and valuable in him, all that was wonderful and good—his entire soul, his whole body, all his thoughts and memories—he would give it all to Volodya if it would help keep Volodya from looking so despondent and nerve-wracked.

But Masha—Masha dared to forbid them to even speak to each other! It was bad enough that she'd been around all day yesterday, but now she'd evidently decided to start openly hounding Yurka, following at his heels, without shame and without hiding it.

Yurka wandered away from the mess hall, listening to Masha's footsteps behind him and growing increasingly irritated. They only had two days left, today and tomorrow, and now they couldn't spend even those tiny crumbs of time together because of her. Because of her, they had to just look at each other from a distance; they had to feel misery instead of adoration. And after Volodya's strange behavior with the boiling water, it wasn't even misery, but alarm.

What did he do that for?! fretted Yurka. *He's doing it because of her. It's all because of her!*

The sound of her heels on the asphalt behind Yurka clanged in his head like an alarm bell. Every time she sighed, he shuddered in revulsion, as though he were hearing not someone's breath but someone's nails running down a chalkboard. His nerves were as taut as violin strings: *And now we can't even talk . . .* , Yurka thought to himself. Behind his back, her low heels clacked. One step . . . another . . . *She's decided she can control us, has she?!* A step . . . another step . . . and another. *And now she's following me around. She forbids me from even standing in front of him!* A step. Another step. Another. *No way. That's enough!*

Yurka couldn't take it anymore. He jerked to a stop in the middle of the path. "What do you want from me?!" he shouted, unable to restrain himself.

"For you to stay away from him. He's a good person, a Komsomol member, but you're a freak and a creep! You're ruining him!"

"Who, me? What about you? Who do you think you are? You don't get to decide who he is or what he and I do!"

"It's not my decision, it's everyone's! The whole camp knows what a good person he was until you got your hooks into him!"

"We're friends! And friends—"

"That's not friendship!" she screamed. "You're leading him astray, you're turning him into a psychopath, you're seducing him! Yes, that's right! You're seducing him!"

"As if you know anything about it!"

Yurka was surprised to see this bring Masha up short. She turned red and stared down at the ground.

"You've gone and fallen in love with him!" he said maliciously.

Masha stood motionless, staring at Yurka. Pioneers were walking along the path past them. Yurka took Masha's hand and led her off to the side, away from the path, so the others wouldn't hear.

"Don't touch me!" Masha exclaimed, once they were off the path.

"Don't stick your nose into what's not your business, and then I won't need to even look at you."

"Stay away from Volodya, or everyone'll find out!"

"You fell in love with him, didn't you? Answer me! Yes or no? One word!"

"I don't answer to you!"

"Yes or no?!"

"Yes! Yes! Are you happy now? Yes!"

"And so you think, what, that if you follow him around and blackmail him, he'll love you back? You think that's how that works?" Yurka laughed cruelly.

"I'm not asking your advice. For the last time, I'm telling you: Stay away from him or I'll tell!"

"And what will that do for you? Can you even get it through your thick skull what'll happen to him if they find out about all this? Do you realize this will destroy his life? He'll be kicked out of his institute, and the Komsomol, and his home. Everything he ever wanted to do will be taken away from him, and all because of you! To hell with the institute or the Komsomol, though: What if it's worse? What if it's the loony bin? Or prison? Did you even think of that?!"

Yurka couldn't stop. His fury was no longer boiling inside him, it was gushing out uncontrollably. He was on the verge of hysterics. He was shaking. He had lost control of his body. Without realizing what he was doing, he grabbed Masha's shoulders and shook her, hard. He bellowed, "Did you think about how he'll remember you after that? How much he'll hate you? Is that what you want? Is *that* how you love him?!"

Masha was screaming now, too, but from fear. This was what pushed Yurka over the edge. He was about to throw her to the ground, but suddenly someone grabbed his arm and roughly shoved him away. Volodya.

Yurka and Masha had been yelling way too loud, so it was no surprise Volodya had heard them while he was finishing his breakfast in the mess hall. Finding them wasn't hard, either: half the kids from the athletic fields had come running to watch when they saw the altercation. At least there weren't any of the senior management among the spectators, just Lena and Ira Petrovna.

Volodya dragged the kicking and bucking Yurka aside while Ira stood protectively in front of Masha.

"What's the matter with you, Konev? Are you crazy?" barked Yurka's troop leader.

"Volodya, tell her! Tell her everything!" begged Yurka when he saw Ira.

"Calm down!" ordered Volodya.

"Ira, this piece of trash fell in love with him. She's been running around after him for half the session, and now she's totally lost her mind. She's following him and threatening to say all kinds of crazy stuff about him if I don't back off."

"Konev, what is wrong with you? Have you lost your mind yourself?!"

"Volodya, nobody's going to believe me! You tell them—tell them everything: how she followed us to the river and how she went into your room late at night. Come on!"

Volodya pulled him aside and spoke to him very softly: "You are hysterical. Let's breathe in and out . . . and in . . . and out . . ." Apparently trying to calm himself as well, Volodya took a deep breath in and let it out slowly.

But Yurka was physically unable to breathe evenly. He was eyes were teary and he was shaking with rage. "But it's true. Tell them, please," he whispered hotly.

"You left me no choice. But you go to the first aid station and take some tincture of motherwort or whatever Larisa Sergeyevna gives you for this."

"I'm not going anywhere!"

"Yura, Leonidovna's going to call all of us onto the carpet anyway. Please, go to the doctor, let her confirm that you are overworked and had a nervous breakdown. We'll tell everyone the show drove you to hysterics and you took it out on Masha because she was following you."

"But I'm not tired! I miss you! We're going together! Please. You also need to go see Larisa, right? Because what was that you were doing in the kitchen? Why were you doing that?"

"That's not important right now. Go to the first aid station, you need the doctor to certify that you—"

"We're going together!" Yurka repeated, interrupting him. "There are some bushes by the first aid station—"

"Yur, this isn't the time! What if Masha tells on us? I can't leave! Maybe she won't say anything if I'm there. And if she does, then at least there's a chance I can make something up right on the spot. Go by yourself, please. Don't pour more oil on the flame, you'll just make it worse."

In the end, Yurka didn't do any more pouring. He resisted some more, but eventually gave in.

At the first aid station, he described everything as they had agreed he would: he said he'd evidently gone into hysterics because of the show and yelled at Masha.

He was indeed called onto the carpet. There, too, Yurka recited everything as per the story Volodya had invented. Nobody asked him any strange, unnecessary, or personal questions. Everyone looked at him with sympathy. Not even Olga Leonidovna got angry. In fact, she was the one people got angry at: she shouldn't have given children such a heavy burden. In the waiting room, Yurka found out that Volodya and Ira had also been called in. And that later Masha had been invited in, too, of course. But it looked like management wasn't going to make a big stink about it. And that was good, because it meant Masha hadn't told on them. Yet.

There was one more piece of evidence that nobody knew anything about what had happened. This proof was provided by the Pukes.

As soon as Yurka appeared on the movie theater porch after his session on the carpet, Ksyusha beckoned him over, calling, "Yur! Yurchik! Come here!"

Yurka shot her a dark look and shook his head. But Ksyusha, and then Ulyana and Polina along with her, got up and ran over to him. They grabbed him by the elbows and led him off to a corner of the theater next to the stage.

"What's going on between you two?" whispered Ksyusha.

"*Something*'s going on between you two!" said Ulyana, nodding.

Polina just stared at him silently, her eyes burning with curiosity.

"I don't want to talk about it. It's private."

"Oh, come on, we're going to find out about it anyway," said Ulyana, trying to persuade him.

"It was Masha. She got up to something, didn't she?" asked Ksyusha.

Polina was nodding encouragingly.

"We just had a fight, that's all," said Yurka dismissively. "Nothing special."

"Because of the piano?" Ksyusha narrowed her eyes speculatively.

"Oh, well, that's boring, then," sighed Ulyana.

"But tomorrow's the last day, Yura!" Polina burst out unexpectedly. "Make up with her! You have to make up with her! Tomorrow is it! Then it's get on the bus and go back home. Don't part on that note."

"And speaking of notes, tomorrow you have to play music together!" said Ulyana, backing Polina up.

"Not together. We take turns playing. And just one time," explained Yurka, irritated. "As if you didn't already know that."

"Yur, speaking of music," said Ulyana excitedly, "can you play something from *Athena and Venture*? Just real quick, before rehearsal starts?"

"No. I don't know anything from that."

"A pop song, then? What about, say, 'The Last Time' from the Jolly Fellows album? I really want to sing! Play something, won't you? Please! Come on . . ." She started humming and danced a few steps.

"Sorry, Ul. Not in the mood. Some other time, okay? Or . . . hey, look, Mitka's here." Yurka turned around and caught Mitka's jealous stare. "Ask him. He'll bang out whatever you want on that guitar."

Yurka ran over to Volodya after extricating himself from the Pukes. Volodya had come back to the movie theater while Yurka was talking with the girls and was sitting in the audience, in the middle of the first row.

While he was still walking, Yurka asked, "Did she blab about us?"

"She didn't say anything like that in front of me."

"But when she was with the director?"

"I don't know. There's no way she's brave enough to tell the director, and if she did, I wouldn't be here right now. What worries me is this: she and Irina left together afterward."

"Do you think she told Irina?"

The door creaked open, revealing a red-eyed Masha in the doorway. Without answering Yurka's question, Volodya got up and went onstage. But Yurka understood even without words: she may well have.

Masha tortured the Moonlight Sonata for a while, then went and helped Ksyusha with the costumes until the end of the day. Volodya was with the actors, rehearsing scenes and working on individual lines right up until dark. Yurka played, then finished painting the stage decorations and preparing the props. He forced himself to switch into robot mode again; it helped that there was a ton of work to do, making it easy to find something to keep himself busy.

That night it drizzled. Yurka couldn't sleep. The calming effect of the tincture of motherwort had already worn off by lunch, and now, at night, as soon as Yurka got in bed, the worry he'd worked so hard to suppress seized him again, making him feel even worse than he had during the day. Had Masha told Ira?

Somehow Mitka, the radio announcer, had managed to make his way into the Troop One boys' room. He and the rest of the boys were all sitting on their beds, getting ready to go toothpaste the girls and warming their tubes of toothpaste in their armpits. Yurka chatted with them to try to distract himself. They tried to get Yurka to go, too, but he refused.

"That's your loss! You're going to miss something really fun!" Mitka made one last attempt to convince him.

"Trying not to laugh while you finger paint? What's fun about that? It's way more fun to look at the results. As long as you use Pomorin, of course." The Bulgarian brand was a favorite for toothpasting because its formula left a particularly nasty rash.

"We don't have any Pomorin. Irina confiscated it. Ah, it's too bad . . ." lamented Pasha.

"Get a load of you!" Yurka, shaking his head, started digging around in his suitcase. "Where's the joy in toothpasting with regular old toothpaste? But you're in luck, because I've got some of the best toothpaste in the world right here!"

To everyone's glee, Yurka stood up and brandished two whole tubes of Pomorin.

"Yurets! I owe you for life!" Flushed with joy, Mitka pressed his hand to his heart.

Yurka sent them off with a little advice. "Choose your victim carefully," he warned, guessing who Mitka wanted to toothpaste. The boy's crush on Ulyana was common knowledge. "The show is tomorrow, and a certain someone will blow her top if she has to perform with a rash covering half her face."

"I'll comfort her," said Mitka with a wink.

"Comfort her, my foot. You've gotta learn how to talk in front of her first!"

Mitka lost the gift of speech anytime he even glimpsed Ulyana. But of course he assured all the boys that everything was moving along just as he intended.

"Draw something on Masha for me," Yurka whispered to Mitka as the boys left. Mitka winked conspiratorially again in reply and disappeared out the door. The rest of the toothpasters tiptoed after him.

Yurka fell back on his bed. He listened intently to the hollow plunks of water droplets falling onto the roof. He looked up at the dark ceiling. The boys who hadn't gone on the toothpasting expedition were keeping him awake, snoring and grinding their teeth in their sleep. The grinding was incredibly irritating. Yurka completely failed at trying to make himself ignore it. He plumped up his thin pillow, and tossed and turned, and fought off the thoughts that kept stubbornly creeping into his head, but each passing minute saw him more mired in wakefulness.

How long has it been since we've seen each other? And how much longer will it be? Tomorrow's the last day of the session . . . tomorrow's the end! No, to hell with all this thinking. Just listening to Vatyutov's teeth grinding is better than this . . .

Vatyutov moaned, rolled over, and finally went quiet. The rain kept changing, first petering out, then coming down harder.

As long as the rain stops by morning, thought Yurka. *The bonfire's tomorrow. The whole camp will be there. Maybe we can slip away from the crowd and talk? At least just say goodbye? This is so stupid, avoiding each other because of that idiot! I hope someday she suffers, too, from the same kind of stupid, mean, jealous . . .*

A rhythmic noise cut through the chaos of sound. Yurka froze. He listened. Then it vanished.

The head of his bed was right against the windowsill. Yurka sat up and turned his left ear toward the window. Had he imagined it? He hadn't. Someone really was drumming on the windowpane. He looked out the window and saw a figure standing there, holding a flashlight whose dirty yellow light barely diluted the darkness. The person was dressed like a ninja, all in black: pants, jacket, cap . . . and glasses. Volodya! As soon as he saw Yurka, Volodya's shoulders sagged with relief.

Yurka, barely able to keep from jumping for joy, pressed his nose to the glass. He brought up his hand to open the window, but Volodya furiously shook his head no. He reached into his pocket and took out a piece of paper. He pressed it to the windowpane and lit it from the side with his watch. "Unfinished barracks. Now!" read Yurka, and nodded. Volodya mouthed the words, "I'll wait for you there," then dove back into the bushes.

Yurka got dressed the way his father had taught him: like a soldier, in the time it takes a lit match to burn out. He was also in a hurry because Mitka and the boys would be coming back any minute and Yurka didn't want any awkward questions. He was in such a rush that he pulled on the first things that came to hand—a warm sweater and a pair of shorts—but not so much that he forgot the main thing: to dress like a spy himself in a dark jacket with a hood.

Like a spy, he looked into the window of the girls' room and confirmed that Masha was being toothpasted, and then, again like a spy, he kept checking all around him the whole time he trotted to the unfinished barracks, dreading that he'd see her over in the bushes somewhere. He was gripped by panic, even though he knew for a fact that Masha was asleep back in the cabin.

The path to the unfinished barracks started at almost the very beginning of the Avenue of Pioneer Heroes. It was well-defined, but very narrow, and it went off into the woods and looped around between the trees. Yurka had taken neither umbrella nor flashlight with him, so it was hard for him to make it to the fence around the new building; he kept either sinking into huge puddles or tripping over clods of earth.

In the moonless, rainy night, the empty four-story building looked like a gigantic gray spider with a dozen empty window-frame eye sockets. Out here the lamps worked until midnight, but it was long past midnight now and not a single ray of light fell on the construction debris littering the site: lengths of rebar, spools of cable, and strange pipes that looked in the dark like crooked spiders' legs.

The tall gate wasn't locked. It creaked open, but as Yurka crossed the deserted courtyard, he doubted himself: Had he understood this correctly? Were they really meeting here now? This didn't seem like Volodya.

The narrow door of the main entrance opened easily. But instead of the warm air of a functional residential building, Yurka was met with a stream of damp and cold. The darkness was complete, total, even palpable. Yurka walked forward through it slowly, with effort, as though he were walking through water. Something rustled underfoot, and he looked down. It took him a moment for his eyes to get used to the dark, but then he saw that on the floor a narrow, pale gray strip was becoming visible, like a photograph developing. It glowed against the black background, regular in some places, in others getting narrow or spreading out wide. At some points it curved around for no reason, and occasionally it got brighter, but at other points there were yawning black gaps. Yurka had to crouch down and examine it to figure out what it actually was. It turned out to be nothing supernatural: somebody had spread newspapers across the floor. Yurka's eyes landed on one of the headlines of an issue of *Pravda* from May: "In and Around the Station: A Report from Our Special Correspondents on the Region of the Chernobyl Atomic Power Station."

Yurka walked along the path of newspaper, wondering whether it had been laid out for him as a marker or if the newspapers had been put down to keep the floor clean. Time went by slowly. Strange thoughts came into his head. It was as though Yurka were walking along time when he was walking along the newspapers. After all, every newspaper had its own date, and every article had its own topic, and every page had its own events. Yurka could only see some of the dates, making it all the stranger to step over one thing, then stop on another. The pages, and with them the photographs of people and the events themselves, kept sticking to the bottoms of his shoes. They were clinging to him as though they didn't want to let him go. *That's what happens in real life, too, actually*, thought Yurka philosophically. *The past clings . . . But what if these newspapers are from the future? Not even the very distant future, just a little, even just from the summer of eighty-seven . . . or what if they are from five years from now, or ten years . . . Or maybe from twenty years later . . .* Without finishing his thought, Yurka turned right and entered a room. He just had time to notice that it was even colder here, despite the fact that these windows had glass in them, before someone threw themselves at him and held him tight.

It was Volodya, of course. Yurka recognized his scent. He recognized his warmth. That warmth, Volodya's warmth, was special somehow,: it was utterly dear and familiar and recognizable. Although there's no such thing, of course, as recognizing someone by their warmth.

They didn't speak. They alternated between passionate embraces and tender kisses. They nuzzled each other, now with their noses, now with their lips, everywhere they could find: their cheeks, which were cold, and their necks, which were warm, and their wet hair. Locks of Volodya's hair kept sticking to Yurka's face, and Volodya's glasses were really getting in the way.

But Yurka only wished that that hair would stick to him, tickle him, and get in his way every single minute for the rest of his life—because it was Volodya's hair, after all... those were Volodya's glasses, after all... and this was Volodya, after all! Yurka would have welcomed any discomfort that reminded him of Volodya.

As soon as he held Volodya in his arms, Yurka realized how much he'd missed him. When Yurka had imagined seeing him again, he hadn't realized that his heart would start pounding so hard, or that his eyes would start burning, or that he'd be unable to breathe. He hadn't known that because of all this, he'd be unable to squeeze out a single word, or that once he could, no words would come to him. Or that even if he did manage to speak, even if he said just a tiny little fragment of what he actually thought and what he actually felt, he'd burst into tears. And crying is embarrassing and doesn't help. So Yurka just stood there gasping for breath, holding Volodya tight and being tightly held in return, silently, fearful of every sound: What if their bitter joy were suddenly interrupted? What if this happiness were destroyed? What if they were taken away from each other?

"We've lost so much time!" groaned Volodya, so softly Yurka could barely hear it.

"Yes, we have ... so much ... ," affirmed Yurka, reaching for Volodya's lips. "But you did give her your word, you wouldn't be with me ever again ... "

Volodya had bent his head toward Yurka and pulled him closer, but when he heard that last comment, he jerked away, scoffing. "'Gave my word'... Pfff! That's all it was, just words, meaningless words to a meaningless person. I had to see you again. And I have to tell you something."

"Wait, you were never going to stick to it?" asked Yurka, amazed.

"Of course not," Volodya replied, pressing his forehead to Yurka's. "And don't look at me like that, as though you've never broken your promises. But . . ." He seemed to want to continue but then stopped. Had he changed his mind? Or was it that he didn't dare say it? "Should we sit down?"

Volodya unwrapped one arm from Yurka but continued holding him with the other as he led Yurka over to the far corner of the vacant room. There, by the window, a pile of newspapers had been thrown down on the floor to make a mat that was a finger's breadth thick. There was room to sit on it, but not quite enough to lie down. The boys knelt, facing each other.

"Yura, I'm going to tell you something now. It's not good, but it's important. I don't like saying this, so don't interrupt me, okay?"

"What happened?" Yurka started up, alarmed.

"I think . . . ," Volodya began, then faltered, pausing to slowly collect his thoughts and choose the right words. "I think Masha's probably right. This is all probably for the best . . . That tomorrow we're both going our separate ways, I mean."

No, Yurka wasn't imagining it: it really was bitterly cold and damp all around him in this room. He wouldn't be surprised if his breath started steaming. Or was it the opposite: Was it that everything inside him was frozen?

"What?" Yurka choked out, not believing his ears. "Here I am, not able to see how I'm going to keep living without all this, but you're saying it's for the best? How could that be for the best?!"

"It's for the best for me," Volodya said, then remained silent for a long time.

Yurka studied him as though he were seeing him for the first time. Volodya's words made no sense. Yurka simply did not believe them. He wanted to say many things, but at the same time he knew the best thing he could do right now was not to speak.

After a minute that lasted forever, Volodya continued: "I've thought a lot about us, and about myself. And of course about what I'm going to do about my abnormality. Because it's not normal, Yur! Say what you want, but Masha's right about one thing: it's against nature; it's a psychological aberration. I was able to find some things about this, I read them—a handbook of medicine, Tchaikovsky's diary, an article by Gorky—and you know, what we're doing . . . it really is bad. It's not just bad, it's awful!"

"It's awful?" said Yurka, stunned. "When you hold me, you feel . . . awful?"

"No, no, no! That's not the point! How do I explain this to you?" He pondered for a moment, then said urgently, "It's bad for you! Yes, that's it: it's bad for you. And not just for you, and for me, but for society, too. Take fascist Germany, for example. Gorky wrote that the Germans back then were all sodomites and that sodomy was the seed of fascism. 'Destroy the *homoseksualists*, and fascism will disappear.' That's exactly what he wrote in 1934. It's historical fact."

"But you're not like them. And neither am I! It just turned out that way, that we met . . . and we . . . yeah," Yurka objected hotly. When he heard that ugly, disgusting word—"sodomite"—it was like someone jamming a red-hot needle in his brain. Because he'd heard the word before, and now he remembered exactly when.

He was still very young at the time, just a little kid, and he didn't understand a thing as he listened to his grandmother. She was talking about how, when she was looking for her husband, Yurka's grandpa, she found out that it wasn't just Jews that got sent to the concentration camps; there were also people who had to wear pink triangles. Some of them were even German. His grandma said they were called sodomites, and the fascists hated them and tried to exterminate them just like they did the Jews.

These memories clicked into place just like a missing puzzle piece in Yurka's head. He announced firmly, "And you've got it wrong. In fascist Germany, those 'sodomites' were sent to the concentration camps."

Volodya raised his brows, surprised. "How do you know?"

"I am a Jew, after all. I have heard a few things about the concentration camps."

"All right, fine. But nobody knows anything about it for sure, anyway. There aren't even any books about it in the USSR. There's just the entry in the handbook of medicine saying that it's psychological, and then the statute of the Criminal Code."

"So?" Yurka couldn't believe that this was really happening. He felt it must be some kind of trick. What was the matter with Volodya? He had called him out here in the middle of the night just to dump all this on him. Volodya wasn't asking questions, he wasn't getting advice, he wasn't sharing his concerns. He was just asserting this. What for? To bring Yurka back to his senses? "The statute of the Criminal Code"? What did that statute have to do with the two of them right now? Yurka shook his head in confusion, then offered Volodya the only somewhat logical conclusion he was able to draw from all this: "So you think Masha told someone and you're going to prison for this?"

"No, I don't think that. They'd still have to prove it, for one thing. And it's not prison I'm afraid of; I'm afraid for my family, don't you see? And so that's why I decided . . . as soon as I get back, I'm going to . . . I'll make myself tell my parents everything so they can find a doctor who will cure me of this."

It was like the frost had covered the walls: they glittered, blinding Yurka in the total darkness. The frost crept along the floor and touched his feet.

"And you want to be . . . treated?" whispered Yurka. "How? Where? If it's psychological, they'll lock you in the loony bin!"

"Then let them, if that's what helps. I spent a lot of time on this and found out a little about how it's treated. And there's nothing bad about it. They just show you pictures of men . . . well, like the ones you saw in that magazine . . . and give you a shot that makes you nauseous. They do this many times, and eventually you're supposed to develop an automatic gag reflex. But that's not what got my attention. They also do hypnosis! They can instill interest in girls. They can use it to make you forget about these feelings."

The glittering sheath of ice crawled up Yurka's legs, past his waist, encasing his stomach and chest.

"Have you lost your mind? You're ready to be locked up in a ward with a bunch of psychopaths? You're normal! Living with them will make you go crazy for real!"

"I'm not normal! I want to be free of this, once and for all; it's messing me up! It's not letting me live in peace, Yura! I want to forget everything."

"You want to forget . . . me?! Just like that?! Simply put it all out of your mind, and you're done?!"

"It's not simple, Yur . . ."

"Why are you . . . but you . . ." Yurka felt betrayed. "I . . . I have no idea what's happening here. Why are you telling me all this? So I stay away?"

Yurka leaped to his feet and ran over to the doorway, but Volodya ran after him and grabbed his hand: "Wait! Yur, please, you have to understand, this is all for real . . . it's serious, really serious . . . Please, hear me out. You'll probably leave once you hear the truth, but please at least hear me out."

Yurka went completely still. More than once, Yurka had felt something between them—a sort of veil of things left unsaid. Things that kept them from growing even closer. Things Volodya knew but wasn't telling Yurka. Or that he mentioned but didn't fully explain. Many times, Yurka had thought about asking, but whatever was there, he was afraid it would hurt even more, and then he'd regret the lifting of that veil.

While Yurka was thinking about this, Volodya cleared his throat and began in a whisper: "It's complicated because we were never just friends. You and I had just met, but then everything started moving so fast that I didn't even recognize it when it happened." His voice went hoarse. In that kind of absolute darkness, there was no way Volodya could see Yurka's face, but evidently he didn't even want to look in Yurka's direction, because he turned away and said, loud and clear: "I fell in love with you."

Those words stupefied Yurka. He could hear Volodya's words just fine, but he wasn't able to wrap his brain around them. In love. Did Volodya mean it? "Fell in love"?

But then the frost started melting. The warmth started inside Yurka but then moved outward. Meanwhile, Volodya was still talking, his voice husky, but with every word, his whisper grew hotter: "The way I fell in love with you is the way you're supposed to fall in love with girls! And this whole time I've been wanting from you what a normal guy would want from a girl: little sweet nothings, and kisses, and . . . and . . . and all the rest of it." He looked distraught. "I'm a dangerous person! I'm a danger to myself, but I'm especially dangerous for you!"

"All the rest of it . . ." Yurka had also fantasized about "the rest of it" when he was alone. But he figured that didn't concern anyone but himself, because it was his own body, and Yurka knew a way to solve that problem that didn't involve Volodya at all. Sure, Volodya was an object of desire, but that didn't mean Yurka was going to go act on his feeling. Yurka had known for a long time now, obviously, that people could do "the rest of it" not for procreation but just because it felt good. And after seeing the magazine, he had guessed that there were ways to do it other than the traditional way. Recently, he'd realized that might even mean it was possible to do it with people other than girls. But for him and Volodya to do it? No. No, that was too much. Yurka could deal with his problems himself. And to tell the truth, he didn't even think of it as a problem at all!

But evidently Volodya did. And he was so desperate, he was even ready to go to a doctor—anything to forget. To forget it all. Which meant to forget Yurka, too. But Yurka couldn't allow that! What was he supposed to do? Volodya was terribly afraid of his own desires, but wasn't that because he longed to fulfill them? Was that why he was telling Yurka all this: because subconsciously he actually wanted Yurka to push him to do "the rest of it"? Because he wanted Yurka to convince him that essentially there was nothing dangerous about "the rest of it"? That it was probably just the opposite: that happiness is entrusting yourself to a person who loves you?

And that was the biggest thing of all of it, for Yurka: Volodya had fallen in love with him! As he remembered it, his dark thoughts had disappeared as though he had never had them. Volodya loved him! Could anything in the whole world be more important than that? No! The future, all those fears, this "abnormality"—all of it was nonsense, none of it meant anything, none of it was worth worrying about if Volodya was in love with him. So what if a "normal" man would find this absurd? It made Yurka so happy that he wanted to laugh out loud—so much that he couldn't hold back. He burst out laughing, grabbed Volodya's arms, turned Volodya around to face him, pushed him back on the pile of newspapers, and jumped on top of him, chortling, "What am I supposed to be afraid of you for? What are you going to do, hold me so tight, you squeeze me to death? Go ahead, please, hold me as tight as you want."

"It's not what I'm going to do—I'm not going to do anything to you. It's what I want to do . . . I'm like a maniac or something . . ."

Volodya made a pretty poor maniac. It was impossible to take his threats seriously when he was sitting on the floor, squashed into submission by a Yurka who was holding him down.

"And what do you want to do, exactly?" Yurka knew already, but he wanted Volodya to admit it out loud.

"That's not important. None of it's going to happen anyway." But Volodya was only protesting verbally; physically, he wasn't moving a muscle.

"Yes, it *is* important! Tell me! What?"

"I don't want to do anything that'll harm you! And I won't! Yurka, it's harmful! It is! It's an abomination, it's vile desecration! I wouldn't do that to you for—"

"But what is 'it'? This?" Yurka put his hand under Volodya's shirt.

"Yurka, stop!"

Volodya roughly snatched Yurka's hand away and pushed him off, then knelt on the floor and hid his face in his hands. Yurka had been soaring with happiness—Volodya was in love with him!—but the sight of Volodya, ready to weep, cooled his ardor. Yurka tried to peer between Volodya's fingers to look into his eyes but could only catch sight of Volodya's furrowed brow.

"Come on, why are you acting like this, Volod . . ."

He stroked Volodya's hair, but instead of calming down, Volodya flinched and burst out angrily, "Can you really not understand this? Can you really not conceive of where this might lead? You're not like me. You've liked girls before. You haven't lost everything yet!" Volodya lowered his hands from his face and looked Yurka right in the eye. "Yurka, promise me, not for show but for real: Swear me an oath you'll never break. Promise me that I'll be the only one. Promise that as soon as you get home, you'll get your act together and fall in love with a good girl . . . a musician . . . That you won't be like me. That you'll never look at any other guy the way you look at me! I don't want you to be that way! It's bitter, and it's scary . . . You have no idea how scary it is!"

"Can you really hate yourself this much?" whispered Yurka, dismayed.

"Can you really pretend you don't care? Because I'm sick! I'm a freak!"

Yurka itched to slap him so he'd come back to his senses and stop insulting himself. But instead he said, "I do. I do care. And you know something? When you're a nobody like I am, when you've got nothing to lose, all these terrible thoughts just go away. And I can think clearly. Because, look, what if everyone's wrong?"

"That's stupid! Everyone can't be wrong!"

"But what if they are? Because I see the kind of person you are, I know you. This is me talking here! I can be messed up, I can be crazy, but you can't! You're the best thing there is. You're smart, you're upstanding. I . . . Let everything be my fault, okay? I'm the one who's ruined, I'm as bad as anything—not you! I'm used to everything being my fault! It won't hurt me to be guilty of one more thing; it's just a drop in the bucket."

"You're spouting nonsense."

Yurka didn't bother answering. Nonsense? As long as it made Volodya feel even a tiny bit better, Yurka was willing to both spout nonsense and take responsibility for everything. He was willing to lie and hide. But did Volodya really not need all this? Did he really want to get rid of what Yurka was trying so wholeheartedly to give him? No. That was nonsense!

It was painful to look at Volodya, to see him so despondent now that he'd basically resigned himself to the inevitable. It was terrifying to think about what he wanted to do to himself. And Yurka felt so bad for him. Far worse than he ever felt for himself.

Yurka sat down next to Volodya. He put his arms around Volodya and rested his head on his shoulder.

"What if I say I love you, too?"

Volodya didn't respond; he didn't even move. After a pause, he said coldly: "It'd be better if you didn't say that."

"I just did."

"It'd be better if you forgot."

It was as though Yurka had been stabbed through the heart. No matter how scared Volodya was, no matter how much he was suffering, did he really not understand that hearing those words was simply painful?

"Listen to what I just confessed to you! Doesn't it make you even a little happy?" demanded Yurka. Volodya didn't say anything, but he did smile. Yurka noticed that and continued hotly: "Then I'm going to say something else, too. I also have doubts about a lot of things—there's also a lot I don't understand—but one thing I know for sure: you shouldn't destroy what you've built. If everything ends now, if we just quit on each other, I'll regret it for the rest of my life."

"No. You'll be grateful to me. You're stubborn now, but later you'll learn. You'll realize I was right. Because I'm not just saying this. I know more than you about these things."

"You know more than me? Tell me, then! Tell me already: What is this great thing that you know but I don't! You're always lecturing me, but you can't tell me like it is, Konev's still too stupid! Wait until you get smarter, Konev, then you'll understand!"

"That's not true. I just don't want to scare you, or . . . or disappoint you."

"Then admit it! What happened to you?"

Volodya sighed in resignation and started talking. "You're not the first person for whom I've had . . . this."

He looked closely at Yurka to see his reaction, but Yurka just nodded and said, "Go on. It can't get any worse."

"Well, we'll see about that . . . The first one was my cousin. He came to stay with us while he was getting enrolled in university. We hadn't seen each other for many years. I'd even managed to forget what he looked like, but then here I see him again. He'd grown up, become . . . he'd gotten . . .

I don't know how to describe it. He'd become remarkable. He's older than me; I had always been drawn to him and wanted to be like him. And then I saw him and was just transfixed. Everything that had anything to do with him seemed good and important to me. I lost my head whenever he was near. And all of a sudden, I felt . . . it. And not for just anyone, but for my own cousin!" He turned toward the window, pressed his temple against the wall, and said in despair, "Just think, Yur, think how disgusting I am! Think what this filth inside me is capable of making me do. He was my cousin! My own blood, my family, my father's brother's son. We even have the same name: his first name's also Vladimir and his last name's also Davydov; just our patronymics are different . . ."

"Did you tell him?" Yurka asked dully.

"No, of course not." Now Volodya was speaking softly. "I never told anyone about my cousin, and I probably won't ever tell anyone else, not even my parents. Especially not them. I have never felt as much horror as I felt then, and I probably never will. Because to be any more scared than that would be more than I could take: I'd die of heart failure. It got so bad that when I woke up in the morning, I'd look in the mirror and genuinely not know how I hadn't gone gray yet. I'm not joking and I'm not exaggerating, Yur. I got scared of myself, I got scared of other boys: What if they awakened this filth inside me? And then I started to be scared of absolutely everyone. I haven't always been as closed-off as I am now, you know. And I don't hate people. I avoid them because I'm afraid: What if they see it inside me?"

Yurka didn't know what to say, or whether he needed to say anything at all. He pulled Volodya away from the wall and hugged him hard. He rubbed his shoulder for a while, then went still. Bursts of rain kept spitting doggedly into the fogged-up window. It was now late at night, and it just kept raining and raining. Volodya's breathing gradually went from panicked gasps to slow, even breaths. He began calming down and maybe even dozed off a little; Yurka didn't check, since he was afraid of disturbing Volodya. Yurka was sleepy himself, and as he relaxed, his left hand accidentally fell down onto Volodya's belly.

"Yura, are you testing me? I already asked you to move your hand. I forbid you to touch me there."

Yurka flinched in surprise, then got mad: What did he mean, he forbade him?! Scowling, he retorted, "And I forbid you to put your hands in boiling water!"

"Oh, would you just stop," said Volodya, giving up without a fight.

"The bonfire's tomorrow," said Yurka, petting Volodya's belly through his shirt. "Do you even understand that? Tomorrow is the last time we'll see each other! Maybe even the last time in our whole lives!"

Volodya shot a surly glance at Yurka's hand, then looked pointedly at Yurka. Yurka understood his complaint.

"Fine, have it your way! I'll move my hand! But you know what? I'm going to be leaving so much behind at Camp Barn Swallow that it can't be counted. I'll be leaving half of myself here! And when I get back home, the thing I'm going to regret more than anything else is that I moved my hand. And don't tell me that it's for my own good, that it's for the best, and that I'll be grateful nothing happened, and that *you'll* be grateful nothing happened. You don't even believe that yourself!"

"Of course I don't believe that!" Volodya exploded.

It turned out he hadn't calmed down at all; he was just pretending, and really he had gotten worked up about something again. Now he poured everything out on Yurka's head in a rush:

"You're talking about this 'tomorrow,' but look at the time: it's already Friday. The bonfire's today. Today is the end. As soon as we separate, I'm going to lose my mind from missing you . . ." He heaved a shuddering sigh. "Yura, please, understand me! I'm so lost, I'm so tired of going back and forth! As soon as I make up my mind to do it, to go get treatment, I swing over to the opposite extreme: more than anything in the world I want to keep what we have now! And then I think about you and I get afraid again, because I don't want the same thing to happen to you—"

Yurka interrupted him. "It's too late to be afraid of that, because it's already happened! With you! I've told you a thousand times, I don't know what other words to use. Volodya, if it weren't for you, I wouldn't have started playing again! Music came back to me, thanks to none other than you! Goodness and meaning came back into my life because of you, so you can't be bad. And today's not an end at all, not if you don't want it to be. Volodya, look, I'm not your cousin. And it'll be different with me. I understand you, and I—I love you. And now I know for real, not from books, how hard it is to become each other's first love, how hard it is to *be* each other's first love. But then staying that for each other is easy as pie. Let's do what it takes to stay that way, okay? Because we're friends, first and foremost, and I'm not going to betray you, and I'm not going to abandon you. I'll write you and support you."

The whole time Yurka was talking, Volodya started at him without blinking, his eyes radiating his desperate desire to believe those words, to believe that everything would work out for them.

"I'll write you, too," Volodya said finally. He smiled. "I won't skip a single letter. I'll write twice a week, or even more, and I won't even need a reason."

"There, you see? Now we're talking sense."

"You got that right." Volodya chuckled. "I'm a little less afraid I'll lose my mind now . . ."

Yurka realized, suddenly, that he was freezing. To warm up, he stretched out his goose bump–covered legs and started rubbing them with his hands.

"Oh!" he remembered. "Tchaikovsky didn't write in his diary that sodomites should be exterminated, too, did he?"

"No," Volodya scoffed. "He was one of them. They didn't put you in prison for that back then. But he suffered from it, too. He called it 'feeling Z' and wrote about how—"

"There, see?" Yurka interrupted him, to keep Volodya from getting bogged down in a discourse on suffering and torment again. "He didn't start any wars. Just the opposite! He was a genius." Yurka wanted to shout the word "genius," but his teeth were chattering from cold. He shivered.

Volodya, of course, noticed that Yurka was freezing and started taking off his own jacket, evidently planning to drape it over Yurka's shoulders, but Yurka stopped him. "Better to warm my legs." Volodya nodded and put his hands on Yurka's ankles. His hands were so warm, as though it weren't freezing! He started rubbing his hands briskly up and down Yurka's legs. Yurka felt the warmth spreading through his body—not regular warmth, but that special warmth, Volodya's warmth. He shut his eyes, luxuriating, and so didn't see Volodya lean forward, but he felt the heat on his knee. It was so cold that Volodya's lips on it felt burning hot.

Yurka stared at him, not daring to move a muscle. Volodya caught his eyes and smiled. He slowly breathed out another puff of heat onto Yurka's skin, then leaned over to kiss the other knee.

Yurka couldn't help it: he reached down and took hold of Volodya's shoulders and tried to pull him toward his face. "Kiss me. The grown-up way. Like in the boat."

"Yura, we shouldn't . . . Don't stir . . . that in me. Even without any kissing you're too good at getting me excited, I can't sleep for half the night afterward. I don't want to get all handsy with you again and then regret it."

"But I want you to! And you, you're . . . stirring me up, too; you're over here kissing me on the knee!"

"I know, I'm sorry, I didn't mean to . . . God, I'm even seducing the most innocent, the most—"

"Stop blaming everything on yourself!" Yurka erupted. "You keep creating all this blame and guilt and then heaping it on yourself! Is what we're doing really bad? Does it really hurt anyone?"

"No, but Masha might tell."

"Tell what? She doesn't even know where we are right now. She's sacked out over in the cabin, fast asleep. Look, I don't want to ruin our last day because of her. Volod, it's our last day! What if we never see each other again? What if we really—"

"Masha or no Masha, we shouldn't." Volodya hugged Yurka's head to his shoulder. "This can only lead to . . . to something improper. And I'm responsible for you."

"For cripes' sake! Look, what if after this I go do something bad without telling you—some act of vandalism? Are you responsible for me then? No. Come on, Volodya, quit treating me like I'm a little kid."

"Well, okay. But let's not start up right this minute, okay? I barely got to sleep the night after the boat. We have to get up early tomorrow, and we've stayed up late enough as it is."

"But tomorrow is already here," said Yurka, smiling.

He was warmed up. But now Volodya went quiet. Evidently he was immersed again in yet more worries. But Yurka didn't resist. He wanted only one thing: for Volodya to rest his head on Yurka's chest and then let him think about whatever he wanted as he listened to the beating of Yurka's heart.

They held each other again. Yurka turned his desire to reality, pulling Volodya close and hugging his head to his chest. The nosepiece of Volodya's glasses bit into him, so Yurka pulled them off Volodya's nose without asking. Volodya didn't offer a word of protest; he just put Yurka's hand on his head the way he'd done that time under the willow, so Yurka would stroke his hair. And Yurka was unable to refuse him.

The rain slowed. Falling raindrops tinkled and plinked. Eventually, dawn began striping the sky in the gaps between gray rain clouds. It was time to leave, but ending their embrace, even just tearing away from each other for a few seconds, was too hard. It was all but impossible. As they said their goodbyes, their kisses were many and frequent: kisses on the lips, but not grown-up ones, not like the kisses in the boat.

They threw caution to the wind and left together. But once they reached the intersection of the path to the unfinished barracks and the Avenue of Pioneer Heroes, Volodya realized he'd forgotten to throw away the newspapers he'd spread in the barracks to cover up their tracks. He shook Yurka's hand in parting and turned to head back.

Yurka was still a little angry at Volodya for not kissing him properly, and for not letting him touch his stomach, and for . . . well, there was a lot he was mad at Volodya for. Easier to say that Yurka was just mad about everything.

As he trudged back to his own cabin, he remembered his final threat that he would perform some act of vandalism without telling Volodya. He stopped and looked around, checking that no one was nearby, and raced back to the intersection where he and Volodya had parted ways. He'd remembered that he still had a piece of chalk in his shorts pocket.

The intersection was freshly paved and formed a perfect square, as though it had been created specifically to be an artist's canvas. Yurka thought about what he should write. Maybe the first letters of their first names and the year, like in the lovers' bower? No, writing something like that would be too risky. Obviously the *V* could be hiding Vitya, or Valya, or Valera, or any number of other names, while the *Yu* could be Yulya, not Yura. But then the dwindling rain would hardly wash away the writing by the time the bugle played reveille. And if it didn't, and if Masha did somehow find out about his and Volodya's absence, then things would get ugly for them. No, writing the first letters of their first names was off-limits. But what did he need two letters for? Yurka had never liked the first letter of his name; it was awkward and weird-looking. The letter *V*, though: now, that was a different story altogether . . .

He got the chalk out of his pocket. He bent down and, with a flourish, started drawing the most gorgeous letter in the world, *V*, the first letter of his favorite name. He traced around it, making the lines thicker and then shading them, and then realized that just the one letter all by itself wasn't enough. There had to be a meaning hidden in his "act of vandalism." It had to conceal a feeling: the feeling he'd been afraid to call love, even to himself, up until that night. But love was precisely what it was. Yurka knew that now.

He loved that letter, and he loved that name, and he loved that person, and he lovingly drew a big, beautiful heart around the *V*. He used to laugh at people who drew things like that. He used to think it was stupid, childish. But that was before he'd met his *V*.

Yurka heard footsteps on the path leading to the unfinished barracks. He recognized them and suddenly felt shy. Volodya had finished so quickly! But Yurka wasn't done drawing his heart yet. He pulled the chalk down in a crooked line, intending to bring it to meet the other line to make the point at the bottom of the heart, but out of nowhere he started to feel uncertain: What would Volodya think when he saw it? Maybe he, serious as he was, would think it was silly. Maybe he'd think it was just naive childishness and tell Yurka, "You need to grow up!" And then Yurka would be not just embarrassed but hurt.

To avoid being caught red-handed, he blindly drew a final line with his chalk and then ducked into the bushes. But he accidentally spoiled the heart: instead of a sharp point at the bottom, there was a curve. It wasn't a heart at all. It was an apple. An apple that had the letter *V* inside it.

Volodya noticed the letter. He stopped. His shoulders shook—was he laughing?—and he shook his head back and forth a few times. Yurka thought Volodya would leave after that, but Volodya stood over the drawing for a good minute, examining it from various angles, as though he was trying to commit every flourish and every little detail to memory. Yurka was getting sopping wet in the sodden bushes, but he had no complaints. He admired Volodya as the older boy stood over that uneven, misshapen heart.

Volodya moved to take a step, and Yurka's heart skipped a beat: he couldn't be about to scuff it away, could he? But Volodya had no intention of scuffing or trampling anything. He gave the heart a wide berth, walking all the way out in the grass. He could've walked along the edge of the paving stones; it would only have smudged the heart a little, just a teeny, tiny bit, just a centimeter of it. That's what Yurka would've done. But Volodya walked around the heart, treading on the wet, muddy grass.

CHAPTER SIXTEEN
THE SHOW

The morning of the show, the morning of the last day of Session Two of the Barn Swallow Pioneer Camp of the summer of 1986, emerged overcast and gloomy. By the time breakfast started, the sky was completely dark; a north wind had chased in a mass of heavy gray rain clouds, which hung directly over the camp, so fat they looked fit to burst. The only question was when they'd let loose. But Yurka—like Volodya, and like the entire cast—had no time to think about extraneous matters. Work was going full steam ahead; they had no time left for anything, not even sadness. Although Yurka was occasionally visited by sad thoughts, of course. How could he not be, after that nighttime conversation, after everything that had been said?

Yurka finished painting the stage decorations, set them up in their places, touched base with the actors, double-checked the cues for the sound effects, told Alyosha Matveyev what he needed to do during the show, and carried chairs from the mess hall to the theater because there weren't enough seats in the audience for everyone. In between all those tasks he also managed to run through his lines, rehearse the scene with Krause a couple of times, and practice the "Lullaby," which it seemed he could again play even with his eyes shut.

On top of everything else, Olga Leonidovna also showed up to rehearsal first thing in the morning. She spent a long time walking around the movie theater with Volodya, discussing something with him. The conversation made Volodya completely despondent; he told Yurka that the educational specialist had demanded that he sit in the audience with her and the camp director. She had said that the show was the Pioneers' own work and she needed to see what they were capable of when the troop leaders weren't helping. "Will you sub in as director for me today?" Volodya asked.

Yurka agreed. He wasn't upset by the responsibility that had fallen to him. He knew the script backward and forward, and he already had a ton of responsibilities anyway: running the lights, prompting the kids if they forgot their lines, making sure the curtain was open and closed at the right times, and so forth. Overseeing the entire show didn't really add much extra work. Plus it had already become a habit for Yurka to keep himself busy to avoid his own sad, longing thoughts. Right now he was avoiding them with all his might, but despite his best efforts, fragments of his conversation with Volodya kept coming back to Yurka periodically, first throwing him into a fever, then giving him chills.

One part came back to him most of all: "I've thought a lot about us, and about myself. And of course about what I'm going to do about my abnormality." Yurka's heart went painfully tight. At that moment he was moving the stage decorations for the first scene out from backstage and issuing instructions to Alyoshka and Mikha, who were helping him. He stopped and looked over at the stage, where Volodya was explaining something to Vanka, who was playing one of the Germans.

"Why do you treat yourself like this?" Yurka asked Volodya silently. "In what way are you 'abnormal'? Have you even seen yourself? How can you think that?" He shook his head dejectedly.

Yurka and Mitka were checking that the curtain opened and shut smoothly. Volodya's voice sounded in Yurka's thoughts: "I spent a lot of time on this and found out a little about how it's treated." A shiver ran down Yurka's spine. He stood still, then took a deep whiff of the dusty air, recalling how he and Volodya had kissed for the first time, wrapped up in that very curtain. Yurka started shaking as soon as he imagined the doctors eradicating those memories from Volodya's head, those feelings from Volodya's heart.

"You're not the first person for whom I've had . . . this." What was he like? That first one, the other Volodya Davydov? Of course Yurka couldn't help wondering about him. Was that Volodya as good as his Volodya? He must have been, because Volodya couldn't fall in love with a bad person, right? Yurka felt ambivalent about this other Volodya. If he, Yurka, had been Volodya's first love, then maybe Volodya wouldn't have considered himself such a monster, wouldn't have taken all of this so hard . . .

After breakfast he went to the mess hall to get the chairs for the theater. He heard the clattering and clanging of dishes in the kitchen, and with them Volodya's words: "I don't want to do anything that'll harm you! And I won't! Yura, it's harmful! It is!" And then remembered Volodya's hands over the vat of boiling water and understood, in a burst of realization like an electric shock. At the time, Yurka couldn't figure out why Volodya was doing that, but now it all made sense: it was punishment! Volodya deliberately caused himself pain in order to punish himself! But why? What an idiot that boy was! Did he really need to punish himself for these feelings, these good, exalted feelings?

Was that why Volodya had been so stern about forbidding Yurka to touch him? He kept telling Yurka to move his hand away; he didn't want to kiss Yurka for real . . . But what would've happened if Yurka hadn't moved his hand, if he had kissed Volodya for real, despite Volodya's resistance? Because Yurka wanted so badly to experience that kind of thing with Volodya . . . He didn't see anything shameful about it, it was simply an expression of his love, but Volodya obviously regarded it as something that would ruin both of them. Or—how had he put it? That he was afraid of defiling Yurka? But that just made no sense, and it also made Yurka a little mad: How come Volodya got to decide everything without even asking him? Why was he so intent on being the only guilty one?

Nice try, but no, thought Yurka, grinding his jaw. *I can make decisions myself. I can tell the difference between good and bad. And no matter what Volodya says, these feelings are the best thing that's happened to me my whole life. They can't ruin anyone or anything!*

But he didn't end up finding a time to get Volodya alone to talk. That whole morning all they could do was exchange sad or knowing glances or murmur work-related phrases as they prepared for the show. It wasn't until right before the show, when the audience was already starting to take their seats, that Volodya finally came to Yurka, who was in the supply closet with the rest of the cast, getting into his outfit for the performance.

Yurka was having a sense of déjà vu as he stood in front of the mirror, trying, with shaking hands—he was already in the throes of stage fright—to tie his neckerchief. Then Volodya approached, put his hand on his shoulder, turned him around, and started tying the red knot at Yurka's neck. It was all exactly the same way it had been before Summer Lightning, except that now they were in a tiny room that was crowded with people. Yurka looked around in fear, searching for Masha, but didn't see her. And what was wrong with this, anyway—with Volodya helping him tie his neckerchief?

"Yur," said Volodya quietly. "I'm really looking forward to your 'Lullaby.'" Even more quietly, he added, "It's the only thing I'm looking forward to . . ."

Yurka took a long, searching look into Volodya's sad eyes. "I'll be playing it just for you. Promise you'll watch me the entire time."

Volodya nodded. "Of course." He smoothed the ends of Yurka's neckerchief and turned around to the rest of the boys in the supply closet: "Does everyone remember I won't be here backstage with you? Listen to Yura, he's in charge!"

The boys nodded and Volodya left. Olezhka ran over to Yurka and gazed, entranced, at his neckerchief. He had evidently understood Volodya's order literally, since he paused and waited expectantly. Finally he asked, in a whisper, "Yuwa, is it twue that the Pioneews won't take someone like me, who can't say theiw *r*'s?"

"What? That's stupid! Who's telling you that?" Yurka couldn't restrain himself.

"Oh, you know . . . I heawd it fwom lots of people."

"Of course the Pioneers will take you! Grandpa Lenin himself said his *r*'s different, and he wasn't just a Pioneer, he was the leader of the world proletariat! So it'll all work out for you, too, Olezhka! Don't you listen to anybody, you'll—"

"So I don't have to listen to *you*?" Olezhka narrowed his eyes shrewdly, grinning.

Yurka hadn't even finished rolling his eyes before Olezhka darted away.

By one o'clock the audience was filled to bursting. There weren't enough seats for everyone even with the extra chairs from the mess hall, so some people had to sit in the aisle. The houselights went down and the auditorium went silent. Then Volodya came out onstage in front of the closed curtain. The honor of saying some introductory words fell, as was proper, to the artistic director. And, as was also proper, he began, "Esteemed audience members, we offer for your consideration a show marking the anniversary of our beloved Pioneer Hero Zina Portnova Barn Swallow Pioneer Camp..."

Volodya recited the memorized words in a serious but rather indifferent voice. Yurka had already heard the monologue during rehearsal, so he didn't listen to it now, instead helping the actors get ready for their first scene.

Volodya finished delivering his official welcome and handed the floor over to Polina, the play's narrator. In a clear, expressive voice, she began reciting the poem that was ubiquitous at all Pioneer camps, Zheleznov's "Pioneer Heroes," about how the Soviet people fought valiantly and saved everyone from fascism, but at great cost to themselves.

Mitya was working the curtain. He was standing at the ready, his gloved hands gripping the rope, and he was getting antsy. He whispered to Yurka, "Well? So you're going to nod, right, when it's time to open it?"

"Are you sure you don't need help?" Yurka wasn't convinced Mitka could handle the curtain all by himself; he'd have to open and close the curtain at least thirty times, after all. Since it wasn't practical to completely switch out the sets every time there was a scene change, they had divided the stage into two halves. The left half was for indoor scenes, while the right half was for scenes that were set outdoors. And because the script maintained a regular alternation between indoor and outdoor scenes, only the right half of the stage, the outdoor part, had to be covered by the curtain whenever there was an indoor scene, and vice versa.

Mitka was more serious than Yurka had ever seen him. "I can do it myself!" he insisted, sneaking a peek at Ulyana, who was warming up for her entrance. Yurka realized that the curtain had become a way for Mitka to prove his manhood; still, Yurka had his doubts.

"But, Mitya, it's only easy to draw the curtain at first. You're going to have to draw it a hundred times during the—"

"It's fine!"

"Mitya, if we shit the bed here, even just one thing..." Yurka expressed himself in exactly the words that were running through his brain. And why not? Volodya was elsewhere, and none of the senior campers were around, either, so nobody was there to tell him off for it.

But Mitka was stubborn and declared firmly, "Yura, I'll do it myself!"

There was no time to argue. The moment of truth was upon them. Yurka was very worried, even though his entrance wasn't for another whole act, because he was in charge today, and Volodya was counting on him, and Yurka had to show everyone what he could do. It felt like he'd put part of himself into the show, and he was invested in its success.

The Young Avengers had already taken their opening positions and were getting ready for curtain. Polina was starting the final stanza of "Pioneer Heroes," which called on everyone to always remember and honor the young heroes who'd died for their country.

Yurka took a deep breath, trying to calm his agitation. He opened his eyes and nodded to Mitya. The rope creaked and, in perfect accordance with the plan, the curtain slid up, revealing the left side of the stage: the indoor side. The first scene was where Zina Portnova and her nine-year-old sister, Galya, arrived in the village in late June 1941 and found out the war had started. As the narrator, Polina announced that the village was quickly occupied and that Zina soon met Fruza Zenkova—played by Ulyana—and joined the ranks of the other brave young people of the Belarusian SSR in the Young Avengers.

The left side of the stage was quite picturesque: the crew had fastened a big picture of the inside wall of a wooden hut to the backdrop, hung propaganda posters on the wall, and arranged suitcases and duffel bags on the floor. They had even brought over dishes and pots and pans. Masha, her hair pulled down over her face to hide the rash that covered her cheeks after she was toothpasted with Pomorin, started playing the Moonlight Sonata. The Young Avengers had gathered at a table with a map and were planning their sabotage. All the play's main characters were in this scene, and they all had at least one line, meaning that if even one of them made a mistake, the entire scene would go off the rails. So far everything was going smoothly, but Yurka, who was scrupulously following the actors' lines in the script, was prepared to prompt them.

"Zina," said Ulyana as Zenkova, the secretary of the Avengers, turning to Portnova. "You've been working in the officers' mess for a long time now. The time has come to give you a task!"

The leader held a little glass bottle of perfume out to Portnova. (They hadn't been able to find anything else at camp.) "This is rat poison," she explained. "You have to poison their food."

"I will!" Portnova replied readily.

"And now we move on to the next issue. A secret cache of weapons has been found. Ilya, how many weapons do we have in total?"

As Ilya Yezavitov, Olezhka leaped to his feet. "I . . . I . . . ," he stuttered.

Yurka whispered from backstage, "We have . . ."

"We have," said Olezhka, collecting himself, "five wifles, a Maxim machine gun and ammunition, and half a dozen ow so gwenades."

The piano music faded, replaced by the sound of clacking train wheels. Pasha, playing Nikolay Alexeyev, a member of the underground who had a job at the railroad station, ran onstage and into the room. "Men, for several days now echelons loaded with haystacks have been moving through the station. It's strange: no one uses steam trains to transport such flammable cargo. It *is* strange, right?" The Avengers nodded. "Well, I was checking the bridge today and I looked and saw that under those haystacks they're hiding tanks . . ."

Everything would've been fine, but there wasn't a trace of alarm or surprise in Pasha's voice. The actor was just getting through the words as quickly as he could. Yurka huffed angrily, but the Young Avengers notified the partisans of the tanks by radio and made arrangements to meet the next day to hand over the weapons they'd found. The curtain slid closed.

"Guys, why are you so sluggish? You've got to pull it together, we can't let Volodya down!" hissed Yurka when the actors came backstage.

Ulyana actually flared up at him: "We're already doing the best we can! But instead of gratitude, all we get is criticism! You know what, Yurka—"

"Ulya, no time to talk: Get to the outdoor half, on the double!"

The forest stage decorations were already in place: the crew had attached drawings of fir trees to the backdrop, along with the large outline of a train station complete with low outbuildings and the station bell. The members of the underground hurried over to their hiding place, a small hollow log, to hide the weapons, looking around apprehensively the whole time. But there was no log onstage! There should've been, according to their plan, but there wasn't! Had Alyosha forgotten to set the prop?

Some helper Matveyev turned out to be! He begged and pleaded to join in, but what happens! Yurka thought angrily, waving his arms to indicate they should hide the weapons behind the piano. They understood and set the weapons there.

Meanwhile, on the indoor half of the stage, the part now covered by the curtain, chaos reigned. The kids were getting ready for the next scene, in which Zina poisoned the soldiers in the mess hall. They set out a table, covered it with a white tablecloth, and took down the posters. The scene in the forest only had three lines, so it went by like a flash. It was time for the next scene.

This was chubby little Sashka's fateful hour: he'd been entrusted with playing the first German to die.

Mitka heaved on the rope and the curtain slid away, revealing an officer's mess with German officers sitting at the table. Upstage, Zina surreptitiously poured poison into a pot of soup, then started ladling it into bowls. Masha played the dark, gloomy passage from the middle of the "Internationale." The officers each had a spoonful of soup and then fell to the ground. Sasha, of course, overdid it, shouting and writhing so much that the audience tittered.

Zina was seized immediately. She started shouting that she'd had nothing to do with it, that the soup was fine, and that she'd prove it. She ate a spoonful of the poisoned soup, and her legs buckled as she fell unconscious to the floor.

Villagers appeared onstage, picked Portnova up under her arms, and took her upstage to where a set piece resembling a porch had been set up. The villagers arranged Zina next to it. Her grandmother and sister appeared. Her grandmother started fussing over the still-insensible Zina, while little Galya clutched her tightly, started crying very believably, and said in a thin voice between sobs, "Zinochka, I'll be left all alone without you! Leningrad is starving, and our mama and papa are there . . ."

The action continued to play out on the porch while Sashka, having finished his dramatics, ran offstage.

"Sasha, I'm begging you, a little less emotion! At least don't shout so much."

It was as though Sashka, wiggling happily and red in the face, didn't even hear him. But Ulyana peppered Sashka with questions: "So? How's it going?

How's the audience?" Then she added smugly, "I was too preoccupied to see, you know, because I'm a lead."

Yurka scoffed.

"Oh! Fine," the chubby lad assured her happily. "Olga Leonidovna and Pal Palych look pleased, but Volodya looks strange, like he's not paying attention even the littlest bit!"

"No way!" declared Ulyana.

She and Sashka tiptoed over to the curtain and peeked out from behind it at Volodya. Yurka remained where he was, making sure that the outdoor stage decorations were being set up for the next scene. There wasn't much that could be messed up there: all they had to do was throw a pile of "coal" on the ground and attach a drawing of the pumping station to the backdrop. They didn't even have to remove the previous scenery of the forest.

Ulyana came back offended and hissed angrily at Yurka, "Konev! Here you are, riding our backs with your 'Don't let Volodya down, don't let Volodya down,' but Volodya doesn't even care! He couldn't care less about this show!"

"That can't be!" Yurka was actually perplexed. If anybody cared about this show, it was Volodya!

"It sure can!" scowled Ulyana.

The stage was set, so Yurka had a free moment to peek into the audience. It was true: Volodya wasn't even looking at the stage. His face was tilted down, toward the notebook in his lap, and his brow was furrowed in concentration while his fingers drummed on the armrest. He was nervous. How Yurka wished he could sit beside him right now. But he had to show everyone—not just the administration and Volodya, but himself—that he could do it, that he could be counted on, that he could make his own decisions, that he could keep things running smoothly, both for himself and for the actors.

Yurka went backstage. Ulyana, fanning herself with the script, nodded toward the audience. "See? What did I tell you?"

Yurka said stubbornly, "Ulyana, it's not that he doesn't care, it's that he's nervous! If we botch this, we're in for it. Volodya too! You know that already. So give it your all!"

Onstage, the narrator's voice began: "It is now 1943, two years since the Fascist invasion and occupation of Zina's village. Zina Portnova has recovered from eating the soup she herself poisoned and continues her work with the Young Avengers. In order to stop the Red Army's counteroffensive, Hitler's forces have started sending enormous numbers of troops and resources to this part of the front. Troop trains thunder along the Vitebsk-Polotsk line day and night. But their motion is being hindered: steam trains need water to make steam, and almost all the water-pumping stations along that railway line were destroyed, either by the Soviet Army or by partisans. Only one pumping station has remained intact, one that had gone unnoticed among the villages and fields near the little town of Obol until it was too late to put it out of commission."

The right side of the stage was revealed, showing a pumping station with a German soldier standing next to it: Pcholkin, wearing a uniform jacket and holding a toy rifle at the ready.

A girl playing Nina Azolina approached him. She was a pretty girl, a Young Avenger who acted like she was serving the Germans faithfully. Pcholkin the German started yelling at her, but the deputy commandant who was courting her came running at the noise.

Vanka was playing the part of the deputy commandant, Müller. He ran up to the German guard and started shouting at him in German. His German wasn't all that great, but he was doing the best he could. Yurka had written that line especially for him. *"Entschuldige dich bei der Dame! Schnell!"*

While he was turned away from Azolina, shouting at the guard, Azolina sneaked a bomb disguised as a lump of coal into the coal pile.

Polina resumed her narration: "Three days later the water station was leveled to the ground. It took two weeks to rebuild it, during which the Germans were kept from conveying eight hundred troop trains to the front. The Germans began to suspect it had been the local residents, not organized partisans, who blew up the station, so they increased the guard on strategic infrastructure and set more patrols on the streets."

The next scene was Yurka's favorite. It was impressive, but it required a lot of attention. The entire cast had put their heads together to come up with a way to depict it onstage. "If only we could do it as a movie, so everyone didn't have to just imagine the fire and smoke . . . ," the kids had mused.

Yurka darted over to the lighting console and readied himself to give the signal for the sound effects at the right moment. He looked over at Matveyev, who was standing next to the stage decorations for the outdoor half, holding the ends of some strings.

Yurka tried not to dwell on the fact that this scene was the last one in the first act, which he was bringing to a close with his "Lullaby." The main event of his whole day was going to happen in just a few minutes, but Yurka wasn't mentally prepared for it.

On the left side of the stage the crew had put back the set for the Young Avengers headquarters: a typical village hut with a porch, and on the ground by the porch a small sandbox where Galya Portnova was playing.

"Galka, you remember, right?" asked Zina. "As soon as you see fascists or police, you sing your favorite song, 'In the Field a Young Birch Stood.'"

Galya nodded. Zina went into the hut. The meeting began. Olezhka as Ilya Yezavitov took the floor: "The Fascists are afraid of us, but that doesn't mean we are out of danger!"

All of a sudden, Galya's thin little voice pealed,

*"In the field a young birch stood,
In the field, long-tressed, she stood . . ."*

Upstage, three Germans walked across the stage and then exited behind the curtain. Ulya, as Fruza Zenkova, the chairman of the Young Avengers, ran over to the porch, verified the soldiers were gone, came back to the meeting, and began listing the facilities in Obol that had been seized by the Germans and had to be destroyed: the power station, warehouses, and town factories.

After the shouted line "All of them must be destroyed!" Yurka looked Mitka, who, drenched in sweat, uncovered the outdoor half of the stage, revealing a village scene with huts and vegetable gardens, along with four large flats depicting an electrical power station, a flax mill, a brick factory, and a warehouse. A string was attached to the back of each flat, and Mitka held all four strings. Yurka rested his right hand on an AV console and got ready to give the signal to the person handling sound effects and Alyoshka.

Polina narrated: "On August third, the Young Avengers dealt their heaviest blow to the enemy: at eighteen hundred hours exactly, the power station was blown sky-high." Yurka chopped his hand down, giving the signal, and then three things happened at once: there was the sound of an explosion, a red spotlight lit up the power station, and the flat with the power station painted on it fell down. Gasps came from the audience. Yurka perked up and lifted his hand, ready to give the next signal. The narrator announced, "This task was accomplished by Zina Luzgina." Onstage, Katya, who was performing that role, stood up from the bench she'd been sitting on inside the hut.

"Fifteen minutes after the power station, the flax mill was destroyed, complete with the drying chambers, storage facilities, and machine room." Yurka chopped his hand, giving the signal. There was the sound of an explosion as the second flat with the flax mill painted on it glowed red, then fell down. "This task was accomplished by Nikolay Alexeyev." Pasha stood up from the bench.

"An hour later, the brick factory was blown to bits. This task was accomplished by Ilya Yezavitov." Olezhka, his chin raised proudly, stood up. Once again Yurka gave the signal, and once again came the explosion, the red light, and the clatter of a flat falling to the ground. Then, suddenly, Olezha's high but confident voice rang out over the audience: "For the Motherland!" Yurka turned to look. He couldn't believe his ears: it really was Olezhka! At the beginning of the performance, he'd been nervous and kept messing up his lines, but then his delivery became more and more confident until now, when, for the first time Yurka could remember, Olezhka had pronounced a clear, ringing *r*.

Then the excited Petlitsyn sprang up from his chair. He was early. He was supposed to wait until after Polina's narration: "Five minutes after the explosion of the brick factory, the peat processing plant blew up. This task was accomplished by Yevgeny Yezavitov." Yurka gave the final signal, waited for the sound and light, and watched the fourth flat fall over, then rushed to the piano.

He cautiously peeked out from behind the curtain. Onstage, the Young Avengers who had caused the explosions were still standing in their places. The audience was still rustling and exclaiming in excitement. Volodya saw Yurka and smiled and nodded. Yurka's chest swelled with pride. He ducked back behind the curtain, grinning: they'd really laid on the pathos and fervor! He hadn't expected this much of a success himself! And here he was amidst the thundering audience, and the lights, and the kids' solemn faces, and over it all was Masha, proudly pounding out the "Internationale" on the piano.

"No one was caught that day," continued the narrator. "On August nineteenth, 1943, a station warehouse was burned down, destroying twenty tons of linen that was ready to be shipped to Germany. The fire then spread to a manufacturing warehouse, destroying ten tons of grain allocated for Fascist troops! But this time, shortly before the fire, Ilya Yezavitov had been seen near the warehouse . . ."

Olezhka walked all the way across the stage and exited behind the curtain. The remaining actors stood where they were.

"Ilya left in time and joined the partisans. The Germans noticed that Ilya went missing from the town of Obol right after the attacks. His escape was what ultimately convinced the Germans that there was an underground organization of local residents in Obol and that the acts of sabotage were performed by them, not by the partisans."

"The authorities' response to our infrastructure attack was too weak," pronounced Zina Portnova loudly. "The Germans rounded up a few suspects but quickly released them. Too quickly. They're up to something!" She got up and left, just like Olezhka.

The narrator intoned the last sentence of the first act: "Zina Portnova left and joined the Kliment Voroshilov partisan troop. On August twenty-sixth, 1943, the Gestapo arrested almost all the members of the underground resistance that were left in town, along with their families."

"That's it! It's time!" Yurka started shaking. He was standing in the wings near the piano, all cleaned up, hair combed, in a perfectly tied neckerchief, white shirt, and gray trousers. Masha was just getting up from the piano and glared angrily at him. But he didn't care. His heart was beating hard enough to break through his rib cage and his fingers had gone numb. He couldn't straighten them. He knew that any second now Mitka would slowly and smoothly cover the left side of the stage with the curtain and uncover the right side of the stage, where the piano was.

Yurka looked out into the audience. There were so many people out there! How many times had he played the "Lullaby" in front of the cast without being afraid? But the cast was different: he wouldn't quite call them family, but they were like the boys from his building back home—his people, familiar. It was also true that before Camp Barn Swallow Day he'd played out on the outdoor stage, where anybody walking by could've heard him, like Pal

Palych, and all the troop leaders, and even the Pioneers who were sneaking out during quiet hour. But that was just practice. Only a few individual people were listening, and they wouldn't have cared if he'd made a mistake. But this was it, now: he had an audience!

The second it fully dawned on Yurka that he was about to play his song, his "Lullaby," in front of everyone, his memory ricocheted back to a bad perm and enormous glasses, a table covered in exam papers, and a verdict: "Weak!" He was worthless. He couldn't do it. And if he couldn't do it back then, after he'd trained for several months, what would happen now?

The curtain slid up, the creaking rope indicating that it was time for Yurka's performance.

If only I could rip out this stupid heart, maybe I could at least breathe, thought Yurka. He heaved a shuddering sigh and approached the piano. His cotton wool legs were capable of bending, even of straightening—but his fingers still weren't.

It had felt so good, back then, on the outdoor stage! The cook had been banging the pots and pans while the phys ed instructors lolled around on a bench loudly doing a crossword puzzle. But the main thing was that Volodya had stood behind him and tried to keep him from playing by putting his hands over Yurka's eyes. And Yurka hadn't been afraid in the slightest ... But right now he was, even though it was all the same people here in the movie theater with him: the two phys ed instructors, and the cook, and even her pots and pans.

And Volodya was here, too.

Yurka stood stretching his fingers and trying to concentrate. He pretended that Volodya was standing behind him, tittering silently—although did Volodya even know how to titter?—and covering Yurka's eyes with his warm hands, and that everything was going dark.

Yurka squinted his eyes shut, and everything really did go dark.

"Pull it together. You're not at an exam. You're onstage. Everything is fine. There's no perm. There never was such a thing as that perm in your life! But there was such a thing as Volodya. And all this right here is for him."

Inhale ...

Just watch me the whole time, like you promised, came the thought, full of entreaty. Yurka knew that this thought, sent out into nothingness, would still find its target. His shaking stilled, and his numbed fingers came back to life and began to do as he bid them.

. . . exhale.

The moment he touched the keys, everything disappeared; the voices in the audience went quiet. It was as though he himself sank into darkness. All that remained was a single, solitary gaze. Yurka didn't need to turn around to feel it. The music, too, remained.

Yurka played as though in a fog. The slow, lingering melody alternated with bolder echoes of the main theme, and it seemed like his heart was beating in sync with them. The music filled Yurka completely, penetrating the most guarded recesses of his soul and raking through it, pulling everything out of it in a melody that was sometimes frenzied, other times tender and calming: sadness, and longing, and fear . . . and love. As Yurka let the music in, it passed through him, washing away his emotions. The sounds spoke for him, and he knew that the person these feelings were for would understand. The music was saying everything for Yurka: the love he felt, and the yearning he would suffer, and how fiercely he didn't want to part, and how unbelievably happy he was to have met this person. The music promised that Yurka would wait for him without fail and would keep hoping even when there was no hope left.

Yurka lifted his hands up from the keys. Only then did he realize he'd finished. A rising ovation thundered at him from the audience. Yurka couldn't comprehend how much time had passed. He flinched, turned toward the audience, and immediately sank into Volodya's eyes, which were sad and happy all at once.

The rope creaked and the curtain slid down, hiding Yurka from the audience. Polina came out onto the edge of the stage in front of the curtain and announced, "End of Act One. There will be a fifteen-minute intermission."

Yurka's heart was hammering so hard in his chest that he thought everyone around him must be able to hear it. Had he done it? Had he played well?

The envy in Masha's eyes was his answer. Seeing that Yurka had noticed her expression, she quickly turned away. But Yurka couldn't care less about Masha right now. He wanted to laugh out loud, happily, joyfully. He covered his mouth with both hands and then did burst into laughter. He went offstage and hid by the edge of the curtain so nobody would see him and think he'd lost his marbles.

Someone grabbed his elbow and dragged him away. Yurka turned around: Volodya!

"Hey, what do you think you're doing? They'll see!"

But the hallway behind the stage was empty, and the actors' muffled babble could be heard from behind the closed door of the supply closet. Volodya opened the door to a long, small room lined with shelves piled with stuff: the prop room. Volodya shoved Yurka in, shut the door, and held him tight.

Yurka stood with his hands by his sides, breathing in the dense, dusty smell and blinking rapidly, trying to get used to the semidarkness. He couldn't move a muscle. Volodya buried his face in Yurka's neck, breathing heavily, and his heart was beating as loudly and feverishly as Yurka's had been just a minute ago after he finished the "Lullaby."

"Thank you," breathed Volodya.

When Volodya said that, his warm breath washed over Yurka's neck, and it tickled, which almost made Yurka giggle. But he didn't. He wasn't in any mood for laughing anymore. He was just really sad.

And that was just how Volodya was holding him: sadly. And desperately. He squeezed Yurka tight, clutching fistfuls of Yurka's shirt. As though this were the last time . . . as though if he let him go, he'd never get to hold him again . . .

Yurka got a lump in his throat and his eyes started burning. He wanted to say something, or at least get his hands free so he could put his arms around Volodya, too, but he couldn't do any of those things.

"Magnificent, Yura," said Volodya, without letting go. "You did great. That was magnificent."

Yurka smiled. "Well, I don't really have a choice, you know. I have to show you that I can be counted on—that I can make my own decisions."

Volodya held Yurka out at arm's length and studied him intently. "But I never said that you—"

"But you think it! You blame yourself for my actions, you think of yourself as some kind of terrible evil . . . and you decide for me when it comes to figuring out what's good for us and what's bad!"

Volodya didn't respond. He just frowned. Yurka, realizing that this was neither the time nor the place to make Volodya even more upset, reached out to hold Volodya again.

They stood like that for almost the whole intermission. Yurka couldn't sense the passage of time. He only came to his senses when they heard the trampling of feet behind the door.

"It's starting. You have to go," Volodya whispered sadly.

"Uh-huh," said Yurka dejectedly. "Volod, the kids are hurt that you're not looking at them. Start watching them, okay? They really are trying."

Volodya nodded and pulled his hands away. No matter how much Yurka wanted to stay here forever, in such a loving embrace, he had to let Volodya go and return to helping the actors.

He ran out of the prop room and was in the wings by the time the curtain slid up to reveal the left half of the stage. The stage decorations were the same as before: the Young Avengers' headquarters in the hut. The actors were sitting inside around a table. Galya was sitting outside on the porch steps, winding bandages and singing "In the Field a Young Birch Stood." Zina ran over to her and kissed her on the cheek.

"Is the medic going out on rounds soon?" she asked. And when her sister nodded, she continued happily, "Galka, I'm headed out on a job. Now, don't you worry: I'll be back this evening."

The narrator said, "The partisans had sent Zina back into town to establish contact with those of the Young Avengers who were still alive."

Villagers started coming out onstage, almost all the extras in the whole show. Zina, looking around warily, walked up to a few villagers and acted as though she were asking them something. Whenever one shook his head no, Zina would continue dejectedly on to the next one, again looking around furtively before asking. In this fashion she ended up in the middle of the stage, where she stopped. At the narrator's next words she opened her eyes wide as if fearful.

"In 1943, thirty of the thirty-eight members of the underground were captured and executed. On November fifth, in the village of Borovukha, near Polotsk, in the Belarusian SSR, Yevgeny Yezavitov and Nikolay Alexeyev were executed. A day later, so were Nina Azolina and Zina Luzgina. The

Fascists tried to beat information about the underground resistance out of them—who its members were and what they were planning—but they failed."

As the names of those who had been executed were read aloud, the actors playing them got up from the table in the hut and walked away. Their empty seats were covered by the slowly moving curtain. The last two members of the underground resistance left alive, Ilya Yezavitov and Fruza Zenkova, jumped up from their seats and ran through the crowd of locals gathered upstage, then continued offstage. As they did, a little girl from the crowd stepped forward and pointed at Zina.

"That's her—there's your partisan! She's strutting all over the village free as you please!" The Germans seized her on the spot.

That was the end of the scene. The curtain fell.

The show was going beautifully. The kids had acted the most tragic scene well, with great intensity. There were even sobs in the audience. But Yurka's good mood was gone. Those last ten minutes with Volodya in the prop room had left him aggrieved and negated all the joy of the smoothly running show and his perfectly played "Lullaby." Why, oh, why had he revisited their conversation from the unfinished barracks?!

Yurka rubbed his forehead as though summoning more suitable thoughts to his brain, because it wasn't over yet: Krause was about to appear. Yurka's entrance was coming up.

He looked out into the audience. Volodya was looking at the stage, but his eyes were unreadable. They were empty. Pal Palych called out to Volodya, asking him something. Volodya started, then nodded and forced a smile.

Yurka tucked his tie into his shirt, draped the German officer's uniform jacket over his shoulders, and went onstage, into the left half that was still covered by the curtain. He sat down at the table and leaned back in a chair languidly. It was strange, but he didn't feel any agitation at all. It was as though he'd left all his worries and fear back there, at the piano, and right now all he had to do was play his part, just say a few lines . . .

Polina's voice was hoarse from fatigue as she recited, "Zina was tortured for over a month, but she didn't reveal anything. Soon a new Gestapo officer took over her case, Oberleutnant Krause. He used a different interrogation tactic . . ."

The curtain slid away. Some Germans, holding Zina by the arms, brought her onstage and sat her down opposite Yurka.

"My brave Fräulein, I am aware that your parents remain in Leningrad. And I am also aware that your beloved city has fallen. A new flag flies above it. But I assure you that all you have to do is agree to a small compromise and share a few bits of information with Hitler's army command, and I will personally ensure that such a brave Fräulein as yourself will have a chance to see her family again . . ."

Zina didn't speak. She just looked at him sullenly. Yurka got a heavy pistol out of the table drawer and turned it over in his hands, declaring, "My brave Fräulein, deep in the heart of this small mechanism lies one single solitary round. It is not large. But it is deadly. All my finger has to do is twitch, completely by accident, and there will no longer be any need for long, drawn-out conversations. Ponder this, my brave Fräulein. Your life is priceless, but it would be so easy to simply end it with one careless move . . ." Zina gave the pistol a long, pointed look, so the audience would notice. "Ponder this carefully, Fräulein," Yurka repeated.

He put the pistol down on the table. Without taking his eyes off it, he pulled a pack of cigarettes out of his jacket pocket and extracted a cigarette. Suddenly the silence was broken by a loud shrieking of brakes. Krause/Yurka started and turned around to face the window drawn onto the back wall. As a result, he had turned away from Zina. *Come on, Nastya!* thought Yurka. *Grab the pistol!*

But Nastya didn't. She'd been very concerned about getting this scene right, so finally the confused Yurka turned around to look at her and saw that she was looking out into the audience at Volodya, apparently hoping he would be watching her. But he was watching someone else instead. That someone was Yurka. Volodya was biting his lip and frowning as though something were hurting him, and looking at Yurka with a peculiar look that was heavy, and haggard, and pleading. Yet, when their eyes met, the corners of Volodya's mouth twitched up for just a second.

Time sped back up. Portnova grabbed the pistol and immediately shot Krause. Yurka collapsed for real, coming down with a crash and hitting the back of his head on the ground. Everyone in the audience gasped. Volodya made as if to stand up. Trying not to grimace from the pain, Yurka flashed him a smile, indicating that everything was fine. The back of his head sure hurt, though. He'd have a lump there.

Sashka the German came running as soon as he heard the shot. This was his second death scene, and the entire audience clearly knew what was coming next. Portnova's second bullet got him. While Portnova was stepping over the moaning German soldier, more of them came running onstage, holding their automatic rifles at the ready. Portnova took off running, but the sound of shots rang out and she fell down. She had been shot in the legs. She had left a bullet for herself, so Zina pressed the barrel of the gun to her heart and pulled the trigger, but it didn't fire. She didn't get a chance to try again: the Germans grabbed her and pulled her offstage. The curtain closed as Masha started playing the "Internationale."

"Ready to paint, girls?" Yurka asked as he got up. The actors nodded and sat Nasya/Portnova down in the chair they'd prepared for her, then laid clear plastic sheeting over her clothes and quickly painted white gouache paint over her hair and gray paint on her eyes.

The stage decorations for the execution were quick to set up: the crew just added a drawing of a brick wall to the village scene background that was already on the backdrop. That was all—that was the entire set for the last scene of the show. The extras playing villagers went to stand out along the edges while the Germans gathered in the middle, near the execution wall.

Vanka, who was supposed to go get Portnova and lead her to be executed, was standing with the extras, daydreaming. Yurka muttered a curse and hissed his name as loud as he dared. He didn't notice. His neighbors tugged on his sleeves and he looked at Yurka, but it was too late: the curtain had already opened. Yurka cursed again, grabbed Krause's uniform jacket from off the back of a chair, and put it on, and then he, not Vanka, led Portnova to her execution.

Polina narrated: "In the torture chambers of the Polotsk prison, Zina was put through agony: her tormentors put needles under her fingernails, and burned her with hot irons, and poked out her eyes, but Zina withstood all these tortures and never gave up her comrades or her motherland. Although she was blind, she used a nail to scratch a picture on the wall of her cell: a heart over a little girl with braids and the caption "sentenced to death." On the morning of January tenth, 1944, after a month of torture, seventeen-year-old Zina, who had been blinded and whose hair had gone completely gray, was led to her execution."

Nastya walked over to the wall, limping and stumbling. Yurka had insisted she limp, since Zina had been shot in both legs and it was unlikely she had been given medical care. Portnova stood with her back to the wall, Yurka was given a toy rifle, and the sound of automatic rifle fire rang out. Zina fell.

There was complete silence in the audience and onstage. Masha held the pause, then started playing the Moonlight Sonata.

Polina said the words that brought the show to a close: "Two thousand German soldiers had been billeted in Obol, where the Young Avengers and Zina Portnova lived. Members of the underground had located the German gun positions, counted their soldiers, and tracked their movements. Over the course of their operations, several dozen enemy troop trains, with all their ammunition, equipment, and manpower, were prevented from reaching the front. Hundreds of vehicles used by the German military were blown up by mines laid by the Young Avengers. Five key infrastructure enterprises that were going to be utilized by the Germans were destroyed. In the Obol garrison, several thousand of Hitler's men met death at the Young Avengers' hands. 'It's as terrible here as it is at the front,' one German soldier wrote home.

"Thirteen million children died in the Great Fatherland War. Of the thirty-eight Young Avengers, thirty were executed. Ilya Yezavitov and Yefrosinya Zenkova remained among the living. Zinaida Martynovna Portnova was posthumously named a Pioneer Hero by the Vladimir Lenin All-Union Pioneer Organization in 1954. On July first, 1958, by decree of the Presidium of the Supreme Soviet of the USSR, she was posthumously named Hero of the Soviet Union and awarded the Order of Lenin."

Polina walked offstage. The curtain closed. After a few moments of silence, the theater erupted in thunderous applause.

The audience was gone. The only people still in the theater were the cast and the administration. Yurka, dejectedly surveying the mess left backstage after the show, wondered who would pick it all up, and when.

But right now there wasn't time for that. Volodya, Olga Leonidovna, and Pal Palych came onstage to join the actors. The educational specialist beamed in satisfaction. "Great job, everyone! The show turned out very well! I thought it'd be much worse, given how little time you had," she praised them. But then she had to sour it all by adding: "I have just one observation, but it's very important: it looked like your Portnova didn't leave to join the partisans, but ran away in shame after she betrayed her comrades."

Yurka's right nostril twitched. He was barely able to keep from telling her what he thought of her. That Olga Leonidovna, she sure knew how to spoil the mood! But Volodya's exhausted look brought him back into line immediately.

The camp director, on the other hand, was openly delighted. "Hem..." He clapped his hands. "Your performance was excellent. Good work! I especially noted the success of the scene where the factories get blown up. Whose idea was that?"

Several people looked at Yurka, but he shrugged: "We all came up with it together."

"Hem... Fine, very fine. Good teamwork is doubly good!"

"Yes, Volodya, you've done great work!" Olga Leonidovna went all nice again. "You succeeded in gathering and organizing everyone..."

"Thank you, of course, but this was all a shared effort," replied Volodya. "You helped a lot with the extras, too, Olga Leonidovna, but I just sat the whole show out in the audience."

"We wouldn't have done it without Yurka!" Ulyana interjected suddenly. "He was running his feet off backstage, helping everyone and making sure everything was running smoothly!"

"And he played the piano really beautifully!" Polina said encouragingly.

"And he kept his head when Vanka kept not shooting Zina!" added Ksyusha.

Yurka was stunned at first but then felt the color flooding his cheeks. He was only rarely praised, and never in front of the administration, and definitely never by the Pukes! Without knowing how to react, he looked helplessly at Volodya, who was smiling.

"That's right, Konev, this is a pleasant surprise! Not like last year," said Olga Leonidovna. "Friendship with Volodya is having a positive effect on you!"

Off to the side, someone started huffing indignantly. Yurka stole a look and saw Masha scowling and glaring at the educational specialist.

"Well! In honor of such an event"—Pal Palych clapped his hands again and turned to Matveyev—"Alyosha, get the camera! In honor of such an event, we will . . . ahem . . . have our picture taken!"

Alyosha nodded and ran off backstage. He came back a minute later and thrust the camera into the director's hands, saying, "Pal Palych, maybe it'd be better for me to do it? You know I have experience, remember . . ."

"No, Alyosha. No, it's an expensive new piece of equipment, so let's have me do it myself."

Pal Palych examined the camera as though it were a UFO. Then he nodded to himself with yet another affirmative "Hem" and began arranging the kids:

"So then. Those of you who are taller, get in the middle. Shorter ones sit on the bench. No, Sasha, you get on the edge, by Yurka. Now, then . . . Volodya, hold on: Where are you going? Let's have you sit on the bench in the middle, too. Konev, don't follow him! You stay where you are!"

"Wait for me!" Mitka shouted from offstage. "I'll be right there. I'm just changing my shirt . . ."

A minute later he came out from backstage looking a little silly: flustered, sweaty, and disheveled, and holding Yurka's red cap. When Yurka saw him with it, he decided they should swap: he'd pulled his neckerchief out from underneath his shirt and arranged it on his chest for the picture but then decided that a Pioneer neckerchief didn't go with a Fascist uniform jacket. He tossed the jacket to Mitka.

"And I'll take that," Yurka said, taking his cap from Mitka and plopping it on backward, satisfied. Apparently a red baseball cap went with a Pioneer neckerchief just fine.

Mitka stood next to Yurka. Yurka sniffed, then held his breath. He'd realized why Mitka had changed shirts: clearly he'd sweated buckets hauling that curtain up and down.

"Get ready . . . ," said the director.

Yurka saw Volodya shake his head as though he was thinking, *Ah, the hell with it.* Volodya jumped up, moved Mitka over, and stood next to Yurka.

"Volod... hem... Now, what's this?" said Pal Palych, letting air out through his pursed lips in reproach.

"This is even better, Pal Palych!" Volodya assured him.

"Hem... ah, well, yes. That is, yes. That is better. So. Everyone get ready... Three... two... one..." And he clicked the shutter.

CHAPTER SEVENTEEN
THE FAREWELL BONFIRE

After the show the sky cleared. The clouds, which never had shed their rain, floated off to the east. The speakers poured out music all over the whole camp. Kind, good, lyrical children's songs from movies and cartoons played all during lunch and after it, only going quiet right before the assembly to allow the head troop leader to give the command: "Campers, attention! To the ceremonial assembly dedicated to the closing of the session. Forward, march!"

The Pioneer troops, dressed up in their white shirts and red neckerchiefs and flight caps, formed into three columns and marched toward the main square. Two of Troop One's columns were headed by girls: Ira Petrovna, happy and more beautiful than ever, and Masha, the troop commander. A task with a lot of responsibility—carrying the troop banner—was entrusted to Yurka, leading the third column.

Proud, with his hair combed, his clothing neat and tidy, and wearing white gloves, Yurka yearned to see Volodya as soon as possible: he'd never been given such an honor and he'd never been as proud of himself. He assumed his position at the assembly and focused on Troop Five, which was just now coming onto the square, bringing up the rear of the long chain of people. A pleasant warmth spread through his chest when he saw the touchingly agitated Olezhka, whose hands visibly shook as they held his troop banner. Yurka shifted his gaze to Alyona, who was unchildlike in her seriousness. She had played the little girl Galya Portnova in the show, but in real life she was commander of her troop. And then Yurka's gaze rested for a very long time on Volodya's serious and solemn face. Volodya saw him, raised his brows slightly, and smiled. Yurka gave a small nod in response.

Bright rays of sun pierced the occasional clouds, falling through the thick forest foliage and the leaves of Yurka's apple tree and landing on the flag-bedecked main square. The bust of Zina Portnova, clean and white, looked down sternly from her pedestal at the Pioneers, assembled in a large arc. On the flagpole behind her the camp flag billowed proudly: a red barn swallow on an azure background. Overhead, in the clear sky, the little white puffs of parachutes slid slowly through the blue down to earth. Far in the distance, almost all the way to the horizon, the airplane that the parachutists had jumped out of was leaving a white trail that echoed the shape of the barn swallow's wings on the flag.

"Campers, attention! Ready, front!" shouted the head troop leader. "At ease! Troop commanders, prepare to give your reports!"

Masha and the other troop commanders assumed their positions in front of the tribunal where Pal Palych and Olga Leonidovna stood and began taking turns stepping forward to give their reports.

Masha threw her hand up in the Pioneer salute. "Comrade chairman of the troop council! In preparation for the ceremonial closing assembly of Session Two of camp, Troop One is in formation!" Masha said loudly and clearly. "Reported by Troop One commander Sidorova, Mariya!"

The head troop leader gave the salute and replied, "Report accepted."

After all the reports had been presented, the director gave a speech to open the ceremony. Then it was Olga Leonidovna's turn to speak. She was far more genuine than she had been at the beginning of the session, but year in and year out she always wound up her speech with the same exact words: "The barn swallow is a bird that, like our Pioneers, comes back every year from wintering in warmer climates to return to its native nest..."

Smiling, the educational specialist surveyed the campers with an unusually affectionate expression. She was speaking to everyone, without exception, but Yurka knew better: he wouldn't be coming here again.

There was the sound of a needle rustling on a record, and then from the speakers, scratchy and off-key, issued the melody every Soviet citizen learned as a child: the Pioneer anthem. Every person there flung up a hand in the Pioneer salute. Yurka watched the flag come down, bringing their session of camp to a close, as he and everyone else sang about campfires and midnight-blue skies.

He still thought the song was meaningless and pretentious, but he now realized something else: what was important about the anthem wasn't the words. Not at all. What was important was that the act of singing the anthem was supposed to unite all of Camp Barn Swallow, everyone from great to small. And everyone was indeed singing: the old (to Yurka) Communists, the younger Komsomol members, the school-age Pioneers, and the youngest Little Octoberists from Troop Five, along with their troop leader. Volodya was standing facing Yurka, looking at him and smiling in a way that was tender but sad. Yurka thought in passing that Volodya had forgotten how to smile without sadness.

Yurka's eyes started welling up. He was tired of thinking about parting. He was tired of grieving. His eyes were red and burning after his sleepless night. His weariness and the tension from preparing for the show were making themselves felt. The weather, in defiance of all sadness, was almost artificially clear and bright, but it didn't make Yurka feel any better at all. It was as though the weather was challenging him to relish his last day, as though it was telling him, *Nothing like this will ever happen again.*

"That's true, it won't," agreed Yurka mentally. He wouldn't be going to Pioneer camp next summer. He would never sing the anthem or put on that neckerchief again. There was no telling how often Yurka had looked forward to wearing it for the last time. The older he had gotten, the more he hated the thing. The noose. Yurka hadn't felt proud of wearing his Pioneer neckerchief since middle school and had always tried to find a way to take it off as soon as he could, so everyone would think he was grown up. But as soon as he really did grow up, everything turned upside down. The day had come, the day he realized, with smothering sadness, that he had finally done what he'd wanted to do for so long: he'd grown up. His childhood was over.

It hadn't ended when Yurka stopped playing with his toys. It hadn't even ended when he'd encountered true injustice for the first time and let music be taken away from him. His childhood had ended recently, this summer at Camp Barn Swallow, when he met Volodya. Love had engulfed him, with all his thoughts and emotions, and it had overcome all his senses, to the extent that Yurka—Yurka, with his sharp ears!—hadn't heard the heavy door of his childhood clanking into motion and crashing shut behind him. Because childhood was a time when life was clear and simple, when there were set rules, when there was an answer for every why and what-if. But

Yurka had stopped being clear and simple to himself when he fell in love. He'd encountered questions that no one could give him an answer for. And he didn't believe that anyone, not even his parents—not even doctors like the ones Volodya wanted to consult—could answer them.

Now, finally, he saw why grown-ups go back to Pioneer camps as troop leaders, why they sing the Pioneer anthem with all their hearts, why they proudly don their neckerchiefs and flight caps: it's all so they can be, maybe not back in childhood again, but very, very close to it. But Yurka would never be allowed to come back as a camper, since he was too old; nor would he be allowed to come back as a troop leader because of his record. He would never come back again.

For the first time in five years he sang "The Pioneer's Call: Always Be Prepared" absolutely sincerely.

The flag had come down. The closing assembly was over. The speakers poured out the tender, sad words of a song from Yurka's favorite movie, *Passenger from the* Equator. Elena Kamburova sang the song, "Who Dreamed You Up, My Starry Land?," as the troops of Camp Barn Swallow gathered in little knots of people. Yurka turned his white gloves back in to Ira Petrovna and left his troop, heading toward his old hiding place by the unfinished barracks, where he still had an old pack with a few cigarettes left. He looked around to see whether Masha or Pcholkin were following him again, but the Little Octoberists and Pioneers on the square were busy with other things.

He walked along the Avenue of Pioneer Heroes to the intersection where even from a distance he could see his beloved *V* inside the apple, whole and untouched. Yurka thought about that letter *V*, and then about that person *V*, and then—speak of the devil!—Volodya caught up to him.

"Yura!" he said as he approached, panting a little. "Where are you going?"

"I . . . ," Yurka faltered. He remembered he'd promised Volodya he wouldn't smoke anymore. Then he remembered he'd already broken that promise. But now deceiving Volodya felt completely wrong, so he admitted, "I'm going to get some smokes from my hiding place."

"Yura!" Volodya said accusingly. "But you—"

"I know! I know I promised not to smoke anymore. That's why I'm going to get them now: I'm going to throw them away! Honest."

Volodya nodded approvingly. "Well, then . . . good job." Then he suddenly switched topics: "It's hard to believe we're going our separate ways tomorrow, isn't it?"

Yurka frowned. "Don't. I don't want to talk or think about it. Not at all."

"Okay. Then I'll get to the point. I just remembered how after the last-bell ceremony in high school, our class buried a message for future graduates under a tree in our schoolyard . . ."

"A time capsule? What did you write?"

"We talked about our time, our goals, what we were doing to build Communism, what other people were doing. We charged those future readers to remember the feats accomplished by the Soviet people. But I don't want to talk about the message from our class. Let's leave our own. Want to?"

"For the future builders of Communism?"

"No," laughed Volodya. "For ourselves, of course."

"For our future selves?" Yurka grew animated. "That'll be great! But I have no idea what to write."

"It doesn't even have to be a letter, it can just be things that remind us of important events . . . For example, the script of the show, my notebook, our notes . . . Help me figure out what else to put in it. We'll stick it all in the capsule and then in say ten years we'll meet here and open it. Think how interesting it'll be to come back as completely grown-up people—you know, as people who've made their way in life—and hold things from the session we spent together at Camp Barn Swallow. What a good memory of this summer that'll be!"

"Yes, something that was important to our . . . our friendship . . . important to us . . ." Yurka pondered. Then he exclaimed, "The music! I can put the music for the 'Lullaby' in it. Maybe all that will still be important in ten years."

"Of course it will! Especially when you become a pianist. But you keep thinking about what to put in there, anyway. I've got to go."

"But when do we bury it? Where?" asked Yurka, lowering his voice. They were alone on the avenue, but he was still anxious: What if somebody was in the bushes, spying on them? "Tonight? Let's ditch the farewell bonfire, it's going to be such a madhouse, nobody'll notice we're gone . . ."

"Yes, during the bonfire's probably best. I'm still buried in things to do," Volodya replied in almost a whisper, emulating Yurka. "But we'd better not just disappear. I'll try to ask permission to go, if I get a chance."

"But where, Volod?"

"The willow," he whispered. "We'll go through the forest to get to the shallows."

"It rained last night, the river's probably higher."

"Can you check? I've got to go now. We'll meet at dinner. And make sure to bring things for the time capsule tonight."

"I'll remember," Yurka promised happily.

How to pass the time? What to do to keep himself busy until evening? How to live until then? It wasn't fair: time had become the most precious of all precious things to Yurka, but he had to waste it trying to distract himself with all kinds of nonsense—whatever would keep him from thinking about parting from Volodya. It was still too early to pack his bag, and packing wouldn't take more than half an hour, anyway. Yurka hadn't brought that much with him. Should he take a walk around the camp and say goodbye to Camp Barn Swallow and then go check the river?

Yurka thought about what to put in the time capsule as he headed out for his walk. He looked around, trying to think, but as soon as his gaze landed on some spot or other that was painfully familiar, he'd lose his train of thought. There was the movie theater, where so much had happened . . . There was the power shed, shaded by green thickets of lilac . . . There was the merry-go-round that had been drowning in white dandelion fluff but was now blanketed in yellow and green again . . . There were the athletic fields, now covered in people, some exchanging addresses, writing them in accordance with tradition right on each other's Pioneer neckerchiefs in ballpoint pen, others sitting and hugging as they said their goodbyes. Despite the crowd, it was unusually quiet for a Pioneer camp. All the campers looked hushed and sad, and spoke softly, and walked instead of running. *They're probably just saving their energy for the bonfire*, Yurka thought. But he was subdued from sadness, too. Just one thing was making him edgy: he hadn't seen Masha even once since the assembly ended. He'd been looking around the whole time during his walk but he'd neither seen her distant silhouette nor heard her voice.

"What if she's planning something?" Yurka whispered anxiously to himself. He kept walking.

There was music coming from the benches by the courts. It was the radio he and Volodya had taken on their hike. The radio was competing with the song coming out of the camp speakers as the Pukes, Mitka, Vanka, and Mikha all took turns turning the radio dial, trying to get rid of the static. Yurka ran his hand along the chain-link fence around the tennis court and then batted at it. The fence jangled. He thought back to the middle of the session, when he was angry at Volodya after their conversation about adult magazines.

The song "The Last Time," from the Jolly Fellows album, came hissing and sputtering out of the radio, telling him how time would go by and lovers would forget each other. Yurka was already heartily sick of the song.

"Yura! Konev, get over here!" Polina called, waving her arms. "Let's sign your neckerchief, too!"

Yurka considered it: Well, why not? Let him have something to remember them by! He took off his neckerchief and handed it to the girls. In exchange, they gave him theirs and lent him a pen.

Yurka wrote the same thing carelessly on each one, without bothering to figure out which neckerchief was whose: "Thanks for the best session in the whole of Camp Barn Swallow. Konev, Session Two, 1986." But then his conscience got the better of him, because the girls were all writing carefully, putting some effort into thinking of what to say.

"What should I write, Pol?" Ksyusha asked.

"I wrote, 'Wishing inspiration for our pianist!'"

"Then I'll write, 'To the best assistant troop leader. Keep it up!'"

Yurka felt abashed. He had noticed that over the course of the session the Pukes had changed a lot. Or maybe it was Yurka who had changed, and the girls had always been this way? All of a sudden he'd stopped thinking of them as snakes and scourges, or thought it a little less, anyway. Yurka suddenly had the idea of at least asking them what numbers their schools were, because after all they also went to school in Kharkiv. And he could ask Vanka and Mikha, too, and Mitka.

So he did.

"We go to thirteen," the girls said almost in unison.

"Hey, and we're in eighteen," said Vanka happily. "That's also in the Leninsky District! We're not far from each other!"

"Really? That's near the Southern Railway. We can get together and see each other! Do you have phones at home?"

Yurka was barely able to keep himself from giving a low whistle of surprise and admiration. Yes, those Pukes really had changed! Earlier they had turned up their noses at Vanka and Mikha, but now it looked like they were actually flirting.

"So, Yur, by the way . . . you promised me a certain person's address . . . ," said Ksyusha with a wink.

"What person's?" interjected Mikha.

"Whose?" Vanka corrected him.

"Vishnevsky's," snorted Ulyana. Ksyusha scowled.

"Well, I . . . I have it," announced Mitka, clapping his pocket. "Right here. And, uh . . . and his phone number, too," he added, seeing the surprise on everyone's faces.

Mitka had clearly gathered up all his courage for the last day of camp. As soon as he finished giving Ksyusha the address, he led Ulyana off to the side and whispered something to her that made her smile radiantly.

"Pol—look." Ksyusha glanced over at Mitka and Ulyana, then winked slyly.

Yurka, anticipating some kind of rude jibe from Ksyusha, decided to show some male solidarity and distract her. But how? And then he realized: he could kill two birds with one stone.

"Hey, Ksyush, by the way—do you know where Masha is?"

Ksyusha smirked. "Why? Do you miss her already? Did you and she maybe have a little thing going?"

"What? Me and her?!" said Yurka, his temper flaring. "No way. Never!"

"Oh, sure. You're just together all the time."

"I'm only asking because I'm glad she's not here. You have no idea how sick I am of her!"

"Yeah, right. Everyone can tell you're—"

"We saw Masha over by where the final bonfire's going to be," Polina interrupted softly.

Despite the interruption, Ksyusha clearly had a mind to poke Yurka's sore spot again: she narrowed her eyes and opened her mouth.

But she was interrupted again. From the athletic fields, where the Troop Five girls were playing badminton under Lena's watchful eye, came a painfully familiar child's voice: "You'we planning something naughty again, awen't you!"

Well, that didn't last long, thought Yurka. *It's like he never said that r yesterday!*

Pcholkin was darting through the middle of the court, keeping the girls from playing and bumping into them, and Olezhka was chasing him.

"Hey! Yuwka!" Olezhka caught sight of Yurka and the group and ran over to them, almost crashing into Vanka. "Yuwka! I saw Pcholkin wunning off with matches fwom the kitchen!" The panting Olezhka looked very concerned.

But Pcholkin was long gone. And instead, an angry Lena was approaching, hands on hips and tailed by Sashka, who was chewing something.

"What happened now?" Lena asked Yurka.

He shrugged. "Olezhka says that Pcholkin stole matches from the kitchen and is planning some kind of sabotage again."

Lena rolled her eyes and sighed. "That little scoundrel! I'm so sick of—" she began, then cut herself off. But seeing all the kids' mischievous looks, she added, "He doesn't even let me off easy on the last day!"

Yurka snorted. "He should study to be a construction engineer. He's always building up to some kind of prank."

"As long as he doesn't blow himself up with whatever he does! Yur, could you maybe go find Volodya, please, and tell him? I have to stay here with the troop."

"But where is he? Why are you alone with the kids?"

"He's in the woods, helping get the final bonfire ready."

Yurka didn't want to go find him. There would be a lot of people there, too, and then that little spy Masha would probably be shadowing him . . . So what was left for Yurka to do, then? Just look at him some more, like he'd been doing all these days? So that today, on the last day of session, he could finally just be tortured to death by thoughts of their parting? No. That would only make it harder for him. But he couldn't refuse Lena, either!

"By the way... why *are* all you great big lunks sitting here instead of helping the troop leaders get the bonfire ready?" said Lena, frowning.

She reminded Yurka so much of Ira Petrovna in a bad mood that Yurka was actually taken aback. He hadn't known that Lena could also be stern like a typical troop leader.

"Nobody asked us," mumbled Mikha lamely.

"Do we need to help?" said Vanka, surprised.

Out of the corner of his eye, Yurka noticed Mitka and Ulyana sidling into the bushes, trying to escape.

"You always need to help! Get over to that bonfire," barked Lena. Then, after the group had moved some distance away, she shouted after them, "And tell Volodya about Pcholkin!"

Yurka resolved firmly that he was not going to help with the bonfire. He made his excuses to the rest of the kids and headed over to the path to the river. But then he gave in to a sudden impulse and went back to Olezhka, put his hand on the boy's shoulder, and said, "You've done a really good job! I believe in you. You're going to be an excellent Pioneer and then the best Komsomol member ever!"

A wide, proud smile spread across Olezhka's face. He declared, "Thank you, Yuwka! And you'we going to be an excellent pianist! I believe in you, too! Pwomise you won't quit playing music, and I'll pwomise not to be lazy with my speech thewapist like I used to be. I'll twy as hawd as I can!"

"Okay, I promise!"

"And I pwomise, too!"

Yurka winked at him, ruffled his hair, and headed for the river.

He left the courts and headed slowly down the path leading to the beach. His head was completely empty and his soul was, somehow, completely calm. It was as though Yurka had frozen inside, gone numb, but he liked the feeling. He just walked slowly through the sparse trees, the square pavers passing underneath him one by one.

The thing keeping him from falling into utter despair was hope. It burned inside him, bright and warm, like a torch in a pitch-black cave. Yurka was certain that he and Volodya would see each other again. And Masha wouldn't be there, and nobody would forbid Yurka from being near Volodya in whatever way he wanted.

When the path of gray concrete pavers ended, a narrow, sandy path continued on. It was smooth and even, but it wasn't long, only about ten meters down to the beach. Yurka turned off toward the boathouse and was about to walk to the willow, but he couldn't just pass by that dearly remembered place. He moved the wooden gate aside, slipped through the boathouse, and walked down the dock, which creaked underneath his feet. The boats rocked back and forth on the water. Yurka went straight to the one he and Volodya had hidden in. It felt like the boat had happened an eternity ago, but he remembered that kiss so clearly, as though it had just happened. Yurka touched his lips with the tips of his fingers; his lips were warm, as though someone's breath had warmed them.

It took effort for him to make himself turn around and leave the boathouse. The flood of thoughts that came rushing to his head here made him feel both sweet and sad at the same time. They were what he wanted to leave in the time capsule, all these moments: the boat underneath the canvas, the kisses in the curtain, Volodya's warm words, his happy smile, his quiet but deeply sincere confessions . . . He wanted to leave them here, shut the lid tight on them, and bury them in the ground so he could be sure they'd be preserved, never to be forgotten. So that in ten years, when they met again, they could dig it all back up and be right back here again, the last summer before his childhood ended.

Yurka made it to the willow easily. The previous night's rain, contrary to expectations, hadn't raised the level of water in the river very much, although Yurka still had to pull his shorts up high to make it across the shallows. The ground under the willow was damp; the rare rays of sun that penetrated the branches hadn't had a chance to dry and warm the ground yet.

It was getting on toward dinner, but Yurka didn't want to go back. He wanted to sit here alone, all alone, gazing unseeingly at the river. He was amazed to see the amount of movement in it: the lazy current, the smooth ripples of waves, the bright flashes of evening sun reflecting on them . . . It all seemed neither chaotic nor meaningless. Yurka stayed on the riverbank right up until the bugle, trying to understand the systematic interplay of waves in the river current and determine what meaning there could possibly be in it. But he eventually did get up off the ground and make up his mind to go back. He had promised to tell Volodya, after all.

By the time he had gotten back across the shallows and made his way to camp, another bugle call announced the end of dinner. Yurka raced over to the mess hall and saw Volodya among the crowd pouring out. The troop leader, surrounded by the little boys of his troop, was looking around. Seeing Yurka, he waved.

"Here." Volodya handed him two little sweet poppy seed pies. "Why weren't you at dinner?"

Yurka swallowed, salivating: he had only now realized how much his walk had sharpened his appetite. "Thanks!" he said, and in a lower voice, he added, "I went to the willow. The shallows are fine, but the ground under the willow is cold and damp."

"Got it. I arranged with Lena for her to take the kids to the bonfire and then get them to sleep herself. She wasn't thrilled but she agreed, so that's all taken care of. We'll sit at the bonfire with everyone for a little bit and then head to the willow with the capsule. Just get permission from Irina!"

Masha came out of the mess hall. She noticed them standing next to each other and scowled, glaring right at Yurka. But he just rolled his eyes, then remembered to ask Volodya: "Did anybody tell you about Pcholkin yet? About his sabotage?"

Volodya smiled. "Right. It's funny, actually: Alyosha Matveyev had been tasked with getting the matches and bringing them for when we light the bonfire. Pcholkin found out about it somehow, got them from the kitchen, and brought them himself. Olezhka just assumed that Petya was planning an act of sabotage and wanted to catch the hooligan. Turns out Olezhka's a partisan, too! Seems like he really got into his part in the show."

"How about that! Pcholkin? Pcholkin helped? It's suspicious, almost . . ."

"I thought the same thing at first. But then Pcholkin announced that it wasn't fair for Olezhka to get all the glory, not only for being great in the show, but also because everyone was encouraging him and praising him for working so hard on being accepted into the Pioneers. Petya wants some glory as well, and there are things to praise him for, too."

"Well, now! You've trained him well!" Yurka giggled.

"What've I got to do with it? It wasn't me . . ."

"Oh, yes it was." Yurka nodded fervently. "You're his troop leader, which is pretty much like his older brother. You set an example for them. Everyone changes, and when there's a troop leader like you around, the only way to change is for the better."

Volodya's cheeks turned pink, and Yurka was abashed. He'd wanted to say different words to Volodya—ones that did not, of course, include "troop leader" and "older brother." But there were people there. And Masha. Yurka was trying to say "I love you" without saying the word "love." He was so sick and tired of all this damned secrecy . . .

The Pioneers were singing their anthem about soaring campfires and midnight-blue skies. Evening had come. It really was midnight blue. And it was no exaggeration to say the bonfire was soaring up into the inky sky, throwing sparks so high, they mingled with the stars . . . Whenever a point of light winked out, you couldn't tell at first whether it was a spark going out or a meteor burning up.

It took the troops a long time to get into formation. It took them a long time to walk to the broad clearing in the forest. It took them a long time to take their seats on the benches arranged in a circle.

The opening song, the anthem of the session, had already been sung once, but now everyone started it up again, sitting like first graders with their backs straight and their hands in their laps. It was the official part of the evening. As long as the administration was at the farewell bonfire—the camp director, the educational specialist, the phys ed instructors, the musical director, and the other adults—the Pioneers were inhibited and bored. But Yurka knew the adults would leave soon and then there would be . . . well, maybe not mayhem, but it would get a lot more lively. In the meantime, nobody was even allowed to stand up from their seats. The only thing left for Yurka to do was sing and look around for Volodya.

As per tradition, Troop Five was directly to the bigwigs' left, while Troop One was to their right. So Yurka didn't have to crane his neck and peer around; he just had to turn his head a little. Volodya wasn't looking at him.

His stern gaze was directed at the boys in his troop. They were sitting quietly and sadly; they probably didn't want to part from their friends, either. But they were the ones who would definitely be coming back!

It didn't take long for the bigwigs to wish everyone a good evening and depart. Olga Leonidovna threatened that if the Little Octoberists got back to their cabins any later than nine thirty, or the Pioneers any later than eleven, she wouldn't let them into session next year. Then she left, too.

Everyone immediately burst into lively activity and moved to sit wherever they wanted, but still without mixing up the troops. Someone produced a guitar, which changed hands several times among those who could play. At first everyone sang fun children's songs. Then they switched to pop songs. In unison the Pukes demanded Modern Talking, but even if somebody knew the music to one of their songs, it turned out that nobody actually knew the words. Volodya suggested some Time Machine, which earned him an indignant "Eww!" from over half of the Pioneers. Yurka didn't suggest anything. As a result, they all sang Alla Pugachova hits and songs from the Jolly Fellows album again.

Despite all this demonstrative fun, the sadness was literally tearing its way out of Yurka, no matter how much he tried to stuff it back down deep inside. And he wasn't the only one feeling sad: almost everyone there was too. After all, this was the last evening for everyone, not just for him, so everyone was sad right there with him.

The last evening is special for many reasons: everyone becomes kinder and gentler, everyone tries to think about what's most important, to be with the people they care about the most. Everything feels a little different: the sky is so very starry, the smells are so very pungent, the faces so kind, the songs so sincere, the voices so pretty. And everything really is that way, because you're seeing it all for the last time.

Someone passed Mitka the guitar.

"It's always very sad to say goodbye," he said as he took the instrument. He strummed it with his thumb and said musingly, "Well, what about this one . . ." He cleared his throat and looked around at everyone sitting around the bonfire, pausing on the daring couples who were holding hands or hugging. He chuckled and looked tenderly at Ulyana. "This one goes out to everyone who fell in love this summer."

As soon as everyone heard the familiar song's first few chords, the protests began. The wave of indignation washed along the rows of people. "Mitya, don't! Play something else!" begged Ira Petrovna. Zhenya, who was sitting next to her, nodded his agreement.

Yurka recognized the song, too, and burst into hysterical laughter. He appreciated both the joke itself and how cruel it was. Before Volodya, he might've done something like that himself . . . but now . . .

In a low, husky voice, Mitka began singing the lovers' final, parting duet from *Athena and Venture*:

> "You'll wake with the dawn's first ray,
> When you sense it's my time to leave;
> I'll always be there in your memories,
> We're parting forever, though it's hard to believe . . ."

It was as though something snapped inside Yurka. He was hurting, but he was also jeering at himself. This song was the last drop, the just-to-be-sure shot to the head—as though his own private sadness weren't enough! He would've covered his ears with his hands if it wouldn't have looked so stupid.

They were only on the second verse, but to Yurka it felt like an eternity. He was unable to regulate his sadness anymore. It engulfed him. The only thing he was capable of making himself do right now was not look at Volodya.

> "Storms wrack the seas and rage in my soul;
> I cannot accept that we're parting forever . . ."

The Pukes were huddled together, swaying slightly in unison. Ulyana was beaming as she sang the woman's part of the duet—she had finally been allowed to sing something from *Athena and Venture*. Even Mikha, sitting next to Yurka, was sighing sadly (or maybe sniffling).

> "The sea's forlorn waves roll and surge;
> In your deep brown eyes there is grief.
> How I wish I could stay here with you!
> We're parting forever, though it's hard to believe . . ."

Yurka had deep brown eyes, just like the doomed heroine of the song. He couldn't help it: he looked at Volodya. Volodya was listening, mesmerized, eyes looking directly ahead into emptiness. He was whispering the words, singing along, but Yurka could clearly read Volodya's lips: *"You'll always be there in my memories."* Volodya wasn't saying this as a message to Yurka—he was saying it to himself—and Yurka caught a glimpse of utter, impenetrable despair in his eyes. Volodya was not glad he would never forget. Yurka understood this, and his heart went painfully tight from this understanding, almost like it was stopping for a few seconds. No matter how optimistically he announced that he would always remember, that he would never forget, was that really a good thing? After what Volodya had told him in the unfinished barracks? Maybe it really was better to forget, or at least try to get it out of his head, make himself try to . . . but no. No. Of course not. He wouldn't be able to.

Meanwhile, Mitka kept dragging out that endless song. The faces around the bonfire, illuminated by the flickering scarlet glow, were filled with melancholy and with good, tender sadness. It seemed Yurka was the only one who felt that everything good was going to end when camp did.

Volodya focused his gaze on Yurka, and their eyes met. Drowning out the guitar, the Pioneers sang:

> *"Our words make the very heavens shake,*
> *So frightening it is to say them aloud . . ."*

"You'll always be there in my memories," whispered Volodya. There was no way Yurka could have heard him, but in Yurka's heart the words nevertheless rang out in Volodya's voice, clear as a bell.

Then, suddenly, Yurka realized that the line Volodya was whispering was supposed to go the other way around: "I'll always be there in your memories," and that now it was Yurka's turn to say the next line of the song . . . say those words . . . make that promise . . . "We're parting forever, though it's hard to believe."

But Yurka didn't want to! He didn't want to sing that, or to say it, or to even think it, but of their own accord, his lips whispered, "We're parting forever . . ."

The song ended. The other campers took the guitar indignantly from Mitka, complaining that they didn't want to sing such sad songs anymore.

Volodya gazed unblinkingly at Yurka, and it seemed like the world around them simply didn't exist. Yurka couldn't tell what emotions were behind Volodya's eyes. This was more than despair and sadness; it was almost physically painful for Yurka to look into those eyes.

Volodya abruptly stood, walked over to Yurka, and reached over as though he wanted to take Yurka by the hand, but he caught himself. "I'm going to help Lena after all. I'll take the kids to the cabin and come right back . . ." Then, lowering his voice to a whisper, he said, "In about twenty minutes, come out onto the path to the beach, but make sure nobody sees you. We'll go the long way, through the woods, so nobody tags along."

Once Volodya and Lena had led Troop Five away, Mitka picked up the guitar again, but Ira Petrovna convinced him not to sing any more sad songs. "Then let's do girls' choice! Maids, invite your squires!" Mitka called out, and strummed the first few notes of the immediately recognizable "Ferryman."

Yurka wanted to move so he was sitting somewhere on the very edge of the clearing and wait quietly for Volodya to come back, but Ksyusha walked up to him. "Yura, shall we have a dance?"

Yurka didn't have any energy left to be surprised. He nodded automatically, took Ksyusha's hand, and led her to the bonfire where the other couples were dancing. Ksyusha put her arms around his shoulders, but this time she didn't do it the way she had at the other dance—she didn't hold him like a Pioneer. If something like this had happened earlier, Yurka would've burst with pride, but now he felt nothing. He just turned in circles, moving his feet to the rhythm of the music, holding Ksyusha by the waist. He was like a robot. He didn't even understand the question right away when she asked him, "Yurchik, listen . . . So a certain someone told us about how Masha and you are having some issues, and you—"

"No duh we're having issues!" Yurka broke in. "But there's no 'Masha and me.'"

"Really?" Ksyusha said, feigning surprise. "Is it true you fought that time because she's stalking you?"

"She just follows me around; the one she's stalking is Volodya."

"No way!" Ksyusha was so surprised that she bumped into a nearby couple—Nastya and a beet-red Petlitsyn—and stepped on Yurka's foot.

"Well, yeah," said Yurka simply. He cast his eyes around the clearing and saw Masha sitting all alone on a bench by the bonfire, her hands in her lap, staring at the ground. She looked so sad and lonely that for a second Yurka even felt sorry for her. But then he realized that Masha's sadness was nothing in comparison to the time with Volodya that she'd made him lose and the fact that now they were parting. She vanished from his thoughts immediately.

"She's stalking Volodya? What a nightmare! Where'd she get that idea?" said Ksyusha indignantly. This was definitely news to her. "What kind of idiot do you have to be to go after a troop leader like that? Or anybody, for that matter; doesn't have to be a troop leader . . . Doesn't she have any pride?"

"Sometimes people who are in love behave very recklessly," Yurka replied. For some reason, this made him smile. He remembered his own first and most reckless act: when he'd kissed Volodya, back then, behind the power shed. But how was all that working out for him now? Was that fleeting, transient happiness worth such a painful parting, one he'd recall for the rest of his life?

After they danced, the Pioneers played a game of babbling brook, lining up in two rows facing each other, clasping hands with the person opposite them, lifting their hands high to make a tunnel, and taking turns running through the tunnel, still holding hands with their partner. After the game, somebody started trying to get everyone to jump over the bonfire. Yurka was asked, too, but he declined. He was paying careful attention to what Masha was doing. She had apparently cheered up a little when Svetka from Troop Three called her over to the bonfire to join in the game. Thanks to that, Yurka was able to slip away unnoticed. Or so he thought.

When he got to the beach, he had to wait. Volodya was held up for about ten minutes. As soon as Yurka started to think they'd missed each other, he made out the familiar silhouette in the darkness. A silhouette with a backpack.

"You ready?" asked Volodya. "Nobody saw you?"

"I don't think so. Everyone's playing babbling brook. I specifically waited until Masha couldn't see me. What's in the backpack?"

"A shovel, the time capsule, and the things we're putting in it. And a blanket, too . . . in case we want to stay there a little while. Shall we go?"

They turned onto the winding little footpath skirting the beach. It was dark in the woods. They could hear the voices of Pioneers and the crackling of the bonfire from over in the clearing. Usually when they went to the willow, Yurka led the way, because he knew the woods better, but this time Volodya went first, lighting the way with the flashlight as he picked out their path. Yurka couldn't shake the feeling he was headed to his own execution.

They were going to where they'd say their goodbyes. They were going to the willow to spend their last minutes together, say their last words. And now even the little spark of hope that had kept Yurka warm all day was all but gone, flickering on the edge of winking out completely.

"Stop that!" Yurka ordered himself. "We will meet again! We're only parting temporarily!"

He knew that the minutes before something you dread often seem to expand and take longer, so the trip to the willow should have seemed long, but there they were already, going around the boggy pool and coming out of the woods to the steep riverbank. All they had to do now was walk back through the woods for around five minutes, and then they'd be at the shallows.

Yurka wanted to stop and turn back, as though if they didn't go anywhere now, they wouldn't have to part or say goodbye. He held his hand out to Volodya so they could hold hands with fingers intertwined, but he almost fell down from fright when voices burst out from behind them:

"Volodya! Yura! Helloo-oo!" Ira Petrovna, lighting her way with her flashlight, was hurrying to catch up with them. Ksyusha and Polina were behind Ira, and behind them was Masha. "Where are you going?!"

Volodya kept his head. Without a word, he pulled off the backpack and pulled out the time capsule: a tin, the kind people use for storing buckwheat, wrapped in clear cellophane. "We're going to bury a time capsule. It's right here." He held out the tin.

"And why didn't anybody tell me anything?" said Ira angrily.

"Yura, did you not ask permission?"

Then it hit Yurka like a ton of bricks: he'd forgotten! He was embarrassed; Volodya had warned him, after all, that he needed to ask permission. "No . . . I'm sorry, Ira Petrovna, I wasn't thinking again."

"He wasn't thinking!" Ira said. "But you are my responsibility! What if something happens and I don't even know where you are!"

Volodya sighed and requested quietly, "Irin . . . let's step over here for a moment . . ."

The troop leaders moved several paces away. The girls didn't say a word. Yurka looked sullenly at Masha: How on earth had she figured out where he and Volodya had gone? He'd seen with his own two eyes that she was distracted! But it wasn't enough that she followed them again, the backbiter—she also had to give them up to Irina! And why had those two nosy little snakelings tagged along?

It never occurred to the two arguing troop leaders that even though they were standing at a distance, the wind was blowing from them to Yurka and the girls, who could therefore hear every word of their conversation clearly.

"Vova, maybe Konev's got nothing but air between his ears, but *you* could've said something to me, at least!" Ira chided him. "And this time capsule: it's a really fantastic idea. We could've buried one of our own, you know—as a troop. That's not comradely of you, Vov. We're Komsomol members, we should be helping each other!"

"I'm sorry, Irin. I didn't do it on purpose. It's just that this idea came into my head out of the blue, literally this afternoon. And we had a whole bunch of things to do. You know the drill . . . I'm sorry, okay?"

Ira softened a little. "Okay, okay. Maybe we'll get a chance to do our own first thing in the morning tomorrow."

"So how about it: Will you let Konev go under my supervision? Komsomol member's honor: I'll bring him back to you no later than one a.m., safe and sound."

Ira crossed her arms tightly, shifted from foot to foot, and cast a doubtful look at Volodya. "Vov, one a.m.'s too late."

A gust of wind blew in from the river and carried off the next part of their conversation. When the troop leader's words were audible again, Ira Petrovna, now much more amenable, was inquiring, "Did you tell Olga Leonidovna?" Volodya shook his head no. "Just be careful. If anyone from admin notices, I won't be able to help you."

"Do you really think they have any attention to spare?"

"Well . . . not really, to tell the truth. But wait! Vov, if they notice, they'll write it up in your character reference."

"To hell with it. They can write whatever they want. So will you cover for me, Irin? We won't be far—just here in the woods."

"Well . . . okay, I'll cover for—"

Volodya was already turning around to walk away when Masha shouted at the top of her lungs, "Don't let them go! I know what they're going there to do! Irina, they're abnormal! They hug and kiss! They have to be punished! We have to tell Olga Leonidovna!"

Her shouts resonated in Yurka's ears. His eyes went dim. Volodya froze in mid-stride, only his pupils racing back and forth. His panicked gaze flickered from face to face. Irina, mouth agape, looked first at Yurka, then at Volodya. Then she fixed Masha with a glare.

"Ha!" Ksyusha barked out a laugh. In the silence that had enveloped the woods, it rang out so loudly that everyone flinched. After a moment's pause, she convulsed in mocking laughter. Gasping for breath, she groaned, "Now, that's rich! She's gone completely off her rocker! Polya, are you hearing this? Are you hearing what she's saying?"

But Polina, unlike her friends, was serious. "Yes, but, Ksyusha, it's our fault. We should've made friends with her, but we . . . I also . . . I know people go nuts from loneliness. They talk total nonsense but they completely believe what they're saying! My grandma's like that . . ."

Yurka couldn't believe his ears. Never mind his anger at Masha's betrayal; he still didn't like the way the girls were reacting. Like it was something so crazy to believe.

"Are you serious?" Ksyusha asked, hiccupping and gasping. "You think . . . you think she's gone off the deep end?"

"Would a normal person really follow somebody around and then say something like that?" Polina replied. "But Masha's always alone and she never sleeps at night! How many times have we seen her sneaking away after lights out?!"

"I . . ." Masha looked scared. "I'm te-telling the truth," she stammered out.

"Irin, she really was stalking Volodya, though," said Ksyusha, who had calmed down. "I didn't believe it myself at first. So she leaves the cabin and runs around, who cares. I thought she was with Konev. But then this . . ."

"She left the cabin?" whispered Ira Petrovna, taken aback.

"Yes," confirmed Polina, eyeing Masha with suspicion. "Half the troop could tell you the same thing."

"That's true, Irin." Ksyusha nodded. "Probably need to tell Olga Leonidovna. Telling these kinds of lies—it's vile! She should be kicked out of the Pioneers for this!"

"Don't! Think what a black mark it'll be on her record! But this—well, okay, so she went a little cuckoo, it happens. Once she gets some sleep she'll settle down. And I won't leave you alone any more, Mashka, so don't worry...," Polina assured her. But nobody paid her any attention.

Masha choked out a sob. Ira Petrovna walked up to her and demanded sternly, "Masha, what are you saying? This is completely over the line..."

Masha's lips started trembling and she sniffed. But she was unable to restrain her tears. "It's true, Ir... Iri..."

"It's utterly ludicrous!" Ira shouted. "Spreading this kind of slander, and about a troop leader! About an exemplary Komsomol member! How on earth did you even come up with something like that? Kissing a—good God! How can you even bring yourself to say something like that? Because even imagining it—it's abnormal, is what it is!"

Masha burst into sobs. Yurka was stunned by what Ira had said. Yes, Volodya was her comrade and her friend; yes, she thought she knew Volodya. But this thing that was happening to him and Volodya, this love, was it really so horrific that nobody could believe even hypothetically that it might exist? Because there were people who loved like that: there was one right here—Yurka; he was "that" kind of person—and there was another one standing right over there, in a stunned silence, adjusting his glasses with a trembling hand.

Yurka recoiled. What kind of world was he living in? What a wrong, stupid, unjust world it was. And it was the world that was wrong, not Yurka.

Still, if he'd been in Ira's place as recently as a month ago, he wouldn't have believed it, either.

Meanwhile, Masha was now sobbing uncontrollably. Ira shook her head in reproach. Ksyusha piped up again mockingly: "Get a load of her! She's the liar, but now she's all weeping and moaning! It takes one to know one, right, Mash? Why don't you tell us: Is there something about *you* we don't know?"

"Stop it!" barked Yurka. "What are you attacking her for? You can't humiliate her like that, no matter what she said!"

He'd recovered somewhat from his shock, and he felt sorry for her. He wasn't defending her; she had been shamelessly despicable and vile. But Yurka had also seen how Volodya's face changed when nobody believed Masha: his brows had shot high in amazement, and for a second the corners of his mouth had twitched up.

Ira Petrovna stopped and took a breath. Then she took hold of Masha by the elbow. "Come on, sunshine. You're going back to the cabin for a nap. I'll forgive you this one time, but if you keep spouting this story, I'll take you right to Olga Leonidovna and tell her everything about these abnormal fantasies of yours . . ." She dragged Masha back toward the bonfire. "Ksyusha! Polina! You're coming with us. And you're going to keep your mouths shut, too. Volodya! Yurka will be back in the cabin by one a.m.!"

"Irin, don't tell Leonidovna," came Polina's voice as the group headed away. "This is all our fault, we didn't make friends with her, we didn't listen to her . . ."

"She was totally fine last year, she really was just normal when she and Anka were friends . . . ," said Ksyusha, her voice barely audible.

"We'll see. Depends how she behaves. Masha, if you say one word . . ." The end of Ira Petrovna's sentence died away in the silent woods.

CHAPTER EIGHTEEN
THE LAST NIGHT

Volodya stood stunned, unmoving and unblinking, staring at the path the girls had just taken.

"Hey! Everything okay?" Yurka walked over to him and snapped his fingers in front of Volodya's eyes. It took a couple of tries, since his palms were still sweaty from fear.

He knew he couldn't allow Volodya to retreat into himself right now, as that would be the death blow to their final evening together.

"I don't know . . . ," said Volodya, as though he were coming out of a trance. "I'm going to have nightmares now about Masha's outburst, but . . . I can't believe we got out of that."

"And the main thing is that we *did* get out of it! Or . . . do you think maybe we didn't? Do you think she'll tell Leonidovna?"

"Who, Irina? No," he replied with certainty. "Otherwise she would've dragged us off with her. Or did you mean Masha?" Volodya added warily. "Do you think Masha will tell her?"

"Nah, she'll be too scared. It's fine telling Ira about something like that, but telling Leonidovna and the director's way scarier."

"It *is* scarier, but that doesn't mean she won't do it!" insisted Volodya. "If she tells anyone, it'll be them. They're older, they're more experienced, they know this kind of thing does exist. Not like Irina."

"Okay, so fine. Let's say she does tell them. What then? In that case, I'm the victim here, and they'll ask me whether that's really what happened. And I'll say Masha's lying! And you will, too, and Ira—I mean, everybody will say Masha's lying! We know Polya and Ksyusha won't be able to keep quiet, they're definitely going to blab. So the way it'll end up is that there'll be nothing to charge us with because there are no victims."

"That's true, too. There's no crime here."

"Okay then, so are we going to the willow?"

Volodya nodded, turned off his flashlight, and went off the path directly into the woods. "To make sure nobody else can tag along," he explained. "Even though that's unlikely now . . ."

After a couple of minutes, when they were going around the steep riverbank, he paused and set the alarm on his watch. "Did you leave anything at the bonfire?" he asked.

"Why, are we not going back there?"

"Going back is bad luck, remember?" Volodya smiled and started walking again.

Yurka managed to collect his thoughts somewhat as he trundled obediently along behind Volodya. He felt guilty, because he was the one who'd gotten them in trouble, after all: he hadn't gotten permission from Irina, nor had he kept track of Masha . . .

"That Masha's a real pest," he said. "She was the one who sent Ira after us. It couldn't have been anyone else. And then the Pukes went gallivanting along behind her. I thought she was busy playing babbling brook and didn't see me leave."

"No need to justify yourself, Yur. We've already seen how good a spy Masha can be. By the way, I was amazed that you stood up for her. That was a good thing you did."

Yurka winced. "I don't even know what came over me. It was like I suddenly felt sorry for her. What do you think: Will Ira go tattling on Masha to Leonidovna? I mean, accusing a Komsomol member of something like that is no joke . . ."

Volodya scoffed. "I wouldn't bet on it. Just imagine the mess Irina will have to deal with if she does. And also, she's just a troop leader: she doesn't have any kind of pedagogical role like a teacher or anything. And on top of that, today's the last day: tomorrow Irina won't have any kind of official position in relation to vis-à-vis Masha anymore. And Leonidovna doesn't need this kind of bureaucratic hassle, either." Volodya snorted. "She had more than enough of you last year. So why do you ask?"

"Well . . . What Polya said was actually true . . . ," Yurka mumbled lamely. "People would condemn Masha . . ."

"Are you worried about her?" Judging by the tone, Volodya was even more surprised.

"Well . . . ," he said slowly. "I mean . . . even if she is evil on two legs . . ."

"Come on, Yur. She's just a girl in love. Her love isn't evil in and of itself."

Yurka groaned wearily. "Look who's talking about evil, Volodya! That love is precisely the kind that is evil. It's ours that isn't. Masha blackmailed you, after all! She tried to force us apart, and now here she is pulling this nasty, vile maneuver on us."

"No, Yura," insisted Volodya stubbornly. "She just doesn't know how she should love. She's in despair. She should be pitied, treated with—"

"I'm in despair, too! And I don't know how I should love, either!" exclaimed Yurka. "But somehow *I'm* not the one sneaking around spying on you! I'm not trying to do these nasty, awful things!"

"That's because your love is reciprocated. Why don't you tell me who was still throwing apples at me not all that long ago, huh, Yur?"

Yurka tried to think of something to say in reply but didn't come up with anything before they reached the shallows.

They had to take their trousers off to cross the river. During the day, Yurka had been wandering around here in shorts, so he'd just pulled them up, but now the prospect of sitting half the night in jeans that were wet all the way past the knees didn't seem very appealing. The water in the river wasn't that cold, but his legs were covered in goose bumps the moment he came out on the other side of the river. Volodya dove quickly into his tracksuit bottoms, but Yurka had to struggle a bit with his jeans. He was rewarded with several mosquito bites as a result. He cringed as he put on his shoes: his wet feet squelched disgustingly in his sneakers.

As they walked along the far riverbank toward the willow, Yurka asked, "What did you say to Ira that made her let us stay out all the way until one a.m.?"

"I reminded her that I covered for her and Zhenya when she asked."

"Oh, so you do know . . . ," said Yurka, surprised.

Volodya sent him a sideways glance. "Zhenya and I shared a room. How could I not know?"

"So what do you think about it?"

"About what?"

"About the fact that Zhenya's married but he's seeing Ira."

Volodya shrugged. "He loves her. I don't know if anybody else sees it, but it's completely obvious to me. Yesterday they had yet another fight and I was stuck in the middle as their go-between. Irina would come and complain to me and ask if she was doing the right thing."

"Oho! So you've turned into a couples counselor now?" laughed Yurka.

"About right," Volodya shrugged dismissively. "Almost a full-blown matchmaker. But I didn't want to; Zhenya made me."

"So? What did you tell her?"

"I . . . I told her to think about her own life and not look around to see what everyone else thought. The people around you will always judge you, always say something, but maybe it's worth just not caring what other people say, at least sometimes. Because if she's happy with him, then let her be with him."

Yurka stopped short. "Did you actually tell her something like that?"

Volodya also stopped and turned to him with a smile. "Yes."

"Is that what you really think?"

"Yes."

Something started simmering inside Yurka, something between anger and hurt. The memory of their conversation in the unfinished barracks was still too fresh. "So that's what you think . . . Huh . . . ," he said slowly. Then he added angrily, "But at the same time you're convinced you're some kind of monster and can't allow yourself to be happy, right?"

"That's totally different, Yur—"

"That's exactly the same thing!" shouted Yurka. "You were saying you're afraid to cause me harm, and that's the exact same way Ira's afraid of harming Zhenya. You look around at everybody else, just like she does, and you think you're bad just because the people around you do! But you won't listen to me when I try to convince you otherwise! Why not?!"

"You don't understand—"

"I understand everything! Stop treating me like a child! You're only two years older than me! Look how I've changed. That's you. You changed me. Just three weeks ago I was afraid to even get close to a piano, even though everyone tried to talk me into it: my mother, my father, my relatives . . . They even tried to force me to play! But you were the only way I could get over my fear. But now you can't get over your fear, even though I'm asking you to! I'm asking you to do it for me! So don't go saying I don't understand it. I understand perfectly why you're so afraid. I'm afraid, too! But I can overcome that fear—" He broke off and breathed out a ragged breath, as though all his fury had suddenly evaporated. Then, quietly now, with lowered eyes, he added, "Because I fell in love."

Volodya froze and looked at him in astonishment. Then Yurka felt uncomfortable with what he'd said and how he'd said it: it was like he'd dumped everything on Volodya, and so harshly, too . . . He knew this was neither the time nor the place to talk about everything in a big heart-to-heart, but on the other hand, when would it be?

And now it was apparently Volodya's turn to be lost for words. He just grabbed Yurka's hand and pulled him forward, to where they could see the slope down toward the water and the lush foliage of the willow.

Once they were inside the tent of the willow's branches, Volodya pulled the blanket out of the backpack and tossed it on the ground. Then he got out the time capsule, his notebook, and a pencil. He said, "All right. We need to write something to ourselves when we're ten years older."

Yurka sat down on the blanket. Volodya joined him and pulled off his damp sneakers. Yurka did the same. Then he took the pencil and notebook and wrote on the last page, "No matter what dont loose each other."

"Look at these mistakes, Yur!" grumbled Volodya. "'Lose' has one *o*, not two, and you need an apostrophe in 'don't.'" Yurka looked at him reproachfully. Volodya added guiltily, "But that makes no difference right now! No, don't correct it; it's actually better this way. You can see it was written by the young hooligan Konev." Yurka could hear his smile in his voice. "Then you'll remember him ten years from now . . . And now it's my turn. Here, shine the light over here."

With one hand Volodya took the notebook and held it as he bent low over it. With his other hand he wrote in neat, compact handwriting, "No matter what, don't lose yourself . . ." Then his hand started shaking. Yurka, forgetting he might blind Volodya, shone the flashlight on Volodya's face. He jerked away from the beam of light but not before Yurka saw that Volodya's eyes were wet.

"Volod, don't cry, or else I'll start up too . . ."

Without waiting for him to finish, Volodya seized Yurka's shoulders and drew Yurka in, holding him tight. Volodya buried his face in Yurka's neck and mumbled something unintelligible.

Yurka choked at the pain that had flared up again. Maintaining his self-control with some difficulty, he put his arms around Volodya. The only word he could understand of Volodya's feverish whispering at his neck was a quiet "Yurochka..."

If this had lasted even a minute longer, Yurka would've lost it, too. The helplessness and grief were making him want to either cry or scream. But Volodya quickly got hold of himself and said, "You're right. This isn't doing us any good right now. It'll wait, it'll all wait till later."

He picked up the notebook again and kept writing. Yurka sniffed as he held the flashlight on the notebook so Volodya could see. "Stay just the way we were in '86. Volodya will graduate from his institute with honors and take a trip to America. Yura will go to conservatory and become a pianist."

"Done," said Volodya. Then he asked, "What else should we put in the time capsule?"

Yurka extracted a damp sheet of paper from his jeans pocket: the music he'd copied out for himself so he could practice. "Here's the 'Lullaby.' It's the most precious thing I had during this session." He put the music into the time capsule.

Volodya rolled his notebook into a tube and put it in. The notebook had the corrected script with all the notes, with his own personal thoughts jotted down over the course of the session as well as his wishes for their future selves.

"And one more thing," said Yurka, digging in his pocket. "Here. I think this should go in, too." He produced a white lily, now crumpled and missing a few petals—the lily Volodya had given him. Volodya nodded and placed the flower carefully at the very top of the time capsule, sitting on the notebook.

"Is that everything?" Volodya asked quietly.

Yurka thought for a moment: Was that really everything? Or was there something else that should be left here for safekeeping? Yurka shook his head. "No. There's one more thing."

Yurka clutched the Pioneer neckerchief knotted around his neck and tugged at it fitfully, trying to untie it. But his hands were shaking, and instead of loosening the knot, he made it even tighter.

Volodya reached over silently to help him. Yurka said gloomily, "How ironic. When I was accepted into the Pioneers, a Komsomol member tied my tie on. And now a Komsomol member is taking it off."

A cool breeze touched Yurka's bare neck, making him shiver. Volodya misread the reason for Yurka's reaction: "Are you sure you want to put it in the time capsule?"

"Yes."

"But your neckerchief only costs fifty-five kopeks, you know. We agreed to only put our most precious things into the time capsule," said Volodya sarcastically.

"That was what it used to cost. Not anymore."

Volodya smiled and said, repeating Yurka's own words, "Get a load of that! So how much does your Pioneer neckerchief cost now?"

"It's priceless." Yurka saw Volodya's smirk and clarified, "No, not because of the story of duty it tells; because it's a piece of my childhood."

"Will you help me?" asked Volodya. He took Yurka's hand and put it on his own neckerchief, which was ironed, and crisp, and neat, and warm from his body heat. After both their neckerchiefs had been taken off, Volodya took them and knotted the ends together. Yurka remained silent. He studied the strong, tight knot and guessed that Volodya had imbued some kind of secret meaning all his own into it, but figured it was unnecessary to ask about it.

Volodya sighed, put the neckerchiefs into the time capsule, put the lid on, and said, "It looks like you really have grown up, Yura."

The rain-dampened earth yielded easily, and even with their child-size shovel they were able to dig their hole quickly. They put the time capsule in. Yurka watched the clods of earth slowly covering up the tin's little rectangular lid. Too late, he remembered that his neckerchief was where the Pukes had written their addresses. Mikha and Vanka, too. But this thought flitted out of his head as quickly as it had entered it. Right now that was completely unimportant. Volodya was way more important. Yurka watched him take his penknife and cut something into the bark of the willow tree right over the place the time capsule was buried. Yurka trained his flashlight on the tree, moving the circle of light around on the trunk, revealing a small, uneven set of Cyrillic initials appeared inside it: *Yu+V.*

Seeing those letters was painful, because in just a few hours this spot, on this tree trunk, underneath this tent of willow branches, would be the only place where he and Volodya would remain together. In real life they would be headed off their separate ways, to their separate cities, which were almost a thousand kilometers away from each other.

Yurka stopped caring then about what Volodya thought of himself or what Volodya was afraid of. It became imperative for Yurka to hold Volodya close. So he did. He pulled Volodya tightly to him, with no intention of letting go, even if Volodya tried to get away. But Volodya didn't push him away. On the contrary, it was as though he had just been waiting for this moment. He eagerly hugged Yurka back, pressing close and breathing shakily. "Yur . . . I'm going to miss you so much . . ."

Yurka wanted to ask him to be quiet so as not to hear such painfully sad words. And besides, why couldn't they stay here forever, under their willow? Why couldn't he hold on to Volodya forever, breathing in Volodya's own dear, familiar scent, so they would never, ever part?

Volodya clutched Yurka so tightly, he rumpled Yurka's T-shirt. He stroked his warm hands along Yurka's back and breathed on his neck, making Yurka cringe from the ticklish sensation. Then Volodya abruptly leaned in and kissed the hollow under Yurka's earlobe. Yurka shuddered, then recoiled. He remembered how Volodya had insisted he didn't want all this touching, all this tenderness, and now here he was doing it himself . . .

He removed Volodya's hands and sat down on the blanket, wrapping his arms around his knees and then resting his chin on them.

"Yur, what's wrong?" Volodya sat down next to him. "What did I do?"

"Nothing." Yurka shook his head. "It's just . . . you and I have so little time left, but I don't know what I'm allowed to do. Because you forbid me from doing anything."

Volodya moved very close, put his arm around Yurka's shoulders, and drew him in. "What do you want to do?" he whispered.

Yurka turned his head and rubbed noses with Volodya. "To kiss you. Is that allowed?"

"That's allowed."

Volodya closed the distance between them himself, pressing a warm, tender kiss to Yurka's lips. Yurka squeezed his eyes shut, found Volodya's hand, interwove his fingers with Volodya's, and held on tight. He felt as though the moment he let go of Volodya's hand, the moment he let that kiss end, then everything would end: his feelings would fizzle out, his heart would turn to stone, the air would turn to jelly, and the whole world would stop dead.

But the kiss did not end. Volodya's lips parted and the kiss became wet and soft. Yurka opened his mouth, too, and sighed. He felt like smiling. It was so sweet that all those irrelevant mournful thoughts vanished immediately. The murmur of the water in the river, the rustling of the wind in the leaves, even the loud beating of his own heart—all of it went quiet; all of it ceased to exist. The only thing left was that dizzyingly real kiss and the distinct desire ringing in his head like an invocation: Let this kiss never end.

Yurka didn't know how he ended up lying on his side on the blanket. He only knew the kiss had ended because a cold chill had just touched his wet lips. He opened his eyes. Volodya was lying next to him, one arm around him, looking at him: his cheeks, his lips, his eyes. Yurka thought for a moment that maybe he had fallen asleep for some amount of time, but no—only a couple of minutes had passed. He'd just lost track of everything. It had been so good, though. He wanted more.

Volodya turned to lie on his back and looked up at the sky through the willow leaves. Yurka studied the way the weak light outlined Volodya's profile in a silvery silhouette. Then he moved closer. Volodya didn't move; he just sighed heavily. Yurka moved even closer, and still closer, until his whole body was pressed up against Volodya's. He almost asked permission to put his arms around him but then cursed at himself: "To hell with all that!" As soon as tomorrow came, he'd regret he hadn't taken Volodya in his arms, but by then it would be too late. "To hell with awkwardness and shame!"

Yurka laid his head on Volodya's shoulder and put his hand on his chest. He opened and closed his fingers hesitantly, stroking him. Volodya shuddered.

"Yur . . . you're too close."

"Too close to what?"

"To me." He put his hand over Yurka's as though he were going to move it away but reconsidered and held it instead. "I really like it when you do that . . . We had almost a whole month, but we didn't do hardly anything . . . We didn't even lie down together like this . . ."

"Well, you wouldn't have let us. But we still have today left."

Volodya turned his head slightly and buried his nose in Yurka's hair. He inhaled Yurka's scent. He let Yurka's hand go and lightly stroked his neck, then his ear. Yurka gasped with pleasure. Volodya chuckled, then whispered, "You want so badly to be touched . . . It's like you're electrically charged: the sparks fly even if I barely touch you." He sighed. "Same thing for me, though," he admitted.

Yurka wanted to touch Volodya, too. And although he knew Volodya would immediately resist him, he resolutely lifted the edge of Volodya's shirt anyway, to touch Volodya's stomach with trembling fingers. Volodya flinched, biting his lip. "Don't, Yur," he protested half-heartedly, but he didn't move Yurka's hand away.

Yurka was quaking on the inside as he cautiously stroked Volodya's smooth, warm skin with just the very tips of his fingers. "It's like you're afraid of me," Yurka said.

Volodya shook his head. "I'm afraid of myself. You were wrong when you said I can't overcome my fear and change. The hard part, actually, is holding myself back from doing the things that . . . the things I'll regret later."

"And what makes you so sure you're going to regret them?"

"Because they'll cause you harm."

"Here we go again! Harping on that again, huh?" Yurka sat up and glared down at Volodya resentfully. "We have one hour left to be together, but you're still thinking about whether you might hurt me. But I'm already hurting! Any more of this and I'll lose it; I'll lose everything: you, myself . . ." He paused and took a breath. "At least here, at least this one day, be the way you want to be, Volodya. For me. I want to remember you at your best, as special, as my first. And I want to be that for you!"

Volodya stared at Yurka, flabbergasted. He propped himself up on his elbows, then sat up, too. "Yur . . . ," he said, then his voice caught and he spent a moment clearing his throat. "I'm such a degenerate. I keep thinking about just the wrong thing—"

"No, it's the right thing, dammit! That's the right thing!" insisted Yurka, cutting him off. "Volodya, I've left too much behind, here at camp—"

"I understand—"

"—but I want to leave it *all* behind!"

Volodya stared at the ground and was silent for a minute. Then he fixed Yurka with a penetrating gaze: "But this'll be forever, Yur. You'll never be able to forget it. Or undo it."

"Why would I want to undo it? Or forget it? What is there to be afraid of? Nobody's going to know about it, after all. You and I are the only ones who'll know what we did—and that we did it for real. So that even twenty years later we can be positive all this was real."

"Yet another shared secret?"

"Not another one. The only one. The biggest and most important one."

Volodya remained silent for another minute, searching Yurka's face and eyes carefully as though trying to find doubt in them. But Yurka returned his gaze, stubborn and resolute.

"Are you absolutely sure, Yura? I . . . It's . . . Listen. At any moment you can tell me to stop, and I will."

"Okay."

"No, not 'Okay'. You promise me that if you start having any doubts at all, even for a second, you'll tell me."

"I promise."

"Close your eyes."

Yurka closed them obediently. He caught his breath, anticipating Volodya's touch, but on the contrary, Volodya drew back. Yurka could hear Volodya fussing with the backpack. Yurka froze, barely breathing, afraid to weaken the resolve it had been so hard for Volodya to build. Volodya drew near again, squeezed his arm gently, and then tenderly kissed Yurka's neck, his lips just barely touching the skin. It tickled again.

"Will it hurt?" Yurka blurted out of nowhere.

Volodya chuckled. "We won't do anything that could hurt for you. I told you, I won't ever demean you—for anything."

"Demean me?!" said Yurka angrily. "How can you say something like that! I love you and I'm ready for anything! I'll—I'll kiss the hell out of you, from head to toe!"

Volodya burst out laughing.

"No?" Yurka was flustered. He knew he'd sounded naïve, but he hadn't been sure what else to say. And he was in no hurry to open his eyes, so he was just guessing at Volodya's reactions. "Then I'll do something else instead. I'll do anything, anything at all, I just . . . I just don't know what . . . Will you tell me?"

"Oh, my dear Yurochka." Yurka heard the smile in Volodya's voice. Volodya stroked Yurka's cheek and kissed his nose. "For now, just sit down. And help me a little."

Volodya dug around in the backpack again. When he was finished, he turned back to Yurka and whispered, "Can I kiss you again?"

"Volod, you don't need to ask permission."

"Right . . ."

He pressed his lips to Yurka's. This time the kiss wasn't as long and tender as it had been a few minutes ago; now it was quick and insistent.

Volodya was very close to Yurka, but he wasn't pushing Yurka away. On the contrary, he pressed close. Yurka embraced him awkwardly, somehow rucking up Volodya's shirt in the process. But he didn't tug it back down, instead running his hand boldly along Volodya's back near his shoulder blades. Volodya was hot. Yurka buried his nose in the little hollow at the base of Volodya's neck between his collarbones and inhaled, drinking in the beloved scent. He gathered his courage and kissed a bare patch of skin there, making Volodya shiver and take a ragged breath as he raked his fingers through Yurka's hair.

"Volod, wait." Yurka opened his eyes and looked up at Volodya. He reached up and, without asking, took off Volodya's glasses and put them on the ground next to the blanket. Volodya squinted comically. "It's like you're helpless to defend yourself without them," said Yurka.

"Not 'without them.' Against you." Volodya kissed him and turned off the flashlight.

And a few minutes later Yurka had forgotten who he was and where they were. He couldn't understand what he was feeling. It was both pleasant and strange at the same time; it was absolutely unfamiliar, not remotely like anything else. He did remember he could say stop, but he didn't speak. He didn't want to stop. And he didn't have the strength to speak anyway.

Yurka soared and plunged. With Volodya, it was easy to rise up to such heights that there was no oxygen, leaving him dizzy. And it was equally easy to hurtle down with Volodya onto burning sand, or dive into boiling water and drown in it. Yurka felt a compression, a smothering, as though he were about to explode into smithereens. His heart was pounding in his temples so loudly that he could hear nothing else. But Yurka wanted to hear Volodya, to find out whether he was just as breathless, whether this was all just as strange to him. Was it as sweet-smothering-hot all at once for him, too, or was it different? And what was he, Yurka, allowed to do? What *should* he do? He wanted to move, but he was afraid of ruining everything, of doing something wrong. He gathered up his courage and held Volodya, pressing in as tightly as he could. Then he lost himself completely in sensation; he forgot how to breathe; he went deaf from the hammering of his heart.

And then, just as the sensations were becoming almost unbearable, there was a release.

When he came back to himself, Yurka held Volodya close and pressed his forehead into his shoulder, listening to Volodya's heavy, raspy breathing. Volodya had relaxed, too. When he seemed about to draw back, Yurka held him even tighter, saying, "Don't leave. Let's sit here a little longer, okay?"

Volodya obeyed. He pressed his body, still burning hot, into Yurka's and gave Yurka a kiss right on the earlobe. It tickled again, but it was pleasant.

They sat like that for a little while, silent and completely still, until they began to freeze. Volodya moved away and turned around. Even though it was dark and he couldn't really see anything, Yurka started feeling awkward. His cheeks burned. He was probably beet red all over.

"Everything okay?" asked Yurka in a shaky voice.

"Just got a little stain over here." Volodya yanked at his shirt as he turned back to Yurka.

The pale rays of the moon pierced through the willow's narrow herringbone leaves to fall on Volodya's face. He was unusually darling, so tender and abashed, as he rubbed his shirt and smiled, his cheeks flushed.

"If only we could do that our whole lives, huh?" Volodya asked quietly.

Yurka nodded. "You said something about next time. When will that be?"

"When we meet. I'll come see you, or you'll come see me. For a long time. For a whole summer."

Yurka's heart leaped and filled with hope: Volodya had said that so firmly, without a hint of doubt.

"Yes! It'll be so great," said Yurka excitedly. "I'll play on the piano to wake you up, and you'll always be losing your glasses . . ."

"But I wear them all the time and haven't lost them in ages now." Volodya looked around, squinting. His gaze landed on his glasses, lying on the grass, and he reached over and got them and put them on. "Almost squashed them," he noted with relief.

"Well, and I haven't played in ages before this summer," Yurka reminded him.

"But you will, right?" asked Volodya, and held him close, more tenderly than he ever had before. He had his arm around Yurka's shoulder and kept stroking and squeezing it.

"Ha! If I do, you won't last three days, much less a whole summer! You have no idea what torture it is to live in the same apartment as a musician. It's constant, continual music! And this isn't pretty little compositions; this is sounding things out, and hitting wrong notes, and sometimes playing the same part or even the same note over and over. And all this is loud, so you can hear it in the whole apartment. No, you have no idea what hell it'll be!"

Volodya couldn't stop smiling. All of a sudden he took his glasses off again. He put them on Yurka's lap, then buried his face in Yurka's hair and whispered in his ear, "Oh no, it seems I've lost my glasses. You have no idea what hell it is to live with someone who's always losing his glasses!"

It got hot again from Volodya's breath.

"I'll find them for you."

"And I will love your music."

"And I will love you . . ."

The alarm on Volodya's watch went off, tearing them away from their beautiful fantasy where they lived under the same roof, where every morning they woke up together, where they ate breakfast together, where they talked and watched TV and went out together. Where they were always together.

"What time is it?"

"We still have a little time," said Volodya, resetting his alarm.

And indeed, they had just a little time left. They sat side by side in utter silence, completely still, simply enjoying their last moments together. No matter how much Yurka wanted "a little time" to last longer, it ticked away all too fast.

The watch alarm beeped loudly, a shock to their ears. And not only to their ears: to their hearts as well. Yurka knew that Volodya also felt it; otherwise he wouldn't have had tears in his voice as he said, "Well. We came here to say goodbye."

And he wouldn't have stood up, and he wouldn't have reached a hand down to Yurka.

Yurka didn't want to take it, but he did. Volodya pulled him to his feet.

They stood facing each other, barefoot on the cold grass. Yurka was motionless, even limp, as though bereft of will, emotion, and thought. The river roared in their ears. With one hand, Volodya stroked his cheek; with the other, he squeezed Yurka's fingers tight.

I wish I could see his eyes in this dark, Yurka thought. As though hearing his wish, the moon came out from behind a cloud. But it didn't get any brighter. The glow of the thin crescent just highlighted the outline of that beloved face. Yurka tensed: he had to memorize everything, all the images, sounds, and smells, know them better than he knew his own name. They would be more important to him than his own name.

He folded Volodya in an embrace, pressed tightly against him, glued himself to him, grew into him. Volodya embraced him back.

"Goodbye, Yurochka . . . until we meet again . . . ," he whispered, his lips warm.

The hours after that were meaningless and went by in a blur.

Yurka didn't know or notice how much time passed, where he was, what he did. He had no awareness of what was happening around him. His thoughts had remained completely behind, there under the willow, there in that memorable last night, holding Volodya close, feeling his warmth, breathing him in.

But his last memory from that summer was nevertheless not the sound of Volodya's voice, not the words of farewell, not the rustling of willow leaves. Rather, it was the picture he saw out the window of the bus: a wave of Volodya's hand, and out past that the sun, and the summer, and the camp, and the fluttering red flags.

CHAPTER NINETEEN
PEN "PALS"

It wasn't the best time to come back here. It had been pouring rain for a week now, and Yura knew from the weather report that it was going to keep raining just as long. But he hadn't had a choice. It was the end of his tour, and his plane ticket back to Germany tomorrow was right there in his wallet. So there had been no other time for him to visit Camp Barn Swallow.

Half-frozen, soaked from the constant drizzle, Yura looked at the moss-covered sculptures, and the abandoned athletic fields, and the crumbling walls of the mess hall. Then the clouds gathered and the camp went dark, as though the sun had sunk over the horizon. But it hadn't: it was six o'clock, too early for sunset in September. Yet too late for reminiscing. Yura gave his head a shake. *No more wasting time. I've got to get where I was going, do what I came to do.*

Stumbling in the tall, wet grass, he went back to the path leading to the river beach. Part of it was paved with big gray pavers, but as soon as he got past the junior cabins, the pavers were replaced by a narrow, steeply sloping path of sand.

Yura looked down at the path made of concrete pavers, with sedges and dandelions growing in the cracks, and remembered the newspapers that had been spread on the floor in the unfinished barracks. What was it he'd thought back then? *But what if these newspapers were from the future? Not even the very distant future, just a little, even just from the summer of '87 . . . or what if they were from five years from now, or ten years . . . or maybe twenty . . .* Yurka smiled sadly. Now he knew.

The rest of the year 1986 had gone by in a fog. The initial period was unbearably sad. When Yurka got back to Kharkiv, it was as though he'd landed in some completely foreign, unfamiliar world. It seemed that everything around him was a bad dream and that all he had to do to get back to

Camp Barn Swallow was simply wake up. But no matter how hard Yurka pinched himself, how much he tried to lie to himself, this was his reality, here in the stifling city, inside his old apartment's same four walls. The only things Yurka had from that June when he had been so happy were the photo tacked to the rug on the wall by his bed, and the memories, and Volodya's letters.

"When I got back to my room and unpacked my things," began Volodya's very first letter,

> I thought it was completely nuts that I didn't have anything to remember camp by. Because it's true, Yur, we left everything in the time capsule except our troop pictures. When Olga Leonidovna went to pass the pictures to Lena and me for us to hand out to the kids, our bus had already pulled out. You would've cracked up if you'd seen Leonidovna running after us. The bus driver didn't see her and we had to yell at him to stop. Imagine that. Did you imagine it? I can actually see you smiling.
>
> I hope you got your troop picture, too. I'm sending you my picture of Troop Five. Send me your picture of Troop One in return. Only if everyone in your troop is in the picture, of course.

Yurka and Volodya exchanged pictures by mail, and Yurka managed to attach the photo of Volodya's troop to the rug hung on the wall behind his bed. He had decided it had to be exactly there, because the windows of his room were to the east and the first rays of the sun fell precisely on that spot.

Volodya had a fake smile in that photo. He looked calm and collected, but tense. Olezhka stood next to him on one side, chubby Sashka on the other. The boys were frozen at attention, all ironed and washed and combed. Behind them rose the statue of Zina Portnova; above them stretched the cloudless sky. Yurka looked at that photo every morning, thinking each time how artificial it looked. Only Yurka knew exactly what Volodya was hiding behind his smile and the shining lenses of his glasses.

Volodya's letters were the only way Yurka made it through the first couple of months. Of course, he tried as hard as he could to hide his sad longing from everyone: he smiled for his parents, he hung out with the guys from his building, he ate, he drank, he went to visit his grandmother, he helped his mom around the house and his dad in the garage. But in his thoughts Yurka was always returning to Camp Barn Swallow, and he counted the days from letter to letter. In them he found confirmation that Volodya really existed, that he was still with him, that he apparently still loved him. But they were separated by almost a thousand kilometers between Kharkiv and Moscow. It was so unjust! Yurka had always assumed love could conquer anything, but distance turned out to be immune to love's power.

Finally, by the time winter came, it got a little better. Yurka had resigned himself to all of it, and his pangs of sad longing eased, as though the first cold snaps had touched his heart with frost, too.

Now, as Yura stepped from one concrete square to the next, it was like he was moving along a timeline from one year to the next. The next paver was almost as good as new, unbroken, without a single crack or weed. And at the start of 1987 their relationship had been just the same, just as clean and whole, even though they'd been longing for each other for over half a year by then, in their separate cities, comforted by the only thing they could do to span the distance.

Volodya wrote often, about everything. At first Yurka's parents were surprised: What was with all these letters? Why were there so many of them? Why did they come so often? Yurka explained, of course, that it was his pen pal, a friend he'd made at Camp Barn Swallow who lived in Moscow, and so the only way they could be friends was like this, at a distance.

And Yurka knew that, just looking at the letters, the boys really did seem like nothing more than friends. They formulated their thoughts in such a way that nobody could suspect anything was amiss.

Yurka learned how to read Volodya between the lines. He knew when routine phrases were hiding references to their mutual past and individual present. Without seeing Volodya's gestures, just imagining them, Yurka could decipher Volodya's mood in the letters, in the handwriting, in the smudges and inky fingerprints on the paper. He knew what word had made Volodya sharply poke his glasses back up and which word had made him frown. Yurka imagined Volodya's room, and Volodya himself, sitting at his desk at the window. He imagined Volodya at his classes, where he listened to his instructors and chatted with his classmates. The only thing he didn't know was what exactly all those people were talking about. Volodya didn't write much about those conversations. He was secretive, afraid of saying something wrong, despite the fact that now people were allowed to talk about a lot of things.

In a speech he gave in February 1986, Gorbachov had publicly mentioned the new concepts of "glasnost" and "democratization" for the first time. But Yurka didn't truly understand all that, all the changes related to perestroika and the new way of thinking, until 1987.

Those concepts were everywhere: out on the street, and on television, and inside people's homes. The progressive majority was genuinely trying to make it happen, although many Soviet citizens didn't trust perestroika, and some were afraid of it. But the loudest, most insistent calls for change didn't come from the grown-ups; they came from the children. Their insistence rang like an alarm bell throughout the entire country. Who would've thought: Pioneers criticizing adults, and boycotting the All-Union Pioneer Convention's formal resolution ceremony, and asking whether the Pioneers as an organization should even exist at all. Somewhere inside Yurka, he was starting to sense that if children were being allowed to critique the status quo, then big changes really were coming. And indeed they came.

The year 1987 saw the legalization of businesses and co-ops. The shortage of domestic goods got worse, but foreign goods appeared and markets started opening up. Girls passed around rare copies of the highly coveted fashion magazine *Burda Moden*, printed in Russian in Germany; it had only recently started coming out in the USSR. Young people went around in bright, eye-popping parachute pants and jackets with snaps and studs. Yurka managed to get ahold of a pair of high-waisted, balloon-legged Pyramid jeans, ones with the actual camel patch on the rear pocket, and he was very proud of them. But none of these new foreign treasures made him as happy as the photo from Camp Barn Swallow his mom had brought home one day from work. It was the one Pal Palych had taken after the show. Yurka put it in a frame and spent hours turning it over in his hands, examining the faces of everyone in the cast as they stood in the theater opposite the stage. Although the most pleasant face of all to examine was of course Volodya's as he stood with his arm around Yurka in the photo.

The Komsomol still held sway as the formal organization uniting Communist youth, but other, informal groups of young people started to pop up, too. There were rockers, who ran around the city at night; metallists and punks, who were the most aggressive; and a new generation of "hippars," peaceable hippie types who liked worn jeans, strings of beads, and friendship bracelets. In one of his letters, Volodya wrote about the "Lyubers," the outwardly civilized-looking, muscular guys from the Moscow suburb of Lyubertsy who were determined to rid Moscow of "informals," "cleansing" it of anyone who, in their opinion, dishonored their "correct" way of life. The Lyubers beat up the informals, forcibly cut their "too-long" hair, and tore off any clothing with trinkets and frills.

Volodya emphasized, "They don't pick on me," obviously to reassure Yurka. But Yurka just laughed: Why would they?

There were no Lyubers in Kharkiv. But Yurka, who considered himself neither an "informal" nor a "formal," bowed to fashion and grew out his hair to his shoulders. He stopped spending a lot of time with the guys from his building. He and his father watched the revolutionary new TV program *Outlook* every Friday, and he wrote Volodya three times a week, and three times a week Volodya answered him.

Volodya's handwriting revealed much to Yurka. It was usually neat and compact. But when Volodya was agitated, the letters were slanted and the tails of the letters that went below the line were long and narrow, like dashes. When Volodya was angry he pressed down with the pen so hard that he tore through the paper. But one letter arrived written so nicely it was almost calligraphy. Yurka noticed immediately and asked Volodya never to rewrite his letters again and to always just send them as he'd written them, even if there were crossed-out words, or smudges, or even inkblots. *Those are more genuine*, Yurka thought. *More alive.*

Soon they developed the habit of coloring the corners of their envelopes, so that when they were looking in their mailboxes they could immediately recognize each other's letters. Yurka was the one who started it. One time he decided to write the childish "Waiting for your letter—the sooner, the better!" and started writing the letter *w* in the top left corner, but, thinking better of it, he changed his mind and colored over it to cross it out. In reply, he got a letter with the same marking.

And so they lived through all of 1987. Yurka half-heartedly studied for winter exams at the technical college he'd started just so he wouldn't have to go into the army to do his mandatory two years of service, and in December he asked to visit Volodya. But he knew it would be a no. Back in '86, Volodya had already written Yurka, saying, "I won't come visit you, and I won't invite you to come visit me, until you are accepted into conservatory." And as Yurka thought, when Yurka asked to see him, Volodya just reminded Yurka of what he'd said back then.

Yurka had been vacillating about the piano, full of misgivings, but every day his desire to continue his studies grew. Volodya's ultimatum was the push he needed, the last straw, and Yurka obeyed and began studying. It was a little scary. Yurka blamed himself for giving the piano up. And once he'd cleaned all the junk off his piano, put the photo from Camp Barn Swallow on it, and sat down to play, he began harshly cursing himself for ignoring his mother, father, and everyone else who'd tried to convince him to start playing again before his hands forgot.

Yurka quickly saw that he wouldn't be able to get himself ready to apply to the conservatory on his own. He told his parents, so his father found him a tutor. It turned out that the tutor was the meanest, least popular teacher from Yurka's old school. It took Yurka a lot of effort to understand that the hated Sergey Stepanovich yelled at him only because he was so genuinely invested in Yurka's future and talent. Because Sergey Stepanovich did yell at him like crazy before they even began, reminding Yurka of how lazy and arrogant he'd been at school and saying Yurka still didn't even know the basics, so he definitely didn't have enough experience to improvise yet. And once he'd heard Yurka play, he issued his verdict: "Not even average. Poor. Poor minus." But he reassured Yurka's mother that Yurka did have talent. What he told Yurka, however, was that if he wanted to develop that talent, he had to stop showing off and finally start listening to people with more experience.

Yurka communicated this to Volodya. Volodya offered a few scant words of praise. Volodya usually sounded quite unemotional, if not downright indifferent—he was afraid of someone reading their letters. He closed each letter with a note asking Yurka, in veiled language, not to talk openly about what had happened between them, and he kept his own emotions to a bare minimum. But sometimes they broke through despite him. And it was exactly these rare moments that Yurka remembered better than everything else.

Sometimes I miss Camp Barn Swallow so much, it's all I can do not to lose my mind. I don't remember one specific thing, it's the entire summer, as a whole. These memories are kind of confused. I remember events but I don't remember faces or voices.

But that one night when we cut a certain something into the bark of the willow—that, I remember in detail. Yura, how are you? Are you doing okay? How's your health? Are you sleeping well? Do you have friends? Did you get a girlfriend yet? You don't write anything about that.

When they replied to each other in their letters, they never explicitly addressed the questions that had subtexts. For regular questions they'd write something like, "You asked why I'm still not playing. My answer is that it's because . . ." But for special ones, they developed a special rule: Ask and answer them only in the last paragraph. Volodya's question about Yurka's condition was written in the last paragraph, and Yurka answered him in the last paragraph, too, briefly, but in a way that he knew would be perfectly clear:

Recently on TV they were showing reruns of the live Leningrad-Boston teleconference that first aired when you and I were at Camp Barn Swallow. And one of the Soviet women, answering an American woman's question about whether we in the USSR have TV shows about sex, said "There's no sex in the USSR, and we're strictly opposed to it!" Did you hear about that? Absolutely hilarious. The guys from my building—by the way, I see them about once every hundred years; they're all the same—are always repeating "There's no sex in the USSR" any chance they get. And you know what? I'm getting a little tired of it.

Yurka wasn't lying. He knew perfectly well even without any TV or newspapers just how false that claim was, even though he didn't engage in the supposedly nonexistent activity again himself, either in 1986 or in 1987.

Yura took another step. Another square concrete paver, another year: 1988. A year that flew by insanely fast. A year in which he and Volodya were again unable to meet. If the paver really had been a newspaper, then the most attention-grabbing headlines would've doubtless been "Shortages Increasing: Essential Goods Beginning to Disappear from Shelves," "AIDS Epidemic! Number of Infected Grows to 32," and "Richter, Diaghilev, and Tchaikovsky, too? Famous Homosexuals of the USSR and Russia."

A liberal, uncensored media was coming into being. In newspapers and magazines, people started bringing up topics that used to be not just unacceptable, but unimaginable! The concept of "prostitution," for example. Now there were articles saying not just that it existed currently but that it had apparently always existed, in the eighties, and in the seventies, and in the sixties! (By 1989, there was even a Soviet movie about prostitutes: *Interdevochka*.) Yurka watched Yeltsin on TV and saw *Little Vera* at the movie theater, where he saw sex on the big screen for the first time.

Yurka continued getting ready for the conservatory entrance exam, studying music both new and old as well as composing his own pieces. Inspired by his memories of Camp Barn Swallow, he wrote a melancholy melody and sent Volodya the sheet music with a note: "This is about the unfinished barracks. Remember?" Then he waited, so nervous his hands shook, to see what Volodya would say. To his great delight, Volodya's answer came quickly:

> I asked a classmate of mine and she was able to play your melody on the piano. Yura, I liked it so much! Please write more music! Write about the willow, about our theater, about the curtain . . . I mean, write about whatever you want—the main thing is that you write!
>
> A friend of mine has a Japanese tape recorder. I'll borrow it for a day and ask my classmate to play it again and I'll record her playing. So that'll be great, to be able to listen to your melody over and over again, whenever I want! To remember camp, and of course to remember you.

In 1988, people began talking openly about homosexuality in the USSR. Yurka found out about a new epithet: "blue," a slang term for "gay man."

The newspapers were filled with articles about great figures of world culture "who were also." People talked contemptuously about "homosexuals," making jokes and ridiculing them. But Yurka didn't think of himself as one of them. For him, everything was the same as it had been before: he loved someone, and that person apparently loved him, too, and that was that. But Volodya, on the other hand, was starting to fall apart: "Do you have a girlfriend? Yura, get a girlfriend," he advised, but Yurka couldn't figure out whether he was being playful or serious. In the very next letter, though, the advice turned into a demand, which was then repeated every time, bounding with its slanted, narrow cursive handwriting from letter to letter.

"You ask about it as though a girl was some kind of house pet," said Yurka, deflecting Volodya with a joke. But then he added, seriously: "See how many good people are one of 'them'? Wait, no—not good people: great people!"

But Volodya wasn't to be placated. And the last straw for him was when the AIDS outbreak in Elista was announced on TV:

> Yura, do you know about AIDS? It's this disease they have in the West. It's fatal. Prostitutes, bums, and 'they' get it. It takes people who get it a very, very long time to die, and they suffer horribly," wrote Volodya, pressing so hard that in a few places there were tiny holes in the paper. "Nature invented an incurable disease to exterminate people like me! It means I have to go to the doctor before it's too late, otherwise on top of everything else I'll get it, too! And how much harm will I cause then? Because you heard about what happened in Elista, right? Some hospital missed that a patient had AIDS and infected five adults and twenty-seven children with an unsterilized needle! And it looks as though those aren't even the final figures! And, Yura, that patient was just like me; how else could he have gotten AIDS?!

Yurka replied that Volodya was just having a panic attack and that he needed to calm down and stop taking responsibility for all the world's problems. He wrote that the disease didn't just pop up out of nowhere, and that he knew Volodya knew it perfectly well himself; that the disease was a virus, and a virus kills without choosing its victims because it's inanimate, it doesn't care. But Volodya wouldn't budge. His fear of getting it grew so strong that it imprinted itself in his mind and his mentions of his own "disease" became more and more frequent: "It's the cause of all my problems. I have to go to the doctor for treatment. And it's high time you got a girlfriend. Otherwise, who knows . . ."

Yurka ignored the comments about a girlfriend and "who knows." He knew that with letters alone he'd be unable to calm Volodya down; they needed to see each other, or at least talk. Yurka begged Volodya time and time again to find a person with a home telephone whom Yurka could call from a phone booth, but Volodya always refused.

Yurka, worn out as he was by Volodya's panic, didn't spare a thought for himself. Desperation flowed from every single line of Volodya's letters, and even though Yurka knew it was temporary, and that Volodya would eventually calm down, his fear was weighing down Yurka's heart like a millstone. Yurka would've done anything to make Volodya feel even a tiny bit better. He would've accepted and forgiven him anything—except "treatment."

Sometimes Yurka succumbed to Volodya's panic, too. Then he would go get the picture of the group in the theater and look for a long time at him and Volodya: weary, overworked, and sleep-deprived, but beaming, because they were together. They were at each other's sides. That photo was a genuine, delicate treasure in black and white, the most important thing in the world. When Yurka looked at it, and remembered what had happened in the past, and imagined how he and Volodya would meet in the future, he calmed down. They had been afraid of a lot back then, too, but they'd still been together and been happy. And if they'd been happy once, it meant they'd be happy again!

As Volodya's panic continued, Yurka gradually realized, with a sickening sense of helplessness, that he was indeed going to have to give Volodya the world's best calming remedy: the picture of the theater group. Copies had been passed out at Yurka's mom's factory, since that was the easiest way to get the pictures to the kids, but Yurka knew that Volodya didn't get one, since, like some of the other camp employees, he had no connection to the factory that sponsored the camp and was from a different city. Hoping that once Volodya saw them together and remembered, he would come back to his senses, at least a little, Yurka took the photo out of the frame and, with heavy heart, mailed it to Volodya. Yurka didn't comment on this act at all, continuing to write about the same thing in different ways:

> On TV they said AIDS is transmitted through blood. And my father says that to avoid getting it, you have to keep from getting cut, and you have to stay away from other people's cuts—that is, from their blood. And you have to use only your own needles, and bring your own scalpels to operations. My mom says you have to bring all your own scissors and clippers when you go to the salon. But none of those things apply to you, do they? No! So everything is okay, you don't need to do anything. Just take a sedative and get some sleep.

What Yurka really wanted to ask Volodya about was sex. Was Volodya having it with anyone? And if so, was he using a condom? But he was embarrassed to write that kind of thing. So instead of questions, he sent Volodya a few booklets his dad had brought home from the hospital. Every single one of them had "AIDS is sexually transmitted" written on it in giant letters.

On top of everything else, Yurka was starving for information. If the Elista outbreak really had been caused by one of "them," then what did they do with the guy? Had they tried to cure him—not of AIDS, which was obviously incurable, but of "that disease"? And if so, how? And what even was it, anyway?

It was useless to ask Volodya, but Yurka had to feed that hunger for information somehow. So he took a desperate measure: he asked his father.

"It's a mental disorder," replied his father tersely, hiding his face behind the newspaper.

"Genetic or acquired?" Yurka demanded.

"I don't know."

"But you're a doctor! And you talk to other doctors!"

"I'm a surgeon." His father suddenly put down the paper and studied Yurka's face with his stern, doctor-examining-a-patient look: "Why are you even asking?"

Yurka sighed heavily and dropped his gaze to the floor. Telling the truth about Volodya would be a betrayal. But as far as he was concerned—no, despite his love for Volodya, Yurka still couldn't describe himself that way to himself, much less to his parents.

"I'm just curious," he scoffed. "It's true, though: Look how many of them there are!" He nodded at the radio, which was playing a song by the deliberately shocking Valery Leontiev.

A disgusted expression similar to Yurka's own distorted his father's face. His father hid behind the newspaper again and muttered, "It's abnormal, in any case, and you'd be best keeping your distance from people like that. They could start to affect you psychologically and make you get off track."

"How do you treat it?"

His father lowered the newspaper again to look at him and frowned.

"Yura, I'm a surgeon!" For the first time in a month his father raised his voice. "They used to treat it in special clinics, but I don't know exactly how. And I know even less about what they do about it now, or whether they even do anything at all. Everything has been turned topsy-turvy. Those blues should be isolated from normal people, but instead they're performing onstage. Have you seen that Leontiev?"

It was a rhetorical question. Yurka was still just as information-starved, but now, after his conversation, he felt almost dirty. He left the conversation empty-handed. On the radio, Leontiev—the flamboyant performer his father hated so much—was finishing up his song about Afghanistan. It wasn't topical anymore: the war in Afghanistan had ended, and the USSR's troops had been removed that spring.

The hysteria over the AIDS outbreak in Elista made people forget, temporarily, what else was happening in their country. The shortage of food products was getting worse. Stockpiled cases of canned fish were stacked in the corners of Yurka's family's kitchen. His mother pickled every single vegetable from his grandma's garden and got on his nerves by constantly repeating the rumors that soon the salaries at the factory where she worked would be paid in what the factory manufactured: ball bearings. His father got into the habit of reading the crime news. He'd hide his face behind the newspaper without saying much, and more and more often he just smoked his dwindling supply of cigarettes in complete silence. Yurka quit smoking, but he, too, read about the constant shootouts, the arson, and people being tortured with irons. When the words "racket" and "racketeering" became commonplace, when even regular people found themselves having to deal with the mafia, that was when the entire Konev family first started seriously considering emigrating to East Germany. But in 1988 it was still too hard.

The concrete paver of 1989, all shot through with cracks and overgrown with weeds, crunched under Yura's boot. That year had been overflowing with anxiety because Volodya had calmed down far too abruptly and quickly, and also because Yurka had taken and failed the conservatory entrance exams, and because of his family's search for ways to leave the USSR. The Iron Curtain had fallen and all paths were open to Yurka, but the past didn't want to let him leave, while the future didn't want to let him in. That whole endlessly long year, as he waited for something different, Yurka was tormented by a premonition: "You think it's bad now, but just you wait. It's going to get worse."

The smell of vinegar would permeate the apartment for weeks on end. Every day, Yurka's mother would watch the dubbed Brazilian soap *Isaura: Slave Girl* while boiling either jam or jeans (doing a homemade acid wash). Commercials appeared on TV for the first time. More and more new TV programs kept appearing. Yurka watched his father's beloved *600 Seconds* and *Fifth Wheel* out of the corner of his eye.

The airwaves were also filled with something fundamentally new, something even more strange and suspicious: performances by the faith healer Allan Chumak and the hypnotist Anatoly Kashpirovsky. Of the latter, who had been popularly nicknamed "Koshmarovsky"—"Nightmare-ovsky"—Volodya wrote, "Hypnosis is a charlatan's trick, it doesn't actually work . . ."

To which Yurka replied by asking, "In the unfinished barracks you were saying hypnosis was what would help you, so how are you coming to this conclusion now?"

But Volodya responded evasively: "A friend of mine went to one. He had another problem, not like mine: he can't sleep. And since it couldn't solve his problem, there's no way it'll solve mine."

Yurka started to suspect that Volodya didn't have any such friend and that he'd tried it himself. On the one hand, Yurka knew hypnosis wasn't as dangerous as other "cures," like getting shots to induce nausea, so he relaxed somewhat. But then he got panicky all over again: if Volodya had gone to that kind of doctor, he might go to another kind of doctor, too. So he began to focus on convincing Volodya to wait before going to a psychiatrist.

In the midst of these negotiations, as tense as trade talks, he forgot how angry he'd been at himself for failing the conservatory entrance exams. What would've once been a huge blow to his self-esteem before was unimportant now. Yurka knew he'd try again next year, and that if he failed then, he'd try again, and eventually he'd get in. Trying to get in and not making it—that wasn't a failure. Quitting his studies was the failure. But an even worse failure would be letting Volodya mess himself up.

Not even a month went by before Yurka's fears began to be substantiated. Volodya's letters were different. His handwriting had changed! Whereas Yurka used to be able to recognize Volodya's mood from the way he wrote, now Yurka was haunted by the distinct sensation that the letters were being written by someone else entirely. Volodya's handwriting was now looser and bigger. But what was even scarier was that he'd started making basic spelling and punctuation mistakes, which would have been completely impossible for the Volodya Yurka knew. But before asking Volodya directly whether he'd gone in for treatment, Yurka reread all Volodya's letters several times to catch anything he'd missed before. Yurka was trying to pinpoint when exactly Volodya had changed, to guess what had caused the change—because despite what Volodya had seemed to think, the AIDS outbreak in Elista had nothing to do with either of them, and in his heart of hearts Yurka thought this reason was so stupid that it couldn't possibly be the cause. But no matter how many times he sat down to reread the whole heap of Volodya's letters, no matter how carefully he read, he was unable to discern a cause or even a date when Volodya had suddenly changed. Eventually he began to doubt whether there had ever even been a reason, and whether Volodya had actually changed at all . . .

There was no help for it. Yurka started asking to come visit and inviting Volodya to visit him. But Volodya refused to either come visit or let Yurka visit him. Yurka even threatened to come anyway, but the threats had no effect. Apparently, Volodya had guessed that Yurka simply didn't have enough money for tickets, and so he replied in broad, sweeping handwriting: "Yura, do you remember our agreement? I won't come see you or invite you to see me until you get into conservatory."

Yurka was dumbfounded. The conservatory?! In his last paragraph, he scrawled, "Did you mean that about the conservatory? I'll still have so long to wait! Volod, I miss you, I really want to see you. What's going on? Because I can tell something's off. Be honest: Did you go to treatment?"

Volodya's response was some time in coming. Yurka had grown tired of waiting and was about to write Volodya again when he saw the familiar colored-in corner of a letter in his mailbox. He opened the envelope with trembling hands and took out the letter. In the last paragraphs he read, "I wanted to lie to you, but I realized I can't. You don't deserve lies. But I was in no hurry to talk, either, until I'd made up my mind for sure.

> Yes, Yura, I did confess to my parents. I would've had to do it at some point anyway, but what happened at Elista made me do it now. It was scary to talk and hard to begin. The thing I was most afraid of was that they wouldn't take the news seriously, like the way Irina didn't believe Masha that time. But they believed me. They were in shock, of course. I really disappointed them. But the main thing is that they understood: it's as much a problem for them as it is for me. It took my father a long time to find a doctor who'd give me treatments unofficially so my records wouldn't show I'd been to a psychiatric clinic. And also because he'd started his own business and made a name for himself in certain circles, so there was his reputation, too... You get it.
>
> The doctor and I talk for a long time at our sessions. He prescribed me some pills and said that if I have people I'm close to, people I can be open with, I should both tell them about the disease and let them know I'm in treatment for it, in case I need their moral support. He also told me to start looking at the pretty girls around me. Just look at them for now, not meet anyone or go on dates. This is so I learn to see their beauty. It's funny, Yur, but I see it perfectly well already,

and in fact I think a lot of girls are pretty, but . . . not a single one of them attracts me. But that's just right now, I hope . . . not permanently . . .

Yurka read the letter and felt the hair raising on the back of his neck. He was scared, both for Volodya and for himself. Inside him, his hurt shouted, "He wants to cure himself of me! Of his love for me! He wants to forget everything! After all the times I asked him not to go, he still went, he still did everything his way! He betrayed me!"

But once his emotions calmed a little, other thoughts occurred to Yurka. Volodya hadn't betrayed him. He had told him the truth. He was still thinking about Yurka. He needed him! Volodya's letter was a cry for help, after all. He needed support. Yurka realized that Volodya had it even harder now: the fact that Volodya's parents knew, and were even paying for his treatment, made it Volodya's responsibility to ensure the treatment was a success. But what if it wasn't, or what if it took a long time? If Yurka, his single, solitary real friend, didn't support him, then he'd be the one betraying Volodya. However much it hurt him—however much he doubted that Volodya even needed treatment—he had to help.

Yurka spent a long time composing his reply to Volodya's letter. He wasn't satisfied until the fourth version:

> Volodya, you know perfectly well that you're my only close friend. I asked you not to go. I won't lie, I'm not happy you did it, but I trust you. If you decided it was your only choice, that you'd only feel better by going to a doctor, then I support you. But I'm also even more worried about you now. Tell me how everything's going. Are you sure it's not causing you harm? What kind of pills are you taking? Do they help? How?
>
> I'll say it again, and I'll keep saying it over and over: you are my only friend, my best friend, my dearest friend. You can be honest with me about everything. Absolutely everything, always. Don't feel awkward about any of it, okay?
>
> I'm really looking forward to your reply. I want to know everything about you. If I can help in any way, just tell me, and I will.

This time the letter from Volodya took two days longer to arrive than usual, leaving Yurka plenty of time to wear himself out worrying. "We just talk. The doctor asks me about everything. It was hard for me to open up to him. It's too personal, after all. But he's a psychiatrist: I can trust him with what has been tormenting and terrifying me for so long. And these conversations really are making me feel better. The pills are just sedatives. Thanks to them, I've stopped having panic attacks and I've stopped washing my hands in burning-hot water—remember that old habit? Looks like this treatment really is helping me!"

And no matter how much these letters scared Yurka, no matter how much they made him feel like Volodya was growing more and more distant from him, Yurka was glad for his friend. If Volodya was feeling better, if it was helping Volodya, then all Yurka could do was support him. And he did, that whole year.

That autumn, the international news hit like a thunderclap: the Berlin Wall had fallen.

The physical boundary between East Germany and West Germany no longer existed. Officially, the two countries weren't planning on reunifying for a long time, but Yurka's uncle heard from his friends in the government of East Germany that unification was going to happen, and not in the distant future but soon. He wrote Yurka's mom that the whole family had to pull it together and get to the East German consulate first, because immigrating to Germany would be even harder once the countries united. His mother went.

Listening to her, Yurka was astonished at how difficult it was. For the time being, the only way they could immigrate was as a Jewish family. For that to happen, then at least his mother, if not all of them, had to have the word "Jew" showing in her passport as her designated ethnicity, and she had to be a member of a Jewish religious community. But the ethnicity listed in his mother's passport was Russian. And despite all Yurka's grandma's efforts, Yurka's mother had stubbornly refused to join any Jewish organization. The only thing she'd agree to do was let Yurka be circumcised. Yurka's grandma had changed both her first and last names back at the beginning of the war, and on top of that all her German documents, including her marriage certificate, had been destroyed. His grandpa's life had come to an end in

Dachau, which meant that Yurka's mother and Yurka were legally eligible to be treated as victims of the Holocaust, but they still had to prove they were related to him. The only relative they had in Germany, the uncle on his grandfather's side, was his mother's cousin, and Yurka's cousin twice removed, so it wasn't clear whether this relationship would be of any help to the Konevs. The one thing that was crystal clear, however, was that they'd have to track down and replace a great many identification documents. In spite of everything, though, none of them—not Yurka, not his parents, not the uncle—lost faith in their return to their historical motherland.

Meanwhile, a terrible time of shortages began in the USSR. The stores ran out of everything, even soap and laundry powder. Staples like macaroni and buckwheat kasha were nowhere to be found. Yurka's family, like all the rest, began getting ration tickets for sugar. Yurka's father began to work longer and longer hours; sometimes he was stuck at work for whole days at a time. His mother was bedridden from a long bout of pneumonia. Yurka, already used to standing in hours-long lines, stood even longer now in lines of enraged citizens, reading his German textbook while freezing and listening to people talking about the coal miners' strike: half a million people beating their helmets on the pavement.

In Kharkiv, everything was more or less calm, but Volodya wrote that in Moscow it wasn't just the coal miners but all the rest of the Soviet citizenry, too, tired of always being half-starved, that was going out to demonstrate. And Volodya, always with his keen interest in political events, went right out with them.

As he stepped onto the next square concrete paver, Yura looked at its blank surface, wet and glistening, and for some reason felt like any minute now an ant would run out onto it from the grass, and then another one, and then more and more of them, until the entire paver was crisscrossed with long lines of ants, the way the entire year of 1990 had been crisscrossed with lines. There had been lines everywhere, for everything you could imagine: vodka, cigarettes, food . . . They stretched out from stores and kiosks; they stood unmoving in front of the conservatory's administrative offices; they swelled to kilometer-long columns at embassies.

The whole country was in a fever. In every news program Yurka saw the same thing—he could've recited it from memory: "Alcoholism and crime rates have grown to epic proportions," "Profiteers are getting fat," and "Refugees from Nagorno-Karabakh are hiding everywhere." The programs spoke about how the cigarette shortage made the populace run riot: they went on strike and stopped production lines, they burned and looted stores, and they overturned bigwigs' cars. People started referring to the Soviet Union contemptuously as sovok, "dustpan."

But Yurka felt that the TV news reports must be exaggerating things. Yes, all that did exist, but life didn't seem quite that doom-and-gloomy to him. In some ways it was just the opposite, blooming with vibrant color: now there were uncensored, nongovernmental radio stations that played so much new music that it seemed like Yurka never heard the same song twice. At dance clubs he knew that people were dancing the lambada, although he didn't go out dancing himself or look up girls' miniskirts; he just sat at home, working hard on his German and continuing to prepare for his conservatory entrance exams. Now he was practicing on his own: his family couldn't pay the tutor anymore since his mother had been cut to part-time and his father hadn't gotten his pay in several months. But Yurka worked hard, putting in as much time as he could at the piano. He mentally prepared himself for another failure. This time, though, this time—he got in!

"I did it!" Yurka wrote in his next letter.

> I thought they'd fail me again, but I finally did it, Volodya! Just like I promised you! And now that I've made it, everything's different in my mind. I used to dream about becoming a pianist, but now it's not a dream anymore, it's a goal. And what I really want now is something else: not to play music, but to write it. My dream is to become a composer. I dream of writing something special, something that doesn't just sound good but is full of meaning. And in the last paragraph of his letter, Yurka reminded Volodya of their agreement: I remember you promised we'd meet as soon as I made it into conservatory. So there you go!

For days there was no reply, but Yurka chalked it up to issues with the postal service. When the answer did come a week later, Volodya was so happy for him that Yurka smiled as he read. But Volodya wouldn't agree to meet, saying that he had absolutely no time since he'd failed one of his exams and the retake was scheduled in September. He had to study for that, plus he had to help his dad with the business, and also it wasn't a good time to be in Moscow, what with all the demonstrations and riots and strikes.

"And another thing," wrote Volodya. "I want to ask you to hold off on our meeting for a while, since I'm afraid it might have a negative effect on my treatment. Because, Yur, I remember you . . .

> I'm learning how to control myself. For example, at the last session the psychiatrist brought in some pictures of . . . well, pictures he thought I'd like. Then he started asking me to say what I could possibly like about them, how I could even like them, but get this: of the twenty pictures he showed me, only one caught my eye! And even that was probably just because it really reminded me of our last night at camp. Then he gave me other pictures, of women this time. And this time he also asked me to look at them closely and talk about what specifically I liked about this one or that one, and what I didn't like at all. And he gave me some homework.
>
> You asked me to be very honest. It's a little hard to do, but I'll try. Because we're grown-ups, after all, and even though this is something people don't talk about in polite company, it's different for us—we can understand each other. So anyway . . . he gave me some pictures to take home, pictures that are the kind I'm supposed to like later after we've cured my disease. He said that sometime when I'm by myself I should try to relax and take a good long look at the prettiest ones, so that . . . Well, you get it . . . so I learn how to get real physical pleasure from looking at them and imagining things . . . And Yur—! What a relief! I did it! I thought only about what I saw in the picture, and I was able to! I was able to do it!

It took Yurka an effort of will to suppress the emotions Volodya's letter called forth. What helped most was the realization that this was the lesser of two evils: he knew that if Volodya hadn't been suffering from these problems, he would have been in a relationship with a real person by now and would have been doing real things with that person, not just imagining things when he was alone.

So they didn't broach the topic of a visit anymore. Their letters to each other went flat and neutral. Yurka finally accepted that the treatment was helping Volodya and making him happier. Yurka should've been glad, but in reality it made him uncomfortable. It seemed as though once Volodya had rid himself of his fear, he'd also rid himself of his thoughts about Yurka: he had forgotten him, stopped loving him.

That letter was the last one that year in which Volodya wrote about anything personal.

In October, the thing Yurka's uncle had been saying would happen did happen: the unification of Germany. The Konevs went to the embassy, stood in line for five hours, and finally succeeded in submitting their documentation.

Three families that Yurka's parents knew had already managed to leave for the West, and it made Yurka's mom go from difficult to completely unbearable. Almost daily, her voice dripping with poisonous envy, she counted off the names of coworkers who had gotten out: "The Mankos left. The Kolomiyetses left. Even the Tyndiks left! Never mind that in America they're nothing, while we have full right to German citizenship! We waited too long to try! How much longer will it be now? Until we die of hunger?!"

Yurka's dad could never refrain from a weary, reluctant, half-whispered rebuttal: "You don't have to be a citizen to move to Germany."

In November the only people in their building that the Konevs were friends with left. This turn of events devastated Yurka's mother.

"I'm an engineer!" she fumed constantly. "I have an advanced degree! I gave my whole life to that damn factory! I ruined my health! And what do I get in return? I get my salary paid in ball bearings! But Valka, that trashy street vendor with her dinky little stall, eking out a living bringing in crappy clothes from Turkey—that Valka, she gets out! She's living it up!"

She didn't blame Yurka's father, although his salary hadn't been paid in months; she blamed the German embassy and the world as a whole. Her health really had taken a turn for the worse. She'd started having lung problems. The unrelenting illnesses and poverty had finally and irrevocably ruined her once kind disposition. As though she were seeking yet another piece of proof of how bad things were, she even asked about Yurka's pen friend, "the one from Moscow": How were they faring out there in the capital? "Just as badly as we are?"

Yurka shrugged vaguely. "Probably so . . ." But he couldn't add any specifics. Volodya's family wasn't suffering. Volodya's father had really thrown himself into his business. He'd started a construction company and in less than a year had started pulling in such a profit that Volodya's mother didn't need to keep working. Volodya himself continued his studies at MGIMO while also devouring economics textbooks on the side so he could start helping his dad as soon as possible.

Smiling, Yurka wrote Volodya: "Now there's an irony of fate: the country is falling apart, but you are building it back up."

When he said the country was falling apart, Yurka meant it literally. In 1989 and 1990, one by one the republics of the Soviet Union began to declare independence. This Parade of Sovereignties was the beginning of the end of the USSR.

In the letter before last, Volodya had joked, "Who knows? Maybe by next year our different cities will be in different countries. Wait while I settle some things here and establish that my treatment worked, and then I'll come see you while we're still citizens of the same country." In answer to the "you are building it back up," Volodya said modestly:

> I'm doing what I can to help, but there's not much use for experts in international law here. On the other hand, I know English. I got a bunch of textbooks on market economics and Pops scrounged up a couple of books on how to run a business. 'It's called management,' he explained. So I'm sitting here, studying. It's important. The country's transitioning from a planned economy to a market economy, and nobody knows how to do business in this new environment. But I'm going to know. My brains will be our company's advantage. Now don't you dare think I'm bragging! It's too early to brag.

"Citizens of the same country," Yurka repeated aloud. He felt his heart drop like a stone. He was in no hurry to inform Volodya that the German embassy had finally accepted their documents and moved them to the next stage. Yurka was afraid both of jinxing his application and of breaking the bad news to Volodya any sooner than he had to. Yurka had written Volodya about Germany more than once, but he'd talked about it casually, as an aside, with no faith that he really had a chance. But now, all of a sudden, it hit home that they really might end up in different countries after all. Maybe even on different continents. Because even if Yurka didn't end up living in Germany, Volodya had always dreamed of hightailing it out to America. And Volodya was so stubborn that if he really, truly wanted to do something, he did it. Yurka knew that.

He'd no sooner opened Volodya's latest letter than he knew it had been written hurriedly, in a panic. It was wrinkled and full of blots, and the letters tilted over onto each other, and the lines of writing weren't even but slid down at the end:

> That filth is crawling back into my brain again! The pills only help every so often, and I can't repeat my earlier success with the pictures because I keep getting distracted thinking about that! And I've started having dreams again! Today I had such a vivid dream that when I woke up, I almost lost it. Why isn't this real?!
>
> I dreamed I was standing on a platform at a train station and in the crowd of people coming out of a train car I see U. She smiles and I put my arms around her. We go down into the metro. We're standing on the escalator, going down, but instead of looking around to admire one of the most beautiful metro stations, U. looks only at me. It's like she doesn't care where she is or what's happening around her; all she cares about is me. We go to the VDNKh pavilion and sit by the rockets that are on display and stroll around the fountains. It's hot. She puts her face and hands into the water. Then we take the metro back home. I lay my jacket over our knees

and hold her hand tightly underneath it. We're at my place. There's nobody else home. I fold out the sleeper sofa. She gets a jar of cherry jam out of her bag and puts it on the table.

Yurka knew that "U." was "you" and "she" was "he." Volodya was writing about him. Yurka could tell Volodya was panicking. He knew how bad Volodya must be feeling and that Volodya was scared. But at the same time Yurka couldn't stop smiling: Volodya was dreaming about him! And even though joy was completely inappropriate at the moment, he couldn't keep his emotions in check when he wrote his reply. Once he'd sent it, he bitterly regretted what he'd said: "I don't give a damn about secrecy! I'm not 'she'! And I still love you! And also . . . we submitted our documents at the embassy. I'm probably moving to Germany soon."

He sent that letter at the end of December. Three days later he got a telegram from Volodya: DO NOT WRITE ME THIS ADDRESS ANYMORE. WILL WRITE YOU MYSELF LATER.

The concrete paver for 1990 was the last one. After that, the ground broke off in a sandy cliff. The year 1990 was when his and Volodya's relationship suddenly broke off, too.

CHAPTER TWENTY
IN SEARCH OF LOST...

Volodya's telegram was a shock for Yurka. Why couldn't Yurka write? What happened? Yurka's thoughts ricocheted from bad to worse: *Volodya's parents read my last letter, realized who I was to him, and now blame me for messing up his treatment! Or maybe it's that Volodya himself wants to get rid of me and my interference? Because I was the one he dreamed of, I'm getting him off track. Doesn't he need me anymore?*

Yurka's guilt, and his fear for Volodya, kept him from disobeying and writing to ask what had happened. Logic calmly reminded him, "No matter what, Volodya's too grown-up now for his parents to punish their son for something somebody else said." But his fear whispered, "Volodya and his father are in business together, and that means he's still dependent on his father." And the very worst times were when his hurt feelings tormented him: "Volodya was looking for an excuse to break off our relationship, and I'm the one who gave it to him. He really doesn't need me anymore. He never did." He barely listened when his memory pointed out, "Volodya's getting paranoid again. This has happened before, more than once."

Still, Yurka waited for that "later" to arrive and for Volodya to write him. But no letters came.

Yurka was exhausted by doubt and uncertainty. Nothing could make him smile. His apathy made itself felt in every way. He was sleeping badly and eating badly. He was taciturn and soon became completely withdrawn. He was indifferent to everything and even lost interest in music. He made it through the interminably long winter. In the spring of 1991 he was briefly drawn out of his stupor by good news from the embassy. His mother, beaming with genuine delight, ran right into the kitchen without even taking off her coat and shoes, shouting, "We're approved!"

"I'm leaving! I'm actually leaving!" Yura was happy, for the first time in a long while.

But soon his happiness evaporated. He was leaving! But what about Volodya?

In May they found out their departure date and other details. There was no time to waste. Despite Volodya's request not to write, Yura sent him a brief note: "We're leaving in July. First they're sending us to a distribution center, then from there they'll transfer us to our permanent place of residence. I don't know the permanent address yet, but here's a temporary one."

May was coming to a close, but Yura still hadn't heard from Volodya. His heart pounded like crazy every time he approached the mailbox: maybe there was a letter! He startled every time the doorbell rang: maybe it was a telegram! But he never got an answer.

Once June started, Yura had no choice but to borrow money from friends and go to Moscow himself.

He stepped off the train and plunged into the chaos of Moscow. He definitely did not like it. It was like a seething cauldron: too aggressive, too noisy, too dirty. Everything from the pavement to the sky was plastered in posters of Yeltsin, Zhirinovsky, and other candidates in the upcoming election for president of the RSFSR—the first such election ever. Half the city's parks and squares were taken over by demonstrations and rallies, but even if you didn't take those into account, Moscow was still too dirty and too loud. The city looked to Yurka like one big street market where people haggled over clothes when they weren't haggling over rights and freedoms. Street vendors were everywhere: in the squares, in and around the metro stations, and even standing in rows along the sidewalks of busy streets, next to the panhandlers and lines of people. Throughout the city, high above the political posters, hung banners advertising the Russian production of David Henry Hwang's *M. Butterfly* by the Soviet Ukrainian director Roman Viktyuk: the first show with homosexuality as a theme. And all this was engulfed by the endlessly scurrying populace.

Yurka had never been in the capital until this moment. He'd previously dreamed of visiting Lenin's mausoleum as soon as he got there, but once he arrived he completely forgot about it and went straight to Volodya's metro station.

He more or less figured out where he was on the map and was so concentrated on the purpose of his trip that he paid no attention to the beauty—or ugliness—of the metro. Or to what Volodya's apartment building looked like: a yellow, four-story, Stalin-era building with stone balconies and picturesque ivy growing up the sides. Or to what Volodya's courtyard looked like: shady and quiet, with a statue of Pioneer girls poring over their books. Or to the smell of Volodya's building entrance. Yurka only came back to his senses and began to notice at least some of the things around him when he found himself at the door to Volodya's apartment.

He rang the doorbell. Nobody opened the door. He pressed his ear to the door: silence.

Yurka settled in to wait. He remembered that Volodya's mom didn't work anymore, which meant she had probably stepped out for a little while and would soon return. It was getting on toward four o'clock and he was counting on the fact that in a couple more hours somebody would definitely be showing up. He tensed at every rustle, hoping it was one of the residents of the hallowed apartment coming up the stairs. But nobody ever came all the way up to the fourth and last floor; nobody went to Volodya's door. One grumbling old granny did shuffle past Yurka and survey him suspiciously, but she ducked into the apartment next door without a word.

An hour later, the granny cracked her door open, without undoing the security chain, and yelled rudely at Yurka: "Who are you? What are you sitting here for?"

"I'm waiting for someone," he said, and turned away. Then, thinking better of it, he jumped up: "I'm a friend of Volodya Davydov. He lives here. Do you happen to know if anybody's coming home soon?"

"You go on home, then. They're not coming back."

"What do you mean?"

"The whole family left. Six months ago now," replied the granny, continuing to drill a hole in Yurka with her gaze. "Just before New Year's."

Yura's throat seized up. He croaked out: "But why?"

"How should I know? They didn't tell me," answered the granny sharply. But she made no move to close her door.

"Have the other neighbors said anything?" asked Yurka, trying to get the woman to at least share some rumors. *I mean, she is a granny,* thought Yura, *and grannies are all equally nosy, no matter where you are in the USSR. This one's probably no exception.* He was right.

"People talk, but how much of it's worth listening to?" said the old woman, frowning. A minute later, though, she broke her silence: "Lev Nikolayevich got mixed up with some bandits. He borrowed money from them and then couldn't pay them back. He signed the apartment over to them and he and his family escaped."

"Lev Nikolayevich?" This was Volodya's father. "What about Volodya? Are you sure they weren't after him?"

"I saw it myself. More than once. A car would stop at the entrance and Lev Nikolayevich would get in. Then he'd get back out. Then the bandits started coming right up to the apartment. They'd come banging on the door at all hours of the night. I'd call the police, but they'd be long gone by the time the police showed up."

The first thing Yurka felt upon hearing this was relief: he had spent so long blaming himself for Volodya's disappearance, afraid he'd outed their relationship to his parents and revealed that the treatment didn't work. But now it turned out Yura had had nothing to do with it. The thing that was the real reason for Volodya's disappearance—or rather full-on escape—was far worse: his family had been run out. And the granny's story was entirely plausible, because in those days it was impossible for businessmen to get by without borrowing money, but the only people who had money were the bandits. So there were only two ways to keep afloat: either borrow from a bandit, or become one. The sudden upswing in Volodya's family's income was confirmation of that, he realized: it was impossible to just start out from zero with the kind of thing that's as long-term as construction and make that kind of income after just one year.

"And what about Volodya?" Yura asked hoarsely. "Did he leave with his parents? Because he's grown, he's in college . . ."

"You tell me. You're the one who said you're his friend."

"We haven't seen each other in a long time, I haven't—"

"And there's no telling what's wrong with that Volodya, anyway," the granny interrupted. "He was a good boy. He always said hello, helped me carry up the shopping. But then at the end he got all jittery. Always peering around wide-eyed. Stopped saying hello."

Yurka feverishly cast about for his next move. How would he find Volodya now? "Where might they be? Do you know?"

The granny shrugged so hard that the security chain on her door clinked.

"What about relatives or friends?" said Yura, inspired. "His cousin! He had a cousin with the same exact name! Where do their relatives or friends live?"

"I believe they had someone in Tver," replied the granny. "Now, you go on along. You can't wait for them. They're not coming back."

Yura asked a couple more questions, but the granny had no answers. He asked about the institute—"He was a student. D, did he really just quit?"—but on that note their conversation ended.

Yura flopped down on the top stair like a rag doll. He stretched and limbered his fingers, which had gone numb from the shock, and stared at the gray floor, trying to sort out the fragments of thought wheeling through his head: *They escaped. Bandits. They're hiding. If they're hiding, then they've hidden well enough not to be found. Tver. Is Tver far? The institute. I have to go to his institute. I have to get ahold of myself. This is my only chance to find him. There'll be no chance later.*

He forced himself to collect his thoughts and stand up. His gaze shifted from the concrete floor to the padded, pleather-covered door of Volodya's apartment. His heart went tight. Yura realized that he would never, ever get inside this apartment. He'd never see Volodya's room. Even if nothing of Volodya was left inside the apartment anymore, even if the couch he'd slept on wasn't in his room anymore, even if the nightstand he'd put his glasses on every night before bed wasn't there, even if the desk he'd sat at wasn't there, then at least the window Volodya had looked out of when he was writing Yurka letters was still there. Yura wanted to look out that window. It felt like that would bring them closer together. Or at least if he could see the marks Volodya's furniture had made on the floor. They'd prove Volodya really existed,. Yura hadn't just been imagining him.

I will find him! I will! His feet moving reluctantly, he made himself walk away down the stairs.

In hopes of finding letters from the Davydovs' friends or relatives, Yura broke open the door of their mailbox. The blood pounded in his head as he saw that there were two letters there! But his hope faded as quickly as it had blossomed: they were his own letters. The second-to-last one, in which he'd declared his love, and the last one, in which he'd said he was leaving in July.

Then, despite the hopelessness of the situation, Yura's spirits lifted just a tiny bit. It hadn't been his fault, after all, that Volodya had sent that last telegram telling him not to write anymore. He hadn't even read the letter that Yura had been so worried about. There was hope after all that Volodya still loved him, still needed him. But this also meant he didn't even know that Yura was leaving soon.

Yura left Volodya's apartment building and went straight to Volodya's institute, where after some effort he found out that Volodya had collected his records and documents and left. And that this had also been just before New Year's.

Yurka spent the whole way to Kursk train station, where he'd get his train back to Kharkiv, trying to decide whether to go to Tver or not. "It's not far. But I don't have much money left. But if I don't at least try, I'll never forgive myself. I'll never forgive myself for it."

The metro was loud, thundering and clattering. On the opposite seat a young man put his jacket down on his girlfriend's lap and tentatively squeezed her hand. It was just like in Volodya's dream, except that this pair didn't have to hide their hands.

It's a sign, thought Yura. So he transferred to another metro line and headed for Leningrad Station, where the train for Tver left from.

Once he got to Tver, he stopped at a post office, bought a phone book, and began calling all the Davydovs one by one. He called over half the numbers, but nobody knew a Vladimir Davydov. His heart skipped a beat when a girl finally said Vladimir was home and called him to the phone. The seconds of waiting stretched into minutes, or hours. It was like Yura had gotten lost in time and space and couldn't tell whether he'd really been waiting for a long time at all. But his wait finally came to an end: Vladimir answered. Yura's heart fell. This Vladimir Davydov was an old man.

Trying not to lose heart, Yura ran his finger down the lines of text in the phone book. A few lines down was something that made his finger tremble: the name Davydov, Vladimir Leonidovich.

Yura stood for half an hour in the telephone booth, the receiver glued to his ear, cursing through gritted teeth: he couldn't get through. The line was busy. It was getting late, but the phone kept giving him nothing but those short, rapid beeps. Yura decided it was time to pay Comrade Davydov a visit.

The entrance of the old Khrushchov-era building reeked of cats. Yurka rang the doorbell. A girl replied from inside, without opening the door. She heard what Yura had to say and called the Vova who lived there to the door. A young voice answered her. The lock clicked and the door opened, revealing a tall, broad-shouldered man of about thirty.

"I'm looking for Volodya Davydov."

"Yes? What can I do for you?"

"It's not you, it's probably your cousin. He lived in Moscow, he had dark hair and glasses, I was at camp with him," babbled Yura, digging in his pocket for the single photo he had of Volodya, in which he was with Troop Five. "Volodya was a troop leader there in '86. The Barn Swallow Pioneer Camp, outside of Kharkiv. I . . . hold on a minute, I've got a picture of him here . . ."

"Don't know who you're talking about," answered Vova brusquely.

"Hold on a second—here's the picture." Yura held the photograph out to Vova, but the man didn't even look at it.

"Don't know who you're talking about," he announced again, and shut the door, pinching the photo between the door and the doorframe. Yura pulled the bent photo back out, straightened it, and saw with dismay that the corner had been torn off.

That was it. The end. Period. But Yurka couldn't bring himself to believe it. He thought he must still have a chance; he just wasn't looking in the right place. He thought he could find Volodya if he just had a little more time.

The only thing left to Yura when he got back to Kharkiv was to pin his hopes on others. He wasn't going to be able to meet the new residents of his apartment, if there even were any: the Konevs' apartment had been state-owned, not theirs, so they hadn't been the ones who sold it to a new owner. Yura wrote a note to the new residents, asking them not to throw away any letters that came to him but to send them to his temporary address in Germany, and left it with the neighbors in the apartment next door to give to them. But he didn't hold high hopes: the neighbors were alcoholics and had always feuded with his parents. In a P.S. to the note Yura added that soon he'd send a letter to this address with a new permanent address in Germany.

He asked his buddies from the building the same thing: to stop by his old apartment every so often, in case the new residents were there, and tell them everything, and also to check the mailbox from time to time, in case a letter from Volodya came.

And that was it.

He did the work of gathering his things and getting ready to leave in a kind of daze. The airport, the flight, the transfer to the distribution center—it was all a blur, too.

And then there he was. It was 1991 and he was in Germany. He hadn't done a single thing to get there, while ever since Volodya had been little he'd dedicated his whole life to getting out to America.

Did he? He has to have. It'd be too unfair otherwise! Yura thought. *Maybe he's already there?*

For a long time he felt utterly foreign in the country. He was ashamed of his accent and cringed every time he heard the word "immigrant." The tone was always disgusting, demeaning. And he was a Russian immigrant to boot. That's what the Germans said, anyway, despite the fact that the entire world had been following the collapse of the USSR and everyone knew that Russia, Ukraine, and Belarus were different countries now. And Yura was not Russian. But what was he—what *could* he be, here? A quarter German, a quarter Jewish, and half Ukrainian, with a good knowledge of German language and history and a lively interest in culture. But knowledge of the language, culture, and history couldn't change the fact that he was an immigrant; in fact, he was something even worse, essentially a refugee. He felt disdain and contempt for himself and hated himself for it.

Trying every day to convince himself that he had no other choice—he had to forget Volodya—Yura lived through his first month in Germany. But it felt to him like surviving, not living.

August had a fantastic beginning: Yura made it into the conservatory immediately, on the first try. But a short while later, on August 19, 1991, a heavy blow awaited him.

He was sitting in his room, testing out a new piano his uncle had given him, when he was startled by someone pounding on his door like a crazy person. It was his mom. She started shouting so loudly that her voice temporarily drowned out the music: "Yura! Come here, quick! Yura, there are tanks in Moscow! Gorbachov's been overthrown! Good Lord, what's happening? Tanks!"

Yura, unable to believe his ears, moved slowly into the living room, overcoming the awful resistance of the air, suddenly thick as soup. He lowered himself onto the sofa in front of the TV and sat there until late at night. And the next morning, too, and all the next day, the images stood before his eyes: Yeltsin on a tank, the crowd around the Russian White House and on Red Square. Later, the press conference held by the State Committee on the State of Emergency, and Yanayev, whose hands shook so badly, he couldn't hold the piece of paper. Yura's hands were shaking just as badly. He was starting to panic. Worse than he ever had before. The kind of panic that had probably tortured Volodya when he was unable to control himself and thrust his hands in burning-hot water.

"What if he never went anywhere? Neither to America nor to Tver? What if he's in Moscow? What if he's there, at the White House? What if those bandits hounding his family were mixed up in politics? What if Volodya's involved with them, with the coup? He used to go to some kind of demonstrations . . ."

That night, things got even worse. The White House was attacked and there were tanks driving along the Garden Ring. When Yura saw people throwing themselves at the tanks and someone was killed, his whole body shook. In the dark of night it was hard to make out who exactly had been killed. It was a young man, with brown hair, no glasses, but he still looked a lot like Volodya.

What if it's him? What if his glasses got broken and that's him? Yurka heard himself thinking, but knew he was just being hysterical. He knew that in the multimillion metropolis of Moscow, there were hundreds of thousands of young men whose build and hair color were similar to Volodya's. But he was scared anyway until the man's identity was confirmed.

Yura wrote to his friends from his building and asked them again to go to his old apartment and see whether any letters had arrived there for him. If they had, he asked them to send the letters on to Germany. He got his answer a month later. His friend wrote that the apartment was still vacant and there were no letters in the mailbox. He also shared the news of what was going on in the country, but Yura had no response to that. He just asked the friend again to make sure and check the mailbox every once in a while.

In December of 1991 the USSR ceased to exist. Yura watched on TV as the Soviet flag over the Kremlin was lowered and the Russian flag raised in its place. Along with the flag of the USSR, a curtain seemed to come down, signaling the end of his old life, and it was like a new curtain lifted up along with the Russian tricolor to reveal a new scene. And that's when Yura realized that not only was his childhood was good and truly over but the place it had occurred was gone, too. It had given him the gifts of love and friendship and then left, taking everything with it. Before him lay a different time, a new time. And a completely different life. Just like Volodya himself had written once, it was time for Yura to stop looking back at Volodya and learn to live a normal life.

It didn't take Yura long to find out that in his new town, just like in all of Germany, there were a lot of Russian speakers. Although they had no official organizations, they supported each other. It was from them, as much as from the TV, that Yura's family found out what was happening in Russia and Ukraine.

It was hard for Yura to adapt to his new life. Once the academic year started, he began associating with Germans as much as possible, even though they seemed like people cast from a completely different mold, with no similarity whatsoever to people from the former USSR. And entering into a relationship with anybody wasn't in the realm of possibility. He felt lost, like nobody needed him, like he was extraneous and powerless. He tried to fit in with everyone around him, to be like the Germans in his classes, to lose his accent. But he still stuck out, even if he didn't open his mouth. He still thought about Volodya. He still remembered how much he loved Volodya. And he still didn't like women.

However, it didn't take Yura long to find out that the attitude toward homosexuals in Berlin was totally different from what it had been in the USSR.

Now, back at Camp Barn Swallow, the sandy path cut down steeply from the cliff to the river. At times Yurka slipped and slid down the sandy slope. That was how 1992 had been, too: life carried him forward of its own accord. Yura continued to be a model student and didn't do anything but study, but everything around him changed. It changed so much it became unrecognizable.

That was the year that the thing Volodya had been so afraid of happened: Yura started checking out other guys. He didn't set out to find a partner or even to meet somebody who was like him. But one evening an openly gay man, a member of Berlin Pride, came to a college party. He liked Yura, and although Yura didn't find the guy sexually attractive, that didn't keep them from becoming friends. A little while later, Mick told him about the gay community and invited him to the district where their people hung out and partied in Berlin.

The next weekend Yura went to Nollendorfplatz. He came out of the metro, walked along the square, and started walking down Motzstrasse, but before he'd taken more than a few steps he stopped short, flustered. What he saw was nothing he'd ever wished for or dreamed of, simply because he had never been capable of even imagining anything like it. It was a parallel world, one that was noisy, crowded, bright, and free. It was as though Yura had landed on an amazing new planet where there was a permanent celebration, where he was not a stranger, where it felt like they'd even been expecting him. Dozens of songs played in dozens of clubs. Hundreds of people were strolling all around him. Some of them, like Yura, were walking by themselves, looking around for someone in the colorful crowd. But the majority of people were in same-sex pairs. They were free and uninhibited, almost to a point that felt vulgar. They walked around holding hands, and they kissed right out in the open, in front of everyone, and nothing happened to them! No disapproving glances, no curses, nothing! Yura couldn't believe this was really happening. He froze, eyes wide in amazement. All he could do was blink, look enviously at the strolling pairs, and sigh, "If only Volodya could see this." Later, Mick would confirm that this was normal here, that this was a place where the war Yura didn't even know was being fought had already been won. Still, as someone born and raised in the USSR, Yura was sure that as long as he lived, he'd never be able to make himself walk openly down the street like that, holding hands with a guy.

The asphalt was wet and gleaming from a recent rain. At his feet lay bright stripes: the reflection of a bar's neon sign. A rainbow flag. Yura lowered his gaze to stare at them, then he released a shuddering sigh and stepped onto the reflection on the ground. He gathered his courage and walked along the rainbow, following it into the bar where he'd arranged to meet Mick.

He slipped inconspicuously to a seat at an empty table, ordered a beer, and drank it down in a single go. Not fifteen minutes had gone by before he was surrounded by a group of a dozen-odd people whom Yurka would soon come to think of as nothing other than his real family. The group included women, and men, and people Yurka didn't know how to refer to. They were excited, full of joking and laughter, as a few of them described their plan for staging an action code-named Operation Civil Registry that was going to make a lot of noise. The gist of it was that on a specific day, August 19, 1992, a whole bunch of same-sex couples were going to apply for marriage licenses at the same time all over the country. All their applications would get written rejections, of course, and then the couples would sue. Drunk not on beer but on the atmosphere, Yura immediately agreed to participate. A "husband" was found for him on the spot, whose name Yura only remembered once he read it in his marriage license application. Everything happened so fast that it wasn't until Yura got the official written refusal to accept his application that he realized for the first time what a strange position he'd have been in if his application had been approved.

The pile of mail containing the refusal from the civil registry office held another letter for Yura as well, from his friend from his building back in Kharkiv. The guy had moved to another neighborhood a long time ago, but he sometimes came back to the neighborhood where he and Yura grew up, to visit his mother. This is what he was writing about. His letter shocked Yura.

"I went to visit my mother recently. She said that some guy had been looking for you. I didn't see him myself, but my mother said he had glasses. Is that the guy you were expecting?"

Yura sent a brief response: "What did he ask? What did she tell him? Did she give him my address and phone number in Germany? Did the guy leave his contact information?"

Another month went by before he got his response: "My mother did not give out your address or telephone number. She just said you'd gone away to Germany. He didn't say anything about himself."

Yura put in a request: "Go to my old apartment and find out whether that guy went to see them and whether he left his address with them. And make sure you take any letters! If there's still nobody there, break into the mailbox."

There was no answer for a long time. His friend was living his own life, wrapped up in family and work. He wasn't about to run around from one end of the city to the other at Yura's beck and call, of course. And he didn't answer until later, the beginning of November: "The guy went to see them. He didn't leave his own address but he took back his own letters."

Volodya had sent more letters! But irritation pulsed through Yura: Why hadn't Volodya left his address? Why had he taken the letters back? Had that "You'll be better off without me" nonsense kicked in again? Yura's irritation grew into fury. If Volodya had been there, Yura would've hit him.

Enraged and hurt, he fled to Nollendorfplatz. He hunkered down in a bar, tossing back drink after drink. By the time he was seeing double, an old acquaintance came up to him: Jonas, his erstwhile "fiancé," his partner in submitting the marriage license application. Yura was so drunk that the next morning he couldn't remember how he'd ended up in bed with Jonas. But it didn't keep their fling from turning into a relationship. And neither did the memory of Volodya.

Way back in '86, he and Volodya had agreed to meet at Camp Barn Swallow ten years later. But he didn't show up, because life got busy and he finally started getting some recognition for his music. Playing at concerts and continuing his studies—but now as a conductor as well as a pianist—Yura was reaping the fruits of his labor. But it was Jonas who made him finally forget their agreement.

Jonas was a gay rights activist. He promoted and supported the gay community's civic life. He tried to respect what Yura was doing with his life, but it became clear pretty quickly that either he didn't like Yura's music specifically, or he didn't like piano music in general. He said it didn't do anything. It was just noise.

But they still went to the theater and the opera together. Once, while they were traveling in Latvia, Yura saw a poster in Russian advertising Roman Viktyuk's Russian-language production of *M. Butterfly*, and even though Jonas didn't speak a word of Russian, Yura insisted they go see it together.

The production made a double-edged impression. The nudity was off-putting, as well as the way the acting descended into affectation, and the fact that it was based on real events—and fairly recent ones at that—was shocking. But the story's ambiguity was appealing, and so was its moral that love has no gender. Above all, though, was the simple fact that it was in Russian. Yura was hearing the language onstage for the first time since he'd left.

M. Butterfly reminded him of what had been happening the first time he saw the posters for the show, back in '91 in Moscow. It reminded him of the person Yura had gone to Moscow for. And after seeing that show, Yura's dream of writing a composition full of meaning returned to him. The image of the main character who puts on women's clothing and feels free in it was one that followed Yura for many years. Jonas thought the whole idea of it was just self-mockery, absurd. But Yura disagreed.

For him this was the beginning of a period of creative inquiries, experiments, and mistakes.

Yura and Jonas were too different, and they both knew it from the beginning. But maybe it was just this diametric opposition of their personalities, temperaments, and interests that attracted them to each other. A year after their relationship began, they moved in together. At first they were still able to forgive each other's flaws and make room for each other's interests, but the longer their relationship dragged on, the harder it got for each of them to accept the other's disdain for the thing that gave his life meaning.

Jonas spent all his time and energy organizing gay events, gay parades, and gay trivia contests. He wanted gay people to have the same rights as heterosexuals. But Yura couldn't see how activism would help much: to accomplish something meaningful, he was sure that Jonas needed to be a politician. What's more, he didn't understand the constant discussions of discrimination. The whole time he'd lived in Germany, he hadn't encountered discrimination in his professional life. Not once. And no, Yura didn't hide his orientation, and it never even occurred to him to hide Jonas. It was just that none of his colleagues ever asked about his personal life, and Yura wasn't about to advertise it for no reason.

"Gays can't get married. That is discrimination," Jonas would say. "Why are we forbidden to do what's allowed for straight people? We're fighting for rights equal to what hetero couples have. We're citizens, too, just like them! You should be out there fighting for your rights too. Nobody's going to do it for you."

Maybe it was his Soviet upbringing, or maybe it was just his temperament, but Yura didn't think he needed marriage. What's more, the provocative nature of gay parades irritated Yura. And Jonas's most active project, the creation of gay neighborhoods, was something that Yura thought of as actively harmful. He didn't mind that gay neighborhoods existed—they were nice places to make friends and hang out—but he also thought that making more of them was exactly the wrong thing to do.

"You're literally fencing gays off, putting them in ghettos. Like in America, where they have white neighborhoods and black neighborhoods, just here it's gay neighborhoods. You shouldn't be expanding the ghettos, you should be getting people out of them entirely."

One thing Jonas did that Yura completely agreed with and supported was the gay trivia contests, because the contestants were originally from various countries, including ones where homosexuality was a capital offense. "If you really want to help people," he told Jonas for the hundredth time, "create psychological resource centers in schools and universities. But if what you want is to accomplish these goals of yours, you have to go into politics. It's the only way."

After six years of fruitless attempts to learn to accept and love each other as they were, each of them with interests the other considered character flaws, their relationship started to fall apart. Their love, so bright and exciting at first, grew pale and feeble, then faded away completely. Their irritation at each other's interests carried over into everything else. Jonas's good looks, which had taken Yura's breath away when they first met, were no big deal now. Flaws like the mole on his temple, which Yura had earlier stubbornly ignored, now caught his eye constantly, prompting his disgust. Yura even started being irritated by Jonas's walk, his habits, his gestures, the way he dressed, even the way he ate. And Yura could see in the way Jonas looked at him that Jonas liked him less and less, too.

And maybe Yura did say things wrong and have the wrong opinion sometimes about what Jonas was doing, but Jonas blatantly ignored Yura's music.

He tried to be out whenever Yura was at home perfecting a new piece; he never asked Yura to play him something; and he never once went to the concert hall to see Yura perform.

With increasing frequency, the most relaxing thing for them to do together was to keep quiet. Then not talking became habitual. Soon even the sound of the other's voice was irritating. Almost every conversation about music or the community ended with them making a scene. Then they stopped wasting energy on fighting. And then they stopped wasting it on sex. That's when Yura asked Jonas to take his things and go. Thus ended that which Yura had once thought eternal.

It was June 30, 1998. Way back in '86, he and Volodya had agreed to meet at Camp Barn Swallow ten years later. But Yura had forgotten about the meeting under the willow. He'd failed to show up for it two years ago. Indeed, he now realized, he'd forgotten about a lot of things, and given up a lot of things. He had ruined his relationship with his parents, who were unable to accept his orientation and treated him more like a distant relative than their own son: his mother was cold toward him, and his father avoided him entirely. He'd stopped hanging out with his Russian-speaking friends—at least, the ones who weren't part of the gay community—and he'd sacrificed momentum in his musical career, in which he should've been investing a whole lot more time and energy. Now it was as though he'd come back down to earth from heaven and remembered that, apart from Jonas, there were other things in life. And more than anything else, he started thinking again about his unfulfilled promise.

Although back in 1991 there'd been no chance of finding Volodya once he had vanished, now, since the advent of the internet, it was at least hypothetically possible. Yura knew Volodya would have eventually gone back to Camp Barn Swallow. He didn't believe it, he didn't assume it—he knew it. So, aided by the internet, his first task was to find the camp. The second task was to go there, even though the meeting time had already passed.

Yura had forgotten the way to Camp Barn Swallow. To be precise, he had never known it in the first place: the Pioneers were always brought there by bus. Yura remembered the bus number—410—and that it was near the village Horetivka. But he was unable to find that one single village out of the hundreds of thousands of them all across the former Soviet Union. Yura went to all the Russian-language internet chat forums he could find and posted in them about the village, asking whether anyone knew where it was or what had happened to it. He didn't get many replies, and even the ones he did get were useless. A few people knew of a similarly named village, but it was in Moscow oblast in Russia. Nobody knew anything about a Horetivka near Kharkiv in Ukraine.

Yura began to buy maps and study them closely. But the village wasn't on them. Tired of the constant dead ends, he began to ask himself whether a village like that had ever existed at all. Maybe after so many years he'd forgotten its actual name and in his head he'd distorted it until it was unrecognizable?

Since his mother had worked in the factory that sponsored the camp, he asked her whether her former colleagues remembered where the camp was, but they either didn't know or didn't remember. He scoured the internet for images of a voucher for a session at Camp Barn Swallow. He didn't find any. He researched the 410 bus, looking for similar numbers, like 41, 10, 710, 70, and so forth, just in case he'd misremembered. But the ones he found didn't go anywhere that even remotely resembled the places Yura needed.

After his futile attempt to find the place, he started looking for people: the Pukes, Vanka and Mikha, Pcholkin, Olezhka, and anyone and everyone else he remembered, even Anechka and his nemesis Vishnevsky. But maybe they didn't have computers or internet access, or maybe they connected to the internet with dumb usernames at internet cafés; at any rate, Yura failed to find them either. He wrote the guys from his building asking them to find out the phone number of Public School 18, then called it looking for the Pukes. But the money he spent on international phone calls was wasted. Every time he asked himself what he still hadn't done to find what he needed, what he hadn't tried yet, he came up with something else to do. And once he'd tried it, he couldn't believe that it, too, had failed: "It's just not possible that I can't find anybody!" But it was.

In the end, it looked like the only thing left for him to try was actually going back to the Motherland. There he'd be able to dig around in archives and find people using telephone books and speak with people affiliated with the factory. So, unwilling to give up, Yura began planning to take some vacation time soon and travel to Kharkiv. But his plans were canceled by a phone call from his parents. His father spoke to him for the first time in four years. What he said was bad. Yura's mother was sick and might not get well again. The many long years of employment in an unhealthy workplace were making themselves known.

For the next two years, Yura forgot about his plans and about his desire to find Camp Barn Swallow. His mom was slowly fading away as her disease progressed, and the treatment wasn't having the expected results.

The only thing that saved him from the bleak atmosphere at his parents' was music. It became Yura's anchor, helping him accept the inevitability of the loss.

He finished his conducting degree and accepted the head of the conservatory's offer of a position as one of its piano teachers. During the day Yura taught music and played for the students, while at night, sometimes, when he went to his parents' place, he played for his mother.

She died in the spring of 2000. Yura's father was devastated. Although he'd never exactly been open and sociable, now he withdrew far into himself, speaking less and less and applying himself to the bottle more and more. Yura, gazing at him, realized bitterly that even after so many years, after such a shared loss, the single family member who was close to him neither accepted nor forgave him, his son, for who he was.

Time moved ruthlessly on. Yura recovered from his sorrow. He began performing in concerts and writing music again. Relationships flickered in and out of his life, but none of them were as long or as strong as the one with Jonas. It was lonely. He caught himself thinking that he wished his home were as loud as it used to be, that people were always coming over again, that good smells came from the kitchen, and that he could feel someone's back against his side when he was falling asleep. Never mind that he'd often fought with the owner of that back. As soon as Yura hit the thirty-year mark, his loneliness became almost physical; it was his constant companion, one that short dalliances or one-night stands were unable to rid him of.

All this time, Yura had watched Jonas from a distance, as though it had nothing to do with him, trying to track what his former lover was up to. Yura sometimes felt that it was those last words he'd said, during their last fight, that had prompted Jonas to take an important and useful step: he'd joined the Lesbian and Gay Federation in Germany. Next, Jonas had gone on to become a member of the Social Democratic Party of Germany. And then, at the end of 2000, Yurka saw that Jonas and his colleagues had achieved their main goal: two of four political parties voted to legalize same-sex unions at the federal level. The other two parties opposed it, but it became law all the same.

The law went into effect in 2001. It specified partnership, not marriage; for the time being, gays and lesbians had access only to a minimal series of rights. But little by little the law was expanded. And not long ago, in January of 2005, a new expansion had been enacted, allowing gay people the right to register partnerships with citizens of other countries. In some ways, the news of these expansions just felt like mockery to pathologically lonely people like Yura. Still, he couldn't help being proud of Jonas and all he had achieved.

The next year, 2006, was a new stage in Yura's career. He began planning his first big tour of Russia and the Commonwealth of Independent States, and it was going to end in Kharkiv. Although he'd previously lost hope, his knowledge that he'd be going back to Ukraine prompted him to try to find Camp Barn Swallow one more time.

He still didn't have much hope of success, but he began his search all over again all the same, going through all the Russian forums again, writing in all the chat forums again, searching for nostalgic websites. And on one of them he finally found a scanned copy of a voucher for a session at Camp Barn Swallow! From the person who published it, he found out that the village of Horetivka really had existed. That person didn't remember the exact location, but he did give a general explanation of what highway to take to get there. All that remained was to lay out a route and find it. Yura couldn't do that in Germany, since Horetivka wasn't on a single map. But once he found himself in Ukraine, in Kharkiv Oblast, he went out to find it himself. And he did.

Yura didn't arrive in Kharkiv empty-handed; he brought with him a dream he'd fulfilled. He had composed his magnum opus, the one he'd written Volodya about so long ago. A symphony, one that wasn't just beautiful, but full of meaning. It was about freedom. Yura had allowed himself to be dramatic and old-fashioned. The symphony began in complete silence, broken by a faint, stifled, cracking tenor. Moment by moment the singing intensified, becoming louder and more confident, until a choir joined in, but the choir didn't drown out the man's voice; it elevated it. After the choir came the strings, accompanied by piano, and at the very end, the dramatic, grandiose wind instruments came crashing down on the audience. When he first heard it onstage, Yura seemed to become free himself, although the center of the symphony was neither him as the conductor nor even him as the composer but the tenor, with his stifled, cracking voice.

For a long time Yura thought that his inspiration had been *M. Butterfly*. But today, now that he'd come back to Camp Barn Swallow and remembered his past, he realized that the muse of his most important work wasn't some character from a play, someone he didn't actually know, but someone else entirely. Someone he'd once known very, very well.

The path ended when it hit a lot of overgrown bushes. Yura stepped onto the sand of the beach and got a faceful of a terrible stench from the river. Back then, especially after it rained, it had smelled unbelievably delicious here, of summer freshness and mushroomy dampness. But now the woods had grown thin and scrubby. On the trees, the yellowing, dried-up foliage was wet and heavy. The smell of putrid standing water was strong in the air. As Yura walked past the turn-off to the boathouse, he frowned: through the sparse trees he could clearly discern a heap of boards and debris. That was all that remained of the dock. Yura didn't have time now to turn that way and examine the remains of the place where he'd had his first real kiss. He kept going.

As soon as he arrived today he'd begun fretting about whether he'd be able to get across the river to the willow, but all his doubts vanished as soon as he stepped through the rusted chain-link gate that used to separate the beach from the woods. The river wasn't a river anymore. All that remained of that once deep and mighty tributary of the Donets River was a swamp, a little green stagnant swamp choked in duckweed. It made the old Soviet sign at the entrance to the beach—depicting swimmers in deep waves and the caption BEWARE OF STRONG CURRENT!—look like a mean joke.

Yura didn't know how or why the river had dried up, but he suspected it was because of the construction on the far riverbank. Maybe the river had been in the way, so they'd filled in the bed? Or built a dam? To hell with it. Yura didn't have time to think about it now.

He turned off to the left, hoping there was a chance he'd still be able to find the shallows. The little trail, which hadn't been much even back in the day, was long gone by now. Yura had to make his way through the vegetation. He reached the path along the high riverbank and stopped. The sandy bank had eroded and crumbled, but he could still walk on it. Yura went up to the very edge and looked down: ten or so meters of sand, then nothing but that same duckweed and stagnant water. He remembered the still pool where he and Volodya had once swam together. He heaved a sigh. Their lilies were all dead, because the shallow pool where they'd grown had dried up and turned into stagnant muck, like the river itself.

Yura looked at the far bank. The bank he was standing on was higher, and from here he could see not only roofs and the wall around the cottage community; he could see some of the cottages themselves. Many of them were still under construction, but there were a few that were done—and clearly inhabited. The billboard near the entrance to the village proclaimed: *Sales of elite cottages and townhouses. Comfort and convenience await you at The Barn Swallow's Nest. LVDevelopment LLC.*

Yura made his way to the shallows and stopped, considering. The water had disappeared completely here, which was no surprise, considering that this was where the water had always been low. Still, he was wary, fearing that the wet sludge wouldn't hold him up and he'd get stuck in it. But he had no choice. He had to get to the willow. Or had he come this whole way for nothing?

Although who knew? Maybe it had all been for nothing. After all, so many years had passed. Maybe both the willow and the time capsule were already gone. Why had he even come here, anyway? Why had he come looking for something that had been lost and forgotten ages ago? But he had to go back, sooner or later. Maybe it was too late for them, but for Yura himself, nothing had actually ended yet. He'd come back to clear his conscience, to bring this to a close, to be honest with himself above all and know he'd done everything he could to find Volodya. He was late, of course, and not just by a day, or a year, but by a whole ten years and then some. And all that might be left linking him to Volodya was preserved here, under the willow. Assuming the tree hadn't been cut down.

His fears proved groundless. It was still there, bigger and more beautiful than ever. Its heavy branches, with lush foliage just beginning to turn yellow, bowed down to the ground. So tense with anticipation he could barely breathe, Yura went down the slope to it. He parted some branches and slipped through to stand in the space enclosed by the tree's drooping boughs. His heart fluttered: everything was the same! Just like then! With just one difference: it was colder, quieter, without the burbling of the river. But the willow still hid Yura from the rest of the world, just like it used to.

CHAPTER TWENTY-ONE
THE TIME CAPSULE

The Cyrillic initials *Yu + V* carved into the trunk had turned dark and rough and were stretched out like an old scar. Tentatively, tenderly, Yura ran his fingers over it. Then he grabbed the shovel. The damp earth yielded to it easily. In just a couple of minutes he heard the shovel clank against the metal lid of the time capsule. He heaved a sigh of relief: it was here! He pulled it out and opened it, his hands dirty from the digging and the rust from the battered old tin. He shook its contents out onto the grass.

First the faded neckerchiefs emerged. Then came the dried-up, crumbling remnants of the lily, along with a Komsomol pin and a pair of broken glasses. But they hadn't put either the pin or glasses in the time capsule back then . . . Yura clutched the glasses, remembering how right here, right under this same tree, he'd once taken them off of Volodya's face, as carefully as if they were a priceless artifact. Mentally, he reviewed his list: it hadn't had glasses, but it had had the notebook. Where was it? But Volodya's notebook, with the scary stories, and the script, and "Yurochka," and the wishes for their future selves, was not in the time capsule. What did come falling out of the capsule next—and this was something Yura never expected—was a neat little bundle of letters tied up with string.

He picked it up with shaking hands and untied the string. His throat went dry, his blood pounded in his ears, and a whole swarm of questions started buzzing in his head: What were these letters doing here? Where did they come from? Volodya must have put them here, of course—who else? But that meant he'd come and opened the time capsule! That meant he'd been here! But when?! The answers were waiting.

The topmost letter, in a standard Soviet-era letter envelope, was addressed to Yura's old address in Kharkiv, with Volodya's old Moscow apartment as the return address. But it had no stamps or postmarks on it. This was a letter Volodya had written but not sent; the contents allowed Yura to guess when.

> I didn't offend you in my last telegram, did I? You always told me that if I pushed you away again, you'd disappear for good. Did I really push you away? Because you disappeared. And if that's what happened, then good for you. You finally learned to keep your word.
>
> But it was all for your own good! My father got into some serious trouble. He got involved with the wrong people. A bunch of criminals. Not willingly, of course. They came to him demanding money in exchange for protection. But my old man's a Soviet-style, principled guy, and he told them to take a hike. They're the opposite, though, completely unprincipled, so they "gave him a taste" and set fire to one of our properties. Then they threatened to hurt our family. Yura, when I wrote you those words, and then sent that telegram, I was trying to keep you safe! Our mailbox isn't inside our apartment, you know! They could've found your letter, gotten you mixed up in everything, too—and you're what's most important to me. I was scared for myself and for my mother and father, of course. But I was also scared for you. It still scares me to think of what they'd have done to you if they'd found out who you are to me. And if they'd started threatening to hurt you . . . What would I have done?
>
> I know now that it wouldn't have been worth the hassle for them; Kharkiv had its own criminal groups, obviously, so ours wouldn't have bothered encroaching on foreign territory. But that's now . . . back then it was different . . . and I wasn't the only one who was afraid of my own shadow. The whole family was terrified of even leaving the apartment.
>
> Well, whatever happens, I suppose it's all for the best. It wasn't what I wanted. I miss you terribly and I don't want to lose you. But it'll be better this way. I want you to get your

> own life in order, I want you not to let me distract you, not to think about me. I want you to find a girl. Because what do you need me for? All you get from me is pain. I hold you back. I get you off track and distract you, when you should be living your own life. Don't think badly of me. And forgive me for everything I've done. I've never forgotten you, even for a minute, but you'll be better off without me.

As Yura's eyes ran along the lines, every word pulled him deeper and deeper into the past. He remembered what he'd been like back then, and what Volodya had been like. Now, in this changed new world, all that seemed forgotten, completely unreal, but back then . . . how important it had been!

Volodya had never sent this letter. Now Yura understood why: Volodya had been afraid for him. Volodya had been protecting him and didn't want to get him in trouble. And because of Volodya's fear, Yurka had spent ages trying to guess what he'd done wrong and why Volodya had cut him off so abruptly . . . but the reason turned out to be absurdly simple: Volodya wanted to keep him safe. Volodya was afraid somebody might hurt Yura, so he thought he would keep Yura safe by abandoning him.

The following three letters had stamps and postmarks. They had been addressed to Yurka's Kharkiv apartment, but the return address showed letters and numbers instead of a street: MU-1543. Military Unit 1543. So Volodya had done his obligatory two years of army service. The first of the three letters was dated the beginning of August 1991.

> I can just imagine your face when with no warning you get a letter from the army. But why not? I'll have to do my army service sooner or later, so why not now? I can't say I like it here; I do regret that I had to go unenroll from my institute just one semester before I graduated. Don't worry, though: I'll enroll again once I'm out. The thing I regret more than that is how it had to end between us. It had to, Yura! It wasn't what I wanted!
>
> I know you're angry at me. But I also know you're reading this anyway. Don't be angry. When I get back to civilian life

> I'll explain everything, you'll see. I'm sad here. Write me at least a couple of lines. But . . . you have to write very carefully. You understand. Write soon. I'm waiting.

But the response Volodya was waiting for would never come. Yura sighed. He'd never gotten these letters because by then he'd already moved to Germany. How awful Volodya must've felt, not to get any response to his letter. But there were two more letters sent from the military unit. Yura opened them one by one.

At the end of August 1991, Volodya wrote:

> I don't know why you aren't answering me. I hope it's just that you didn't get my first letter. Maybe there's a problem with the mail?
>
> It's hard for me here, far from my family and friends . . . and without hearing from you. It's especially difficult because of my problem. My surroundings are . . . having an effect. You're probably asking yourself how I'm dealing with those fears of mine here.
>
> That problem of mine hasn't gone anywhere, of course. Nothing helped. I wrote you about that, you should remember. After the thing happened, the thing I can't tell you about in a letter, the thing that made us have to leave Moscow, my father suggested that for my own safety I should do my army service. He added that in the army they'd make a man out of me for sure. You're the only one who knows I'd had a "relapse." I didn't tell my parents. That's why my father wasn't worried about me, and I convinced myself I wasn't worried, either. Now I remember the last three years and shake my head at how naive I was, thinking that I could get rid of my problem so easily. But now that I'm here, in the military unit, there's no chance of me overcoming it. Although, on the other hand, the army does temper you. There's nowhere to hide from my fears here, I've got to learn to live with them.
>
> Write me soon, I really want to hear from you.

Yura knew Volodya was talking in a coded way about his "disease" and that it was very difficult for him to be in the army, surrounded by men. He also knew that it was hard for him to understand just how difficult it was. In the former Soviet republics everything was much worse as far as attitudes about LGBT people; it had been then, and it still was now. He knew that people's opinions were changing only slowly and with great difficulty, not like in the West. But trying to cure homosexuality as though it was a mental disorder—that was inhuman. The doctors could've caused Volodya irreparable harm! And then the army . . . it had to have been no joke for Volodya, fighting his monsters—thinking that he himself was a monster!—to spend two years surrounded by men. Now Yura was consumed with regret that he never got those letters. He wished so badly he could've gone back and supported Volodya, told him that there were lots of men like him, told him that where Yura lived, they were accepted by society.

The last letter from the military unit was dated March of 1992. It was very short:

"Still no answer. Did you move? Or is it that you hate me? How are you? What's going on with you? Have you met a girl? Maybe you're already married? I really hope so. I hope you've found yourself and your happiness. It's hard for me to believe a whole year's almost gone by. I have leave in April and I'll come see you, Yura! I'll come see you right away!"

That last line made Yura narrow his eyes thoughtfully, calculating the dates: that was when Volodya had come out to look for him but hadn't found him.

The rest of the letters were in regular white envelopes without stamps or addresses. The only notes on them were dates written in pencil.

Yura opened the oldest of them, dated May of 1993:

"Last year I went to Kharkiv. I didn't find you. I went to the address that you always wrote me from, but there were new people living there, in your apartment. They told me you'd moved to Germany a long time ago.

"You did the right thing, Yura. What you did was right. If you didn't take the letters, it's because you don't need them. If you didn't leave me an address, it's because you don't need me. It's probably for the best . . . It wouldn't have worked out for us anyway . . ."

Yura was so frustrated, he hit the air with his fist, almost tearing the letter: "I left my address! I wrote them, I asked them to give him the address, I asked them to pass on the letters. Why did I ever rely on other people!"

He shouldn't have. He should have written his old neighbors himself, a letter every month; even if nobody was living in his old apartment, he should've piled on the letters anyway. But he hadn't.

"I screwed everything up!" he moaned out loud.

He didn't want to keep reading, but he couldn't stop now: "But what I keep wondering is this: why did you go looking for me that time, then? Why did you go to Tver? And how did you even find my cousin's address?"

Yura had been about to quit reading this letter and move on to the next one, but then he thought: *Cousin?!* So that Vova really had been Volodya's cousin!

Yura turned his face away. But the letter drew his gaze back, like a magnet. Volodya's handwriting, the even lines, the compact letters—it was a vivid reminder of what they'd had . . . and of what they might have had.

> Yurka, I was in despair when I found out that the connection between us had been good and truly lost. I'm bouncing from one extreme to the other: I know it'll be better this way, but I can't make myself accept it. I'm still in despair now, which is why I'm writing this letter, even though I know there's nowhere for me to send it. Writing letters to nowhere . . . it's a way of dealing with stress. I read about it in psychology books back when I was still at the institute, but the first time I tried it was in the army. The idea is that you write down your thoughts and worries and then you destroy them. That's how you get some of the weight off your chest. It really helped me in the army. I was assigned to headquarters, so every so often I was able to find time and space to write.
>
> By the way, my unit was basically fine. The guys I served with were good, I made friends with a lot of them. I heard stories, you know, about the kind of awful things that can happen during army service, but I didn't get that—I didn't

even get hazed. I had a different problem . . . you know what I mean. So I poured out my emotions into letters. Letters I didn't send. I wrote to you in them, even though the guidelines of the exercise say you should write to yourself. If you only knew how many confessions I made, how many loving words I said there! And then I burned them all, because I couldn't risk anybody finding out about something like that. But now I'm home, and there's no need to burn everything . . .

I'm feeling really bad right now. But I'm very glad for you. I hope things are better for you there. I hope everything is better . . . the people, and your life . . .

My two years of service went by, and I came back home, but it feels like I came back into a completely different world. The world really has changed. The country has changed. My father started another business. He says I have to help him, but I just can't seem to get back to normal after the service. That's pretty common, though, Vovka was telling me that after his two years it took him six months to recover. Oh, by the way: Vovka!

When he told me some guy had come to his apartment asking about a troop leader from Camp Barn Swallow, and he didn't even let the guy into the entryway, I tore into him and we had a huge fight. I know, I should've warned him you might show up, but honestly, it never even occurred to me you might go see him! I get where Vovka was coming from: he knew about my father's problems, he knew we'd left because we were hiding from some criminals, so he didn't tell you anything . . . But I still can't get over the idea that there was hope we wouldn't lose each other, and we did anyway!

The times I'm living in now aren't good, either, Yur. Something bad started happening in Tver and they're pressuring my father again. My parents want to move again. To Belgorod now; they say it'll be quieter in the outskirts, near the Ukrainian border. But the border's where all the contraband is, so there's no way it'll be quieter for us, and I can't see how they don't understand. My dad won't budge; he refuses point-blank to be partners with a bunch of bandits. Come on—does he think there's none of them in Belgorod and that they won't pressure him there, too?

I had a big fight with my dad about all of this. I've been telling him that we have to get not only out of town but out of Russia. It's not that you can't run an honest business here: it's that with my father's principles—which I actually do share, by the way—you can't run a business at all. I can't get through to him that you just have to take those expenses into account in advance, just make them a line item in the budget. But he will do whatever he wants. I, at least, can do something useful while he's beating his head against the same old wall.

I'm still planning on leaving for the States someday, but there's no way I can do that right now. I've got to finish my degree, to start with; I'll reenroll in the Institute and finish up by correspondence course, and then we'll see. I remember what you thought of my efforts to become a Communist, get into the Party, and earn a good reputation. I remember it and smile: you were so right when you said none of it mattered. Because that's right, now it's all meaningless.

Well, I should finish up this letter to nowhere, my hand is starting to hurt . . .

Yura looked back over the letter hungrily. "If you only knew how many confessions I made, how many loving words I said there! And then I burned them all," he reread aloud. "If you only knew!"

So many years had gone by, but now it was like he was being sent back to that time. While Volodya had been pouring out his feelings onto sheets of paper he then burned, Yura had been waiting for news from his old friend from his building back home. But then he had indeed begun to forget Volodya as he got into a relationship with Jonas. He felt guilty for letting everything fall through his fingers and for not keeping his love alive longer, and it tormented him as he opened the next letter. Volodya had written it almost a year later, in April 1994.

> I haven't written one of these letters in a long time. I don't think I especially need to; I just felt like it. I've recovered from my army service and I'm finishing my degree. I'll get my diploma this June. I'm helping my father with the business, so I've had to postpone my plans for moving to the U.S. Maybe the place I end up going won't even be America. Or will I even go anywhere at all? Right now I definitely don't have time for that. I have things to do. I'm helping my father. He finally learned to listen to me. We buy up land and old uninhabited buildings, mostly in rural areas or on the outskirts. I found a legal loophole that allows us to resell it at two or three times the price.

Another letter was dated February 1995. Yura was flabbergasted as he read the first few lines:

> Get this: I moved to Kharkiv! How ironic! Even though I was the one who dreamed of hightailing it out of the country, you're the one who actually did. But now I live in your city! My father got Ukrainian citizenship and officially registered the company here. We ended up choosing Kharkiv, but not because of my sentimentality—it's just that Belgorod is on the border of Kharkiv Oblast, and by the time we were going to move, we'd bought several plots of land in Kharkiv Oblast, and we already had a small client base established here.
>
> I'm also getting Ukrainian citizenship. There's no such thing as honest business here, either, of course, but I think my old man's finally admitted it's time to send his principles packing.
>
> It's so strange to walk the same streets that you once walked! It's almost as strange as writing you these letters knowing you'll never read them.
>
> I really like your city, Yura. It resembles Moscow in some ways, but there aren't as many people. It's quieter and calmer. I go on walks whenever I get the chance and try to guess whether you also took walks in the same places. I looked for the Kharkiv conservatory for two months before I found it.

How was I supposed to know that, even though you called your alma mater "the conservatory," it's actually called the Kharkiv I.P. Kotlyarevsky National University of the Arts? As I was walking past one of the buildings, I heard someone playing the piano. It was such a nice feeling, as though you were the one playing, although I also knew there was no way it could be you. It's sad. It's like I got a little closer to you while remaining as incredibly far away as before.

Know what? I met a girl. Her name is Sveta. She's really nice. And she's just like her name—"light." She really is a bright light in my life! She was the leader of a city tour I went on, and she showed us how the main Lenin statue in the city, there on Freedom Square, is pointing toward the public toilets. I don't know why that struck me as so funny, but I laughed about it for a long time. And I remembered how you used to talk to the bust of Vladimir Ilych back in our theater.

I like Sveta. She's very positive and cheerful. I'm not getting my hopes up, because I know all I'm feeling for her is friendly affection, but being with her is pleasant. Maybe I could fall in love with her?

Yura smiled, remembering the statue of Lenin and the city where he was born and raised. Was Volodya really living in Kharkiv now? After all this time, he couldn't think of anything more ironic. And Volodya—how old had he been in '95? Twenty-seven? And he still thought he could become normal! Nobody had ever told him that he was normal his whole life, actually, because what would be abnormal for him would be if he did just the opposite and fell in love with a girl . . .

Maybe Volodya's comment that he wanted to fall in love with Sveta was a joke, but Yura sensed the hope in his words. And he felt something else, too, buried way down deep in his heart: jealousy. It wasn't very strong—he barely felt it—but he smiled as he realized how silly it was to feel that now.

He kept reading. The next envelope had April 1996 written on it.

Yura, I screwed everything up! I betrayed her so badly! She's suffering; she calls sometimes, and I do what I can to calm her down. I wish I had someone to calm *me* down. I'm such an idiot! Ever since 1990, if not earlier, it's been all but proclaimed from the rooftops that people like me are . . . well, not normal, of course, but at least not the kind of monsters I used to think they were. No, I still don't accept all of them—I hate the ones like Boris Moiseyev who do drag—but I wish I had tried harder to be accepting. Instead, I had to go and ruin my own life and then go and ruin Sveta's.

I feel bad for her. She's so fun, so lively and funny . . . She's like you. She's bright, just like her name. And I caused her pain. I loved her. Or rather, I thought I did. I tried so hard to believe I could fall in love with her—I wanted it so badly—that I convinced both her and myself.

We started dating a month after we met, you know. It's my fault. I was confused about myself. I couldn't tell the difference between liking her as a person and liking her sexually. We talked so much, went on so many walks. This is probably going to sound stupid, but she was lavishing me with light and warmth. I couldn't resist! I started hoping my disease was curable again, seeing Sveta as my chance to change.

We moved in together. Two months ago her period was late. She told me about it immediately. I felt like I'd been punched in the face. Like an honest man, I said that if she was pregnant, I'd marry her. No question. We told our parents and went to the clinic for a pregnancy test. It's a good clinic, private, you pay out the nose. Sveta and I are sitting there in the hallway and I'm looking around at the pictures of babies and pregnant women. And Sveta's just glowing! She's smiling, flipping through a magazine, and then she holds it up for me to see: a picture of a young family. A happy mama holding a cute little baby and the father behind them, his arms wrapped around them both. Sveta's all "Look,: what a cute little guy!" and what do I look at? The husband! And I go, "Yeah, he's cute." And then it hit me like a ton of bricks: What am I saying?! What am I doing here?! How did I ever manage to get myself into something like this?! What dream am I dreaming here?! What do I think is going to happen?! Am I blind?! Then they call Sveta's name, and she goes into the office, and I run to the bathroom. I thought: Okay, I'll turn on the hot water just to bring myself back to my senses; this will pass . . . it used to help me before, after all . . . but no! It didn't help! It just made it worse. What the hell kind of father would I be? I'm unbalanced, I've got some kind of suicidal tendencies! I hide in the bathroom and burn my hands at the least little thing! What kind of husband would that make me?

For a few days, while we were waiting for the results, I was a bundle of nerves. I felt like I was in some kind of hell. Not even the army was that bad. I had to force myself to do it with Sveta in the first place, you know. I already had to spend half an hour just working myself up to it. Sveta was a big fan of the long prelude, of course, but the prelude wasn't for her. And I realized, if everything was so bad already, then how much worse would it get? There were only two options: either I'd cheat on her, or I'd die by my own hand.

And then we got the test results: false alarm. I was so happy, I didn't sleep that night! But Sveta thought the opposite, she thought I couldn't sleep because I was so upset. My parents told us to get married anyway. They loved Sveta, obviously. Doubtless because she'd apparently cured their fag of a son. Sveta's parents agreed with them. They said, "We give you our blessing. And kids will come with time." But the minute I came back to my senses I told her I wanted to break up. Poor thing, to this day she thinks it's because of that non-pregnancy. She cries all the time and calls me late at night. I don't get to sleep until two in the morning because I'm staying up on the phone with her. I feel bad for her. I never did tell her the truth, and I never will. I'm never going to tell anyone. But I don't know how to deal with it. I know now that it's incurable. I look at other people like me and I don't feel any hatred toward them, or at least I don't think so.

> But other people being this way are one thing; it's different when it's yourself. I can't forgive myself for being this way.
>
> I feel as though I'm living someone else's life. But what's my life supposed to be like? I have no idea. And I can't bring myself to find out. It scares me.

Yura squeezed his eyes shut, then opened them wide as he blew out a huge sigh. His head was buzzing from the emotion saturating those lines and from the sheer volume of information. How much life Volodya had poured into his writing, how much despair and hope. And the whole time Volodya had been writing that—the whole time Volodya had been about to get married, and then calling it off, and fighting himself, and failing to accept himself—that whole time, Yura hadn't given a single thought to his Volodya. Yura had been completely immersed in his relationship with Jonas. He felt terrible. He should've tried to find Volodya earlier! Yura had promised, after all! He had promised they wouldn't lose each other... But he had remembered his promise too late.

There were only two envelopes left in the bundle. One of them had the exact date for once: June 30, 1996. Yurka's hands trembled when he saw the day of their intended meeting at Camp Barn Swallow. That had been ten years to the day after they saw each other the last time.

> I opened the time capsule today. I got out my notebook and read our farewell wishes. None of them came true. We lost each other, Yura. And I lost myself. I didn't leave for the States, and now I never will. Business here's booming and we're opening branches in other cities. My father's retiring soon and I'll take over. It's too late to go out in search of myself. I have to be content with what I've got. Maybe you went to the conservatory and became a musician, at least?
>
> I had no hope, of course, that you'd be here on this day. Well, okay, that's not true: I did hope so, but I knew the chances you'd show up were so small it'd be a miracle. You have your own life over there. And I know very well that the old Yurka I sometimes write to hasn't existed for a long time. You've grown up, you've changed, and my invisible

interlocutor is nothing but an image in my mind, a memory of you that I've been lovingly preserving all these years. I don't even know whether it's good or bad that I can't let you go no matter what. Sometimes I think I'm getting a little crazy, because how could I not be? But it's all just because I'm lonely. It only looks from the outside like everything's fine. Inside, I feel like an old man, even though I'm not even thirty yet . . . No matter where I am, I feel detached from the world, and everywhere I go, I'm different from other people—and not in a good way, either. I've accepted myself and I don't fight my perversion anymore. I wish I could meet someone, my kind of person, a guy I could be honest with. But the more I think about it, the more I know I'll never find a man like that.

I've been putting these letters in our time capsule with some small, weak—but not quite dead—hope that you'll read them someday. Because this capsule is a mailbox, in a sense; it's the only way you'll ever get them. Or is the capsule just my past's grave? I don't know. Enough. I'm going to try not to write my mute interlocutor any more letters.

Yura's insides seized up as it hit him how right Volodya was. They hadn't been able to take care of each other. They'd lost each other and they'd lost themselves. Sure, Yura had become a musician, like he promised. But he hadn't achieved happiness. The only things he had now were his career and his loneliness. And loneliness in your thirties is very different from loneliness when you're sixteen, when you only think that nobody needs you. It wasn't very likely Yura would be rescued from his loneliness, because there was nobody he was close to anymore. His mother had died, his father wanted nothing to do with him, and he had few real friends left: some had started families, some he'd stopped getting along with, and some he'd just lost, like he had lost Camp Barn Swallow.

The last envelope was different from the others. It was contemporary, business letter size, and it was brighter and newer. There was no writing on it, just the year in pencil: 2001. Yura opened it. In contrast to the other letters, which were written on notebook paper and folded in quarters, this one was written on a blank piece of printer paper and folded in thirds.

> This is the last letter. Now I understand clearly that it's time to unburden myself of this habit, too. There's a reason to do this now. It sounds strange: I just bought my youth. But I have to get on with my life. Because when you're always looking back—I remember you every time I write—it's hard to move forward.
>
> I'd really like to be able to say I have no regrets. But alas, that's not the case. I do have regrets—painful ones. Not about you, but about what I did to myself in '89. If I'd known what the consequences would be, I would never have agreed to go get treatment and I would've strangled that "doctor" with my bare hands. How could a doctor not see my habit of punishing myself as an indicator of suicidal tendencies? Because I told him about it! I did! That right there was what needed to be treated, not the fact that I longed for my friend Yurka Konev. He used to say that once we suppressed my inclinations, I'd get out of the habit of burning my hands, too. As if! But that wasn't the only issue. I suffered the consequences of his "treatment" for almost ten years. I was messed up already, but he messed me up the rest of the way.
>
> Still, I'm almost completely free of the habit of punishing myself. Almost. Sometimes, when my panic attacks get really bad, I start getting the old itch again, but I've learned how to dispel those thoughts. Of course, I didn't get rid of them all on my own, but I definitely got by without any charlatans messing with me.
>
> My only real relationship started late, when I was 31. Now I know I never loved him as a person, as himself. I only loved one thing in him: his gender. Just the very fact that he was a guy. My guy! Finally! I would get into such a frenzied euphoria just because he had a man's shoulders,

and arms, and—everything else. He himself as a person, his personality, even his looks, didn't matter to me a bit. We were together for almost two years. Although "together" is relative: we met, went out, talked, slept together, but the idea of, say, moving in together was never even on the table. He was married. I got tired of his vacillating and ended the relationship. And I got the final confirmation that I didn't love him when we broke up: I didn't miss him, just the closeness. But I don't regret he was in my life, not in the slightest. He helped me overcome my fear. I forgave myself and accepted myself. And damned if I don't feel so much better now!

But that's not the only thing that changed in my life. Yura, I'm here! I can't believe it, but I'm here, and it's all mine. We've been developing land in lots of places, so I had an excuse . . . Now I can truly say I've got everything. Everything except . . . well . . . but I've got nothing to lose, so . . .

Yura unfolded the letter so he could keep reading, but something fell out. He picked it up: a black-and-white photograph that had been folded in half down the middle. He opened it and caught his breath. It was that picture, the one they'd taken after the show. Yura had completely forgotten about it after eighteen-odd years. He looked at his young self and at Volodya, whose arm was around Yurka's shoulders. How handsome Volodya had been, though: tall and slim, a little pale, a subtle shadow under his chiseled cheekbones . . . And Yurka looked so funny in the picture, with his crooked grin, and his Pioneer neckerchief, off-kilter as usual, and his baseball cap on backward . . . It was so ridiculous! They were so exuberant in the picture: they'd been so happy then! Never mind their impending separation, never mind that they had basically no time left to be together . . . They'd been happy then, because they'd been together, they'd been with each other, but mainly because they'd hoped and believed they'd see each other again!

Yura folded the picture so he could put it back down and keep reading the last letter. But what he saw made his heart stop for a minute, then pound against his ribs painfully: on the back of the picture, in compact handwriting, was written, "I'm not hoping for anything and I'm not expecting anything from you anymore. I just want to find out how you're doing," followed by a phone number that had been crossed out. Underneath, written with a different pen, were two more numbers, for a landline and a cell phone.

His heart skipped a beat again. Hope flared bright within him. Yura guessed that Volodya had written the message and the crossed-out phone number earlier, in 1996, when he'd put the old letters in the time capsule, but that he'd written the new numbers in later, in 2001. Yura pulled his cell phone out of his pocket, trying to remember how much money he had left on his cell phone account, and slowly dialed the cell phone number with a shaking finger. Then he pushed the call button. It felt as though he were setting off a detonator.

The call was answered quickly. A woman, and not a young one. Immediately the thought flashed through Yura's mind: *Who's that? A jealous wife? But I thought he'd come around on that!*

"Hello, could I speak with Volodya?"

"What Volodya?" replied the irritated voice.

"Volodya Davydov."

After a moment of silence, which felt like an hour to Yura, she said, "You've got the wrong number," and hung up.

Yura figured Volodya must have changed his number. In 2001 the cell phone networks were just getting established and things were always changing: service providers, rates, numbers, and so forth. Volodya had probably gotten a different SIM card since then and this number would have then been given to a different person. Yura double-checked the second number, the landline, on the back of the picture and then dialed it. It seemed familiar to him somehow.

He spoke aloud as he dialed it: "Fifty-five . . . five . . . Strange . . ." He'd definitely seen it somewhere before.

"Hello, this is the front desk of LVDevelopment. How can I help you?"

Yura was taken aback. He turned instinctively to look at the advertising billboard, but he couldn't see it from there.

"Put me through to Volo—ahem, to Vladimir Davydov."

"Vladimir Lvovich is out of the office today. Leave your phone number and he'll call you back."

"Later won't work, I need him now, it's urgent! Give me his cell phone number!"

"Your name, please?"

"Konev. Yury Konev," he answered lamely.

"Your patronymic, please."

"Ilych."

Several seconds of silence followed. The secretary was probably looking for his name in some list of the company's clients or partners. But Yura was beginning to lose patience.

"Yury Ilych, unfortunately I can't give you the director's personal number. Please leave your number."

Yura ground his teeth. He understood that the secretary wasn't supposed to start passing out her boss's personal number to random people, but right now she was the only thin thread of hope Yura had. She was also the only barrier blocking his way. So he said politely, but as forcefully as he could: "Call him now, please. Tell him Konev's calling. Give him my number and have him call me immediately. I really can't wait,: it's extremely important and urgent, and it is for him, too! Tell him it's about Camp Barn Swallow—I mean, about the Barn Swallow's Nest." He gave her his number and warned her that if he didn't get a call in the next ten minutes he'd call back.

Yura waited, staring mindlessly at the picture. He walked around the willow and looked up at the sky, completely covered in gray clouds. The rain, which had seemed about to let up, started drizzling again. Almost no rain made it through the willow's leafy branches, but the rising wind rustled the long, yellow-green tresses.

Yura clutched his cell phone. He kept checking the time. Ten minutes had gone by without a call. But he couldn't bring himself to dial the front desk again: he was afraid Volodya would call while he was on the phone, so he'd miss it. If Volodya even called him back at all.

"What if he's busy? What if he's outside the network? Maybe he's on a business trip or way out in the sticks somewhere and there's no coverage? Or maybe he just doesn't want to talk to me? Because so many years have gone by . . . He did write that he wants to forget all that . . ."

Yura paced back and forth across the little clearing under the willow. Outside the shelter of its branches, it started raining harder. He needed to put everything back into the time capsule and go back to his car. But he was too agitated. The unbelievable thought that he might finally hear Volodya's voice after twenty years kept running through his head.

His blood roared in his ears. Thunder rumbled off to the east. The cell phone's sudden, harsh ring made him flinch. He pressed his phone to his ear.

"Yura?"

Yura froze. For several seconds he forgot how to breathe.

"Yes . . . Yes! Volodya, it's me!"

"Yurka . . ." Yura could hear the smile in Volodya's voice.

"I'm so glad to hear your voice! I read your letters . . . Volodya, I'm so sorry, I screwed everything up! We promised not to lose ourselves, not to lose each other, but we did. I looked for you too late."

Volodya didn't say anything. All of a sudden his tone of voice changed. The speaker distorted it, and Yurka thought he now sounded indifferent.

"Are you at Camp Barn Swallow?"

"Yes, under our willow. Everything around it is ruined, the river dried up, but the willow's still here, even bigger and more beautiful . . . as though . . ."

"As though it were waiting for us," Volodya finished for him.

Yura was pressing the phone to his cheek with both hands, as if he wanted to squeeze through it to get to Volodya. "What are you like now?" Yura asked softly.

Volodya paused for a couple of seconds, then answered. "Well . . . you're clearly not asking about my business or my health. What am I like now? I grew up some . . ."

"Are you far away?"

Volodya snorted. "I'm closer than you can possibly think. Do you want to see me?"

Yura swallowed the lump that had formed in his throat. "Yes."

"Aren't you afraid of being disappointed?"

"Of course I am. Aren't you?"

"Did you become a pianist?"

"Believe it or not, Volod, I did!" Yura smiled. "I did!"

"Then I'm not afraid of being disappointed." There was a pause. "Okay, wait there—"

The call was cut off, replaced by rapid beeping. Yura was left standing there, confused, looking stupidly at the screen of his phone.

He redialed Volodya's number, grateful at the thought that now, after so many years, he could. But Volodya didn't answer.

Why isn't he picking up? Did his battery run out? thought Yura. He bent down over the time capsule and set about collecting the opened letters. Then he noticed one more piece of paper in the capsule. He'd already gotten excited—one more letter!—when he saw he was mistaken. He unfolded the piece of paper. It was the sheet music for the "Lullaby." A sad smile came unbidden to his face: once it had almost ended everything, but then it had been where everything began instead.

He carefully smoothed out the paper so he could put it away with the other papers back in the time capsule, but then he froze on the spot, the music clutched in both hands. He'd caught sight of someone's silhouette through the wall of willow boughs.

Yura stood up mechanically and walked out from underneath the willow tree. A man was standing about ten meters away. From this distance Yura could only see that the man was tall. The man took a step toward Yura. Yura took a step toward him. It was hard to make out the man's features through the misty drizzle, but with each step closer, just like when a photo is developed, his features became sharper and more distinct. Yura's hand trembled. He wanted to look at the picture from the theater and check it, compare the man he saw before him with the man he would've wanted to see. But he wasn't holding the picture. And even if he had been—so many years had gone by! Still, no matter how a person changes with time, there's always one thing that remains, one thing that lets you recognize him: the eyes. And these eyes, even though they weren't hidden behind glasses, were his. Volodya's eyes.

"How?" whispered Yura soundlessly. He looked to the left, at the roofs revealed in a gap in the woods, and thought of the billboard again, and suddenly he understood.

The camp was Volodya's now. This was Volodya. He'd grown up, he'd changed, but it was really him!

Volodya, flustered, was smiling and looking at Yura, frozen a few steps away. It was as though he couldn't believe it. Yura couldn't believe it, either.

Yura wanted to hug Volodya, but for half a second he still hesitated. He briefly wondered if he should ask permission, then decided to hell with all that. They hadn't seen each other for twenty years, and Yura had every right to just go on and hug him, no permission needed. So he did.

And nothing in the world was more important than that moment.

As it had back then, twenty years ago, time stood still around them, holding its breath. All that existed was the two of them, the pattering rain, and the wind whispering in the willow leaves. Volodya placed his hands tentatively on Yura's back at first, as though he couldn't believe this was really Yura. Then he returned the embrace fiercely, heaving a long sigh of relief into Yura's shoulder, as though he were rolling a massive rock off his soul.

After a long minute, Volodya took Yura by the shoulders and held him at arm's length. He studied Yura's face as though still doubting it was really him. Then Volodya glanced down at the sheet music still clutched in Yura's hand, looked back directly in Yura's eyes, and smiled. "Are you going to play me a 'Lullaby'?"

AUTHORS' NOTE

This book contains a handful of details that merit further clarification. In reference to the description of the village of Palanga as being on the border of the Lithuanian SSR and part of Poland occupied by Nazi Germany: in 1939, in accordance with the Molotov-Ribbentrop Pact, Poland was occupied by the USSR as well as by Nazi Germany. In reference to the headline of "AIDS Epidemic!": the word "AIDS" is being used intentionally to emphasize how panicked and uninformed people were at that time. In actuality, here and elsewhere, what is being discussed is HIV infections. Last, in reference to the term "homoseksualist": this is a transliteration of the actual word Maxim Gorky used in his 1934 article, which is different from the Russian word for homosexual. The specific term Gorky used was derogatory and conveyed a belief that homosexuality was a disease.

TRANSLATOR'S NOTE

I believe that US readers who choose to read a story set largely in Soviet times, with largely Russian-speaking characters, are by definition interested in tasting the Russian-language flavor of the text. So names have been rendered in a phonetic approximation, not a formal academic transliteration, to allow readers unfamiliar with the language to get an idea how they might be pronounced. Hence, Pcholkin (not "Pchëlkin" or "Pchelkin"); Gorbachov (not "Gorbachëv" or "Gorbachev"); Pyotr (not "Pëtr" or "Petr"); and so forth. Nicknames are a special convention for Russian speakers, giving valuable information about relationships between people; nicknames express a range of attitudes from tender, to endearing, to mocking. Sasha, Sashka, and Sash are all versions of Alexander; Volodya, Volod, Volodka, Vova, Vovka, and the very affectionate Volodechka are all versions of Vladimir; Yura, Yurka, Yurets, Yurok, Yur, Yurchik, and the very affectionate Yurochka are all versions of Yury. The metric system is also retained.

A word about the Pioneer system: In Soviet times, you really did have to be a Communist Party member to join the social elites and gain access to perks, privileges, and influence. But the process of becoming a Party member started in early childhood. First you had to be a Little Octoberist, the political organization for seven-to-ten-year-olds. Only after being a Little Octoberist could you graduate to becoming a Pioneer, the political organization for kids aged ten to fourteen. Once you hit fourteen, you aged out of the Pioneers and graduated to the Komsomol, the Union of Communist Youth. You could be a Komsomol member for more than a decade while you worked on getting your Party membership, but if you hadn't become a Party member by the time you were hitting thirty, you'd age out of the Komsomol and be kicked out, ending your chances of ever joining the Party. At Camp Barn Swallow, the youngest troop is Troop Five, while the oldest troop is Troop One. Troops Three to Five are the junior troops, while troops Two and One are the senior troops. One reason the character Yura Konev feels out of place at Camp Barn Swallow is that, since he had never participated in the Little Octoberists before his first session at the Barn Swallow Pioneer Camp, he had to go back and start as a Little Octoberist at camp at age eleven, when most Octoberists were under ten. And then every year when he came back to camp and joined the next oldest troop, he was always older than his troopmates. In the events that occur in this book, Yurka is around sixteen years old and in his sixth camp session, when most Soviet kids stopped being Pioneers—and so stopped going to Pioneer camp—at around fourteen.

As for the Barn Swallow camp itself: In Soviet times, people didn't just decide to send their kids to whatever camp they wanted. Every camp was affiliated with some state entity, like a factory or a worker's union, that managed and ran it. The chance for your kids to go to camp was one of the benefits of employment/union membership. It was free, but parents had to get permission for their kids to attend—meaning that parents had to maintain good standing—and had to be issued an official voucher.

Another note: Vladimir Lenin really did say his *r*'s wrong, as Yurka tells Olezhka, although technically Olezhka and Lenin have different forms of rhotacism. Olezhka completely switches out his *r*'s for *w*'s, while Lenin did say his *r*'s, but instead of flipping or rolling them, the Russian way, he pronounced them as a glottal fricative, like the French *r* in "de rien."

Also, please be aware that for copyright reasons, quotes from real Soviet-era songs and poems have been replaced in the translation by invented words and titles.

And finally: The names of places located in present-day Ukraine, including in Ukrainian territory that has been illegally invaded and occupied by Russia, are given according to their Ukrainian names. So the city where Yura is from is Kharkiv, not Kharkov; the name of the village next to the Barn Swallow Pioneer Camp is Horetivka, not Goretovka; and so on.